DREAM TRAIN
CHARLOTTE VALE ALLEN

**GLAMOROUS . . . MYSTERIOUS . . .
ELEGANT . . . ROMANTIC . . . THE
PASSENGERS ABOARD THE ORIENT-
EXPRESS ARE ALL THIS AND MORE. . . .**

JOANNA—A renowned photojournalist, she
embarks on her journey uncertain of her future,
uncertain of her life—and uncertain of the two
different men who love her.

(MORE)

TYLER—A famous British actor and director, he'd fallen in love with Joanna the first time he met her in the States. Now that he's seen her again, he doesn't want to let her go.

LUCIENNE—A beautiful, glamorous woman, she has journeyed on the train to escape from her responsibilities as restaurateur in Paris—and to accept a marriage proposal from a man she doesn't love.

HENRY—A British literary agent, he hides his passion for Joanna beneath his three-piece suits.

LADY ANNE—An aristocratic Englishwoman celebrating her fiftieth wedding anniversary on the train, she is astonished at Joanna's similarity to her daughter—a daughter who has died.

SIR JAMES—Happily married to Anne for fifty years, he too is astonished to find Joanna aboard the train, looking and acting like his daughter.

JACKIE—A young, spirited American boy, he helps Joanna sort things out with his innocence—as she tries to help him cope with his self-involved, rich family.

DREAM
TRAIN

Charlotte Vale Allen

IVY BOOKS • NEW YORK

DEDICATION

This book is for Claire Smith,
who not only "parented" its conception
but served as midwife through a difficult birth.
My gratitude and affection are limitless.
You are, quite simply, the very best.

ACKNOWLEDGMENTS

There are many people who helped in many ways before, during, and after the writing of this book. Some of them are: Sam MacDonald of Air Canada, who was a terrific flying companion and who shared with me the frightening story of her apartment fire; John Reeves, photographer extraordinaire, who patiently answered all my technical questions; Archie MacDonald, valued friend, who assisted with the background research on the Orient-Express; Bruce Hunter, master of the telex, who invariably sorted things out; Mariolina Franceschetti of the Italian Cultural Institute, who unearthed the details of the Special Law for Venice; Renato Piccolotto, chef for the Venice Simplon-Orient-Express, who took me through the stages of food preparation for the train; Giovanna Paschero, operations supervisor for the VS-O-E, who spent hours with me at the depot at Scomenzera explaining the logistics and maintenance of the train; Dr. Natale Rusconi of the Cipriani in Venice, who extended exceptional hospitality; Paola Starace, who gave friendship as well as assistance; Adrian Denham, chief steward on the VS-O-E, for creating a singular opportunity to allow me to ride in the locomotive of the train; Antoine Cadier, train manager, for his help in general; Mariana Field Hoppin and Denny Davidoff, for providing information and good company; my editor, Judy Kern, who is blessed with humor and patience, for her suggestions; the train staff of the VS-O-E, who were kind and accommodating; Caroline Boyle of marketing (U.K.), who made my travel arrangements and answered many questions; CIGA Hotels, Venice for their help and hospitality; and, finally, James Sherwood, whose wish it was to have a novel set on the new Orient-Express, for the trip of a lifetime and an unforgettable experience.

1

THE NIGHT BEFORE SHE WAS TO LEAVE VANCOUVER, JOANNA dreamed again of the fire. She was back in the bathroom, the only place in the apartment she'd been able to get to, with foul-smelling oily black smoke snaking in through the gap between the bottom of the door and the frame; she was back in that little room soaking towels in water before pushing them up against that dangerous gap, all the while screaming for help, hoping the neighbors above or below would hear and call the fire department. Over and over, she'd screamed, *"I don't want to die in here!"* while pounding with her fists on the ceiling, the walls, the floor, praying to be heard and rescued. No one came. Minutes were hugely elastic, ballooning into immeasurable portions of time. She kept on screaming and pounding on the ceiling and walls; there was nothing else to do. When she dared put her hand to the bathroom door, it had grown hot. The fire was eating away at it on the other side. Mouth dry, throat raw from screaming, heart racing, she turned on the shower and aimed the spray at the door, then with her toothbrush glass began splashing water around the room while her voice, automatically now, pleaded with Sally who lived upstairs, and with Jean and Barry who lived downstairs, to call the fire department, to get people to come and save her. Her life had been reduced to a small, highly flammable package she wanted to keep intact.

Forcing herself awake, she sat up in the dark hotel room, her body slick with the sweat of fear, shattered anew at the near loss of her life, and at the actual loss of years of work. The destruction of her clothes, keepsakes, furniture had been upsetting of course. But the ruin of her files of prints and negatives and slides had been a permanent injury. She'd lost moments of time; corners, fragments, features of faces, scenes and events. Her personal vision up to that point had been wiped out by the fire. It was a monumental loss. In some ways what she'd produced in the eight years since the fire was better—more clearly perceived, more profoundly graphic; yet she knew she'd never be able to duplicate the innocence and enthusiasm that had given those early efforts their uniqueness. She often wished—if for nothing else than comparison—she could review those lost photographs, lay them down beside her present efforts and try to track her personal passage in life through the people and scenes she'd chosen to represent a particular day, a time, a mood, or a feeling. The odd print turned up now and then: someone had admired a picture, so she'd made an extra print; the someone called up out of the blue and in the course of conversation mentioned the print; elderly magazines in the waiting rooms of various members of the medical profession upon whom she had occasion to call—she'd come across a piece of her own work and gasp with pleasure at the discovery. She had no qualms whatever about stuffing the magazine into her handbag and taking away retrieved bits of her life.

After a time she switched on the bedside light. Almost eight. There was no point in trying to go back to sleep for the twenty-five minutes left before the alarm went off. She sat back against the headboard, thinking about what had preceded the fire: those four years with Greg. It had been a game, more or less, with both of them playing out preassigned roles. He was the one meant to garner laurels, to harvest crops of success. He was the one who was supposed to shinny up the corporate ladder in a dazzling, spotlit climb. And she was supposed to have been entirely supportive and nurturing during his ascent. It gradually drove her crazy. She refused to accede blindly to his wishes or to surrender her right to her ambition, so they kept their separate apartments, even though it was accepted that they were a couple. There had been times when she'd disliked being known as the other half of Greg. Yet because she'd always been uneasy about her personal attributes, she'd stumbled along with him through the retrospectively clichéd ups and downs of their time together, until the fire.

He'd always had a casual disregard for the things her growing success provided. He'd put his shoes on the furniture; he'd broken a vase she'd carried on her lap all the way from Hong Kong, and couldn't understand her being upset at its destruction; he'd even tapped his cigarette ash onto the floor of her new BMW rather than using the ashtray; after the first year he'd eaten her food without comment; he'd slept in her bed and used her body, also without comment. He'd infuriated her. When they'd argued about his transgression of the moment, he'd invariably pretended innocence, claiming not to understand what it was that had set her off "this time." And the implication that she was someone too readily set off heightened her anger with him. By the time of the fire she'd actively loathed not only Greg but herself for continuing to be involved with him. It was something she simply couldn't understand about herself—her remaining for so long with someone who, once past the initial stages of the romance, had displayed so little approval of any aspect of her.

All it took to end the whole affair was a spark, some ashes from one of his cigarettes fallen down the side of the sofa— he'd had the ashtray perched on the arm, another of his habits that had maddened her. The spark had smoldered for hours, long after he'd gone home, before erupting into flames that had gutted the apartment and reduced to ashes all evidence of her flourishing career, as well as every memento of her past. It was pure luck that she'd been too tired that day, after shooting a cover feature for *Connecticut Magazine*, to lug her equipment up from the garage. So she'd left it locked in the trunk of her car. Those items, and the film from that day's shoot, were all that remained of her equipment. Everything else had been incinerated.

When the fire chief came to talk with her at the hospital, where she was well into the process of detoxification, and he'd revealed to her his findings—that the fire had, without question, started in the sofa—she'd refused to see Greg again. Yes, it had been an accident. But it was one caused by his seemingly permanent disregard for her, and so she couldn't forgive or absolve him. She hadn't even been able to speak to him because had she said anything at all, considering her years of accumulated anger and her ultimate outrage at his being responsible for the fire, she might well have killed him. She'd had repeated visions of strangling him, or running him down with her car; she'd stabbed him, shot him, poisoned him; she'd humiliated him publicly and *then* stabbed, shot, or poisoned him. She wanted him dead and gone, as dead and gone as all the work of her life to that point.

When he'd telephoned, she'd said, "Stay away from me! I don't want to see you or hear one word from you ever again!" Her voice had been low and foreign and tremulous with rage. She'd put down the receiver with a shaking hand and stared for a long time at the ceiling, wondering if she was being unfair, deciding maybe she was, but any more of Greg and there'd be nothing left of her to salvage.

The fact that he took her at her word and made no further attempt to make contact proved once and for all his lack of feeling for her, which only further depressed her. If she could spend four years with a fool like Greg, what was *she*? No matter how many times she went back over the time with Greg, she failed to find any satisfactory explanation for her involvement. She'd been sifting through the clues to her own identity ever since, but still hadn't any viable answers. Her inability to come up with answers in the matter of Greg no longer bothered her to the degree it had in the immediate aftermath of the fire. But every so often—late at night or en route to some assignment—she couldn't help looking back and speculating on the subject. All she knew for certain was that the fire stood as one of the two milestones in her life.

The second was the death of her mother two years ago. She had no nightmares about Lily. And when she thought of her, it was as she'd always been and not as the shrunken cadaver she'd become at the last. Her father and her younger brother Ben—always called Beamer by the family for reasons long since forgotten—and she had all prayed, near the end, that Lily would go soon.

It was, however, one thing to crave an end to someone's suffering and quite another to have a life without that someone in it. With Lily's death, it seemed Jo lost still more fragments, corners, exposure-tested strips of her own past. There were also new questions for which she periodically struggled to find answers. Lily had been her mother, after all, and the most influential person in Jo's life. Lily's absence, the silencing of her voice, left Jo feeling oddly empty-handed. She'd always thought a time would come when she and Lily would sit down together and review their history and, in the process, at last enable Jo to make sense of all sorts of things that continued to bewilder her.

She looked again at the clock. Eight-twenty. She got up and went to the bathroom to shower, leaving the door open as she always did now. Her flight wasn't until eleven, but it took her at least an hour and a half of a morning to assemble herself for the day. She liked to linger over coffee while reading the local newspaper, dipping toast points into her coffee cup, eating mechanically as she absorbed details of the latest front-page disasters, scandals, atrocities, and weather predictions. The news was eternally so bad that, by comparison, she felt quite well. Her health was good, her career hummed along; she was free of having constantly to consider the moods and preferences of anyone else. She set her own pace, often made her own travel arrangements, worked out her articles according to the degree of interest a project aroused in her. She'd left Manhattan after the fire and bought the condominium in Rowayton (on the garden level so she could escape either through the front or the rear patio door in the event of a fire. And when traveling, she refused to stay above the fourth floor in hotels; upon arrival she at once checked the location of the fire exits). She had a home, yet she rarely lived in it.

For six to eight months of the year, for two weeks here or a month there, she made nests of hotel rooms, setting out her coffee and portable one-cup coffee maker, the family portrait she'd taken while still in college, her notebooks and pens, her stock of film, the heavy camera bag, the books and research materials needed for the assignment, her Walkman and the detachable microspeakers. She'd check in, take a few minutes to distribute her bits and pieces, and at once the hotel room would seem less sterile, more familiar. She'd recently begun to dislike hotels, and it took more and more effort to rid them of their sterility.

She'd been in Vancouver for four days doing a feature on Expo 86 for *Worldview*, a trade travel magazine that featured her work two or three times a year. She was considered a dependable source of high-quality photographs and clean prose that didn't suffer from too arch a personal viewpoint. She approached every project with an open mind, prepared to be pleased and enlightened. The result was an increasing number of plum assignments: covers for *U.S. Travel*, for *Gourmet*; features with photographs for everything from *People* to *Architectural Digest*. There were jobs that were strictly photographic, and some were purely journalistic, but the majority required both photos and text, and these were the ones she most enjoyed.

Expo had been one of the really good assignments. The pavilions were clever, even exciting; the grounds were immaculate, the employees friendly, the color-coding of areas well-designed and effective, as were the trains and monorail; the nightly fireworks display complete with laser light show and music had turned her into an eight-year-old, open-mouthed with delight as, through the lens of the tripod-mounted Nikon, she'd watched the bursting flares in the night sky reflected in the water below. She had a hunch that one of her time-exposure fireworks shots might make the cover, although it was often impossible to predict what might make an editor's heart tick over. There were shots she'd been positive would be snapped up for covers that were passed over in favor of less tricky or less exciting exposures.

Anyway, this job was done, and she was looking forward to going home, to eating food she prepared herself, to going upstate to the place in Kent where her parents had moved after her father's retirement, to see her dad and Beamer. She'd been on the road longer than usual, having come to Vancouver directly from a job in San Francisco and, before that, one in Nashville. The last year or so, her assignments had been one on top of another, which meant she had to do her writing in hotel rooms on rented typewriters. She couldn't seem to bring herself to say no, to turn down offers of work. The result was the feeling that she was somewhat less than real, like some arcane form of processing machine, something that absorbed information, captured the visuals on film, then assembled everything into a readily digestible format and sent it off by courier either to her agent or to the publication in question, depending upon the particular protocol. Time off, time to herself, had become, at age thirty-six, vital and elusive.

A number of times of late she'd referred to herself as the mobile cipher, the invisible eye, the sponge in the corner soaking up details and bits of trivia. It sounded amusing, people laughed; but Sally, who was still a close friend, had a couple of months earlier said, "I'm beginning to think you have no idea who or what you are anymore, Joey. You talk as if you're middle-aged and ugly, as if no one in his right mind would find you interesting or attractive. I'd like to remind you that you're still young, and very goddamned attractive. I hate it when you talk about yourself that way." With an encouraging smile, Sally had gone on to say, "People do see you, you know. Whatever you may think, you're definitely *not* invisible."

Sally's remarks had made an impact, because she'd begun to feel vaguely uneasy, even afraid. There were moments when it seemed as if she were actually fading, like a color negative left on a sunny window sill. She felt out of step with people's attitudes and values. She also felt something of a fraud, because most of the people she met encountered her professional self. This was the Jo who, with confidence bred of experience and technical skill, could keep conversations afloat and be sincerely engaging. But without an assignment backing her up, without the camera, the personal self seemed to be in trouble. Her presence anywhere seemed validated by her career, and without her professional credentials to back her up, she not only lost confidence, she also feared she had nothing of interest to say to anyone. She'd arrived at a juncture where she better than halfway believed the Jo who wore the professional hat had taken precedence over the Jo who didn't. And the only consolation she found nowadays was in the small rewards she gave herself at the conclusion of each assignment: clothes, a piece of jewelry, cassettes or books or videocassettes. Things just didn't feel right.

As usual she was too early for her flight, and settled into a phone booth to check in with her agent in New York.

"Did you get my message already?" Grace asked.

"What message?"

"Are you home? Where are you?"

"I'm at the airport in Vancouver. I fly out in an hour."

"Well, listen, kiddo! I've got some great news."

"What?" Jo asked warily. Great news usually translated into another job, and all she wanted was to go home.

"It's the assignment of a lifetime, Jo. They're all set to go. The guy they had lined up to do it rolled his car day before yesterday on the Jersey Turnpike. Nothing major, but he's not going to be going anywhere for a while. I just happened to be over talking to Harry Harris at *Travelogue*, and he was in a total panic, asking did I have anyone who could jump in at the eleventh hour. Of course, I told him you'd be free, and he was ecstatic."

"Oh, God! What is it this time? Bora Bora, or down-home cooking?"

"If I knew how to work a camera, kiddo, I'd do this one

myself." Grace took a breath, then said, "It's the Orient-Express."

"The Orient-Express? I thought that shut down years ago. Does it still run?"

"Sweetheart, it runs and then some. You'll catch the train Sunday morning at Victoria Station in London, and ride it to Venice. Then five days at only the most sensational hotel in Venice, the Cipriani. Then a return ride to London. The Italian Tourist Bureau's involved, too, and they'll be laying on a couple of things for you. The hotel's PR director will have all the info. The hook is a great ride followed by a stay at a great hotel. Say yes, and let me call Harry back."

"Wait a minute! First of all, how long is the train ride? And what do I need? Give me a little something more here, Gracie! I can't just change my plans and agree to this without a bit more input."

"I'll telex Henry in London and tell him to air out the guest room. You know he loves having you stay with him. So that's no problem. When can you get over there?"

"I've *got* to go home, Grace! I mean it. I've been on the road for the last hundred years. I want to see if my place is still there; I want to see my dad and my brother; I want to do my laundry." She paused, then said, "You already said yes, didn't you?"

"Uh-huh. You can't turn this down, sweetheart. Cover feature, plus whatever material Harry doesn't use, he says we can shop elsewhere and that includes all the foreign rights. This could be good for half a dozen markets. Top-dollar fee. And, come on, Jo! The *Orient-Express*! I know people who'd kill to ride that train, me included. Black-tie dinner, the Alps, fascinating people. Then, there's only the most gorgeous city on earth waiting for you at the other end."

"I never have been to Venice," Jo said consideringly.

"Go catch your plane. I'll talk to you tonight, with the details."

"What about the airfare to London?"

"Prepaid executive-class ticket's waiting at Kennedy. Call

me the minute you get home. There's a lot of stuff to go over before you leave.''

"I love having about ten minutes' notice that I'm heading off to Europe. What kind of kill fee?''

"Fifty percent. Think about it on the flight back. You're perfect for this one. I'll bet by the time you call me later you'll be out of your mind with excitement. Gotta go, another call. Think about it!'' she said again, and hung up.

Think about it! Jo looked at her watch. She had plenty of time to walk through the terminal to the bookstore, just to see if they had anything on Venice or the Orient-Express. Nothing on the train, but a Berlitz guide to Venice she paid for, then popped into her handbag before making her way to the departure gate. The nonslip strap of the heavy Lowe-pro camera bag bore down into her shoulder, and she thought longingly of the visits she'd planned to her chiropractor. Now she'd be lucky to see him once before she left. *If* she decided to go. Mentally, she went through her wardrobe trying to think which clothes might be right.

Oh hell! she thought, starting to smile. Of course she was going to go. How could she possibly turn down anything as intriguing and exciting as a ride on the Orient-Express?

2

THE APARTMENT SEEMED TOO QUIET. THE PICTURES ON THE walls were misaligned—proof that the cleaning lady had been there in Jo's absence. Everything felt odd. She had to stop every few minutes and look around, trying to decide what was wrong. Usually, coming home was like arriving at a good party. This time it was as if she'd wandered by mistake into someone else's house.

She opened the windows to let the humid breeze move through the rooms, then stepped outside onto the deck. In the afternoon silence, a family of ducks sat as if dazed on the surface of the pond. The grass had just been cut and the smell of it was powerful. She stood breathing in the scent, looking first at the ducks bobbing on the pond, then at the dissolving clouds.

Although she sometimes missed the frantic pace and perennially menacing atmosphere of Manhattan, overall she'd come to prefer living in Connecticut. The silence at night was broken only by the clacking rattle of late trains passing on the tracks that ran near the lower part of the condominium complex; during the day, if she cared to take a stroll over the grass, she might hear the concert pianist practicing, or someone's stereo, or the laughter and splashing of kids up at the pool. Ordinary, everyday sounds for the most part, the background music she'd grown up with and that, as a teenager, she'd longed to escape. And for those five years when she'd lived in the city, she'd harbored a certain smug satisfaction at having discarded her suburban background. She'd acquired a new and different set of survival skills; she'd grown street-smart and proud of her ability to navigate the subways. She'd concentrated on her work, had done it so well that she'd established a good reputation and earned enough money to buy the BMW which, in truth, had been a frivolous and wildly expensive toy. Keeping it garaged in the city had cost almost as much as the rent on her apartment. In the end, she'd moved the car up to her parents' place, reregistered it in Connecticut, and Beamer had used it more than she had. Until the fire. Then she'd escaped back to the suburbs, using her savings for the down payment on the apartment, and the insurance money to pay for the furnishings and new camera equipment.

She'd been grateful for the quiet of Connecticut. Now, suddenly, it made her uneasy. Everything seemed skewed. Why, if everything was going so smoothly and so well, was she standing outside on the deck watching half a dozen sun-dazed ducks instead of busying herself with all the things she'd promised she'd do once she got home? No answer.

She sat down, her thoughts shifting to London, and to Henry. She had to smile, remembering their first meeting almost ten years before. She'd gone along to his office shortly after her arrival in London, geared up to meet someone middle-aged, very British, and stuffy. Gracie had only said, "You'll like Henry," and had smiled rather significantly, which had led Jo to expect the worst. Every time someone declared two strangers would like one another, the two in question seemed destined to despise one another on sight. But in this case, Gracie had been right.

Henry hadn't been middle-aged or stuffy. He'd greeted her warmly and they'd gone off to lunch, during which he'd chatted companionably, smiling often, while she kept her professional hat fixed firmly in place. He had been very British, perfectly correct in his dealings with the restaurant staff. Yet his correctness had been offset by his enthusiasm for her work and by his habit of meeting her eyes straight on and nodding approvingly whenever she spoke. Gracie had been right: She did like him. She more than liked him, finding him sweetly appealing in his three-piece suit and starched shirt. He had lovely manners, an absurd sense of humor, and a talent for making the person he was with feel important.

"I'd love to have one of your photographs," he'd told her as the meal progressed.

"Anything in particular?"

"I haven't seen it yet," he'd said. "But I'll know it when I see it."

"You will, huh? Any clues as to what it might be?"

"Not a one. I'll be quite forthright about it, however. No fear. I'll ring you, or write to say I'd like a print of this one, please. So be prepared."

"Oh, I will." She'd smiled at him. "I'll be living in a state of suspense from now on."

He'd looked at her for a long moment before saying, "Oh, don't! I'd hate to think of you suffering, waiting for the dreaded declaration. No, it'll be painless, I promise. I'll simply see what I want and inform you. Since Grace sent over the samples, I've been most curious about you. I expected you'd be fat, for some reason."

"Fat!" she'd laughed. "Why fat?"

"Don't know. Something to do, I think, with how very— *comfortable* your photographs are. I envisioned you waddling happily along, spotting something that took your fancy, then clicking away. Needless to say, I'm delighted you're not. Fat, that is. Anything but, actually. And younger, too, than I'd imagined."

"Fat and old. I'm going to have to take a good long look at my stuff. Maybe somewhere inside me there's a middle-aged fat lady." She'd thought, looking at his smiling mouth, that she'd have liked to kiss him. His proximity and his comments and the look of him made her somewhat giddy, and

13

she'd wondered if perhaps he'd inspire her to give up Greg. She didn't at all mind the prospect.

"You know," he'd said a short time later, "I'm about to buy a house. In Chelsea. When next you visit, possibly you'll come stay in the guest room. I'm sure it would be much more comfortable, not to mention less expensive, than a hotel. And I think you and Brenda would hit it off nicely."

"Who's Brenda?" she'd asked, hoping he'd say his sister or cousin.

"My fiancée."

"Oh!" Her giddiness had gone, along with her budding romantic interest. She'd returned to the hotel after the meal feeling like an idiot for having been prepared to become involved with him. She'd chided herself for being too fast off the mark, and had conscientiously shuffled her emotions like an old deck of cards, thereby relegating Henry to his proper place as business associate and friend.

She never did get to meet Brenda. By the time he'd moved into his house, he was no longer engaged to her. Jo got into the habit of staying in his guest room whenever she visited England, always glad to see Henry, safe in her acknowledged involvement with Greg. And Henry had been wonderfully kind, most solicitous, when she stayed with him a few months after the fire. "You're well out of it," he'd said. "I never did care too much for the sound of that fellow."

She'd been so grateful for his sympathy and understanding that she'd never thought to ask why he'd said that. Of course, he'd distracted her with laughter, and outings to the theater; and he'd assured her she could do far better for herself. He had, in fact, instinctively said every last thing she'd been wanting to hear. Dear old Henry. It'd be good to see him; he'd make her laugh.

She shook her head, went inside, and called her father.

"Are you home, Joey?" he wanted to know.

"I got back an hour or so ago. But I'm leaving in a few days for London. I was thinking maybe I'd hop in the car, come up to see you and Beamer tomorrow."

"Oh, hell, Sweetcakes! We're leaving in an hour for

Fishers Island. Didn't you get the message I left on your stupid machine? Christ, but I hate those things!''

"I haven't listened to my messages yet. How long are you going to be at Fishers?''

"A week. The Fullers wouldn't take a no. They've got some female they want me to meet.'' He laughed. "Everybody and his cousin's got some woman they think'll just fill my bill. How long are you over in London?''

"A couple of weeks at least. I'm doing a feature on the Orient-Express.''

He whistled, then laughed again. "Ver-ry nice. Don't suppose you want a traveling companion?''

"I wish. How's everything? How's Beamer?''

"Right as rain. Your kid brother's bitching about wasting valuable time so he's dragging his computer and a whole mess of work along with him. He'll probably spend the entire time in his room, with the poor Fullers' telephone hooked into some system or other so he doesn't miss out on any hot offerings. He'll be a millionaire any minute now. Hey! Make sure you send me a postcard from the Orient-Express. I've always had a yen to ride that train. Does it still go to Istanbul?''

"No, just to Venice.''

"Just Venice. Will you get to spend any time there?''

"Five days.''

"Maybe I'll cancel the Fullers and come with you," he joked. "I haven't seen Venice since the war. I hope for your sake it smells better now than it did then.''

"I'll call you when I get back," she promised. "Give Beamer my love, okay?''

"Okay, Sweetcakes. Have a good time. And don't forget my postcard!''

She hung up and went to unpack her bags.

While the first load of clothes was churning away in the washer, she took the camera bag into the second bedroom, which doubled as darkroom and storage area. She lifted out the camera body and the lenses, and all at once she just had to get out. Grabbing some film from the refrigerator, she

15

shoved everything back into the bag, ran out, and jumped into the car. She felt panicky as she reversed out of her slot, her whole body tensely coiled. The only cure she'd discovered for this malaise, or whatever it was, was to get out and shoot some film.

She drove, the tension easing almost immediately as she was visually soothed by the physical beauty of the area, and ended up at Weed Beach in Darien. She found a slot, pulled in, picked up the camera bag, and headed across the lot to the far end of the beach.

There were many mothers with young children, rows of impossibly lithe teenagers in advanced stages of tanning; radios and cassette players created pockets of music; the air reeked of mustard and of coconut oil. The hot, heavy air hung like a transparent, shimmering curtain.

She walked slowly along the rocky shore, looking out at the boats on the Sound, then down at the crusty tideline. Her attention was caught by something she couldn't at first identify but which was, upon closer inspection, a paperback book that had been taken out on the tide, then washed back in. The cover was long gone; the sun had dried and curled the pages, turning it into something like an extraordinary marine flower. Fitting the telephoto to the camera body, she dropped to her haunches to take several shots of her find.

Then, caught in the rhythm, freed and eased by the complicity existing between eye and camera, she opened the lens full to photograph some of the sailboats. With the glaring sun and wide open aperture, the final shots would seem as if they'd been taken late in the day.

She moved on to a close-up of some odd, stunted bushes; then bits of debris tangled in the seaweed at the tidemark; a medium shot of the slow-moving queue of children patiently waiting to buy Popsicles at the snack bar.

Forty minutes, twenty-four black and white exposures, and she was trudging back through the sand to the car. It was too hot to sit in at once, so she stood looking around, waiting and thinking through the idea that she was not only unprepared to go rushing off on another assignment, she was also

16

very nervous about it. She'd thought she'd come home, potter around the apartment for a few days before going upstate to see her family; she'd thought she'd bring her photo files up to date, and spend some time in the darkroom. Instead, her family was unavailable, she had just enough time to do a little background research before repacking and flying off to London for another of her of-late increasingly awkward sojourns at Henry's house with the redoubtable Suzanne hovering in the foreground and making it clear by means of certain facial expressions that she was less than thrilled at having Jo there.

Jo's prior relationship with Henry meant nothing to Suzanne. Neither did their professional dealings. Jo was another woman and therefore a disruption and a threat. Henry either failed to see or chose to ignore the heaviness in the atmosphere during these visits, and Jo had been planning to stay elsewhere on future trips. But this assignment had come up so suddenly that it simply hadn't occurred to her to get Grace to inform Henry not to expect her. More fodder for her uneasiness. Well, if it got to be as heavy as her last stay, she'd move to a hotel. As fond as she was of Henry, his taste in women was doubtful at best. Brenda had sounded bad enough; Suzanne had absolutely no sense of humor. How could a man like Henry live day after day with a woman who wouldn't recognize a joke if it was lit up in neon? Henry's women made Jo frustrated and sad; they all seemed so—*second-best*, as if he was making do until the one he really wanted came along. And that was ridiculous, because Henry had everything to recommend him. But there he was with Suzanne. God! How could he stand her?

During the flight to London her anxiety returned. It seemed she was doing everything wrong. Why, for example, had she put aside the Nikon at the last minute and packed the Pentax body and lenses? The KX was old and she hadn't used it in years. She should've told Grace she wasn't up to this, but she'd hardly protested at all before letting herself be overcome by the romantic idea of riding the world's most famous train. And "idea" was the key word, because all she'd managed to find on microfilm at the library were a couple of magazine pieces with some interesting facts about George Pullman and his American cars, and about Georges Nagelmackers, who'd created the original Compagnie International des Wagons-Lits. She'd Xeroxed both the articles and brought them along. Aside from this she'd rented a few movies with Venetian settings. And that was the sum total of her research. She hated feeling so unprepared, and wondered if maybe her professional hat was starting to slip. If so, she was in serious trouble because, without it, she'd have nothing going for her.

And what if she hadn't brought the right clothes? The dinner on board was supposedly a gala event, with the passengers in twenties-type finery. She'd packed a two-piece beige silk outfit that was smart, but not especially festive. Maybe she'd buy something dressier in London. But then she'd get stuck with a dress she'd likely never wear again. Come on! she chided herself. There's not a thing wrong with your clothes; there's not a thing wrong with the Pentax. Everything will be fine.

Henry had left the key to the flat in the flowerpot outside the door, as always. She let herself in and discovered a package on the floor addressed to her, with a Post-it note from Henry attached saying he'd be out for the evening but wouldn't be late, and the guest room was ready for her.

She carried her things into the cozy, familiar flat, trying to pinpoint what was different. Certain items—knickknacks, several pictures—were missing; so was the overpowering scent of Suzanne's perfume. Just to be absolutely sure, Jo ventured down the hall to the master suite, where she opened the doors to the wardrobe. Only Henry's clothes. Suzanne, obviously, was gone.

"Great!" she said aloud. "Great!"

Feeling much better, she settled in the guest room.

The package contained a four-color brochure, one booklet titled *Passenger's Guide to Venice Simplon-Orient-Express*, another on the Bournemouth Belle and a glossy dark blue folder stamped TRAVEL DOCUMENTS. The entire package was impressive: the glossy dark blue luggage tags and stickers, the Sealink boarding card, the itinerary typed on beige paper with chocolate trim, a beige card bearing the VS-O-E logo reading: ''We have pleasure in enclosing tickets for your trip to: Venice. The check-in is at: 10.00—Victoria Station.'' Handwritten.

She went through everything feeling as if she'd been given an exceptional gift. The presentation was elegant, and personalized in a way no airline ticket ever could be. *The Passenger's Guide* was loaded with information, including histories both of the Pullmans and of the Continental carriages.

She was starting to get excited, and even more concerned about her clothes because, according to the guide, ''You can never be overdressed on the Venice Simplon-Orient-Express.'' She'd consult with Henry. He had great taste; he'd know if her clothes were right. And now that god-awful Suzanne was out of the way, maybe they'd be able to sit and talk together, in their old comfortable fashion. Suzanne was gone! God! It was too terrific. Maybe she'd have a chat with Henry about his peculiar taste in women and find out why he kept taking up with such wretched types. Sure. Then he'd follow suit by asking what self-destructive impulse had prompted her to stay with Greg for four long years. Game, set, and match. Maybe they both had lousy taste in partners.

Her unpacking done, she wandered through the flat, admiring anew Henry's taste in furnishings and the lovely Victorian details of the place. He lived on the ground floor and rented out the flats on the second and third floors. The rooms were large, with high molded ceilings, everything painted white. The furniture was chunky modern, upholstered in soft gray fabric, with clean rounded lines and down cushions. No clutter, just a few large potted plants, an assortment of antique brass miniatures on a round mahogany table near the front windows, several compelling watercolors, and the large black and white piece of Jo's he'd loved on sight. ''This is the one!'' he'd announced. ''I must have it. If you don't give it to me, I won't be held responsible for the consequences. They'll find my poor shriveled body—after days of searching—huddled in the doorway of the Quali-Print shop where, as everyone knows, you have access to their darkroom. You wouldn't want that on your conscience, would you?''

''God, no, Henry! I'll go back this very moment and have them do you up an eleven-by-fourteen on archival paper. Your poor shriveled body,'' she'd scoffed. ''It'd take more than just days to get you to that state.''

''All right. After *weeks* of searching, they'll find my poor *semi*shriveled body. Better?''

''Better.''

''Truly, Jo,'' he'd said, studying the contact sheet with a magnifying glass, ''this is divine. What a clever girl you are!''

He'd looked at her with such overflowing admiration that for a few seconds she'd been tempted to throw herself at him and bite him on the neck. She'd liked him so much just then her teeth had ached slightly with a sudden brief desire to take large bites out of him.

The shot he'd chosen was one of her own favorites, a hand-held exposure of four old women seated on a park bench. They were smiling and talking, their hands busy with knitting. The foliage all around served as a lacy frame that contained them perfectly. Like most of her best work, the shot had been done on the spur of the moment, one afternoon here in London after leaving Henry's office. She stood back from it now, deciding there was a good deal of Henry's influence in the final product. Henry was such a staunch fan of her work that he never failed to inspire her to go right out and find more subjects for more photographs that would prompt more of his open approval.

There was another note from Henry on the refrigerator door. It read: ''Eat and drink. In anticipation of your arrival, I've taken the highly unusual precaution of stocking the larder. I don't expect to be later than ten, so try to stay awake for a drink and a natter and the latest gen on the assignment.''

She put on the kettle, then opened the refrigerator to laugh aloud at the sight of a roasted chicken with yet another note attached, this one to a drumstick. "Eat me, Alice," it read. She wasn't hungry, but tore off a small, crisp piece of skin to nibble as she looked out the kitchen window at Henry's lovely garden. She'd been promising herself for years that she'd one day sit Henry down in his garden and photograph him amid his flowering bushes. This time, she vowed, she'd do it. She'd get him out there in some of the ratty clothes he kept around for his gardening sojourns, and she'd shoot away until she had exactly the view of him she wanted. It'd be a shot that showed the contrast between his proper British gentleman image and his off-time, faintly crazy, soil-tiller persona. He'd be smiling his rather devilish smile, the one that showed his teeth, and he'd have dirty hands and knees. And, of course, he'd be wearing his "plimsolls," as he referred to what she called sneakers, with his toes poking through.

All at once, she was neither thirsty nor tired. It was only nine-thirty in the morning and the sun was shining. Her spirits considerably lightened, she grabbed the camera bag and her purse, pocketed the keys, and let herself out.

The streets of Chelsea were quiet at this time on a Thursday morning, and she walked along looking at the houses, pausing to take a shot of a row of pastel-painted terraced dwellings, each with its own tidy patch of garden at the front. As she neared the river, she saw a black woman pushing a child in a stroller and heard the woman singing softly. Her voice floated like a butterfly, tilting and directionless, on the fragrant air. Jo was captivated, especially when she got close enough to see the woman's broad, beaming face and that of the tiny Oriental child in the stroller. There was a picture here she wanted; she was also intrigued by the pair. Curiosity and confidence pulled together; knowledge of her abilities gave her a physical and psychological certainty. It came to her every time like a sense of well-being, enabling her to say and do things she was never able to do without the camera in her hands.

Slowing her pace she said, "Good morning," and the woman turned to offer her an unsuspicious smile.

"Is it a boy or a girl?" Jo asked, elated by the huge black eyes the child had fixed on her.

"Girl," the woman answered. "Her name's Mai-Ling. Ain't it, darlin'?" She placed a caring hand on the child's head.

"God, she's adorable!" Jo said, overwhelmed by those immense eyes. "How old is she?"

"Seventeen month. She's a little ting, but soooo smart. Smart, ain't you, darlin'?"

"Are you from Jamaica?"

"You been to Jamaica?" the woman asked avidly.

"Not yet. But I've always wanted to."

"Where you from?"

"Connecticut."

"You visitin'?"

"I'm going to Italy on Sunday, then I'll be back for a week. Work," she explained.

"What work you do?" the woman wanted to know.

"I'm a photojournalist."

"Ah! So that's how come you got the camera, huh, and tings bulgin' in the pockets."

Jo looked down at herself, and laughed. "Would you let me take your picture?"

"What you tink, Mai-Ling? You want dis lady take your picture?"

The child broke into a great smile, revealing her tiny new white teeth—four on the top and four on the bottom.

"Mai-Ling wants a picture," the woman announced.

"If you could just stand right where you are," Jo said, "that'd be great."

"What you gonna do with a picture of the two of us?" the woman asked, amused. "Big ugly black woman and little Mai-Ling?"

"You're not ugly!" Jo said, holding the camera away from her face. "You look wonderful, real. The two of you are beautiful."

"You tink so, huh?" The woman now smiled again, revealing a mouthful of large, startlingly white, perfect teeth. The child, who'd been tracking the conversation, chose that moment to turn in the stroller and put her little hand on the much larger black one that held the stroller's strut. Jo felt that interior leap of excitement that came when she knew an exposure was going to be perfect, adjusted the focus, and got the picture. She quickly took three more shots, then put the lens cap back on, saying, "Thank you very much."

As they started along the street, Jo said, "My name's Joanna. What's yours?" and saw herself back at school, making this same introduction at the start of every September.

"Me, I'm Florella. You goin' put our picture in some book?"

"Oh, no. It's just for me."

"You go takin' pictures of all the people you see?"

"Sometimes I think I'd like to, but no. Have you been in England a long time?"

"Twenty-two years," Florella answered. "Long time. I was here till I was fourteen. But my people they hatin' the winter, so they save up, and we all go home. Me," she laughed, "I save up eight years, workin' chambermaid in the hotel, and come back. I like the winter. An' I like this child here!" She stroked Mai-Ling's glossy black hair and the child at once swung around to offer her an adoring smile. "I got seven of them I cared for," she explained. "Some're grown big now. They come to see me. You have children?"

"No."

"You should," Florella laughed. "Then I come care for your babies."

"I'd love that!" Jo told her, able for a moment to picture a rollicking household populated by happy, noisy children shepherded by this affable woman.

They'd arrived at the Embankment, and Jo said, "I'm going to stay here for a while. If you give me your address, I'll send you prints of the pictures."

Jo got out her notebook. Florella recited her address, then

said goodbye and pushed Mai-Ling's stroller off along the waterfront. Jo watched them go, then turned to survey the view.

Brightly painted tour boats were headed down the river, to the pubs along the route, or to Hampton Court. She took shots of the boats, then turned to focus on the street. People were passing and she held still, waiting for them to move on. She waited and waited, and suddenly realized that the figure blocking her view had stopped and wasn't moving. Lowering the camera, thinking to go around this impediment, she heard laughter, looked up, and saw Tyler.

3

"THIS SIMPLY ISN'T POSSIBLE!" HE EXCLAIMED, GRINNING at her. "But it must be. It is Joanna James, after all!" With that, he gave her a hearty hug, then stepped away, saying, "I'd know that camera anywhere! How absolutely incredible!"

"I couldn't imagine," she laughed breathlessly, "why some idiot was blocking my shot. This really is amazing!"

"Are you in town for a while? What are you doing? Are you going to be free to have dinner with me, Joanna?"

"God, I'd love to! When?"

"How about this evening?" he said quickly.

"Sure. That'd be fine. I don't believe this!"

"I'm not sure I do, either. Where are you staying? Christ! Let me find something to write with." He patted all his pockets, his eyes never leaving hers.

"I've got a pen," she offered, getting it from her bag. "I'm staying at my agent's place." She wrote down Henry's address and telephone number, tore the page from her notebook and handed it to him. "Do you live around here?"

"I'm just on my way to Surrey, but I'll be back to collect you at six on the dot and we'll have dinner. I have quite a number of questions I want to ask you, but right now I must run. I'm spending the afternoon with my son.'' He put his hands on her shoulders and gazed at her as if stunned. ''The last thing I ever imagined happening,'' he told her, then laughed again. ''This is just too fantastic! Six o'clock, all right?''

''Definitely!''

He released her, gazed at her a moment longer, said ''Later!'' and went loping off across the road to his car.

She stood rooted to the spot until he'd driven off. Then, too distracted to take any more photographs, she started back toward Henry's house, marveling over this utterly unexpected turn of events.

She'd met Tyler three years earlier when she'd done a piece on crossover productions—American shows that went to the West End, and British companies that came to New York. It had been a major piece involving extensive interviews both in New York and in London, and Tyler Emmons had been one of the British in New York. An unpretentious man with an impressive acting and directing resumé, he'd agreed to an interview, declining her offer of an expense-account lunch and inviting her instead to a Sunday dinner at his sublet apartment in the West Sixties. After a cheese-and-mushroom omelette, salad, French bread, and a bottle of pleasantly woody-tasting Spanish red wine, she'd photographed him in the kitchen as he prepared coffee. The interview had continued over the coffee and then, suddenly, they'd found themselves making love on the living room sofa. Since she wasn't in the habit of going to bed with her subjects, or with men she'd only just met, she'd made a point of treating the event as an accident, and went on her way determined not to think any more about him. Luck and Gracie prevailing, she'd accepted an out-of-town job shortly thereafter and was able, with distance and time constraints, to remain detached.

Her detachment, however, had suffered considerably when, upon arriving home after a three-week absence, she'd found a desiccated floral arrangement outside her front door and several messages from Tyler on her answering machine. The third and final message had given his London address and telephone number, and an expression of his regret at not seeing her again before he left. She'd dutifully entered the information in her address book but made no attempt to contact him on subsequent trips to London. He was married, and she'd always had a horror of finding herself involved in a sordid affair as the "other woman."

She'd also always had trouble understanding men, the things they did, and why. And for reasons still unclear to her, she'd dealt all her adult life from what seemed to be a disadvantaged position with them. With women, too, for that matter. She could interview anyone, she'd often said; but she found "just talking" hard. She also failed to see the prettiness men claimed to admire in her. If anything, being a so-called pretty woman was a help professionally and a hindrance in private life. The men she'd known intimately seemed to have been more interested in the shape of her face than in any intelligence she possessed. Being in love could be hazardous to one's health, like smoking or drinking too much. She told herself it was preferable to remain detached and in control. And so she'd written off their intense interlude as an accident, but that hadn't stopped her from thinking about Tyler from time to time with something like longing.

That evening had been memorable, she thought as she retraced her steps to Henry's house. The two very brief affairs she'd had since had only fused her attention on that single session with Tyler. She'd eaten his food, asked her questions, taken his picture, removed her clothes, and lay down with him. Then he'd insisted on seeing her safely to her car, waiting until she was inside with the engine going before heading back to that apartment whose details and dimensions were even now indelibly imprinted on her brain. And on those occasions when she happened to be over on the West Side in the city, she'd think of Tyler and that apartment. In her mind, he'd never left. Everything remained precisely as it had been on that Sunday evening.

He'd been so unlike other theater people she'd interviewed, so unlike other men she'd met. And, actually, *he'd* removed her clothes, which had made her feel desirable.

Being expected to undress herself reduced her interest and desire, making what was about to happen seem more like a medical examination than an exciting encounter. He'd undressed her; he'd praised her; he'd made love to her with an attitude of privilege that had moved and disarmed her. He'd been so attentive and so interested in everything about her that she'd fled from the prospect of finding herself locked into a hopeless romance with him.

In the guest room, she stretched out on the bed for a nap, trying to imagine why fate had conspired to put Tyler back into her life. It was purely happenstance. Yet wasn't it funny how, until she'd seen him again just now, she'd remembered everything about him but the way he looked. Other people, even some she'd seen only once, stood very clear in her memory, especially her mother. She could effortlessly resurrect a portrait of Lily that was perfect even to the faint down that was visible on her forearms in strong sunlight. She could close her eyes and see her mother full-face or in profile, her pointed chin and deep-set gold-brown eyes, the massed weight of the hair at the nape of her neck. Beamer looked so like her that sometimes, seeing him, Jo wondered if their mother hadn't managed to relocate herself after death in her son. He even had Lily's same slow judicious delivery of thoughts and opinions, her same sudden ability to break into motion or laughter. He also had a talent for efficiency and neatness that was Lily to the core. Lily would have fifteen people in for dinner, and when Jo went off to bed, the living and dining rooms would be chaotic with dirty dishes, half-empty wineglasses, overflowing ashtrays; the counters in the kitchen would be lined with pots and pans and sticky wooden spoons; the carpet would be crunchy with the crumbs from French bread. Yet no matter how early the next morning she awakened it would be to find everything immaculate, the counters clean, the sinks empty, the carpets freshly vacuumed, as if no one had cooked or served four courses of a meal to noisy, invited guests. That was Lily.

Jo thought she was more like her father, cautious with her emotions, yet committed utterly to the people for whom she

28

cared. Both she and her father were fiercely devoted to home and their concept of it. It had been her father who'd gone about the house with a proud proprietary air, pausing to admire the way, for example, the sun filtered through the fronds of a Boston fern set on a column in the bay of the dining room windows. Often he'd come home from the office to tie on an apron and prepare the dinner. And when Jo and Beamer had been small children, it had been their father who'd overseen their nightly baths, heard their prayers, then tucked them in for the night; while Lily, preoccupied with plans for some forthcoming dinner party, or with some piece of needlework she was in the throes of designing, came in at the last when the children were barely awake to touch her lips to their foreheads before drifting away, leaving behind the fragrance of Chanel No. 5.

Lily, tall and thin and enigmatic, still drifted through Jo's thoughts, a piece of tramlined canvas half-painted in her hands, one of her husband's white shirts, its sleeves folded above the elbows, holding the light, her long legs pushing against the air. Lily, the old-fashioned, wistful-seeming debutante, had in fact been a model of independent progressiveness; it had been she who'd spotted in Beamer an early and powerful talent for mathematics. She'd come home one afternoon, calling for Beamer to come help her unload the many cartons filling the back of the station wagon: She'd bought him his first computer. And it had been Lily who, in spite of her husband's protests regarding the unsuitability and expense of the gift, had given the seven-year-old Joanna her first 35-mm SLR camera. "I think you need this" was what she'd said when giving the gift into her daughter's hands. "You're visual. I know you, and this is who you are."

Well, Jo was who she was, all right. Lily had certainly known about that. With her camera, or in the darkroom, Jo knew exactly what she was doing and who she was. But without the camera, or outside the darkroom, she was having trouble. There were those times of invisibility, when she felt that her eyes were the only part of her that were visible or functional, when she couldn't imagine why anyone would want to spend time with someone who'd become quite so boring or remote as she could manage to be.

Maybe, she thought, turning on her side as sleep overtook her, she was doing too much, or the wrong kinds of things; maybe she was spending too much time alone, although she did enjoy the apartment and was forever shifting the furniture to find arrangements that better pleased her eye. When she thought of the place, the image she had was of herself in the chair in front of the fireplace, her feet on the ottoman, and snow falling beyond the sliding glass doors. The sky was that deep blue-gray of twilight, and the trees surrounding the complex were black filigree against the night.

Tyler. It was just incredible . . .

She heard a quiet tapping at the door but couldn't get herself sufficiently awake to respond. The tapping stopped and she allowed herself to slide back into the welcoming depths of her sleep. Then there was a weight on the side of the bed and a light touch on her arm, and she forced her eyes open to see Henry sitting beside her.

"Hi, Henry," she said dopily. "I thought you were out for the evening."

"Hi, Jo. The client canceled." His hand remained a moment longer on her arm, then was withdrawn. "How are you?" he asked softly, as if she were still sleeping.

"I'm fine. How are you?"

"Splendid, thank you. Your friend's waiting. I've given him a drink."

"Oh, my God! What time is it?"

"Five-fifty. He's early."

"Shit, Henry! I think I'm in a coma."

He laughed and again put his hand on her arm. "Take your time. I'll entertain him until you're ready."

"Oh, thank you." She yawned hugely.

He stood up and headed for the door. Halfway there, he turned back to say, "Good to see you," and smiled—very meaningfully, she thought—before going out.

Ten to six. She jumped up, at once understanding Henry's

smile—she was half-naked, having slept only in her under-pants—and began trying to get ready while at the same time trying to determine how she felt about having held a brief conversation with the man while in a state of near nudity. God! She just couldn't think about it.

Shaky with fatigue, her hands were unsteady as she tried to do something with her hair, abandoned her attempt to put it up and allowed it to hang, then smudged on too much eye shadow. The lighting in the bathroom was dim, flattering; in stronger light she imagined she'd appear overdone. She should've put Tyler off until tomorrow evening. But wasn't it lucky Henry's client had canceled; otherwise no one would've answered the door and Tyler would have gone away wondering why she'd stood him up.

Dressed, she picked up her bag and hurried through to the front of the house, slowing as she approached the living room, to study Tyler in conversation with Henry. The two were standing near the fireplace, drinks in hand. They couldn't have been more different. Tyler had a small bald spot at the crown of his head and had cut his hair very short as if to show he not only knew he was losing his hair, but didn't give a damn. He was taller, thinner, and not as young as Henry. He was, she recalled, in his late forties, although he didn't look it.

Tyler was casually dressed in a pair of blue trousers and an open-necked long-sleeved white shirt. Henry, shorter and somewhat heavier, wore his usual three-piece suit—this one of pale gray. His shirt was white with a pencil-line gray stripe; his tie was of charcoal-gray silk. His hair was closely cropped but abundant. His mustache and beard were neatly trimmed; he had color in his cheeks; his eyes were very clear and very blue; he looked healthy, successful, and amused, as if by some private joke.

She stopped just inside the doorway and waited. She felt awkward, and loathed the feeling she occasionally had of being unequal to certain situations. Her talent and credentials got put on hold and she became someone who automatically stood to one side to observe the proceedings. She blotted her damp palms on a tissue as she waited for the men to notice her.

It was the shifting of Henry's eyes in her direction that alerted Tyler to her presence—and it also reminded her that Henry had, only minutes ago, gazed approvingly at her bared breasts. She blushed as Tyler turned, smiled, said "Aaahh!" and came to kiss her on both cheeks in the Continental fashion that always threw her off guard—the first kiss being expected, the second disconcerting. Henry, she saw, watched with interest and, Jo thought, with something like a proprietary air.

"You look so well, Joanna," Tyler was saying. "It really is wonderful, seeing you again."

"You look very well yourself," she said, feeling like a parrot, and wishing Henry weren't there to hear this inane dialogue.

"A drink?" Henry asked from over by the fireplace.

"I don't think so, thank you, Henry. Not on an empty stomach."

"Something nonalcoholic perhaps?"

"Nothing, thank you."

"Well, in that case." He downed the last of his drink, then said, "I'm off. You know where the key is, Jo dear. Good to meet you, Tyler." He shook hands with Tyler and patted Jo on the shoulder as he passed her. "Lunch tomorrow," he told her. "I'll see you at the office at twelve-thirty."

"Okay. Bye, Henry."

Tyler put his glass down on the coffee table, saying, "I thought I'd give you dinner at my place, if that's all right with you."

"Sure," she agreed.

Outside, he held open the passenger door of his car. "It's a fair distance," he told her, waiting to make sure she got her seat belt properly fastened.

"Whereabouts?" she asked.

"Near Camden Passage. Do you know it?"

"Vaguely. Where all the antique shops are, right?"

"Right."

He drove very fast, whipping in and out of the traffic, passing between cars so closely she just knew they were going to crash. The speed and his aggressive passage along the narrow streets made her nervous. At last, she ventured to say, "I'm afraid I'm a very bad passenger. Would you mind slowing down a bit?"

He glanced over, and for a moment she thought he might take this as a criticism and be offended, but he said, "Sorry, not thinking," and eased back on the accelerator. "I'm not a very good driver," he apologized. "I tend to get distracted, don't think about what I'm doing." He smiled before redirecting his attention to the traffic. "Yours, you'll be happy to know, is not the first complaint. Better?"

"Yes, thank you."

"It really is good seeing you again, Joanna. I thought perhaps I never would."

"How was your visit with your son?"

"Much the same as always. At twelve years of age he has far more important things on his mind than a dreary afternoon visit with old Dad. He was in that dreadful state of being torn between his sense of obligation and a burning need to know the West Indian cricket test scores. We each did our duty, had a walk and some sandwiches at the local pub, brought each other up to date on the events in our lives, then said goodbye. He's a decent boy; heart's in the right place. I love him utterly, hopelessly, stupidly, and try not to let either of us take advantage of my affection for him."

"You have just the one child?"

"Didn't know I had any, did you?" He grinned over at her mischievously.

She smiled, admitting, "No."

"You look sleepy," he said sympathetically. "Jet lag's such a bitch." He glanced again at her. For a very pretty woman, she had no conceit. As a result the impression she'd made initially, and made again upon him now, was contradicted by the way she presented herself. She looked most sophisticated, dressed smartly; altogether she was very nicely assembled. But her self-effacing, quiet manner, along with her shy smile made her infinitely less formidable than she seemed at first sight. She had warm brown eyes and an exquisite complexion. She was also a superb photographer. He considered the shots she'd done of him to be the best ever. He felt they reflected the man he was, rather than the projection of an image he wanted others to see.

"So what are you doing now?" she asked him.

"Just opened with a nice little four-hander I've directed. Comedy-suspense-whodunit. With luck, it'll have a decent run. Not *The Mousetrap*, but it has potential. Good script; cast's better than all right; fair notices. I don't, however, care any more for the business than I did when we met."

"Doesn't seem as if you do," she agreed.

"It's a bloody great relief not to have to put a face on it for you. Most of the time one's bouncing about raving what a marvelous thing it is, what a super cast, what smashing sets. It's such shit! Never mind that! Tell me about Joanna and what you're doing here!"

"I'm doing a piece on the Orient-Express."

"Oh, lucky you!"

"I guess. It doesn't seem altogether real to me. It probably won't until Sunday morning when I'm actually getting on the train. For some reason I'm very worried about this job."

"Do you usually worry?"

"Sure. About every job, although lately I seem to be getting worse." She looked over, taking quick mental snapshots: His face was freshly shaved, angular, his cheekbones high and slanting, his hazel eyes slightly hooded; strong nose, generous mouth, high forehead. He was a handsome man, one Americans would call rugged. She couldn't think what the British equivalent might be. He was easy to talk to. It was as if they'd seen each other only days before, and her reactions to him were almost as they'd been at their first meeting. There was a place inside her that was especially vulnerable to him, as if long ago he had, in advance of their meeting, reserved a spot in her emotions so that when they met she'd have the sense she did of always having known and been aroused by him.

"Perhaps you need a break," he suggested, "some time to yourself."

"Maybe so." Suddenly, she recalled Henry sitting on the bed beside her, his hand on her arm as he talked softly in the darkened room. Good to *see* you. She suffered another brief spasm of embarrassed confusion and felt her face grow hot. Why had it seemed as if the two of them had played out that scene before? Why had it felt, for a few seconds, as if the next logical step would be Henry's slipping into bed with her?

"Here we are!" Tyler announced, pulling up on the wrong side of the street behind a van.

She looked out to see trim white rows of houses lining both sides of a street that was, by London standards, unusually wide. And the houses were larger than those she'd looked at this morning in Chelsea; spacious two-story dwellings most of which had, from the look of them, been recently renovated.

None of what was happening had been planned, and little of what she'd planned—ever—seemed destined to happen. For a moment she wondered if she was entirely awake, or if she wasn't somehow caught in the unraveling threads of a dream.

She felt a bit guilty about Henry, and wondered if he was bothered by her failing to spend her first evening in town with him. But he'd had plans. And they'd been canceled. So where had he been going? He hadn't said. He'd just effected a smooth exit and gone off. Was he seeing a new woman? she wondered. She hoped not. She didn't think she could survive one more of Henry's women. He had the worst taste, really. After Brenda, there'd been Gillian, one of those awful, horsy British women who smell of oats and leather. She'd lasted about six months. Then there'd been a lull of a year or so before the advent of Francesca, who came and went in less than three months. Then, for about two years, Henry hadn't seen anyone in particular. Jo had stayed with him three times during that period and they'd had good, long, heavily conversational visits. It had all ended with Suzanne, who wound up staying for—what? Four years? Jo had privately feared Henry might actually marry her. But now she was gone. No more Suzanne. Thank God Henry hadn't married her.

"Jo?" Tyler tapped her on the arm. "I said we're here. Are you awake?"

"Oh, right. Sorry."

He held open the door and she lifted her leaden body out of the car.

4

TYLER'S FLAT WAS BELOW STREET LEVEL, AND SURPRISINGLY Mediterranean. Running the full length and width of the house, it had terra-cotta-tiled floors, stark white walls, an ultramodern open-plan kitchen that was separated from the living room by a serving hatch, and two large airy bedrooms. The furniture was minimal and plain: a sofa, half a dozen huge floor pillows, a coffee table, and a wall unit in the living room; an immense bed, side table, and wardrobe in Tyler's bedroom; a single bed, chest of drawers, and wardrobe in the other bedroom, which was obviously his son's when he came to visit. The bathroom was also very modern, with a heated towel rack, a tub as well as a shower, and a bidet alongside the toilet. On the walls of the long hallway that ran from the front door through to the living room were framed posters of plays and films in which Tyler had appeared or which he'd directed. The only adornment gracing the living room wall was a large, exquisitely rendered oil painting of a country scene. Its frame was of ornate scrolled gold-painted wood, and bore a brass plaque giving the name of the artist and the title. The artist was Joseph Mallord William Turner.

Jo looked at the engraved name, then stood away to study the painting again, experiencing a flutter in her chest as she took in the details of the placid country scene above which, in the distance, darkening clouds gathered menacingly. Her reaction had two distinct levels: The first was composed of awe, even reverence; the second was one of recognition, not of the painting itself but of childhood afternoons spent at her grandmother's farm.

Her father's parents had lived on what had been, early in the century, a working farm. By the time they'd bought the place, the fields had been reclaimed by wild grasses and weeds. It had been the James family's country home during the early years of their marriage and, after her grandfather's retirement from his law firm in Manhattan, their full-time residence.

Jo barely remembered her grandfather, who'd died when she was five, but she'd adored her grandmother, who'd stayed on at the farm until her death at ninety-two, when Joanna was thirty. And the view from the wide verandah of the old stone house had been very like the one in the painting on Tyler's wall. Looking at it revived the joy of her visits to her grandmother, the summer months she'd spent at the farm as a child. She'd walked with her grandmother through the fields in the late afternoon, feeling the sun on her shoulders and the dry warmth of Granny Emily's hand as they'd made their way at a leisurely pace toward the stream that cut across the northwestern corner of the land.

Granny Emily was the most generously open-hearted person Jo had ever known, a woman prepared to love every newcomer on sight. Smiling, wide-eyed, with tremendous natural enthusiasm, she'd created for Jo some of her happiest memories, the majority of them consisting of revelatory moments when her grandmother pointed out some example of earthly splendor or made some quiet observation about the ways of the world. It was her grandmother who taught Jo how to *see*, to take note of everything around her—the life beneath the wild-growing grasses as well as that beneath the surface of the stream. Always saying "Hush now, look!" she directed the child to be still and to allow her eyes to absorb all the details that might otherwise be missed. There had been many occasions when Jo had sat in one of the wicker porch rockers beside Granny Emily, the two of them silent as they watched a storm approach over the fields. "It's not here yet," her grandmother would say when Jo thought perhaps it was time to go indoors. "Wait awhile and watch." And sure enough, it would take another ten minutes or more before the rain spread itself over the house, forcing them inside. They would sit together on the sofa in the warm-seeming circle of light from the old standing lamp and go through Sears, Roebuck catalogs from fifty years before that Jo had discovered in a box in the attic. "We had a brass bedstead like that when I was a girl," Granny Emily would say of an advertisement. "Twenty-two dollars was a fortune back then. Imagine that!" Or they'd giggle together over the corsets tied onto wasp-waisted women who seemed, in the illustrations, to have no difficulties breathing. "Be glad they've done away with those contraptions," Granny Emily told her. "I'm sure it's why we all dropped like flies, fainting dead away of a summer afternoon."

Granny Emily's heart simply ceased beating one night, according to the nurse-companion who spent eight years with her at the last. "When I go," said Peggy, who'd also adored Emily, "I'd sure like it to be that way. Just close my eyes at the end of a good day and sleep my passage into heaven."

Dragging her attention away from the painting, Jo turned toward the kitchen, where Tyler was uncorking a bottle of wine. I could live here, she thought, and said, "This is a great apartment."

"It has its drawbacks," he said, but without intensity.

"You even have a lovely little patio," she noticed, looking out past the French doors.

"It's bloody cold in the winter," he explained, coming over to give her a glass of white wine. "And there's a drainage problem out there." He inclined his head toward the patio. "On the plus side, there's a laundry room, as well as several other storerooms I haven't quite decided what to do with. And it's wonderfully cool in the summer. It's also, incidentally, tripled in value since I bought it three years ago.

This area's gone very trendy. It was in a transitional stage when I moved in. Used to be mainly West Indians here back in the sixties. Now it's chock-a-block with the British version of yuppies. Come sit down, Joanna.''

He sank down on the sofa, propping his feet on the coffee table. "I'm afraid you're about to learn the truth about me." He smiled at her.

"What truth?" she asked, joining him.

"Aside from stews in winter, I can't cook much more than omelettes. And if I recall correctly, I dazzled you the last time with one of those."

"That's all right. It was terrific."

"Thank God!" He laughed softly, then took a swallow of wine.

"Is it a real Turner?" She shifted around for another look at the painting.

He, too, looked, then smiled and leaned across to kiss her cheek.

"You are such a dear little person," he said affectionately. "It is indeed real. My great-grandfather spent rather a large portion of his inheritance to acquire it. My son will own it one day, and, with good luck, his son after him. It's all any of the men in the family have had in the way of a fortune to pass along."

"I'd say it was a lot."

"I feel that way," he agreed. "Of course, at twelve, Jeremy would prefer to think he'd inherit the Jaguar. I had to explain to him that if I dropped dead tomorrow, by the time he was of an age to drive, what he'd inherit would be a rusting great pile of scrap metal. He had the idea the car would get parked in the garage alongside his mother's and would simply be there, waiting for him. That was assuming I was going to drop dead in the very immediate future." He laughed. "I honestly think he was a little disappointed about that."

"There's nothing wrong with you, is there?"

"Not a thing," he assured her, "beyond the usual ravages of advancing old age."

"You're not that old. It's very nice out there," she said, her eyes again on the patio. "Do you use it much?"

"Not so far this summer, what with the show. We were supposed to have a provincial tour, but the plans were changed and they let us open early because a theater came available. How pretty you are, Joanna."

"Oh, no," she said quietly, automatically, still looking at the patio, liking the disparity of the shadowy enclosed area and the still-light sky above; rich, trailing vines crept down the walls from some unseen garden above. There was something mysterious, even faintly ominous about the damp-looking cement patio floor and the darkly green potted plants massed in one corner.

"Oh, yes," he insisted equally quietly, taking hold of her hand and thereby drawing her attention back to him. "Lovely dark eyes," he said, his hand lifting to touch her cheek, "beautiful skin."

She sat immobilized, listening, waiting, breathing slowly, cautiously. She was fascinated by his interest in her.

He studied her for quite some time, trying to work beyond her denial of prettiness to its actuality. She was, he thought, the embodiment of prettiness: her heart-shaped face enclosed by the incurving sweep of her thick brown hair with its razor-edged fringe falling just to her eyebrows, its darkness contrasting wonderfully with her pale, flawless complexion; her eyes wide-set and perfectly round, long-lashed and almost black; her nose small and well placed, her mouth deliciously bowed, her chin daintily cleft. He had, from their initial meeting, very much liked the look of her. He wondered if he'd ever commented to her on how strongly she reminded him of Louise Brooks as Lulu. He didn't think he had. It was the hair, mainly, that blunted cut, longer than Lulu's but otherwise the same. And the expressiveness of those eyes, the uptilting corners of her mouth. A dear little person, with a dear little face. And, as he well remembered, a most mature and expressive little body; narrow-hipped, small-waisted, with beautiful breasts that were absolutely symmetrical and not too large for her frame.

He knew she was watching him, but for the moment he was too absorbed in studying her, and deriving too much pleasure from the act, to break the spell. He wanted just another few seconds to remind himself of the details, of the appeal of her somewhat stubborn chin and her slightly lowered eyelids. He found even her makeup—a touch of color in her cheeks and around her eyes—rather touching. And what fascinated him most was the dichotomy between this quiescent creature silently sitting next to him and the woman she was when working. The two seemed unrelated. In repose, she didn't appear to be capable of the work he knew she did— especially the photography.

Again he touched the back of his hand to her cheek, watching as he did the way her eyes widened oh-so-subtly in response.

"I saw this woman this morning, taking photographs down by the Embankment, and I thought, 'How like Joanna she is! How very like Joanna.' Then I came closer, and you turned and pointed your camera in my direction, and I thought, 'My God! It is Joanna!' And I told myself it simply wasn't possible. There I was in Chelsea for a breakfast chat with the show's producers. I'm rarely in Chelsea, and rarely first thing in the morning. And who should I see but the one woman on earth I truly thought I'd never see again." His hand stroked her cheek and she thought, irrationally, that he must be a good father because he had a gentle touch, a personal touch, as if he was a man who demonstrated his fondness through his fingertips and open palm. "Joanna," he said softly, taking his caress to her hair.

Her response to his approach was immediate and spontaneous. She was simply ignited. His hand went under her skirt, his mouth opened on hers, and she couldn't think at all. Dazed, she watched him undo her blouse, watched him apply his hands to her breasts, and felt she might stop breathing altogether. He whispered, "Jesus Christ, Joanna!" and reached under her skirt with both hands. She lifted, helping, then closed her eyes and clutched his shoulders as he slid to his knees on the floor and held her to his mouth. Incendiary caresses; then he moved abruptly away from her and she opened her eyes, a maddened accomplice, to see him rising in front of her. Dragging her with him, he sank down on one of the floor pillows, pushed her skirt out of the way and brought her down on his lap, both of them tugging at his trousers. Panting as if they'd just run a race, his hands on her hips brought her forward; he surged to meet her, held her steady, made an entry into her body that was smoothly triumphal, then directed her into a demented dance that ended with noisy finality, followed by sudden silence. She lay against his chest with her head on his shoulder, formless and deadened as if he'd found some hidden zipper through which he'd removed her skeleton.

"I've been wanting to do that for three years," he said, almost angrily, holding her very tightly. "Why the hell did you run away from me in New York?"

She shook her head, unable yet to find her voice, and wondered why she'd allowed this to happen. He'd closed in on her so quickly she hadn't had time to think. It was exactly what he'd done in New York.

"I thought you didn't care, Joanna. I thought perhaps it hadn't been as rare and delightful as I'd thought. You flew away and didn't respond to my flowers or telephone messages. I was inept, or heavy-handed, or had completely misread the signs. I thought I'd made an utter ass of myself."

"No," she said quietly. "None of those things. *I* thought it was casual."

"Oh, I see. Three years later, it turns out you think I'm one of those casual fuckers, so cocky and confident I'll have any woman available."

"That isn't what I thought."

"But how was I to know that? I could only interpret your silence as disinterest, or possibly disgust. It had to be that I'd repelled you, this grunting, sweating, middle-aged man trying to prove himself of interest to a sweet young woman."

"It wasn't that way at all. Is that how you think of yourself?" She found the strength to sit away and look at him.

"Not as a matter of course. But in recent times, yes. I

spoke to you on the telephone and agreed to the interview, thinking you'd be another half-assed journalist intent on self-promotion. Then you arrived and you were nothing of the sort. You were so keen, so bloody aware of externals, so gentle and unassuming, and so totally unaware of yourself. All the while we talked I kept looking for the chinks in the performance, but it was entirely real. You hadn't the least idea how adorable you were. And it hasn't changed."

"Tyler, you were *married*."

He stared at her for a long moment, then gave a bitter-sounding laugh. "No," he told her. "No! Not only did you think I was a casual fucker, you thought I also casually fucked around on my wife. No, no, no!"

He held her face in his hands and said, "I've been married. Twice. My first was a qualified disaster that ended some fourteen years ago. And my second, my poor second marriage, it . . . What happened to it? It was euthanized about five months before you and I met. Neither of us wanted it to end, Joanna, but it had to be put to sleep, rather like a big old family pet that had outlived its ability to do more than eat from its bowl and dream for hours at a stretch in front of the fire. I was devoted to Dianne. I believe it was mutual. God only knows, we went through the wars together. But it all just slowly, sadly trickled away. We outgrew our need for each other. It was *over* when I met you, Joanna." He withdrew his hands from her face and waited for her response.

She couldn't, for a moment, meet his eyes. She shook her head, and the movement caused her hair to swing forward over her face, leaving strands caught in her eyelashes. She didn't want to consider the implications of her flight three years before. It was too humiliating, evidence of her fearfulness and her inability either to trust her own instincts or what she seemed to see without a lens to look through. She'd run away, believing she'd made a bad judgment call. She didn't ever want to be some man's well-kept secret.

"I thought it was because I was there, I was handy and willing," she confessed. "And then afterward, the flowers

44

and all, well, you were just being nice because that's the way you were: nice. It was the kind of thing I thought you'd do.''

"I see. Well,'' he smiled at her, "I am nice. But not *that* nice. I was very taken with you. It seemed not to be reciprocal. A fine kettle of fish, wouldn't you say?''

She smiled at him. "My grandmother used to say that.''

"Did she now?''

"Yes, she did.''

"Are you going to run away again, Joanna?''

"I don't know. I don't know what's happening.''

"What's happening,'' he said, "at this very moment, is pure, requited, unadulterated bloody lust.'' He underscored each word so carefully, so dramatically, that she had to laugh.

"I'm not completely stupid, Tyler. That part I definitely understood.''

"Good! Then understand this: I am forty-nine years old, and my past history is against me. I admit that absolutely. I'm in no position to make rash promises, so I will do my utmost not to promise you anything I can't deliver. I'm also in no position to make expensive emotional mistakes, nor would I ever wish to hurt you in any way. I haven't the foggiest where this is headed, and I have no intention of pushing one way or another. I would simply like both of us to give it a chance, see where we get to.''

She remained very still, wishing, just for once in her life, she could manage to integrate the two too-distinct halves of her self so that her decisions, when she made them, would be rooted in a confidence born of age and experience. Maybe it was never going to happen. Maybe she'd spend the rest of her life relying on her career to give her credibility. She hated the thought of that, even despaired of it. She'd permitted Greg to persuade her into four years of turmoil. All she knew for certain was that never again was anyone going to push her into a commitment about which she had doubts. And she was far too tired at that moment to make a decision about anything.

"What you said before, about the way what happened made

you feel. Was that really the truth?'' she asked, looking at
the remains of their meal on the coffee table.

"Actually, it was somewhat less than the whole truth. If
anything, I understated it. I think we all have these snapshots
of ourselves we carry about in mental portfolios. We see
ourselves as this or that, and we behave in ways we think are
commensurate with those images. Then, when things don't
go quite as we'd imagined they would, it seems those pocket
snaps are invalidated, inaccurate. I was embarrassed,'' he
conceded. "I was under the impression that you and I were
at the brink of something very good. Then, a few weeks
later, I felt like the biggest fool, self-deluding, out of touch,
old. I'm not able to speak for other people, but when that
sort of thing happens, I've a tendency to reexamine events
and my part in them, and to decide I missed something or
performed less than brilliantly. Possibly, it has to do with
having spent the better part of my life either acting or directing actors, playing out roles while trying to keep a grip
on who I really am. Most actors, you know, simply aren't
home. They're grateful to the theater or to films for allowing
them to slip into a persona that seems to fit for a time. I've
always had a vested interest in being myself. It's why I've got
rather a lot of contempt—intermittently, I admit—for acting.''

"Then why do it?'' she asked.

"It's the family business,'' he said with a smile. "My
father and mother were both in the theater. Mother gave it
up when she became pregnant with my sister, but Father
stayed in it to his death. The only one of the three children
who didn't go into the business is my brother Michael.

"It seemed eminently reasonable to me as a child that I'd
follow my father and older sister into the theater. I made my
first appearance at age seven in *A Midsummer Night's Dream*,
and that was that. It wasn't until I was in my mid-twenties
and married to Elizabeth, my first wife, who happened to be
a hugely successful film actress and considerably older than
I, that it occurred to me that pretending to be other people
for money was an absurd way to earn a living. It suited Eliz-

abeth perfectly, because her entire existence was a masterly performance. But I began to feel a fraud, and dishonest. Plus, I'd always loathed the more humiliating aspects of the business: the rigged auditions, the repeated call-backs, the necessity of burying one's native intelligence in order not to offend some director.

"On the plus side, nothing is quite so thrilling as a production that's all of a piece, when everything works and both you and the audience get caught up in the singular magic of a successful production. It's the hook that keeps you coming back. I would rather, however, be a photojournalist."

"Oh, no you wouldn't," she disagreed. "I think maybe we all wind up where we're supposed to be."

"Perhaps. But what you have, what you do is tangible, readily marketable. You're also highly gifted."

"It's strange, you know," she said, thinking back. "When I came to interview you, I was having a lot of trouble because I couldn't get any kind of a fix on you. There didn't seem to be one definitive, distinctive 'attitude' that was intrinsically you. You know? And then, when you got up to make the coffee, you unbuttoned your cuffs and rolled up your sleeves, and there it was."

"There *what* was?" he wanted to know, liking very much the change that overtook her when she talked about her work. She became articulate, confident, even forceful; she seemed to acquire crisper edges and stronger definition. She knew what she was about, didn't grope for words, didn't hesitate; she just allowed her visions to acquire tangibility.

"It. You. I knew who you were because of the attention you paid to grinding the beans, even to warming the coffee pot. I'd never seen anyone warm a coffee pot. It was so *idiosyncratic.* I had the picture then, in my mind. You know? And once I've got that, then actually taking the photograph becomes secondary."

"Are you aware," he asked her, most curious, "that you change when you've got a camera in your hands? It's true. I remember so vividly the way you actually seemed to alter physically. You were like a dancer, bending or stretching to frame the shot you wanted. I can still see you crouching in the corners of that kitchen, clicking away at me and murmuring to yourself as I tried very hard to pay attention to the normally simple routine of making a pot of coffee. Just a little unnerving it was, my dear, witnessing your transformation from soft-spoken, polite interviewer to aggressive, self-assured photographer. Altogether impressive, it was; changing lenses, adjusting the focus, moving closer, then away. I swear, it was as if the camera was some vital prosthetic device and with it in your hands you became suddenly complete.

"I mean to say, I found you pleasant enough during dinner. But the moment you opened your bag to take out the camera, you became positively compelling, electric. Like a sprite, you darted here and there, watching me through the viewfinder, your body sinuously insinuating itself into impossible spaces. And while you were snaking about the place, making me feel more of an observer than a participant, I might add, I was suddenly, seriously attracted to you. All at once, I noticed your hands, and the shape of your face, your ankles. I thought I'd like nothing better than to have you around for months so that I could watch you lose yourself to a process I seemed to know."

"How?" she asked, her head tilted to one side. "I don't know what you mean."

"Your description of the mental processes you go through to take your photographs isn't so very different from directing, you know. Both have to do with visualizing something and then attempting to make good on what you've seen."

She stared at him appreciatively, finding that receptive place inside herself expanding. "I think you're right. I'll bet if you tried, you'd probably take good photographs."

"That's your obsession, my dear. Mine has to do, if you will, with *tableaux vivants*. Similar, but different."

If she wasn't very careful, she thought, she'd fall in love with him. Then she wondered why that would be a bad thing. She knew very little about him, except what he was revealing to her now.

"Did you go to theater school, Tyler?"

"Learned by doing. School of trial and error."

"Maybe," she said tangentially, "no one's ever really completely happy."

"On a professional level," he answered soberly, "I think that would be deadly. If one grows satisfied, one's work tends to become stale. Satisfaction breeds smugness and a certain brand of fear. If you succeed at something, if it works well once, there's a tremendous temptation to keep on doing things that same way, over and over. When you take that route, you lose your freshness, your spark, the excitement generated by risk-taking."

Risk-taking? Was that what she did? She didn't think so. "I'm very tired, Tyler." All at once, the last of her energy was draining away. "Do you mind if I use your shower?" She was horrified by the idea of returning to the Chelsea house, possibly encountering Henry, with the evidence of her love-making with another man still wet on her flesh.

"Oh, terribly," he laughed. "Of course I don't mind. Come. I'll fetch you a towel." He held his hand out to her. "I've talked your ear off and here you are, poor dear, with your bloody jet lag."

He opened the door to the linen cupboard, removed a large sunflower-yellow towel and gave it to her, saying, "This is a good color for you, I think. I'll just clear away the dishes while you bathe, then run you back to Chelsea. You have everything you need?" he asked, his hand on the door.

"Yes, thank you."

He went out and she stood holding the towel, wondering why it was that things never happened when you were ready for them.

5

"WHEN WILL I SEE YOU?" TYLER ASKED, HIS HAND ON HER arm preventing her from leaving the car. "You can't just fly off without making a definite date for us to meet."

For a few seconds she couldn't think. Then she said, "Saturday. But it'll have to be an early night. I'll be packing, getting ready to leave Sunday morning."

"Saturday it is." He smiled at her, but she seemed preoccupied. "Is something wrong, Joanna?"

"Tyler," she began, then stopped, turning to look at him. "Tyler," she started again, "don't count on me. What I mean is, I don't know how I feel, and I never do know until I've had a chance to back away a bit and think things through."

"I see," he said stiffly.

"No, you don't," she disagreed. "It has to do with me, Tyler, not so much with you. I can't go into it right now. It's late and I'm falling asleep on my feet. We'll talk on Saturday. Okay?"

He stared into space for a moment, then turned and smiled, saying, "Of course. I'll see you to the door."

"No, that's all right." She leaned across the seat to give him a quick kiss. "I like you a lot. I liked you three years ago, and I like you now. The person I have the problem with is me. What time Saturday?''

"Six?"

"Great. I'll see you then.'' She got out, walked to the door, fished the key out of the flowerpot, and let herself in.

Henry called out "Hello!'' from the living room, and she walked inside to see him sitting in one of the armchairs, his tie loosened, a glass of white wine in his hand.

"Hi, Henry.'' She leaned against the door and looked in at him. He seemed happy to see her and beamed at her from the depths of the chair. One of the things that appealed to her about Henry was seeing in his face the schoolboy he'd once been. Despite his sophistication and his always proper style of dress, the schoolboy aspect was, to her mind, one of the most likable parts of Henry. He consistently looked as if he'd just emerged from a barbershop, with his hair trimmed in a side-parted style that had lately come back into fashion. His mustache and Vandyke beard were meticulously maintained yet the sight of them made her smile involuntarily because they seemed like a disguise the boy had adopted in order to make himself appear more mature.

"Could I get you a drink?'' he asked. "A glass of wine?'' She shook her head.

"A cup of tea?''

"No, thanks. I've got to go to bed. I can hardly keep my eyes open.''

"Poor you. Have a nice evening?''

"Uh-huh. How're you? Everything okay?''

"Everything is splendid, thank you. Business as usual. Run along to bed now, and I'll see you at the office tomorrow.''

"You love being an agent,'' she said. "How does someone get to love being an agent? All those writers calling up to complain.''

"Not quite. It's certainly not boring. *You're* not boring and you're one of those writers.''

"Henry, I'm one of the most boring people I know.''

"Shame on you,'' he chided. "You certainly are not.''

51

She sighed, then said, "I should've turned this one down. I have an awful feeling it's going to be a disaster."

"It'll be sublime. I wish I were going."

"I wish you were, too," she said, surprising them both.

"Very kind of you." He saluted her with his glass before taking another swallow of wine. "I thought you were off to bed."

"I am. You're so sweet, Henry. You really are. All those notes!" She laughed softly. "Eat me, Alice. Honest to God!"

He gave a self-deprecating shrug.

"You know something?" she asked, desperately sleepy yet anxious to continue talking with him. "You always remind me of a naughty schoolboy. It's what I see when I look at you."

He laughed hugely, then exclaimed, "You've caught me out! That is precisely and specifically what I am. *Hart Minor!*" he declaimed in a low rumble. *"Step out into the corridor and remain there until sent for!"* His laughter grew, sending tears to his eyes. "Hart Minor! You are in disgrace! We do not draw rude pictures in our copybooks! You will see me after class! *Hart Minor*, you are doomed to failure; you are utterly without redeeming graces! You are a filthy, disobedient little slug!" He wiped his eyes on his shirt sleeve. "I was an appalling schoolboy, forever going about with food stains on my jacket, tie askew, blots on my copybooks; sent time and again to Coventry for transgressions against the established decorum. On my last day the headmaster declared it wouldn't in the least surprise him to read one day in the newspapers that I'd been sentenced to Wormwood Scrubs for some truly heinous act against humanity. Christ!" Again he blotted his eyes. "I haven't laughed this hard in decades."

"What is 'Minor'?" she asked from the doorway, quietly captivated by his performance. He'd obviously been sitting drinking wine for some time. He wasn't anywhere near drunk, just nicely uninhibited.

"When you have two or more boys in an English school

52

with the same surname, the younger or the one with lesser standing becomes minor.''

"Oh! I thought it was like junior."

"No."

"I take it Suzanne's gone."

He nodded.

"D'you—miss her, Henry?"

"Not bloody likely. Do you miss what-was-his-name, Greg?"

"No, but that ended years ago. And you were with her for ages."

"History. It's better than five months since she left."

"I used to get the impression she wasn't fond of you having your clients stay here."

"There was," he said with a philosophical air, "a great deal Suzanne wasn't fond of. In the end, I wasn't especially fond of *her*."

"But don't you miss having someone around?"

"Yes and no." He set his wineglass down, got up and came across the room. "Are you aware that your eyes keep dropping shut?" He raised her chin with his cupped hand. "I think we'd best put you to bed, Jo. Come along." He took her hand and led her along the hallway to the guest room. Like a zombie she allowed him to direct her, feeling safe with Henry as she rarely did with anyone else. She stood and watched him straighten the bedclothes, then fold them back invitingly. "There you go," he said. "All you have to do is climb in, close your dear eyes, and go off to Noddy Land."

She laughed but didn't move. "I'm wondering," she told him, "if it's possible—to sleep standing up."

"Possible but not comfortable. Are you going to be able to manage?"

"Oh, sure," she answered, still unmoving.

He stood watching her. Again her eyes began to close. Amused, hands on his hips, he said, "This will never do. You'll ruin my reputation as a hotelier. Imagine having to put the guests to bed!"

Her eyes opened. "What?"

"Don't plan on this as a regular service. Smart top," he said, somewhat hesitantly approaching her.

"You like it? It's Claude Montana. Cost about the same as a small car."

He laughed. "Snaps. Thank God!"

"*Story of O* wardrobe," she quipped as he got her out of the blouse, then unzipped the skirt.

"You're supposed to help," he protested, daunted by her undergarments.

"Never mind, Henry. Just point me in the right direction."

"You're not drunk, are you?" he wanted to know, propelling her over to the bed.

"Only had two glasses of wine." She bumped into the side of the bed, turned and abruptly sat.

He gave her a little push and she obligingly lay down. He covered her with the blankets and watched as she moved beneath them. Then her arm emerged and she dropped her underwear over the side of the bed.

"You're supposed to tuck me in and give me a goodnight kiss," she told him.

"I'd like to remind you I am not your father."

"Hurry up!" She extended her arms straight up in the air and he bent to kiss her on the forehead. "Thank you," she murmured. "You smell good." She closed her eyes again, at once feeling the hum of jet engines in her body.

While he watched, her body visibly settled into a deep and immediate sleep. Stifling a laugh, he turned off the light and tiptoed out to return to the chair in the living room and the last of his wine.

An insistent mechanical beeping roused her. She opened her eyes, trying to figure out where she was and what was making the noise. The only thing on the bedside table, aside from a lamp, was a portable radio. She picked it up and held it as it continued, like some peculiar robotlike little creature, to give off its offended beeps. She pushed and pressed all its buttons and finally succeeded in silencing the alarm. Returning the clock-radio to the table, she saw the note Henry had left stuck to the lampshade. "See you at twelve-thirty. A most enjoyable performance last night. Your hotelier in good faith, H."

She smiled and sat up.

In the guest bathroom there was another note, this one stuck to the mirror. "Hope you're planning to have dinner with me this evening. Unless you have another date, you'll have to. In your absence, I ravished the Eat-me chicken. Cheers, H."

She laughed, peeled the Post-it from the mirror and dropped it into the wastebasket.

Henry kept her waiting for almost twenty minutes. Sitting in the reception area, she began to wonder if his keeping her waiting for so long meant something. It didn't feel right. The receptionist appeared intentionally to avoid Jo's eyes, and as more time passed all sorts of negative possibilities occurred to her: Henry was miffed at having had to put her to bed last night; something had gone wrong with her assignment and he was frantically trying to set it right before he saw her; he was angry with her about Tyler for some reason. She'd never had a date come to pick her up at Henry's house. Maybe he hadn't liked that.

By the time he emerged from his inner office, she just knew she was in trouble of some kind. This conviction was compounded by his failure to apologize for keeping her waiting, and by his curt greeting, which consisted only of a nod. His face was tight, even angry, and he remained silent as they left the building together. Her reaction was to draw herself together inside, and to harbor a mounting anger of her own. Two men now, in the space of just hours, had pressured her in some way. Was it something about her that made them behave this way? She couldn't see that it was.

Without bothering to say where they were going, he walked very quickly, cutting in and out of the midday crowds, toward the restaurant he'd booked into for lunch. His pace and continuing silence heightened her anger. She looked into the faces of people they passed, seeing colors and styles of dress she liked, and wished she'd brought the camera. She'd have preferred to be wandering around taking pictures rather than trying to figure out why Henry was behaving as he was.

And what kind of an idiot was she? she demanded of herself, hurrying to keep up with his wild dash along the streets. She had to be some kind of jerk to give in so easily—the way she had last night, for example, with Tyler. It made her squirm to think what a pushover she was. And there it was! She'd been anticipating this rush of self-hatred since leaving Tyler the night before. It was what she'd tried to warn him about: she was unreliable, except where her work was concerned.

There was a short queue at the restaurant and they had to stand in the foyer with half a dozen others while the hostess seated the earlier arrivals. Jo couldn't look at Henry. He could go to hell. She'd reserve a hotel room for her return stay after Venice. She'd get the article done, then go home without seeing Henry or Tyler. She didn't care if she never saw either of them again.

"What's the *matter* with you?" she snapped finally. "I don't think I want to eat with you, Henry. My grandmother always said you should never eat with people you don't like or who make you uncomfortable. Right now, you're making me very uncomfortable. You haven't said a word to me, just marched me along here."

He looked totally taken aback by her outburst. His eyes stayed on her, but she could tell he was hoping no one was listening. She could also tell he was trying to come up with something to say to her. When he didn't speak, she said, "That's it! I'm leaving!" and turned to go.

She got all the way out the door and onto the street before he caught up with her, catching hold of her arm.

"I am sick and tired of accepting weird shit from people that makes me feel as if I did something wrong I'm supposed to know about, but don't. You kept me waiting for ages, Henry, then you came out and you might as well have snapped my leash, just expecting me to trot along after you. I shouldn't have come to stay with you. In fact, I'm going to go get my stuff right now and check into a hotel. I'm so *tired* of being expected to understand everything.'' She stood glaring at him, ready to storm off.

"Joanna, I'm sorry. It's been a perfectly foul morning, and I'm afraid I simply wasn't thinking.''

"Go to hell, Henry! I have foul mornings every day of the world and I still manage to be polite to people.''

She was so angry her face was scarlet. "Look,'' he said placatingly. "If I've been rude, it was completely unintentional, and I apologize most sincerely.''

"I'm also tired of people not thinking. I don't need this. I *really* don't need this. You were so darling to me last night, Henry. I was totally wiped out and you were an angel. But that was last night and you'd had your wine and were nicely oiled. Now it's today and I'm just another pain-in-the-ass client.''

"That is most assuredly *not* how I think of you,'' he said emphatically. "I apologize for keeping you waiting, and for not speaking to you. I *wasn't* thinking; I was distracted. Please, let me give you lunch and we'll set things to rights.''

"I don't want to eat with you, Henry. At least, not in there.''

"Fair enough,'' he said quickly, gamely. "We'll go somewhere else.''

"Forget it! I'm not hungry. Why do men *do* these things, as if women aren't people, don't deserve the same courtesy you give each other? All you guys slapping each other on the backs, all so full of it. I *hate* men. With all my heart, I hate men!''

"Aahhh, now!'' He smiled at her. "You know you don't really hate me, Jo. Now, I've apologized, and rather nicely, too, I think. I refuse to accept your thesis that men are more polite to each other than they are to women. At least I, for one, don't subscribe to that policy. You've scolded me thoroughly; I am abject. I propose that I pop into one of the take-away places along here, get some sandwiches, then we'll sit down somewhere safely neutral where I will tell you about my morning and you will confide to me the real reason for your anger.''

Accepting her failure to reply as agreement, he hurried into a take-away place and returned in a few minutes carrying a white paper bag.

"There are some benches just along here," he told her.

Luckily, there was an empty one. She chose to sit as far from him as she was able. Smiling inwardly, he doled out the contents of the bag—two cheese and chutney sandwiches and two containers of tea—then, as he unwrapped his sandwich, he observed, "I've never known you to be temperamental. I am very sorry to have upset you. I truly don't know what I was thinking of, treating you in that fashion. Sometimes, I think we do and say things, behave in certain ways because no one thinks to stop us. In that regard, I may be rather spoiled. Certainly no one in the office would dare say a word. I am, after all, their employer. But, Jo, I do believe you trust me. Otherwise, I think you'd have said nothing.'' He gazed penetratingly at her for a moment, then continued. "If that trust didn't exist, you wouldn't have blasted me quite so thoroughly. We tend to display our true feelings only to those from whom we believe we'll receive an honest response. So now, why don't you tell me what's upset you.''

She looked away. The untouched sandwich sat on her lap. She could feel the July heat beating down on the top of her head, soaking into her clothes. She despised herself.

Failing to get any reaction from her, Henry, between hungry bites of his sandwich, said, "I'll enlighten you about my morning. I began the day with a light step, cheery and optimistic. Arrived at the office, and within mere minutes, the crises began. First came the telex having to do with the loss, the actual, physical loss, of a manuscript that was being sent by courier from one of our authors to his publisher. It's been missing for *six* days, and the damned book's already behind schedule. Then, not one but two authors rang up to point out errors we'd completely missed in their contracts. *Then*, the bank manager informed me that a very substantial check we'd paid in from a supposedly highly reputable foreign publisher had bounced sky-high. On and on, climaxing with a hysterical editor screaming—and justifiably—over an author's having removed all the editorial flags from a manuscript, thereby incapacitating the poor editor. Minor madness. You look especially pretty this morning. The sun's turned your hair quite red. You must forgive me, Jo. Surely you know I'd never want to upset you in any fashion."

"How come hardly anybody tries to anticipate the effects of the things they say and do?" she asked, still not looking at him. "I practically kill myself trying not to step on people's feelings, to be thoughtful and considerate. And I wind up every single time feeling steam-rollered. Never mind *feeling* it, I *am* steam-rollered. I just go along and let myself be used because I don't have the brains or something to say 'Wait a minute!' Nobody gives you any time."

"What's happened, Jo?"

"You'd think I was old enough to know better. I like the light," she said confusingly. "Maybe I'll go back to your place and get the camera."

"You haven't eaten, and you haven't said you accept my apology."

"I'm really not hungry. And I do accept your apology, Henry. I can't tell you what happened. It would be tacky and indiscreet, especially since I haven't actually figured it out for myself yet."

"It might help to talk about it."

"I've got to stop letting these things happen to me. That's really what I'm angry about. Anyway," she took a deep breath, "I should go back. I've got notes to make about the train."

"If you're certain. You will have dinner with me, won't you?"

"Oh, sure. Why not?"

"Don't make it sound like a chore, Jo. I'm really very fond of you, you know."

"Since when? You've never shown one bit of nonprofessional interest in me in ten years. Are you sure you haven't decided to be fond of me because of Tyler?"

"That's nasty!" he accused.

"You're right, it is. I'm sorry. I don't know about you, Henry, but I think I'd rather take photographs of the world right now than get bogged down in the middle of it. Honest to God. You have no idea how nice people can be when you're on a shoot. They'll get out of your way, stand back and watch respectfully for ages. Most people think you're doing something really special and they admire that."

"That's because you *are* doing something special. I've only seen the end result, of course, but I imagine people are able to see quite readily that you not only know what you're on about but that you're very bloody good at it, to boot. It is not, however, possible or healthy to stay forever on the outside looking in. Sooner or later, whether or not we much care for it, we're bound to get involved. And it's up to you to control your own life. Now, I won't preach any more at you. But humor me: Eat."

She unwrapped the sandwich, stared at it for some moments, then picked up one of the quarters. "You're being too nice," she complained, most of her anger lost. "How can I keep on being mad when you're being so reasonable?"

"You can't."

She looked over to find him smiling at her.

"Can you?" he coaxed, anxious to be back on good terms with her.

"No." In spite of herself she had to respond to his smile. "Why do I like you, Henry?"

"Because I represent the quintessential best of British manhood."

"Oh, right! How could I have forgotten that? Silly me."

"Eat that, Jo dear, before it goes stale."

"The best of British manhood," she scoffed.

"You have an impressive temper."

"Thank you."

"You're welcome."

6

"GEORGES NAGELMACKERS WAS STRONGLY IMPRESSED BY the American, George Pullman. Pullman's first car, Pioneer, influenced every luxury train coach for nearly half a century. Nagelmackers' meetings with Pullman renewed his interest in his dream of a transcontinental European express."

She put down her pen, giving her eyes a rest while she considered what she'd been reading. Pioneer had been too big and too heavy to be used on the rails existing at the time, so it had sat on a siding for months, a great big beautiful curiosity—until the assassination of President Lincoln. Then, Pullman had offered his carriage to Mrs. Lincoln to carry the president's body. The rails along the route were widened and Pullman's creation moved into history. How, she wondered, had he come up with that idea? Had he done it out of some genuine desire to be of service to his country, or had he made the offer knowing that both he and the carriage would benefit from the attention it was bound to receive on its stately journey? Probably both. Pretty damned clever of old Pullman.

She looked again through the article, trying to find a hook upon which she might hang her own piece. Yes, there was the tie-in between the train and the hotel, but the article needed a viewpoint and she didn't have one yet. Undoubtedly, she would find it once she'd actually been on the train, and it wasn't normally something she worried about in advance. Yet here she was, worrying about it, and thinking it a shame that the dates were a little off, otherwise she could have tied the inaugural run of the Orient-Express on October 4, 1883, to its "second start" on May 25, 1982. Maybe she could use that anyway. She chewed on the end of her ballpoint pen as she scanned the list she'd made of important facts. It all sounded so removed and dry, so unreal. "The Train of Kings, the King of Trains." Maybe that had impressed people a hundred years ago, but nowadays not a whole lot was impressive—to anyone. People had seen and done it all; the most remote places were accessible and a lot of folks had the money for the fare. What could she possibly say about this train that hadn't already been said dozens of times before? Hers certainly wasn't the first piece to be written on the VS-O-E.

Agitated, she got up and went to the kitchen to put on the kettle. While she waited for it to come to a boil, she stared out at Henry's beautiful garden. A long, narrow enclosure, it was surrounded on three sides by high brick walls. Down the right-hand side and along the rear wall Henry had planted tiers of flowers and shrubs, with tall perennials rearmost and low-to-the-ground annuals front-most, and careful attention paid to color. On a circular bricked area halfway down the garden sat a round white-painted metal table and four graceful chairs. A red-and-white-striped Cinzano umbrella sheltered the grouping from the sun. Trees from the neighboring gardens provided shade in the early morning and late afternoon, casting dappled patterns over the grass and flowers.

She wondered if she, like Katharine Hepburn in *Summertime*, might take a humiliating spill in some polluted canal, or be pursued by some fabulously handsome Rossano Brazzi–type Venetian. Oh, sure! That kind of stuff only happened in movies. And hadn't Hepburn developed some kind of permanent eye infection from taking that movie dive into the canal? And why had the Hepburn character gone scurrying home to Ohio or wherever instead of sticking around for more of Rossano? It would've been a different picture altogether if it had been written by a woman, without the corny symbolism of fireworks in the night sky and an abandoned shoe on a balcony. Still, there were moments that were horribly, painfully accurate, like that scene with poor Katharine sitting all by herself at a table in the piazza, watching all the twosomes go by.

The movie hadn't been at all the way she'd remembered it. She'd forgotten about the stunning blond older woman who'd owned the pensione, and the darling little boy who'd followed Hepburn everywhere, getting her to buy feelthy postcards, and trying to sell her pens and stuff. God! That little boy would have to be in his forties now. And Hepburn was pretty near eighty. The amazing thing about movies was the way everyone in them stayed the same age forever. Only the audience got old.

The kettle had boiled and shut itself off. She turned it on again while she got down a mug and a teabag. She happened to glance up as she was about to return the tea canister to the cupboard, and there was another note from Henry.

"Biccies in red tin. Your favourites with the dark chocolate. Courtesy of H. Hart, Hotelier."

She laughed. It wasn't possible to be angry with someone who left notes all over the place. Did he do it for everyone who came to stay, or only for her? She couldn't recall his ever leaving notes for Suzanne, but he may have done at the beginning, and Suzanne may not have been amused. She'd had absolutely no sense of humor, Suzanne. Maybe someone that beautiful didn't feel she needed one. "Who knows?" Jo said aloud, pouring water over the teabag in the mug. Beautiful women were so intimidating. Suzanne had been, for damned sure. And Jo had always wondered how Henry could treat her so matter-of-factly, as if there wasn't anything special about her. For her part, Jo had never been able to think of anything sensible to say to the tall, coolly blond, alarmingly elegant woman. Perhaps it had been because Suzanne had seemed less than interested in anything Jo might have had to say to her. She'd been polite, inquired nicely after Joanna's health, asked did she have everything she needed, then gone on her way—to talk on the telephone in her frightfully-frightfully voice, or to speak in an urgent undertone to Henry in the privacy of their bedroom, or off on one of her astounding shopping sprees. The woman had private resources that were apparently limitless, and she'd thought nothing of spending three or four hundred pounds for a pair of shoes, or a scarf. Jo had been stunned speechless on one occasion when Suzanne had displayed for her—like a teacher with a small child—her acquisitions of the afternoon: two Hermès scarves, a pair of Ferragamo boots with a matching satchel, a "divine little bangle" from Cartier, and an assortment of Chanel cosmetics. Jo had looked over at Henry to see his reaction to these purchases, but he'd seemed only mildly interested and definitely unimpressed.

Then there'd been that time when Jo had been awakened by the sounds emanating from the bedroom down the hall. Suzanne and Henry had been doing something in there—bumping into the walls and furniture, their voices raised but their words indistinguishable. To escape them, and the memory their noise triggered, she'd put on her coat and boots—it had been winter that visit—and had gone to sit on the rear steps gazing sleepily at the frozen garden, waiting it out until they finished their fight, or their lovemaking, or whatever it was they'd been doing.

According to Henry, Suzanne had left shortly afterward. Jo imagined she'd probably taken up with some duke or earl with a "divine little pied-à-terre" in Belgravia. What a bitch! Jo liked most women, found them almost always willing to talk, to confide, to share, and it distressed her to meet someone like Suzanne, who was a woman only anatomically but not in disposition. So, the big question was: What had Henry seen in her? And what did he mean when he said he was really very fond of Joanna?

Carrying her tea, she opened the kitchen door and sat down at the top of the rear steps. It was time to confront her feelings about what had taken place with Tyler.

On a night some thirty years before, Jo had awakened very abruptly, very completely, and had sat in her bed blinking in the darkness, trying to think why she was awake in the middle of the night, when she heard the sounds she then understood had seeped through the layers of her dreams. From down the hall, the sound of her parents' voices came sliding around the edge of her bedroom door, which always stood slightly ajar in order to admit a sliver of light from the chandelier on the landing, which stayed on all night.

She'd crept over to the door, holding her breath, listening to the altered yet recognizable voices of her mother and father as they growled at each other, heaving what seemed to be accusations back and forth. She'd been unable to make sense of the occasional words that came clearly, intact, down the length of the hallway. There'd been a lull and then, to her horror, she'd heard a cry, followed by the unmistakable sound of her mother's weeping.

Very afraid, Jo had gone running silently barefoot along to Beamer's room to find her three-year-old brother crouched among the pillows at the top of his bed, chewing on his fists. She'd climbed into bed with him, whispering, "It's okay, Beamer," and settled down with her arms protectively encircling him. "Go to sleep, Beamer," she'd whispered in the tone she'd heard their mother use a hundred times. And he had. Pressing his wet face into her shoulder, he'd closed his eyes and gone to sleep, while Jo lay holding him for a long time, until the house was quiet and the only noise was of the wind pushing against the windows.

The next morning, just before boarding the school bus, Jo had turned to her mother to ask, "What happened last night? It woke up me and Beamer." And her mother had looked alarmed, saying, "God, Joanna! Don't ask me now! The bus is waiting. I can't answer you now. Ask me again when you get home from school." She'd urged Jo onto the bus, then stood at the foot of the driveway until the bus turned the corner and Jo couldn't see her anymore.

When Jo came home from school, Lily was in the kitchen, busy with preparations for one of her dinner parties. She let

Jo sit in a corner and lick various bowls and spoons, and Jo forgot to ask again. She did remember on subsequent days, but somehow it was never the right time to ask. So she didn't get an explanation. And it wasn't until many years later that an answer of sorts came to her quite by accident, one afternoon in Manhattan. But by then it no longer mattered—at least that's what she told herself—because she was well beyond childhood and innocence, and she no longer trusted people as she once had, with the exceptions of her grandmother and Beamer. Everyone else was suspect. And Greg, whom she'd trusted as best she was able because she'd told herself she'd spend her whole life alone if she didn't trust someone, proved to her that she'd not only misplaced her trust but also was not the best judge of men. She seemed rarely able to understand their intentions.

Henry had made her admit she trusted him. And he was right: She did. She'd never in her life blasted anyone who'd upset her. But she'd sure as hell blasted Henry. And then he'd made her laugh. He could always make her laugh. Right from their first lunch together he'd known how to elicit her laughter. Tyler, by comparison, made her head ache slightly with some of the things he said; it was as if she was required to match his intensity, and she wasn't sure if she was either willing or able to do that. Tyler was thirteen years older than she, lived in England, and traveled almost as much as she did. His love-making had been tidal, seismic, determined. She'd been swept away. His intensity had overcome her. Yet everything had taken place on a primal level; her brain had had nothing to do with it. She hadn't had much opportunity to laugh. And with daylight, she had to wonder how she could have done the things she had the night before. She despaired of having revealed herself so nakedly, of having applied herself to Tyler's body like someone seeking life-sustaining liquid. Christ! She put her head down on her knees and closed her eyes. She truly did like the man. She also liked Henry. Now, out of nowhere, Henry claimed to be fond of her. And when he'd said that, the spot inside her she'd thought to be reserved for Tyler had expanded in anticipation. She couldn't help thinking of her initial and immediate attraction to Henry ten years earlier, and how foolish she'd felt when he'd spoken of his fiancée.

She'd met both Henry and Tyler professionally. And she knew how differently she dealt with people on that level. Maybe they were both operating on the assumption that that was the real her. Then there was Greg, who'd been, at the last, indifferent to her both personally and professionally. Maybe she had nothing to offer anyone, on any level. God! It was so hazardous to care for people. How could you ever be sure what was real?

She raised her head and drank some of the tea. She couldn't see Tyler tomorrow night. She needed some distance, and time to do her work. She went inside to the telephone, and held her breath as the double rings on the other end started. A click, then Tyler's answering machine came on. Relieved, she waited for the tone, then said, "Tyler, it's me, Jo. Look, I'm really sorry, but I'm going to have to cancel out on tomorrow night. I'm way behind on my notes for this job, and I've got to get organized before I leave Sunday morning. I'd love to get together with you when I get back, so call me in a week. Okay? Talk to you soon. Bye."

"So," Henry asked as they walked along the Embankment after dinner, "did you go out and about with your magic camera this afternoon?"

"As it happens, the magic stayed in its bag. I got caught up in reading about the train, and by the time I stopped, it was too late. I had to take a shower, get ready for dinner."

"I take it you're feeling somewhat more relaxed about the job now that you've had a chance to do a bit of homework."

"Somewhat."

"Good. We've had the most marvelous weather this summer," he said, breathing deeply of the balmy evening air. "Some of the shrubs have flowered three and four times. I've been able almost every evening to sit out of doors with a drink and something needing to be read. Even fixed myself dinner once and ate it in the garden."

''What did you 'fix'?'' she asked, well aware of Henry's lack of culinary skills.

''Bangers I grilled with my very own hands, and some salad. Very nice it was, too. I detect a mocking tone in your voice.''

''Oh, heaven forfend! Did Suzanne cook?''

He laughed. ''*Suzanne? Cook?* Good God, no. She simply fetched in hampers from Fortnum and Mason, or some other favored emporium. Cooking would've destroyed her manicure, or undone her permanent wave, or something equally disastrous. She did, however, brew up the occasional pot of tea. She even, once, actually warmed some croissants in the oven. Talked about it for days after, she was that proud. Suzanne, my dear Jo, was the most purely ornamental human being I've ever known; programmed from birth to be decorative above all. And you and I must both admit that she succeeded admirably in that department. For a fairly brainless, entirely superficial, primarily self-interested creature, she was nevertheless a wonder to behold. Especially, I might add, without benefit of clothing.''

''It sure doesn't sound as if you liked her much, never mind her physical charms.''

''Hard to ignore those,'' he snorted, ''but, honestly, I didn't.''

''Then why ever did you stay with her for so long?''

''I couldn't think how to ask her to leave,'' he admitted. ''She seemed quite content to stay, and I thought it would be cruel of me to ask her to pack up her Guccis, her Zandra Rhodes frillies, her Chanels, and all the rest of it, and bugger off.''

With a laugh she said, ''That's not how it was. Was it?''

''Not quite. It was remarkable, Jo, truly. I'd come round a corner, or walk into the kitchen, and there she'd be; and it was mind-boggling to think that this beauty, this satiny, peachy, luscious-looking creation actually lived and bathed in my home, and even took off her clothes and allowed me to be something alarmingly like a dirty old man. It did actually feel that way at times,'' he confessed, looking over to gauge her reaction. "I mean to say, it did seem as if I were taking advantage of a child. Her interest in matters sexual was negligible. My interest in her evaporated fairly quickly in view of that. So." He cleared his throat, saw Jo wasn't going to say anything, and went on. "I never for a moment thought of it as anything more than temporary, but there's no other word but 'fascinating' to describe her habits, and her mannerisms, and her behavior. What would have been gross affectations in anyone else were the *bona fides* with Suzanne. It was, at times, like living with some dotty Kay Kendall character. No matter how she annoyed me, no matter how long she tied up the telephone, or the bathroom, no matter what silliness came out of her pretty mouth, I was perpetually fascinated. When she finally, rather archly, confronted me to say she was leaving, that she was bored silly by me, by my clients and houseguests, by my tedious three-piece suits, by my unspecial automobile, and by my pedestrian attitudes to all things she considered important, I was only mildly disappointed, and tremendously relieved. I thought what a pity it was that the world's longest play was going to end so anticlimactically. All the expensive frippery went into her matched set of Louis Vuitton bags. A chauffeur appeared to carry the bags out to a waiting Daimler, and she was off. Didn't leave behind so much as a hairpin. Farewell, Suzanne, adieu." He swung out his arm in a theatrical gesture, then laughed softly. "What a twit!"

"Did she really say all that about you?"

"Oh, indeed. And a great deal more. Fetched me up good and proper, she did," he whined in Cockney tones. "I was that broken up, I was. Sat right down and drank meself an entire bottle of Pouilly-Fumé for consolation."

"No, really. Did you care?"

"Not terribly, although no one likes to be accused of being boring. It's the same as being told you're sexually inadequate."

"You think so?" she asked interestedly.

"Yes, I do, actually."

"Wow, Henry!" she exclaimed suddenly. "I just thought

of the most amazing thing. You know that movie, *Summer-time*, with Katharine Hepburn, the one in Venice?''

"I know it, yes," he answered, wondering what on earth this had to do with the subject at hand.

"Well, her character's name in that movie is Jane Hudson. And in the movie *What Ever Happened to Baby Jane?* that character was Baby Jane Hudson. That's absolutely amazing. I wonder if it was some kind of send-up or something. I mean, the Hepburn movie was in 'fifty-five and Baby Jane was 'sixty-two. I can't see the connection, though.''

"God in heaven, Jo!" he laughed, his expression one of mixed amusement and disbelief. "How do you *know* these things?"

"I don't know. I just love movies. When I'm home, some-times I'll rent eight or ten of them for a weekend. I love the visuals, the setups, the weird camera angles. And the stories, of course. When we were kids, my mother would drop me and Beamer off at the theater while she went shopping, and we'd sit there, the only two quiet kids in the whole place while the rest of the kids hurled popcorn boxes at each other and shouted all the way through the movie. We both loved it. I still can't stand it when people talk through a movie.''

"I'm not fond of it myself," he said, watching her stop and look at a boat chugging up the river toward the City. Going to stand beside her, he said, "Have you resolved your difficulties of this morning?"

"Not really," she said quietly. "Maybe I'll never resolve them." She turned to look at him. His eyes were a very clear blue in the fading light, his rounded face most pleasant to look at. He was wearing another of his three-piece suits, having bathed and changed upon returning home. "I'll bet you don't own a single pair of jeans," she challenged.

"You win that wager; I do not. I am not one of those tall, lean American men who are singularly well suited to those garments. I am evolving into a portly British type who's most at ease in clothes that don't cling to his every crease. Does this mean," he asked, "that I will never measure up in your eyes, Jo?"

"Oh, sure, Henry. How could I ever be serious about a guy who doesn't own a pair of Levi's? I mean, really."

"Pity," he quipped.

She stared at him. "Are you joking, Henry? You're joking, right?"

"Not altogether. Would you care to go somewhere for a drink? Or would you rather have coffee at home?"

"We could have it in your garden," she suggested.

"Lovely. I even laid in some cream, knowing you take it in your coffee. And fresh-ground beans. I'll allow you to make it. Your brew is far better than mine."

"You just don't put in enough coffee, that's all."

"I could put in half a pound per cup and I'd still serve up something undrinkable."

"When I get back from Venice, I really want to take some shots of you in your garden."

"Whatever for?"

"Because it's something I've always wanted to do, but this is the first time I'm getting the chance. I mean, I couldn't very well pose you in the garden with Suzanne hanging around looking disdainful."

"Contemptuous, I think," he corrected her. "That would be more her style."

"How could you stand her? I'd really love to know that."

"It wasn't all that difficult." He took her arm as they crossed the street. "And you, for example, didn't appear interested."

"*Me?* What d'you mean, me? What do I have to do with anything?"

"Quite a good deal, actually."

"Henry!" She stopped on the pavement. "What're you *talking* about?"

In answer, he kissed her on the side of the neck, then stood looking at her.

Suddenly unsure, she said, "Is it because of Tyler?"

"What?" His eyebrows drew together; he looked mystified.

71

"Nothing," she said, realizing this display of his interest hadn't a thing to do with Tyler.

"I've always found you most appealing, Jo. I was under the impression you knew that and had chosen long since to keep our dealings on a strictly professional basis."

"I *didn't* know that," she told him, starting to walk again.

"My mistake," he said without inflection.

"I didn't say it was a mistake, Henry. I just said I didn't know."

"Well, now you do. I hope I haven't embarrassed you."

"Why would that embarrass me? It confuses me, but it definitely doesn't embarrass me. I seem to manage to do all the really embarrassing things to myself."

"Are you involved with this Emmons chap?" he asked, striving for just the right note.

"Not 'involved.' I've slept with him twice. I don't think that constitutes involvement." Since he'd felt free to make the sexual references he had to Suzanne, she felt equally free to discuss Tyler. Yet hearing her own voice make this declaration was like listening to some woman she didn't know, but about whom she had enormous curiosity. "I've wondered for a long time," she went on, "why it is that making love has to mean something. And I've also wondered why I'm incapable of doing the things I do without fearing repercussions. It should be possible to go to bed with someone and forget all about him the next day." No matter what she did, or how much she wished she could change it, the expression of some man's interest in her was a serious matter, something she was unable to treat lightly. This was a discussion unlike any other she'd ever had with Henry, and beneath the words yawned a potential that alarmed as well as drew at her. She'd been avoiding Henry's appeal for years for all sorts of reasons. Now there'd been a subtle shift in their dealings with one another and she felt it only fair to warn him.

As they entered the house, she said, "I know what I'm like, Henry. I mean, I'm very good while it's all happening. I'm wholehearted about it; I even build imaginary houses that the two of us go to live in. But then I wake up and I know none of it's real, and that it's time to get the hell out.''

"How sad," he said sympathetically. "How very sad that you should feel that way. It's not the way I'd have thought of you."

"Oh, Henry, you really are very sweet, such a kind and funny man." She was so very fond of him, she just had to put her arms around his neck and look closely at his eyes before kissing him on the mouth. To her surprise, he seemed to take her interest in him very seriously. Without another word they went hand in hand into his bedroom where, the silence holding, they went about the business of removing their clothes. They were both so intent, she thought, and yet so unusually comfortable together that she wasn't at all bothered by the need to undress herself. It was as if they required these few moments for final, private consideration of what they were about to do, so that if either of them changed their minds they'd have a clear space in which to say so.

There was no mind-changing. Once they were naked together on his bed, she drew him avidly into her embrace. She'd wanted to do this for ten years. She just hoped neither of them would end up being hurt.

"I could very easily fall in love with you," he told her later, his voice breaking the stillness in the room.

"I live three thousand miles away, Henry, and I come to England two or three times a year."

"It doesn't have to be that way," he said reasonably, stroking her hip, and wondering why this had been ten years in the happening. How dismal! he thought, to have lost years of such exceptional pleasure.

"I don't know if I want to change anything." At once, she saw herself attempting to consolidate her belongings; stacks of cartons waited to be filled as she tried to decide which of her possessions were dispensable.

"Will you hate me in the morning," he asked cannily, "as you hated Tyler?"

"I didn't plan any of this, Henry. Maybe I'm having some

kind of breakdown. I honestly don't know what's happening to me.''

"Perhaps it's something that happened a long time ago and it's just now catching up to you.''

She looked at him leaning on his elbow at her side. "Henry Hart without the three-piece suit." She smiled and took her hand over his shoulder, down the length of his arm.

"Joanna James in the flesh." He returned her smile. "And very nice, too.''

She pulled him close and held on, as if the weight of his body could protect her from her thoughts.

"You're my first, you know," he whispered against her ear.

"Your first what?''

"My first American, of course." He ran his fingertip around her ear.

"And you are the quintessence of the best of British manhood," she laughed, wrapping her arms tightly around him. "The things you say, Henry.''

"All to keep the conversation flowing. There should never be unseemly lags." He raised his head in order to look at her. "This is very nice," he observed. "Are you having a lovely time?''

"You make it sound as if we're at a cocktail party.''

"Oh, good gracious! You mean we're not?" His head swiveled around, as if realizing they were at the center of a crowd.

Her chest heaved, and instead of laughing she was suddenly on the verge of tears. To get past it, she gave his beard a tug and raised herself up to clamp her mouth over his.

7

SHE MANAGED TO USE UP THE BETTER PART OF SATURDAY making notes and reorganizing her luggage. The camera bag was ready to go, and she'd remembered to retrieve her supply of film from the refrigerator. She was beginning to get excited about her ride on the train, imagining all sorts of intriguing people, fabulous clothes, luxurious service, attentive staff.

Periodically during the day, she went into the kitchen and looked out to see Henry in the garden. In an ancient pair of khaki walking shorts, a threadbare white shirt, with worn-through espadrilles on his feet, a tatty straw hat on his head, gardening gloves and shears in hand, he weeded and pruned, watered and fed. At one point she was sure she heard him talking to the plants, then decided it was his portable radio.

As long as he remained in the garden and she was free to watch him through the window, she was able to view events dispassionately. After knowing each other for ten years, they'd made love, and he'd admitted he could fall in love with her. And instead of responding positively, she'd hedged. Standing in the kitchen, watching him through the window, she cared so much for him it made her feel like weeping. But when he knocked on her door just after five to say, "I'm for the bath, Jo. Have you made plans for the evening?" she felt unreasonably apprehensive. She had to fight off her instinct to throw open the door and let him reassure her or make her laugh.

"I'm afraid I have," she lied through the closed door. "I'm sorry, Henry."

"Fair enough," he said, sounding not in the least bothered, and went on to his room.

Having told this lie, she was obliged to delve into her suitcase for a change of clothes and, once dressed, to leave the house. Henry called out to her to have a good time, and she felt like an idiot as she went to catch the number 22 bus to Piccadilly. She crossed the Circus with a crush of tourists and studied the theaters as she went along Shaftesbury Avenue, ending up buying a ticket from a scalper outside the Palace for *Les Misérables*.

Her seat turned out to be a good one, right on the aisle in the center of the orchestra. Since she was early, she had plenty of time to read the copious program notes and to admire the theater, with its cupid lighting fixtures at the base of the first balcony and its marble-and-onyx columns.

She was unprepared for the emotional intensity of the production, for the memorable music, or for the epic and unforgettable depiction of heroic lives and deaths. As she sat, holding a tissue to her eyes, the music clutching at her like beseeching hands, she saw herself wrestling with her mother for possession of a plastic container of prescription capsules. She'd been fourteen at the time, and had come home early from school because she'd been feeling uneasy. She'd walked home and let herself into the house, gone upstairs, and arrived in the bedroom doorway to see Lily's reflection in the mirrored bathroom door. She couldn't have said why, but she'd known her mother was going to take all the pills and kill herself. It had to do with the way Lily had stood there studying the container, the concentrated manner in which her hand gripped it.

Jo had put down her schoolbooks and walked through the

bedroom, stopping in the bathroom door. "Give them to me!" she'd said quietly, causing Lily to start and to stare round-eyed at her as her hand closed tightly around the container. And then they'd struggled physically, Lily sobbing "No, no!" as Jo, with superior strength and determination, bruised her mother's wrists and, in tears, broke Lily's grip on the vial. "I *need* them!" Lily had begged, trying to stop Jo as she'd removed the lid and emptied the capsules into the toilet. They'd both stood and watched as Jo flushed the toilet and the capsules went swirling down the drain—Jo panting, Lily weeping mournfully. "*I* need *you*!" Jo had shouted at her mother then. "It's not fair!"

"You don't know a goddamned thing about what's fair!" Lily had shouted back. "You don't know a *thing* about *anything*!"

"You don't really mean it," Jo had told her. "How can you want to die?"

"Oh, I want to," Lily had insisted with stunning negative power. "I can want to and I can really mean it. And what are you doing home?"

One question, and they were back into their roles as mother and daughter.

"I didn't feel well."

Lily had at once put the back of her hand to Jo's forehead, and in that moment, Jo knew it was over. Lily had abandoned her death plans. And if she'd ever formulated any others, Jo never knew of them. It didn't matter whether or not she did because she'd left Jo with an ineradicable memory and even more unanswered questions. All Lily said then was, "Don't tell your father or Ben about this, please."

And Jo had said, "I wouldn't." Then she'd collected her schoolbooks and gone along to her room where, exhausted, she'd at once fallen asleep.

She wept through most of the performance, then stood and applauded until her palms were stinging as the cast took their curtain calls. She felt wrung-out and as exhausted as she had that afternoon twenty-two years before when she'd done battle to keep her mother alive.

After stopping in the foyer to buy a cassette of the original cast recording, she went reeling back along Shaftesbury Avenue to get the bus to Chelsea. She felt pried open, too vulnerable as she walked up the road to Henry's house, picked the key out of the flowerpot, and let herself in.

The lights were on, but Henry didn't call out as was his custom. He didn't say anything until she walked into the living room to see him sitting in one of the armchairs with a glass of wine in his hand. The TV set was on, but the volume was turned very low. He turned and looked over at her. "Hello. Nice evening?"

"Yes, thank you."

"Had rather an interesting chat with your friend Emmons," he told her. "Most interesting, actually. Care for a glass of wine, Jo?"

"Sure, okay. I'll go get a glass."

"Aren't you curious," he called out after her, "to know what we discussed?"

She paused in reaching for a glass and leaned on the counter with her eyes closed. Please don't let there be a scene! she intoned mutely, then got down a glass.

"Lovely stuff, this." He examined the label on the bottle for a few seconds before pouring some of the wine into her glass. "Cheers! Do come sit down."

Apprehensive, she perched on the edge of the adjacent armchair and tasted the wine, keeping her eyes on him. "What did you do, Henry?"

"Ate leftovers, watched rather a good American film on the tube, talked on the blower for a bit. Nothing tremendously thrilling. And what did you do, Jo dear?"

"Went to see *Les Misérables*."

Growing animated, he said, "Isn't it stunning? Christ, but I adored that production. I could go once a week, every week, for years. I have the album here somewhere." He got up and walked over to the shelves that housed the stereo and his record collection.

"I've got the cassette, if you want to hear it." She pulled

it from her bag and held it out to him, but he was already on his way back to his seat and seemed not to have heard her.

Retrieving his glass, he shifted around to look at her, his expression one of infinite sadness. "Are you playing some sort of game, Jo?" he asked mournfully. "It really does seem as if you are." He looked away. "A very pleasant chap, Emmons. Of course, I've seen quite a number of his productions, films. Decent actor, a shade contrived now and then, but very decent. He's under the impression you're avoiding him. I can't think why he chose to confide in me, although he couldn't possibly be aware of the irony of the situation. I could hardly tell the man I had the impression you were also avoiding *me*. I don't believe I've ever had a conversation remotely similar. It wasn't at all as embarrassing as I've always imagined that sort of conversation to be. In any event, no one's accusing you of anything at all, Jo dear, but an explanation of some sort would appear to be in order. Of course, if you feel you don't have to, well, then of course you shouldn't."

"You're a little drunk, Henry."

"No, I'm a middle-sized fellow, only slightly drunk, to be precise." He laughed, then went back to looking sad. "I felt very bloody sorry for poor Emmons. He's besotted with you, obviously. Half the men in London evidently are besotted with you. Naughty of you, Jo dear." He waggled his finger at her, then smiled very sweetly. "None of my business, actually."

"That is true," she agreed, then sat quietly for a time, drinking the wine and considering what, if anything, she wanted to say. "Okay," she said at last. "Here's the truth. Okay?"

"Okay," he agreed.

"I don't know how much I care about either one of you. I made love with both of you, and I think I'd like to sleep with you again tonight—which is neither here nor there, really. There's this tape in my head that says if I don't hurt you or Tyler, one or both of you will probably hurt me in some way. I looked at Tyler's apartment—he has an honest-to-God

Turner, if you can imagine that—and I thought to myself, 'I could live here.' Then I look around here, and I think, 'I could live here.' When I go home, undoubtedly I'll look at the condo and think, 'I could live *here*.' I sound like a goddamned fruitcake, but I want to tell you exactly what's on my mind right this very moment.

"I picture myself with Tyler, or with you—either one, it doesn't matter which for this scenario—and I imagine hearing low angry voices in the night, but this time one of those voices is mine. And I don't *ever* want to be one of the people behind the bedroom door, hissing out my fury in the dark to someone who only likes me because I have no goddamned shame, because I'm willing to use all the parts of me that make pleasure, because men only seem to want you to shut up and receive, and if you question or resist in any way, they'll burn you down, destroy your history. Now, Henry, does that sound like any kind of game you know about?"

Sobered, he answered, "Yes and no. It's definitely not one I'd be interested in playing."

"Good!" she snapped. "Neither am I."

"I've been tactless and now you're angry with me."

"I wouldn't say tactless, and I wouldn't say angry. I don't see you being asked to explain yourself to anyone. Does this strike you as fair?"

He shook his head. "It does not."

"Right!"

"I apologize," he said humbly, then smiled brightly. "Would you really like to sleep with me tonight?"

"I'll fix you some coffee while you go take a cold shower." She got up and made to go to the kitchen.

"You may find yourself with a very alert drunk," he cautioned.

She had to laugh. "You're making out you're farther gone than you are. I've seen you truly pissed once or twice and you're not even close yet. Don't try to con me, Henry."

"Let's compromise and say a *tepid* shower, shall we?"

80

"Go on. By the time you're finished, the coffee'll be ready."

She didn't hear him come into the kitchen, and jumped when his hands closed over her hips. "Don't *do* that! You scared the daylights out of me."

"Pish tosh! You're made of sterner stuff than that." He lifted aside her hair and kissed the nape of her neck.

"How old are you anyway, Henry?"

"Let's just say you and I are contemporaries."

"Fine. Let's just say that. Your coffee's ready."

"While I was in there, splashing away to humor you, I gave some thought to what you said. I'm most intrigued by your sense of yourself as 'shameless.' "

"You are, huh?"

"Yes, I am. Not that I discount any of the other, highly interesting things you had to say. But for the moment, I'd like to concentrate on your so-called shamelessness."

He turned her around, tugged her blouse free of her skirt, popped open the buttons, and then with one finger unhooked the front of her bra. At once, she crossed her arms over her breasts. "I rest my case," he said quietly with a gentle smile, giving her a kiss on the forehead. "So much for the 'shameless' Joanna James. Given the chance, I could probably disprove a fair number of the other statements you made. I do recall that during your last stay here, Suzanne and I had one hell of a row late one night. If that was what you were referring to, I'm very sorry you had to be a witness to that ugly scene. I don't think I've ever behaved so badly, either before or since, as I did at the last with Suzanne." He paused a moment, trying to gauge her reactions. She continued to stand with her arms crossed over her breasts, her eyes fastened to his. "I'd find myself," he went on, "attempting to introduce some thread of sense into one of our arguments, and then I'd stop and ask myself what in hell I was doing arguing with the woman in the first place. It was pointless and futile, but I rose to the bait at least a dozen times before I gave up and just allowed her to rant and rave over some mythical injury she'd suffered, until she wore herself out. Her complaints and accusations were groundless, not based on anything I'd said or done, but rather on my countless sins of omission, my greatest sin being my failure to have inherited, as she did, vast sums of money. So, if you heard any of that last battle, I apologize. In my own defense, I'd like to say that the most compatible people have been known to disagree; they do argue and raise their voices at one another. It doesn't mean they've stopped caring for one another; it means, purely and simply, that their opinions don't happen to coincide on every issue. And most of the time it's an effective way to clear the air, to get rid of some of the animosity that can build up when you've had rather a lot of exposure to one another. Don't hide, Joey,'' he said, unwinding her arms and holding them away while he gazed at her.

He called her Joey, spoke her name so meaningfully that she was drawn into his mood. She was also moved by the way he seemed to care for her. She was seeing new aspects of him almost hourly, and here, now, was another. Her face and neck aflame, she watched him closely, aware all the while of the possibility that someone in one of the neighboring houses might be looking in at them. There was an element of risk, even of exhibitionism in what was happening between them, and something inside her was both thrilled and alarmed. Henry had released her arms and was pushing the blouse and bra off her shoulders. He unzipped her skirt and tugged down both it and her slip. She wondered how far he intended to go, and how far she'd allow him to go, as she breathed in the aroma of the coffee and the scents of the bath soap and shampoo he'd used. His hair was damp, his skin moist. She was held for a moment to his chest as he lifted her, then he set her down on the edge of the table. Now her back was to the windows and she felt fractionally safer, shielded from view. Her eyes never left his; she tracked his every movement until he bent his head to her breasts. Then, involuntarily, she whispered, "Oh, God!" and had to clutch at the edge of the table to prevent herself from toppling over. When he raised his head, the cool air rushed over her, heightening the sensations he was creating. Their eyes locked again, he placed his hands firmly over her thighs and stood motionless for a minute, two. She moved first, and then his hand slid forward, probing, reaching. His eyes widened, as if to see her reactions more clearly. She saw his pupils dilate, his lips part slightly as she opened. Her hand rose and fastened to the front of his robe; she pulled at the fabric, signaling, and, his eyes still wide, his face came near to hers, then nearer. Someone in one of those houses could be watching as she spread herself on the table, then closed around Henry's hand, his mouth on hers, his beard and mustache soft against her face, his belly smooth, hairless, gently rounded under her delving hand. Oh, yes, she was shameless, she thought, closing her eyes at last, unconcerned by the possibility of spectators, concerned only with stretching to broaden the pleasure, with perpetuating it. Shameless, she reciprocated stroke for stroke, her hands hidden by the robe, as curious to know his limits as she was to know her own. She could feel his muscles bunch and tighten beneath her hands, could feel her own power in the increasing pressure of his mouth and the strength of the hand that continued to grip her thigh before relocating to her breast. They were going to do this beneath the ceiling lights, framed by the windows and door, right there in the kitchen with the coffee still fragrant on the stove and the loud hum of the refrigerator. I could fall in love with you, too, she thought; maybe I fell years ago and relegated the case to the file of situations hopeless or lost, boggled as always by the logistics, and by past history. She was lifting off the table in her eagerness, her python thighs ready to devour him as she got open his robe and stroked him forward. He was strong, she thought, stronger than those three-piece suits would have led one to believe. His hands went under her, holding her steady while she strained to absorb him. Her body wanted to slide away across the smooth tabletop, but he wouldn't allow it. Like some outrageous circus act, she was brought upright once more, her ankles locked like iron around him. An oversized baby cradled to his shaking chest, she was in his arms and laughter was spewing from his lips. "I'm sorry," he laughed, damp circles under his eyes, his lips dipping into the curve of her neck. "This is too bloody slippery! And besides, I don't have the balls to finish this in here." The laughter ebbing, he carried her into the bedroom where, with her help, they got his robe off before turning serious again. "You're marvelous, Jo," he murmured, taking her down on his bed. "Bloody marvelous!"

She kissed the rim of his ear, then whispered, "If you stop again, I'll murder you in your sleep."

She dreamed again of the fire, so vividly that she could feel the heat all down the left side of her body. It burned. The hair on her arms was singed. She'd die this time. No one would come. She wanted to move, to escape the flames that were wrapping themselves like burning bandages around her disintegrating flesh. This isn't real! she insisted, the truth reaching through to the part of her brain that manufactured dreams. She could wake up; she could.

With a start, she came to. The heat was still there down her left side and, turning, she found its source. Henry lay glued to her side, his body generating the warmth her sleeping self had interpreted as fire. Gingerly, she eased away a few inches and at once her skin began to cool.

She lay looking at Henry in the early morning light and thought, with mounting affection, that he was a gentleman even in his sleep. He didn't thrash or snore; he simply allowed rest to come to him. A lock of hair had dropped onto his forehead, accentuating his schoolboy look. She smiled down at him.

The breeze entering through the window soothed her, distancing her from the dream. She continued to gaze at Henry, savoring this rare guilt-free opportunity to consider him. His body pleased her. She saw him at that moment in shades of black and white and gray gradually coming clearer the way a print did in the developer bath. Henry was shorter, more solidly built than Tyler. Tyler had the physique of someone always hungry; Henry's body was well fed, sleek. Tyler's limbs were longer, leaner, less visibly muscular; his hips were shallow, bony. The cushion of flesh extending from Henry's middle to the tops of his thighs was an area without hollows. When she'd joined with him and they'd sat facing one another, they'd joined completely, touching everywhere. They were well matched physically, she and Henry. While their striving together lacked the frenzy of her love-making with Tyler, she felt more an equal participant with Henry and less a recipient.

Ah, if only it could stay this way, she thought, daring to let herself love this man for these few secret minutes, while the only sounds were the hum of the refrigerator and the tap-tapping of the metal loops at the ends of the drapery tiebacks. If only there were no memories, no previous experiences to interfere with the natural flow of emotions. But she wasn't young, she'd long since left home, and she'd learned not to trust the part of her that craved the thrust and heat of men. She loved them best, she thought, from a distance. Still, Henry slept so sweetly, with such touching munificence, his palms resting gently open to accept gifts or dreams.

At eight forty-five she telephoned from the kitchen for a taxi. Then she put her bags by the front door and went to keep watch through the living room window. She didn't want the cabbie ringing the bell and waking Henry. She'd talk to him when she got back from Venice, as she would Tyler. Or maybe she'd never speak to either of them again. She couldn't concern herself with personal situations just now. She had to flip that professional switch and be ready to take notes and photographs, to absorb everything she was about to see.

The taxi came within fifteen minutes. With her bags stored up front beside the driver and the window lowered to admit the morning air, she sat back feeling relieved to be moving away from her involvements with Henry and Tyler, and very keyed up about the train. She was tremendously excited, eager for a look at this famous conveyance. She'd never dreamed she'd get to ride on the Orient-Express. She could scarcely sit still during the short ride to Victoria Station, and felt her heartbeat accelerate as she paid the driver, then opened the door to find a porter waiting to take her bags.

"They're departin' from platform 2 this mornin', I do believe, Madame. Right this way, if you will."

This was it! The adventure was beginning! As they entered the great vaulted station, she couldn't prevent herself from smiling. It was too terrific! There'd be fascinating people from fascinating places. Perhaps she'd even meet some of them.

She followed the chatty porter across the station to the far platform, expecting the train to be there, waiting. But it wasn't. No train, no passengers. There was, though, staff at the check-in area. She was unreasonably disappointed.

"There you go, luv!" The porter swung her bag onto a luggage platform set between two portable waist-high check-in stations fronted with the beige and brown Orient-Express insignia on their uppermost portions, and by the glossy blue and gold-crested Wagons-Lits insignia below. After tipping the porter, who wished her a happy trip, she presented her packet of travel documents to one of the smartly suited young women behind the counter.

While the young woman read the letter of introduction, Jo pumped herself back up again, reminding herself that she'd have an entire week free of complications, free of Henry and Tyler. It really was a relief to be out of all that. And maybe she'd be able to make sense of what had gone on during the past few days, not to mention the peculiar overlapping of her personal misgivings into her professional behavior. The train trip would sort things out, she was convinced. There was something about trains—even crummy commuter trains—that allowed your thoughts to form more clearly.

"Ah, yes," the young woman said. "We're expecting you, Miss James. The train manager's been told you'll be traveling with us today. If there's anything at all you need, be sure to let him know. You'll be in Lucille,'' she went on, consulting a clipboard before making a note of Jo's assigned seat number on a small card. "We do hope you'll enjoy your trip."

Jo thanked her, accepting the seat designation, and asked, "What time does the train actually arrive in the station?"

The young woman glanced at a large clock suspended from the platform overhang. "Within the half-hour, I should think. You are rather early. The station buffet has quite decent coffee, if you'd like to wait there."

"I was told I'd be able to board in advance of the other passengers to get some pictures."

"Oh, certainly. I'll have a word with the train manager and we'll make certain you have an opportunity to do that. You'll have about half an hour or so. I'm sorry it's such a short time, but the Pullmans are in constant service."

"That's okay." Jo looked around. Still no other passengers. "Maybe I will go have some coffee."

"It's really not bad at all. Just over there." The young woman pointed to her left. "If you're back by nine-forty, you'll have tons of time."

"Thanks a lot."

"My pleasure."

Jo queued up in the buffet, got coffee and a buttered roll, then carried her tray to a single table occupied by a young man reading the *Observer* and asked him if the other seat was vacant. He indicated it was, and she was glad to sit down and loop the strap of the heavy Lowe-pro bag over the back of her chair. Every table in the place was full, mainly with young people, all reading.

The coffee was good. She ate the roll quickly, realizing she'd eaten very little in the past three or four days. She'd engaged in a great deal of strenuous sexual activity, but she'd missed a fair number of meals. Which was why her suit felt so loose. She looked out at the station as she drank the coffee. It really was too bad she'd arrived so early. This enforced wait made her realize how sleepy she was, and how bewildered. But she refused to think about Henry or Tyler. According to her watch, the train would be arriving in about fifteen minutes, and she intended to return to the platform in about ten to take some shots of her fellow passengers—the others probably knew better than to arrive too early—and of the train itself as it pulled into the station.

With a jolt, it occurred to her she'd forgotten to take her birth control pill, and fumbled around inside her purse, found the container, poked out a pill, and discreetly put it into her mouth. A swallow of coffee and it was done. No chance of creating a little Tyler or a little Henry.

She thought of the determined way Tyler had come at her on the sofa, the way he'd dived under her skirt, and heat rushed into her face. Then there was Henry, displaying a surprising lusty streak in his kitchen. And what the hell had she been doing? Men didn't make love to invisible women. That was part of it, a not insignificant part of it, now that she thought about it. But, God, the whole business was so messy and complicated! More than anything else she was relieved to be leaving it all behind. She gulped down the last of the coffee, hooked both the camera bag and her purse over her shoulder, and hurried back to the platform.

There were now half a dozen or so people at the check-in stations, all with those small totally automatic cameras, and all, apparently, with Louis Vuitton luggage. Positioning herself against the wall beyond the velvet cord separating the area from the rest of the platform, she got out the Pentax, adjusted the aperture for the very low light level, and took several shots that showed the passengers, two brown-coated baggage handlers, and two security officers who checked each new arrival with metal detectors. Security was minimal, just the personal check by the guards. None of the luggage was inspected.

She relocated near the steel gate that prevented people from wandering down the length of the platform. Almost ten. The train would be along any time now. Turning, she saw a fair-sized crowd waiting to hand over travel documents to the calm, polite young women in charge of the check-in. Several groups of Orientals, quite a number of people who looked

British, not many Americans—which was a surprise. She'd expected the majority of passengers to be American, but it was a thoroughly mixed group. And the number of Vuitton bags was proliferating at an amazing rate. Her old Hartmann had a kind of shabby nobility among all those new-looking cases.

Looking out along the branching network of tracks, she was anxious to see the train, and set to take shots of its arrival. It was awkward that her suit didn't have any handy pockets into which she could pop her spare lenses, but she'd guessed correctly the importance of being well dressed for this trip. Everyone was expensively but conservatively turned out; the men in suits, not a woman in trousers.

10:03. The train was approaching. Her sense of adventure rushing back, she watched the engine through the telephoto until it was in range for a good shot. She framed each exposure so that the clock and platform number were visible in the upper left-hand corner, and switched to the 50-mm lens as the train came to a halt, to get shots of the white-jacketed waiters and stewards as they emerged from the carriages and came down the platform to the front of the train where they stopped to confer with the check-in staff. The men were immaculately groomed in navy trousers with gold stripes down the outsides, white jackets with navy lapels sporting gold VS-O-E insignia pins, gold-braid epaulettes, navy bow ties on crisp white shirts; several wore short white gloves. This was great! She worked quickly, changing back to the telephoto for some close-ups, then a few medium shots of the gleaming brown and beige carriages, each with a crested name plaque: Audrey, Cygnus, Perseus.

She moved to the still-closed gate to have a word with the train manager.

"Ah, yes," he said, admitting her onto the platform and offering his hand. "Good to have you with us. You're in Lucille, seat 14. If you'd care to, you may go through the carriages now. It should be another fifteen or twenty minutes before the passengers begin to board."

She was about to thank him when someone tapped her on the shoulder, and she turned to see Henry smiling at her, holding out a single red rose in a paper cone. Her reaction to the sight of him was fifty percent disbelief and fifty percent delight. It was touching of him to go to this trouble; it was also an impediment to the work she had to do.

"I thought I'd come see you off," he said somewhat shyly. "Couldn't resist having a peek at the train, too."

Her delight won out. "You're so darling, Henry!" She gave him a kiss, accepted the flower, then said, "Come with me. Okay? I want to leave the camera bag in my seat before I get some quick shots of the interiors."

"May I? I don't want to get in your way, but I really would love to see." She was, he thought, more self-possessed and businesslike than he'd ever seen her, and he couldn't help but be aware that she might construe his turning up this way as an unthinking, even feckless, gesture.

"Come on," she urged, and started along the platform looking for Lucille. "In here, Henry." She turned to be sure he was following, then stepped inside, dazed with pleasure at first sight of the interior of the parlor car with the tables set for lunch—white linen, crystal goblets, silver vases of fresh carnations, blue and white porcelain.

"Isn't it fabulous!" Henry exclaimed, looking more the schoolboy than ever. "I'm sick with envy, Jo."

"It's wonderful," she agreed, finding her seat and setting the Lowe-pro bag down on its flowered velour upholstery. She put the rose on the table, dropped her lenses into her shoulder bag, then backed away to take several shots of the tables with the sunlight glinting off the silver and crystal.

Keeping his distance, Henry watched, captivated by this first-time viewing of her at work. She held the camera, her eyes slightly narrowed as she judged the light, the angle, the composition, then lifted the camera, made adjustments, and took the shots. She so visibly knew what she was doing, was so completely in charge of herself, that she appeared to him for the first time neither young nor tentative. She also seemed taller, thinner, and extraordinarily concentrated. He didn't know which intrigued him more, the train or this new aspect of someone he'd thought he knew well. In the few minutes it took her to photograph the interior of the car, his assessment of her underwent a profound and radical shift, and he was at last able to make better sense not only of her but of his long-time attraction to her. He was charmed, impressed, and mildly daunted.

"I won't stay, Jo. I know you've got a lot to do." He watched her turn and remember he was there, and knew he was right to get out of her way. Just as he disliked having someone sitting on the far side of the desk when he was attempting to conduct business over the telephone, he could tell she was torn between politeness and an urgent need to get on with the job at hand.

"Thank you so much for coming to see me off," she smiled at him, "and for the rose. I'll walk back with you," she offered.

"Oh, no need," he assured her. "Have a wonderful time. And don't forget my postcard."

"I won't." She gave him a quick hug and a kiss. He'd bathed and shaved and donned one of his three-piece suits—a navy one that darkened the blue of his eyes—to come see her off. "Really, Henry, thank you for going to all this trouble." She gave him another kiss. "I'll see you in a week. Okay?"

"Okay, Jo." He stood a moment longer looking around, then walked quickly away.

"God!" she whispered, feeling enormously pressured by the time constraints. *"God!"*

Almost at a run, she went to the head of the train and began, hastily and methodically, taking pictures of the various interior details of the five parlor cars and three kitchen cars: brass luggage racks, tulip-shaped glass and brass overhead lights, the mosaic lavatory floor of Cygnus, the Greek dancing girl marquetry panels in Ibis, the marquetry floral frieze and burr wood panels of ash in Ione. The detailing of each carriage was remarkable, she thought, taking close-ups of the light fittings and of the different styles of luggage racks, of the pullman crests, and the pink-shaded table lamps. It was like going back sixty years in time, to when the majority of these carriages had originally been completed. Audrey had carried the Queen, the Queen Mother, and the Duke of Edinburgh to review the fleet in 1953; Cygnus had been reserved for use by visiting heads of state; Ibis had been part of the Golden Arrow; Perseus had been used in Winston Churchill's funeral train; Phoenix had been the Queen's favorite carriage; Zena had been used in the film *Agatha*. Each carriage had a unique and fabulous history.

By the time she got to the end of the train, people were sitting, nibbling the nuts and olives on each table. She found her way back to Lucille and looked appreciatively at the lace seat-back cover as she pushed the Lowe-pro under the table. Three women were already in place at the table at the far end, and a late-fortyish English couple were at the table for two on the opposite side of the aisle to Jo. Keeping the camera close to hand, she got out her notebook, made a few quick notes, then finally unwrapped Henry's rose and breathed in its perfume. The train hadn't yet left the station, but she felt as if she'd already done a full day's work. She'd never before had to do so big a shoot in so little time.

"Just made it!" Tyler announced, all but skidding to a stop at her side. "Thought I'd come to see you off," he said, setting a gift-wrapped box on the table beside the rose. If he saw the flower, he neither questioned nor acknowledged it. He stooped to kiss her just as she was getting to her feet, and the top of her head smartly connected with the underside of his chin.

Both of them apologizing, flustered, she smiled at him, staggered that he'd not only come to see her off, but that he'd also dressed for the occasion in slacks and a sport jacket, even a tie. Here she'd been smugly thinking she'd managed to get away from both of them, and they'd both showed up. She couldn't begin to think what it all meant.

"It's sweet of you to come," she told him, directing him out of the carriage and onto the platform, wondering why she'd been painting such unattractive mental pictures of him. He was very good-looking. And she'd forgotten how his voice seemed to rumble out of his chest and vibrate inside hers. There were women who'd do anything for a chance at this man.

"Almost missed it," he said, indicating the cleared platform. "I wanted you to know I was disappointed about last night. I was very much looking forward to seeing you again, Joanna."

"I'm sorry, Tyler. I just couldn't make it."

"Well, never mind." Taking hold of both her hands, he asked, "You'll be back when?"

"Next Monday."

"Promise you'll ring me as soon as you get back?"

"Sure." She suddenly wondered if the other passengers were watching through the windows. She hoped not.

"Off you go, then." He caressed her hair briefly before giving her a pair of those Continental kisses she never seemed prepared for.

"God!" she laughed nervously. "Just give me one sensible kiss before you go, will you? Every time you do that I feel as if I'm dancing a waltz while everybody else is doing a tango."

He laughed and obliged with a kiss on the lips, then another on the top of her head.

"Better," she said, taking a step back into the carriage. "Thank you for coming, Tyler."

"Enjoy yourself. Oh, what's your hotel?" he remembered to ask.

"The Cipriani."

"Lucky you!" He waved, then started off along the platform, turning to wave once again before going through the gate.

She returned to her seat and looked at the package Tyler had left sitting beside Henry's rose. For a second time, she picked up the rose and sniffed at it. The train began to move.

93

She looked out the spotless window to see the daylight beyond the station approach. Reaching for one of the black olives, she bit into it as they left the station behind and the rails spread wide like the gigantic veins of some immense metal organism.

Well, she thought, now she'd finally managed to leave both men behind. Then she turned to look around, just to be absolutely sure.

8

THE WAITERS CAME ALONG OFFERING CHAMPAGNE. JO
would have loved some, but had to decline in order to remain
clearheaded.

"No?" The waiter looked positively crestfallen. "Perhaps
some juice, or mineral water?"

"Water would be great, thank you."

Cheered by this simple request, he went off.

The three women at the far table seemed to be having a
fine time, laughing in bursts, their conversation animated. Jo
couldn't help being aware that she was the only person in the
carriage, possibly on the entire train, traveling alone. She
concentrated on her notes, taking occasional photographs
through the window—of people at work in their allotments,
of the Queen Anne's lace and wildflowers standing above the
ivy blanketing both sides of the track. She knew she gave the
impression of someone with a job to do. The camera, notebook, and pen were her validation. She also knew the three
women had noticed her, and were speculating quietly, curious about what exactly Jo might be doing. Silly as it might
have been, the familiar cadence of their American accents
was comforting. It was one thing to go on a shoot or assignment in some remote location, but it was something else

altogether to find herself a passenger with a purpose on the world's most famous train. And the temptation to abandon herself to the sheer pleasure of the experience was a strong one. Yet the majority of the people she'd so far seen appeared determined to remain outwardly unimpressed, as if they were accustomed to such attentive service and so unique a means of transportation. Of course, it was a train. But not just any old train. This was eleven million pounds worth of a scrupulously restored train, and the staff at least seemed fully aware of that fact.

Beckenham Station, Shortlands, Bromley South. She wrote down the names, recapturing her long-time fondness for this country. England was, to her mind, a place where truly eccentric people could be left alone to flourish. You could, like Henry, spend five days a week being a businessman and then, at the weekends, put on clothes the Salvation Army would've rejected, and spend six hours on your knees in the garden, talking to your annuals while plucking encroaching weeds from the perimeters. And no one would think it odd or unusual. In the setting of his own creating, Henry was perfectly placed, entirely comfortable. The very first time she'd seen the house, he'd taken her on a tour that had ended in the then rubble-heaped garden.

"I have plans for this garden," he'd told her with a visionary's zeal she'd found lovable.

"You do, huh?" she'd teased him.

"I certainly do. And just remember, you skeptical American upstart—and don't think for a moment I'm unaware of your lack of reverence for that venerable institution the British Garden—that one day you'll be assigned to photograph what I create here for *House & Garden*."

"I'll beg for the assignment, Henry. I'll throw myself at the editor's knees and plead to be allowed to photograph your garden."

"Why is it that Grace's clients are all so irreverent? None of Dearborn's people—whom I much prefer"—he'd sniffed in mock offense—"are nearly so lowbrow."

"That's because most of them are English, Henry. And

96

I'm not in the least lowbrow. I mean, just because I'm not delirious with excitement over the prospect of your garden doesn't mean I won't grovel for the chance to shoot it."

"I may not even allow you to *sit* in it. No doubt you'd leave abandoned Kodak boxes in the grass, litter the place with chewing gum wrappers."

"I don't even chew gum!" she'd protested.

"I expect you'll take it up just to annoy me."

She'd stared at him for a moment, wondering if he could possibly be the least bit serious, and he'd started to laugh, saying, "Had you going, didn't I? Just for a moment, didn't I? I could see you wondering if I'd finally gone right over the edge and was actually serious. Admit it! You were thinking I'd gone round the twist, weren't you?"

"Of course, I wasn't," she lied, her face flushing.

"Ah, Jo dear," he'd sighed still smiling, "I do enjoy you."

She'd thought for a moment he was going to kiss her, and she'd waited to see what he'd do, all the while imagining how she'd ask Greg to leave and the pleasure she'd derive from that. But nothing happened. Henry had looked at her for a second or two more, then looped his arm through hers and said, "Come along and see the flats. The tenants haven't moved in yet, and if I do say so myself, they've turned out very nicely."

The waiters were coming by again, this time offering red or white wine to accompany the lunch, and Jo accepted half a glass of the red from a need to celebrate the occasion. There had never been and would never again be another job like this one. A sip of wine, then she unwrapped Tyler's gift. A package of Terry's All Gold chocolates. He couldn't have known that she rarely ate chocolate, but she was pleased nonetheless by the gesture. Putting the box to one side, she gazed again out the window at blocks of houses with neatly clipped lawns, laundry billowing on lines, flowers leaning over fences, the flowing brick arches of overpasses. How could Tyler possibly know her likes and dislikes? Altogether, the time they'd spent together didn't add up to one full day. She was acquainted with his sexual skills, and the intensity with which he displayed them, and she was more than a little susceptible to his fervent demonstrations. But that was all. It wasn't very much.

Orpington Station, Knockholt, Dunton Green.

A few months back she'd done a photographic essay on an author of children's books who'd designed the production being mounted of the adaptation of one of her books. Jo had driven to the place just near Brewster, New York, where the woman lived, to photograph her sitting in a chair outside at the rear of the house where the snow had been as umblem-ished and glossy as the frosting on a cake. The author lived with her agent, who'd hovered in the background the entire time Jo had been there, as if concerned that Jo might sud-denly whip out a gun and start firing. She'd found his pro-tectiveness endearing. He'd obviously cared very deeply for the woman. She wondered idly if Henry knew her.

A wide bowl of dark mushroom soup with a sprinkling of fresh parsley was set before her. Then came Scottish smoked salmon stuffed with prawns and celery in mayonnaise, new potatoes, and a salad of tomato, cucumber, and melon. The food was very light, simply delicious. She ate slowly, appre-ciating the subtle flavors.

The sun glanced off the brass base of the pink-shaded table lamp. The interior of the carriage hummed with now-muted conversations and the musical notes of cutlery striking against porcelain. As the meal progressed, she felt increasingly cos-seted, especially when the train manager stopped by to ask how she was enjoying herself and if there was anything she needed.

"Everything's wonderful," she told him. "But I do have a couple of quick questions, if you don't mind."

"Certainly."

"How many passengers are you carrying today?" she asked.

"With those we'll pick up in Paris, one hundred and thirty-eight."

"And what's your maximum?"

"One seventy-five, ideally."

"D'you get about the same number on the return trip?"

"Usually fewer northbound. It's something we're working on," he explained, "trying to get more passengers originating in Venice."

"Why is that?"

"Well, Italians tend not to take their holidays in Britain. That's one thing. And it would seem a larger number of people start from London with Venice as their ultimate destination. As I say, we're working on it."

"Do you usually get a lot of Americans?"

"Oh, yes. The Americans do enjoy the train."

"And you run all year?"

"We shut down for six weeks from mid-November to the end of December, then start up again for New Year's Eve."

"That would be fun," she said, imagining being inside the cozy train as a winter snow was falling beyond the windows. "I guess that's it for the moment."

"Anything else, please don't hesitate."

"I won't. Thank you."

She set aside the notebook as the waiter arrived with a huge tray of orange-and-Cointreau profiteroles in chocolate sauce. Her appetite had been satisfied, but she couldn't resist tasting the dessert. She found the sauce a bit too sweet, but the coffee was good and strong and she gratefully accepted a second cup while refusing the offer of a liqueur.

Sevenoaks Station, Tunbridge, Paddock Wood.

Sheep grazed in a field; a passing British Rail train was a noisy blur. She felt herself being lulled by the motion and the intermittent sunshine. The three American women were laughing again, and Jo looked at Henry's rose lying beside her coffee cup. It was a nice setup, the coffee cup with a lipstick imprint, the rose. She arranged it a little more precisely, then prepared to take a shot, aware of the three women's silence as they watched her, one of them murmuring, "She's taking a picture of the flower. Did you see . . . ?" Jo didn't hear the end of what the woman said, but suspected it had something to do with the fact that not one but two men had come to see her off. And rather than feeling elevated at having had such attention paid to her, she was chagrined, and didn't know why. No time to think about that! She got up to go have a look in the other carriages, to see what her fellow passengers were up to.

In one of the compartments in the next carriage, a couple sat reading newspapers, ignoring both the scenery and each other, as if they were riding a commuter train home after a day's work in the city. How blasé, Jo thought. But farther along, a group was standing in the passageway looking out the windows and chatting happily about the food and the scenery and the exceptional service and wondering aloud how much they might tip the staff upon arrival at Folkestone.

Hearing mention of Folkestone, Jo looked out the window to see they were already approaching their destination. She turned and hurried back to her seat to reorganize the camera bag, returning the lenses to their cushioned compartments. Notebook safely stowed, she took a five-pound note from her wallet to give to the waiter when she left the train. Her festive mood increased as the train came to a stop, sat for several minutes, then reversed into Folkestone Central.

As she stepped down onto the platform, she realized with a pang that she'd left both Henry's rose and Tyler's chocolates on the table. And there was no time to go back for them. She had to get shots of the passengers being directed by VS-O-E staff to the Sealink Ferry.

On board, they were shown into a private lounge. A vast carpeted area with deep chairs and settees, it had a bar, and display cases at the rear contained items for sale in the duty-free shop. The staff offered tea or coffee, drinks from the bar. Jo arranged herself in an unoccupied area near one of the windows and sat for a few minutes taking in the details. She didn't want anything to drink and it seemed it would be a while before the ferry departed. She decided to go up on deck to have a look at the famous White Cliffs of Dover and get some fresh air. Lack of sleep was starting to catch up with her.

A couple of men with little automatic cameras were already at the rail, aiming at the view and snapping away. For some reason, those cameras annoyed her. Maybe it was because ownership of them convinced people they knew something about photography—although she hadn't actually had anyone espouse that theory to her directly. Her annoyance stemmed from the fact that the cameras made taking pictures too easy, so people were no longer quite as impressed with professional photography as they'd once been. Or maybe the truth was she resented the high quality of the end product, work done entirely by the camera without the need for extra lenses or any degree of skill on the part of the owner. Secretly, there were times when she longed to rid herself of the load of gear that dragged down her shoulder. And as if in defiance of that shameful longing, she carried with her everything conceivable she might need, from a minitripod, to several cable releases, varicolored filters either to enhance or reduce available light, and the three lenses without which she couldn't work effectively: the telephoto with the macro setting, the medium wide-angle, and the 50-mm. She did have a fisheye, as well as a teleconverter that doubled the length of the telephoto or 50-mm, but she disliked having to adjust the aperture to compensate for the distortion and reduction of light caused by the converter.

With the Lowe-pro bag at her feet, she leaned on the rail and looked out at the water and cliffs. The sun had decided to stay out, but the light was peculiar, diffused, rendering the view fuzzy and remote. But some shots of the other passengers pointing their automatic Nikons and Minoltas and Kodaks at the scenery would be good. She sat on one of the benches, got out the Pentax and a fresh roll of 400 to reload, her eyes feeling gritty. She'd have to find someplace in Venice to print up the roll she'd already shot so she could have prints made from the slides to send to Florella.

There were now five men at the rail, and two women standing back wearing patient expressions as they waited for the men to finish. A good vignette, Jo thought. But as she raised the camera, the wide-angle in place, everyone—as if on cue—shifted out of her way. They'd all been watching her. To cover herself, she left the camera bag on the bench, got up and went to the rail to make a couple of uninspired exposures before going back to sit down.

A number of people emerged from the VS-O-E lounge to stroll along the deck. One couple caught Jo's eye. The man was dressed in a suit, hand-tailored but subdued. The woman, however, was sporting a brilliant green leather outfit, the skirt so tight she could only take tiny steps in her four-inch heels. The suit jacket was closely nipped in at the waist, then flared widely over her ample hips. Screaming, teased red hair, masses of heavy jewelry, and a lot of bright green eyeshadow. Amazing! Jo thought. The suit must have cost a couple of thousand dollars, was probably Italian-made, and would've looked fabulous on someone several inches taller and forty pounds thinner. Jo was delighted. All the other passengers she'd seen were so low-key that the woman stood out almost violently among them.

Bitchy, very bitchy, she admonished herself. She was probably a very nice woman; she just had no clothes sense. One of those people who equated an outrageously expensive price tag with quality and high fashion. And what about you in your little black linen suit? she reminded herself. Perfect for church on Sunday. Talk about conservative!

Back in the lounge she spotted several sets of honeymooners. One young woman nestled against her new husband, her head on his shoulder. The pair were exceptionally good-looking and well-dressed. He was tall and dark with perfectly proportioned features, aristocratic in a rather Edwardian-styled light gray suit; she was also tall, with long strawberry blond hair cascading over her shoulders, and not a bit of makeup. Her dress was of pink Indian cotton, with a long full skirt, a prim lace-covered collar, and short puffed sleeves. The two were visibly at ease with one another, as if the ceremony they'd recently gone through had been no more than a pause for formality during a long ongoing love affair.

Another honeymoon couple nearby seemed, in contrast, light-headed as they laughed explosively and often, periodically clutching at each other's arms as if to be certain they were actually in the same place together.

The three American women were over near the bar, having coffee and reading magazines. Strange Muzak tapes of sixties tunes played softly; the ship's movement was scarcely noticeable. Just as Jo was about to doze off an announcement advised passengers to present their passports to the French officials at the office opposite the duty-free shop. She roused herself and pushed out through the lounge doors to join the line.

It took only a few minutes, then she went to have a look at the duty-free offerings. She picked up a spray bottle of Chanel No. 5 eau de toilette, paid for it, dropped it into her purse, and returned to the lounge, where she unwrapped the bottle, sprayed her throat, then breathed in the fragrance of her mother. As she stared out the window at the glassy Channel, she tried to think why she hadn't bought her usual perfume. Then her thoughts shifted as the scent brought back an image of Lily at her dressing table, putting the finishing touches to her hair and makeup. Jo had been sitting on the end of the bed, watching. Satisfied, Lily had reached for the familiar clear bottle with the black top to place the ritual dabs of Chanel at the base of her throat and behind each ear. Then she'd stood up, smoothing the skirt of her dress. Black it had been, Jo remembered. Black silk, with quite a low-cut neckline that had made Lily's skin look slightly blue.

"He's late again," Lily had addressed the mirror. "Don't you have homework to do?" She'd turned to look at Jo.

"Mother," Jo had said with tried patience, "I'm a junior, for Pete's sake. Don't you think I know when and how much homework I've got to do?"

"Sorry," Lily had said curtly. "Where's Beamer?"

"*He's* doing *his* homework."

"What about dinner?"

"I'm taking care of it. Everything's ready to go. It's not my fault Dad's late."

"No one's suggesting it is." Lily had looked down at her shoes, then again at Jo. "I don't remember being so prickly at sixteen."

"I'm not 'prickly.' If anything, you're the one."

Charlotte Vale Allen

"Why is it," Lily had asked quietly, "that children speak to their parents in a manner we simply wouldn't tolerate from any other living soul?"

"Because children have to behave well for other people. Parents are the ones who have to put up with us the way we really are." Jo had smiled at her, going across to pluck an imaginary piece of lint from the shoulder of her mother's dress. "You look divine. And you know you love me."

"There are times," Lily had relented, "when it's quite a challenge. Where the *hell* is he? We're going to be late. I *hate* being late."

"He'll be here."

Jo had gone off downstairs to take the casserole from the oven, calling out to Beamer, as she went, to come and eat. The two of them had sat at the kitchen table, eating and looking over periodically at their mother, who paced back and forth in the living room, stopping every few moments to look out the front window before continuing her pacing.

They were concocting chocolate sundaes and Lily was still pacing but with a drink in her hand now, when the telephone rang. Jo and Beamer had stared at each other, waiting to see who'd answer. Lily picked up the extension in the living room, and the two of them continued to stare at each other.

"He's up shit creek without a paddle this time," Beamer had whispered. "She'll *kill* him."

"Sshhh! I'm trying to hear what she's saying."

They listened, but Lily wasn't saying anything.

"Five bucks says he missed the train," Beamer wagered, still whispering.

"Sshhh! Wait!"

From the living room they heard Lily put down the receiver. At once, they went back to the melting ice cream and the container of Hershey's chocolate sauce, the torn-open bag of crushed walnuts. The whole time they were fixing the sundaes they kept expecting Lily to come in and rant about the latest excuse. But she didn't. She sat for a time finishing her drink. Then she walked purposefully into the kitchen to put her glass in the sink, announcing as she did, "I'm going

104

out. Make sure you clean up after yourselves in here. Don't stay up too late. And, Beamer, if you don't clean up that room and get all that crap off the floor, I will throw every last thing in there in the garbage. And believe me, I mean it. Joanna, try to limit your telephone conversations to less than three hours.'' She'd whipped the keys from the hook by the garage door, picked up her handbag from the counter, and sailed out.

After she'd gone, Jo had looked at her sundae, decided she didn't want it, and dumped it down the disposal. "You'd better clean up your room, Beam. She means it.''

"I never thought she'd actually go without him," Beamer said, stirring the chocolate sauce into the ice cream. "There'll be a big fight tomorrow.''

Jo had stood over the sink gazing at the mess of uneaten sundae.

"There won't be any fight,'' she'd said, feeling a little sick. "Neither one of them will say a thing.''

Beamer came to sit on the counter beside her, still stirring his ice cream. "I'm never getting married,'' he'd said, taking an experimental taste.

"Sure you will,'' Jo had told him.

"Nope. I never will. You wait, you'll see. I absolutely will never get married. It stinks.''

"No, it doesn't,'' she'd said, feeling miserable now as well as sick. "Some day you'll go crazy over some girl and that'll be it for you.''

"I might go crazy over some girl, but I'll never marry her.''

"Oh? And what if you want to have kids?''

"I'm not having kids, either.''

"For Pete's sake, Beam! You're not even thirteen years old. You can't say things like that.''

"Sure I can. I'm *saying* them. I've spent better than twelve years with the two of them. That's plenty for me, thanks a lot.''

"You don't understand.''

"Oh, and you do, right?"

"Maybe," she'd said. "They love each other, Beam."

He'd finished the last of his sundae and turned to look at her. "Looks more like hate to me."

"You just don't understand."

"Okay. But I'm still never getting married." He'd hopped down from the counter, nudged her out of the way, and got a plastic garbage bag from under the sink. "I'll go clean up my room. I don't want her coming in and throwing out all my good stuff."

He'd left then, and Jo went back to gazing at the mess in the sink, thinking, This isn't the way things are supposed to be.

Turning away from the window, her eyes came to rest on an elderly, distinguished-looking couple opposite, separated from her by an unoccupied banquette. The woman smiled; Jo smiled back. With a hand held to her mouth, the woman indicated she was sleepy, and Jo nodded her agreement. The woman's husband was unaware of the communication between them, his attention on a stack of folders he was reading closely, peering down at them through bifocals.

There was something about this couple that at once aroused Jo's interest. They were in their seventies but seemed—regardless of the woman's mime of fatigue—more alert and aware than the majority of the other travelers. They were dressed simply, but extremely well, he in a summer-weight suit of beige wool with a white shirt and Liberty cotton floral tie, she in a tidy cotton shirtwaist dress with a white cardigan whose trim matched the dress fabric. They were both above average height, had exemplary posture, and had obviously been a startlingly handsome pair in their youth. It was easy to imagine the impact the two of them must have made some years back upon entering a room together. They seemed accessible, and Jo hoped she might have an opportunity to get to know them.

More lulled, she let her head fall back against the seat and closed her eyes.

* * *

Anne watched the young woman across the way close her eyes, and said softly to her husband, "What a lot of equipment she has, Jimmy. Did you see?"

"See what?" he asked without looking up from his reading.

"That dear girl with the camera across the way, the one traveling on her own."

Jimmy glanced up and looked around.

"Directly opposite," she said in an undertone. "I saw her on the platform at Victoria, taking photographs. Then she boarded before everyone else. I think she's doing some sort of photographic essay."

"Hmmmn." He returned to his brochures.

"She does so remind me of Lucia. That same shining hair and lovely, open features, great dark eyes. It must be awkward, being on her own. Lucia did so loathe traveling alone. I don't think I'd care very much for it."

"I expect she's accustomed to it," he commented, for the moment abandoning his brochures to look over at Jo. "Does rather resemble Lucia," he agreed. "Fallen asleep, hasn't she? Bit more petite, but there's a definite resemblance."

Anne looped her arm through his and the two of them sat gazing at the sleeping Joanna. Anne sighed. Jimmy automatically patted her hand. "Done rather a splendid job on the old train, wouldn't you say? Looked much as it did when I rode the Bournemouth Belle as a lad."

"You're not disappointed, then?"

"Should say not. Undoubtedly, they've done an equally bang-up job on the Wagons-Lits."

"Oh, undoubtedly." She gave him an affectionate smile, then looked again at Jo. "If she's on her own at dinner, perhaps we should invite her to join us."

"If you like," he said indulgently, and again patted her hand.

Jo was awakened by another announcement, this one informing those in the lounge that they would be disembarking once the other passengers had cleared the ship. She straightened and smoothed her skirt, trying to come fully awake. Most of the others in the lounge looked a little dazed. She wondered how she was going to make it through the rest of the afternoon, and the evening; she also tried to think how she could possibly photograph every aspect of this journey without, at some point, appearing totally obtrusive. Were she just another paying passenger and not someone being paid to do a job, the sight of some woman jumping up every few minutes to take pictures would irritate the hell out of her.

The female staff, having changed out of their serving aprons and put back on their brown suit jackets, began herding the passengers out of the lounge. Their trip up and down the various aisles and corridors only took a few minutes. And just over there was the train. It was wonderful, simply wonderful: the blue carriages spotless and shining, a staff member standing on the platform outside each carriage to assist people in finding their compartments. Jo unearthed the tag she'd been given at Victoria, and was pointed toward the appropriate carriage.

The cabin steward introduced himself, then escorted her to her compartment. "If there's anything at all you require, Madame, please let me know. I'm Mark, and I'll be bringing your breakfast in the morning. What time would you like to be awakened?"

"Eight, please."

Her suitcase was already in the compartment. She stopped in the doorway and looked in, admiring the space that would be hers until the train reached Venice. Gleaming polished wood with a tiger-lily marquetry design. To the right, curved doors concealed what she knew from the guide was a wash basin. Everything had been arranged like a painting, with bottles of Evian water and drinking glasses positioned in metal loops fixed to a corner of the wall to the right of the window; a copy of the Orient-Express magazine open on the table beneath the window, with a folder of stationery and some leaflets positioned precisely in the center; an ashtray with a small blue box of matches; lace covers on the seat backs; bolsters at each end of the seat; padded hangers;

scrolled metal luggage racks; an upholstered stool; a discreet array of buttons on the wall at what would be the head of the bed when the compartment was made up in its nighttime configuration—to summon the steward, or douse the lights, or turn on the night light. This was, she'd been told, one of the four sleeping carriages that had been air-conditioned, and the air was crisp, even nippy.

While she was standing there completing her visual inspection, the maître d' came by, clipboard in hand, to ask which seating she would prefer at dinner, early or late. She chose early. A note was made of this, and she was given a discreet chit with VOITURE LAQUE DE CHINE printed on the top, and her seat number written in.

She used the wide-angle to photograph the compartment, then opened the pair of curved doors to see they were mirrored inside. Thick white towels with the gold-embroidered VS-O-E logo were folded into a rack; more bottles of Evian water; a shiny blue plastic container of bath soap, as well as hand soap in the now-familiar dark blue glossy cardboard; racks to contain her cosmetics; and the tiger-lily motif had been painstakingly hand-painted above the basin and below the mirrors on the doors to lend continuity to the decorating theme.

Crouched at the extreme end of the seat, wedging herself tight against the window, she got a shot of the basin area, then sat down and looked at the closed and locked doors directly in front of her that someone in the next compartment was trying to open. She smiled, wondering when they'd realize that the doors didn't conceal a closet or some secret locked room but did in fact open to double the space if a large party were traveling in adjoining compartments. The jiggling and pushing kept on for several minutes, then abruptly stopped. During this time, Jo hefted her suitcase onto the seat and got out her clothes for that evening as well as for the next day, hung them on the hangers provided, put her cosmetic bag by the basin, then closed the suitcase and tried to get it out of her way. It was too large to go onto the overhead rack, and if she pushed it under the small, fixed table, there'd be no room for her legs. At last, she placed it against the pair of locked doors and propped her feet on it; it made a handy ottoman.

While she found the compartment exquisite in design, and thought it would be very comfortable for two people sitting side by side, she couldn't imagine what it would be like for two adults attempting to dress or undress, or to sleep in such limited space. And speaking of sleep, where was the second berth hidden? Probably, the rear of the seat cleverly lifted up, or something. She made a note to ask the steward about it.

The train was moving. She sat by the window, looking out every few moments, while she flipped through the Orient-Express magazine. It had been left open at a double-page painting that illustrated the route from London to Venice: a bold black line punctuated by red circles at London, Folkestone, Boulogne, Paris, Basel, Zurich, the spur to Chur, St. Anton, Innsbruck, Bolzano, Verona, Venice. The painting was nicely done, depicting the Tower of London in the upper left-hand corner, then snowy Alps, and a gondolier mid-canal in the bottom right-hand corner. Sixteen hundred-odd miles.

Next she opened the small portfolio to look at the postcards and writing paper. Everything she'd seen so far was tastefully discreet and of top quality. She got out her notebook and pen to jot down a few facts. Passengers were requested not to take the towels, since the stewards would be charged at journey's end for missing items. Passengers were also asked not to drink the tap water, hence the stock of Evian.

She paused to consider the contrast between this train and the ones she often rode into Manhattan. Those commuter trains were so totally *plastic:* orange molded seats, booze posters, seats supposedly designated for the disabled and elderly that were invariably occupied by those neither old nor handicapped. And the view in the immediate foreground was of garbage littering both sides of the track and, nearer to Manhattan, derelict buildings with tin sheeting over the windows. This, she thought, running her hand over the plush seat fabric, was the zenith of train travel: windows without so much as a smudge on them; fittings that shone from regular attention; staff anxious and evidently happy to see to one's every need. If there was something she wanted, say from the cabin-service menu—some Beluga caviar perhaps, and an aperitif—all she'd have to do was press the call button and someone would come at once.

A quiet tapping at the door roused her. It was the maître d' who with an apologetic smile said, "Perhaps Madame was not aware of the time change. We are now at the second sitting."

"Time change?"

"Yes, Madame. One hour ahead. I have taken the liberty of rebooking, since I am certain Madame would not wish to miss dinner."

"Oh, thank you. I'll be right there. I'm awfully sorry."

"Not at all, Madame. There is no need to rush. You did wish to dine, yes?"

"Definitely. I really appreciate this. I'll be along in a few minutes."

"Very good, Madame. I hope," he smiled congenially, "you had a good sleep."

She'd managed to sleep for close to two hours. She got the shades drawn over the windows and then, trying to keep her balance, hurried to change clothes. She'd have liked to shower but there were no bathing facilities on board, aside from the basin in each compartment.

Fifteen minutes later, feeling half-assembled, she slung the camera bag over her shoulder and took a final look at herself in the mirrored doors. She hadn't ever had that consultation with Henry about her wardrobe for this trip. A pity. She wasn't at all convinced the two-piece beige silk was dressy enough.

When she emerged, Mark, the steward, was in the corridor.

"I'll lock your compartment now," he informed her. "If

you plan to stay late in the bar car, I'll give you the key. Otherwise, just come and I'll open the door for you. And could I have your passport, please?''

"Oh, sure." She ducked back inside, found the passport, gave it to him, then had to stop to ask, "Which way is the dining car?"

"To your left, through the bar car. Enjoy your evening," he said pleasantly.

On her way down the corridor, holding on to the walls for support, she looked into the lavatory at the end of the carriage. Gleaming dark wood paneling, marble counters, beveled-edged mirrors; the room was pristine, scentless.

The entrance to the bar car was being used as a display area for VS-O-E gift items. Ties and scarves were draped over the brass handrails; photographs showed other available items. The car was full, the noise level high. People stood at the bar. White-jacketed waiters deftly carried trays of drinks to those seated in the armchairs and settees. A very large man in a tuxedo sat at the grand piano to the right of the bar area, playing innocuous renditions of old standards. Most of the male passengers were in tuxedos; the majority of the women wore evening dresses. Jo didn't see anyone in twenties-style gear, but there was one standout couple: a Japanese pair; he was perhaps in his early fifties, wearing a well-cut tuxedo and dress shoes with heels built up a good two inches; his companion, much younger and stunningly beautiful, had on a white silk kimono embroidered with white and gold threads, and a scarlet obi. The kimono looked as if it had never been touched by bare hands. The silk was matte, flawless, liquid as milk. The young woman, with her sleek cap of thick black hair, had captured the attention of the majority in the bar car.

As Jo picked her way through the crowd, people greeted her with smiles; a number said good evening. People were talking across the aisles; there was much laughter; the atmosphere was entirely festive—a party on wheels, whizzing through the night. Jo returned the smiles and the greetings, got to the far end of the car, and managed to open the door without either hitting anyone or falling off-balance in her high heels.

The maître d' greeted her at the front of the Chinese carriage as if the sight of her gave him great pleasure. With a demibow followed by a flourish, he said, "This way, please, Miss James," and showed her to a table for two halfway along the carriage. She sat down facing another empty table for two, then looked around to find people at nearby tables smiling at her. She smiled back, suffering through one of those piercing moments—like the one poor Katharine had had alone at her table in the piazza, watching all the couples go by—when her status as an unaccompanied woman was close to unbearable. She felt as if a small rock were lodged at the bottom of her stomach and her insides were churning around it in protest. Rather than invisible, she felt too conspicuous. It took someone, she thought, with great self-confidence to ride this train alone. It was a vehicle meant for twosomes; it required another person to whom one might turn to comment upon the people, the clothes, the food, the wine, the service. She busied herself organizing the camera bag under the table, notebook and pen close to hand. As she did, she wondered how many women had boarded this train alone, convinced they'd have magical, romantic encounters only to discover, as she was in the process of doing, that the presence of so many pairs could be dealt with in one of two ways. Either one toughed it out, concealing one's disappointment, or one made an attribute of one's aloneness and elected to respond positively to the curiosity and attention paid by those with sufficient generosity to extend welcoming smiles. Well, she'd smile and have a good time, she told herself, because there was no point in succumbing to the lure of self-pity. She smiled at the handsome elderly couple she recognized from the ferry, then picked up the gold-tasseled blue menu to read the offerings.

Escalope of sea bass with caviar and vodka to begin, followed by a fillet of beef sautéed with truffle sauce, spinach flan, and spring vegetables in a light puff pastry.

The waiter came to ask if she cared for something to drink.

"Some water, please."

"You would like *eau minerale*, or Perrier?"

"Mineral, please."

"Very good, Madame."

The car was a work of art: black lacquer panels with predominantly green designs of shrubs and trees, bits of color here and there in tulips, birds nesting in a tree, the red rooftops of a pagoda; more highly polished brass; dusky pink and white upholstery on the armed dining chairs, a complementing fabric in the curtains gracefully looped back from the windows.

Her eyes again met those of the elderly couple and it appeared they were about to speak to her when the attention of almost everyone in the car was drawn to the latest arrival, being shown to her seat by the charming Giuseppe, the maître d'.

The latecomer was a woman whose presence seemed to generate electricity. Somehow unaffected either by the motion of the train or the knowledge that she was being watched, she moved fluidly on very high heels, leaving in her wake a wonderfully rich fragrance of exotic flowers. She was wearing a black evening suit, exquisitely cut to show off her small waist, slim hips, and long, shapely legs.

Along with everyone else, Jo watched her take her seat at the facing table. An exquisite-looking woman, she had long almost black hair, pale skin, and dramatic makeup that accentuated her round light blue eyes and sensual mouth. She lit a cigarette, then shrugged off her jacket to reveal a white lace camisole top underneath. Beautiful shoulders and arms; her skin looked as if it had been polished, the tops of her breasts enticingly revealed above the scalloped lace. Jo was mesmerized. This was the sexiest woman she'd ever seen. She told herself she really had to stop staring so blatantly. But just as she thought this, the woman looked up, studied Jo for a moment, then smiled before turning to speak to Giuseppe, who'd lingered by the table as if he too found the newcomer riveting. He bent his head, listening intently, then straightened, nodded, spoke, listened again, nodded once more, and approached Jo.

"Mademoiselle," he said in an undertone to Jo, "wonders if you would care to join her for dinner since she sees that you are both alone."

Jo looked over at the woman, who smiled again at her, and underwent a moment of anxiety, unable to imagine what she could possibly find to talk about to someone so beautiful throughout an entire dinner. She felt the coil binding of the notebook under her fingers, collected her professionalism, and returned the smile. Think of it as an interview, she told herself.

"I am Lucienne Denis." The woman offered her hand as Jo sat down opposite with her notebook and camera. "Much better not to eat alone, eh?"

"I couldn't agree more," Jo said and, taking hold of the woman's hand, introduced herself.

9

"EXCUSE ME JUST FOR ONE MOMENT," LUCIENNE SAID, and picked up the menu to scan the wine list. Then without bothering to look around, she made a lazy gesture with her hand that at once brought Giuseppe back to the table.

"We will have the St. Émilion," she told him, then asked Jo, "You will have some wine?"

"I'd love some, thank you," she answered, to Lucienne's obvious satisfaction.

"So," Lucienne said, retrieving her cigarette from the ashtray, "what is it you are doing with all this?" She indicated the camera and notebook.

"A travel feature for an American magazine."

"You're a journalist, eh?"

"Primarily a photographer. Do you have a career? That's a wonderful suit."

"You like this? Good. I like it, too. You are interviewing me, eh?"

Jo flushed. "Not really. Just curious."

"No matter. My career . . ." She paused to take a final puff on the cigarette before putting it out. "I have a bistro in Paris. Chez Lucienne. You know Paris?"

"Not very well. I don't get there often, but next time I do, I'll be sure to come to your restaurant."

"Ah, well, you will have to make a reservation four or five weeks in advance."

"Really?" Jo was impressed.

"I make exceptions," Lucienne said with amusement. "If you are planning to be in Paris, you telephone to me and arrangements will be made. It helps," she laughed, "to know the owner."

"Are you from Paris?"

"No, Canada."

"Oh, really? Where in Canada?"

"I was born in Quebec."

"I love Quebec City," Jo told her. "I was there about four years ago, to do a feature. It was one of the best times I've ever had. Where in Quebec did you live?"

"We lived in the bush, eh, far from anywhere. My papa, he worked with the lumber company."

"I can't imagine you living in the bush," Jo said. "You give the impression of someone who'd know her way around a city, who'd never lived anywhere else, especially not in the bush."

"You think so?" Again Lucienne smiled. "Why do you think this?"

"Oh, well, your clothes, for one thing, and the way you wear them. I don't know. Just everything about you. You seem very urban."

"Urban?" Lucienne looked puzzled for a moment, then laughed. "I like this. Urban," she repeated. "My parents they send me to a Catholic boarding school in Quebec City." She made a face. "At sixteen I ran away."

"My God! Where did you go?"

"I worked in a bowling alley. Very exciting." Again she made a face.

"And then what?" Jo asked, anxious for details.

"You are very curious, eh?"

"Always," Jo admitted disarmingly. "Do you mind?"

117

"No, I don't mind. Other people, I think maybe they mind?"

"Sometimes," Jo allowed.

"Me, I don't mind. I leave there to go to work in a restaurant, save my money, because I have decided I want to go to Paris. When I am twenty, I work on a ship and go to Paris."

"What did you do on the ship?"

"Ah! I cook for the crew. A terrible job, very hot. You have been on a ship?"

"A couple of times."

"This was a—cargo ship. That is right, cargo?"

"That's right. Were you the only woman?"

Lucienne laughed again. "No. There were four. I would not go to be the only woman."

"It sounds like you've done some pretty amazing things."

"Maybe so."

The waiter came with the wine, opened the bottle, then awaited Lucienne's approval. She sniffed the cork as well as the neck of the bottle, studied the label, then said, "Good." The waiter exhaled as if a crucial test had just been passed, and poured a small amount into her glass. Again she sniffed; then she tasted; then nodded. Happily, the waiter poured the glasses full.

"Salut!" Lucienne touched her glass to Jo's, and drank.

The red wine was very dry, very smooth.

"Did you ever get in touch again with your family?" Jo asked.

"Oh, yes. I was very angry with them, you know, for sending me to live with the nuns. But once I am free, I write to them to say I'm happy now, everything is okay."

"And what about your restaurant? How long have you had it?"

"When I am twenty-eight, I start my bistro. *Et voilà*, the rest, it is history. So"—she lit a fresh cigarette and shifted the direction of the conversation—"you will be staying in Venice?"

"For five days, at the Cipriani. And you?"

"You have been before?"

"No, never."

"You will *adore* it! The Cipriani is very fine, very good cuisine. I stay also at the Cipriani. I am to be married soon in Venice," she announced, having decided she liked this young American woman with all the questions.

"That's terrific! Congratulations."

Rather than appearing elated at the prospect, Lucienne seemed offhand. "You think it's good to be married?" she asked, as if Jo's opinion was of importance. "You are married?"

"No. The staff seems to know you." It was Jo's turn to redirect the conversation.

"I like the train," Lucienne said simply. "I come quite often to meet with Paolo in Venice. Sometimes, if he has business, he comes back with me to Paris. You like this train? It is your first time?"

"Yes, and I love it. It's fabulous."

"Yes." Lucienne looked around with a pleased, even proud, air. "When you are at the Cipriani, you will meet Renato. He is the chef who prepares the food for the train. You speak Italian?" Jo shook her head. "No matter. You will meet him, see how they make the menus."

"How do you know him?" Jo asked, finding this far easier than she'd anticipated. Lucienne wasn't at all difficult to talk with; she was, in fact, most responsive. At this latest of Jo's questions, her gleaming shoulders lifted in a delicate little shrug. "I am impressed very much with the food on the train, so I ask who it is who makes the menu, and when I am in Venice, I go to the hotel to meet this man, see his kitchen. He is young, but very good. Very modern methods they have for preparing the food. Then," she laughed, "very traditional method for taking food to the train. It travels by boat. Old and new together. Very good."

Listening to Lucienne, Jo couldn't help thinking what a good thing it was that she'd had no preconceived notions about this journey, because every aspect of it so far had been unexpected. She couldn't imagine any other set of circumstances that would have placed her in the company of this beautiful yet agreeably accessible woman. Lucienne struck

119

her as quintessentially French, with that impeccable flair for clothes, and the dramatic features, that French women seemed to have genetically. She was, Jo imagined, someone who probably always looked good, even when climbing out of bed first thing in the morning. She also had the ability to make Jo feel as if her opinions and impressions were of significance, so that rather than being intimidated as she'd feared at being in the company of someone who attracted so much attention, she actually felt very much at ease, as well as grateful for the woman's spontaneous invitation to join her. She was also glad to have no particular need to wear her professional hat. It was an easy pleasure to share in the give-and-take of thoughts and information with someone so surprisingly forthcoming.

The waiter returned, asking if they were ready to order.

Lucienne retrieved the menu, studied it for a minute or two, then said, "I will have the smoked salmon." In an aside to Jo, she said, "I am not in the mood for sea bass."

"I've never had it," Jo replied, "but they served seafood for lunch. I think I'd prefer a salad, if that's possible."

"Certainly, Madame." The waiter noted their selections. When satisfied there were no other substitutions to the set dinner they cared to make, he went off.

Jo again looked around the car, noticing two middle-aged blond American women, both in beaded evening dresses, who seemed to be having a grand time. They clinked their wineglasses together, laughing. Farther along, waiters were presenting two sets of honeymooners with bottles of wine, making inaudible explanations as they did. Jo watched as the wine was poured and then both young couples raised their glasses in the direction of the elderly couple across the aisle from Jo. She turned to see the older pair lift their glasses in a toast to the newlyweds.

They were a remarkably attractive twosome, most distinguished, and Jo could just picture them on a tea plantation in Kuala Lumpur or some other exotic locale. He had the look and bearing of someone accustomed to being in authority. And his wife had the manner of a woman who'd dealt efficiently and well throughout her life with household staff.

Noticing that Jo was watching, the woman leaned over to say, "We spent our honeymoon on the train, you see. And Jimmy's very sentimental."

"Not at all," Jimmy disagreed. "One simply doesn't have honeymoons every day."

"We're celebrating our fiftieth anniversary," the woman went on, unfazed.

"Oh, that's wonderful!" Jo looked over at Lucienne and the two of them drank a toast to the couple.

Lucienne smoked her cigarette and watched her dinner companion talk with the old English couple, finding this American woman most engaging. Initially, Lucienne had thought she was perhaps in her late twenties, this Joanna. But upon closer inspection, she raised her estimate to the early thirties. She was not in the habit of inviting strangers to dine with her, especially not women who invariably sought, in some fashion, to compete. Joanna not only seemed uninterested in competition, but was openly complimentary, and her admitted curiosity was charming because of the interest she showed. Qualities, perhaps, of a journalist. But Lucienne saw something more. This Joanna was well groomed, her clothes were very good, but altogether she had an aura of gentleness and a sense of fun that made her appear younger than she was. Studying Jo as she continued her conversation with the English couple, Lucienne decided her new friend had a veritable gift for engagement, for compassion. This, in Lucienne's experience, was rare. But Joanna very much liked people. And as if to confirm this mute evaluation of Lucienne's, Jo now swung into conversation with the two blond American women who seemed most eager to confide to her the difficulties they had had in bathing and dressing for dinner in their shared compartment. Lucienne sat back, lit another cigarette, and was content to watch Joanna charm everyone with whom she spoke.

"We fell all over each other," one of the women declared with a laugh.

"She's not just kidding. We deserve prizes for getting dressed, I'll tell you."

"I was wondering how two people would manage in a compartment," Jo said with a smile.

"It ain't easy, sister," the first woman said. "But we wouldn't've missed it for the world."

The first courses arrived then, and to Lucienne's amusement, Jo said, "This is so beautiful, I just have to get a shot of it," and proceeded to take a picture of her salad.

"This is something you do often?" Lucienne asked as Jo was putting away the camera.

"I'm afraid so. It's the sort of shot editors love. And so do I. Even if they don't use this particular exposure, I'll look at it sometime when I'm going through my files, and it'll remind me of the entire evening. I'll think about that darling couple celebrating their fiftieth anniversary by sending wine to the newlyweds, and I'll remember those two women from New York. And of course I'll remember you. Did you hear what they said, the two women?"

Lucienne shook her head.

"They're doing the 'Big Three': the Concorde, the Orient-Express, and the QEII. The trip of a lifetime." Lowering her voice, she said, "I'd bet anything the two of them were show girls once upon a time. I can just see them in some nightclub, all done up in skimpy little costumes with feathers and spangles. Can't you see it?"

"Maybe," Lucienne allowed. "Or dancers, eh?"

"They have that glamorous look. Anyway, I'll remember them, and the fact that you're on your way to get married."

Lucienne frowned slightly and started on her smoked salmon. "I am not so sure," she admitted after a few moments. "Six years I have been saying 'not now' to Paolo. Then, in April when he was in Paris, I said, 'In July.' Now it is July and I think maybe it is not such a great idea."

"Why not?"

Lucienne gave another delicate little shrug, wondering as she did why she was revealing so much to this woman. Yet why not? What could be safer than a discussion with someone you met on a train, someone you might never see again?

"It is very complicated," she said. "I am thinking this moment about Chez Lucienne, about my regular clientele, and about the chef who is very temperamental. I am hoping they will do the deposits correctly. Too many things."

"And if you don't do everything yourself," Jo said sagely, "you can't be sure everything's being done right."

Lucienne's eyes widened. "Precisely! You are this way?"

"I don't know." Jo thought about it. "Maybe I am. Sometimes I'm not altogether sure what I'm like. And the only person I have to worry about is me."

"So maybe you are this way after all."

"Could be," Jo said, quickly eating the lightly dressed salad that had been arranged like a flower, with cuts of avocado intersecting leaves of curly lettuce. "Don't you want to get married?"

"Sometimes I think yes, sometimes I think no. You are happy with your life, eh?"

"Yes and no."

"I am the same." Lucienne took a morsel of smoked salmon into her mouth, drank some of the wine, then gazed appraisingly at Joanna. "You are—*mignon*," she smiled. "You understand French?"

"Only a little."

"You are gracious. This is not a usual quality of young women. I am very happy to meet you."

"Thank you," Jo said quietly. "I'm happy to meet you, too. I was starting to feel conspicuous, and you rescued me. It's very kind of you to invite me to join you, and very kind of you to say such nice things."

"It is not kind. The truth is not a kindness."

"No," Jo spoke slowly. "But how many people even know what the truth is, let alone tell it to other people?"

"Ah, yes. Well, I am in agreement with this."

"D'you mind if I ask you something?"

"Already you have asked me everything," Lucienne smiled at her. "I don't mind."

"Doesn't it bother you, traveling alone?"

"No. I prefer it."

"Why?"

"Because it is an occasion when I have no need to think of other people. It is a time only for myself."

"That makes sense."

"But of course it does. You must always take the time to be with yourself, enjoy your own company. You dislike to travel alone?"

"Not usually."

Again Jo looked around. Most of the others were finished with their main courses and were being presented with dessert. Everyone seemed to glow. Much laughter, the throb of conversations beneath the perpetual noise of the train itself, the chimelike music of cutlery against porcelain, clinking glassware. It was like a dream, or a scene from another era; it was unlike anything else with which she was directly familiar. She thought again of the way both Henry and Tyler had showed up to see her off, then looked at the woman opposite and decided she preferred her present company. It was what she needed just then. She was able to be herself with Lucienne in ways she couldn't be with either man. Maybe it wasn't possible to be completely one's self with any man unless you were so sure of your identity, your priorities, your needs, that others lacked the power to influence you. But was that entirely true? What about Lily? *Who was it who put a camera into your hands and said, "This is who you are?"*

"What is it that you think?" Lucienne asked.

"Sorry. I was thinking that nine times out of ten women are easier and more satisfying to be with than men."

"Some women. Some men. But I will drink a toast with you on that!" Lucienne said, and touched her glass to Jo's. Then, pleased with themselves, they laughed.

The food was superb, and both of them made small appreciative sounds as they ate, then laughed some more, and drank more of the wine.

"This is so great!" Jo said happily when the waiter brought

their dessert, an iced meringue with three different kinds of fresh red berries.

"You are not going to take a photograph?" Lucienne teased.

"Nope. I'm just going to eat it. I love fresh berries. I love this train!"

"After," Lucienne said, "we will go to the bar car. This you will love, too."

The bar car was only half full now, the atmosphere rather subdued. It took only a moment, once they were seated, to see that the cause was the corpulent pianist, who was playing a rather somber version of "Autumn Leaves." He finished the piece with a rippling arpeggio, then sailed into a medley of Viennese waltzes. It was all wrong, the first element of the trip that was totally out of synch.

"I have not seen this one before," Lucienne said. "Usually, the music is very lively, eh? People sing, they dance. Not like this."

A cheery young waiter came over and Lucienne ordered a cognac. On impulse, Jo asked for Grand Marnier. She'd already had several glasses of wine, and realized belatedly that she'd allowed Lucienne to pay for it. "This is my treat," she told Lucienne. Her reward was a sudden smile that seemed composed of equal parts pleasure and surprise.

The three American women Jo recognized from Lucille and from the ferry were seated directly behind the piano player and were trying, without success, to get him to play something a little more upbeat. Opposite the three women were the two blond widows Jo was still convinced were former show girls. A French couple with a young son of perhaps ten or eleven sat in stony silence.

"What d'you think?" Jo asked Lucienne, quietly indicating the French pair. "I think she's his third wife, at least, and the boy's his only son. He has the name, but she has the money. She hates him for having the name, and he hates her for having the money. The boy wishes they'd get a divorce so he can stop tagging along with them everywhere they go and just stay home and hang out with his friends.''

As Jo made up this history, Lucienne studied the family, and when Jo had finished, she nodded once slowly and said, ''That's good. I like it. Now tell me about the four there.''

Jo looked where Lucienne indicated, taking stock of two American couples, Texans, from what she could hear of their accents, and probably parents traveling with their daughter and her husband. The daughter was a billowy, curly-headed blonde in a frilly, fussy, full-skirted dress; her husband was in a navy suit, very Ivy League, and looked thoroughly bored. The mother was a petite, good-looking blonde, exquisitely dressed in white silk, and the father was in black tie.

''Okay,'' Jo said. ''The father is in oil. The mother's been taking night courses at the university for the last couple of years, working on her master's in something esoteric, like, say, medieval history. The chunky one's her daughter, and the guy with her is her husband. The parents are old money, at ease and discreet. The daughter managed to snag a husband, probably by telling him she was pregnant. She's never done a thing in her life except spend her parents' money— and she's very good at that. The husband probably works for the father and likes the parents but can't stand his wife and would do anything to get out of the marriage, but he likes to spend their money, too, and doesn't want to give it up, so they're stuck together. The daughter's a real piece of work; she's the kind who'll drive around a shopping center for hours until she finds a parking place right in front of the store she wants to go to.''

Lucienne laughed, saying, ''You are too terrible. Did you also make some story for me when I came to the dining car?''

Jo blushed. ''Actually,'' she confessed, ''I thought you were some French film star, but I couldn't think who.''

''I like that,'' Lucienne declared. ''I don't mind to be mistaken for a film star. Do you see the little Japanese in the very beautiful—what do you call it?''

''Kimono.''

''Yes. Now, I tell you my story. You see he is very much

older. And this is not his wife. He wears a wedding ring, but she does not, eh? He has the company in Tokyo that makes the machines to answer the telephone, and she is the one who sits at the reception to greet visitors. He buys her the clothes and takes her always when he travels, so that everyone will think he is a very great man with a most beautiful young wife. He thinks no one can see that he has special shoes to make him tall. You see this?''

"I did!" Jo laughed behind her hand.

"Ah, look!" Lucienne said. "See these two!"

Coming up the aisle was a very slim woman in a perfect beaded and scalloped twenties dress that was sleeveless and had a scooped neck. Around her neck and hanging almost to her knees were several ropes of pearls, and her hair was concealed by a beaded cloche; even her shoes were right, with sculpted heels and rounded toes. Her partner was wearing a white tuxedo, white shirt, and white bow tie.

"They must have shopped for months to find those clothes," Jo said admiringly. "I'd love to get a shot of the two of them, but I wouldn't dare. It's too intrusive."

"You are wise," Lucienne approved.

"More like experienced," Jo said. "There are times when you just can't jump up and start taking pictures."

"Something is happening." Lucienne tapped Jo on the arm.

The piano player was rising from his seat. There was a sudden conference among the three American women and then the oldest of them slipped onto the bench, flexed her fingers, and started playing show tunes. The other two at once began singing along, and the car sprang to life. Others began to clap and to join in the singing.

"This is better!" Lucienne said happily. "She is great, eh? And the one who sings, not the tall dark one, but the *petite* in the gray, she has so much fun. You see?''

Jo directed her eyes to the woman Lucienne had spoken of, an attractive woman with high cheekbones, large eyes, and tremendous energy, who sang out in a good strong show voice; she laughed gaily and applauded with enthusiasm between numbers. "I can never remember the words," Jo said, her eyes still on the singer, who had a long neck and very short boyishly cut dark hair. Diamond rings on both hands, as well as diamond earrings, yet none of it was ostentatious. Her outfit was like a Pierrot suit, the top with several layers of ruffles around a wide drawstring neck, the trousers fitted at the waist and hips but loose in the legs.

"She reminds me of someone, too," Jo said, "but I can't think who."

People sang and clapped along; more drinks came; drinks were sent to the singers and the woman at the piano. Then the two women were not only singing, they were, in seeming defiance both of gravity and the lurching of the train, dancing in the aisle while the others cheered. Jo and Lucienne clapped, too, and there was a moment when it occurred to Jo that she'd had a great deal to drink, and she looked around, hoping she wasn't disgracing herself. But no. Everyone seemed happy.

The French woman took her young son off to bed, the husband trailing reluctantly after. Then, not five minutes later, the husband returned and joined with the two women dancing in the aisle. The sullen-looking young Texas woman and her blue-suited husband got up, too, as did one of the honeymoon couples.

"There will be trouble," Lucienne said in an undertone. "Did you see that? He has taken the wife and boy to bed, now he returns. She is the type who will not be happy with this. She is one who will blame the two women who sing and dance."

"How can you tell?" Jo took a sip of her second Grand Marnier.

Lucienne made a knowing face. "It is not so difficult when you are accustomed to dealing every day with many people."

"You really love it, don't you?" Jo guessed. "Is your fiancè expecting you to give up the restaurant when you get married?"

"He doesn't say it, but I think it is what he hopes."

"And you don't want to do that."

"I don't think I am *able* to do it," Lucienne sighed. "I make decisions late at night sometimes, eh? It is quiet, Chez Lucienne is closed, and I am alone. Then I make decisions, because I am tired, because I am soon to be forty, because it has been a long day. But in the morning, I think forty is not so very old, and I am not tired, there is work to do, and I have great pleasure in the work. You have not been married ever?"

"No. I used to think it was inevitable, that I'd do all the things I wanted to do, and at the end would be marriage. Now I'm not so sure anymore. I mean, I'm not unhappy the way I am. I love my work, just the way you do. And for the most part, the men I know only seem to be interested in my willingness to sleep with them. Who I am, the way I am, none of that's a big part of what they want somehow. Maybe I'm not explaining it all that well. I don't usually have so much to drink."

"I think you explain it *very* well," Lucienne put her hand on Jo's arm. "You are most truthful. It is a long time since I talked with a friend."

"Me, too. I'm the same way you are about making decisions at night. The one thing I know for sure is that it doesn't matter what I tell myself after the sun goes down, because when it comes up again, everything'll be different."

"Yes," Lucienne said softly.

The piano player had returned. The three American women were preparing to leave, as were the majority of the others in the car. Jo looked at her watch to see it was almost twelve-thirty.

"I had no idea it was so late," she said. "I think I'm going to have to go to bed now. It's been a very long day."

"Then you must go," Lucienne smiled tiredly.

"Thank you so much for asking me to join you. I've had a terrific time, really terrific. Maybe we could have lunch together."

"That would be good."

"Okay. Well, I'll see you in the morning." Jo picked up the camera bag.

"*Bonne nuit*, Joanna."

"Thanks again."

Stopping at the bar to pay for the drinks and to tip the young waiter, Jo looked back down the length of the carriage to see Lucienne light a cigarette before lifting her cognac. The half-dozen or so remaining passengers were all covertly eyeing her as they got ready to leave. From this distance Jo was again struck by her new friend's glamour, by the feline grace of her posture, by the exquisite structure of her body, by the beauty of her pale skin, dark hair, and light blue eyes, and also by the unseen barrier that seemed to hold her locked in isolation. For a few seconds it seemed to Jo as if she'd never seen anyone so visibly cut off from others simply by dint of her physical beauty. She was tempted to go back and stay until Lucienne was ready to go to bed. But then Lucienne seemed to decide that the time had come. She finished the brandy, stubbed out her just-lit cigarette and reached for her bag.

Jo hefted the Lowe-pro onto her shoulder one last time and started back toward her compartment.

10

WITH THE SHADES DRAWN OVER THE WINDOW AND THE BED made up for the night, the dimensions of the compartment seemed much reduced. It was also extremely cold, and she got down on her knees, pushing past the stool and her suitcase to close the air vent. The motion of the train also seemed more pronounced, throwing her off balance, so she had to undress in stages. It took quite some time before she was finally in her nightgown, with her clothes hung away.

Face clean, teeth brushed, she was eager to climb between the crisp sheets. The night light above the bed cast a cobalt-blue glow, allowing her just enough light to see potential obstacles, and she lay down, at once even more aware of the train's motion. Recumbent, she became a part of the train, her entire body sensitive to the track bed. She wished she'd thought to bring on board some Dramamine, or even her Valium, because with the undiminished cold of the compartment and the lurching rush of the train over the tracks, she was very uncomfortable. But her medications were in the bag she'd checked through to Venice.

It was odd to think how readily she'd slept earlier, and how difficult she was finding it now. If she didn't get some sleep, she'd be a wreck by the time she got to Venice. But the more she yawned and thought about how tired she was, the less able she was to get to sleep. She turned from side to side; she even tried switching off the night light but had to turn it on again at once; it was simply too unrelentingly dark without it.

She drifted on the surface of sleep, and her thoughts were drawn toward Henry. In that state of being neither asleep nor awake, he once more acted out his passion, while she was both observer and participant. She watched and responded to the descent of his hands as they shaped her breasts, measured the span of her waist and hips; her appetite grew as he displayed his approving pleasure. She noted his surprise as she revealed her inability to be passive or detached. They surprised each other, she saw from her vantage point of distance. Henry's approach to her was direct yet refined; like an avid botanist examining the intricacies of some peerless floral specimen, he delved ever deeper into its core until, jubilant, he found its heart behind closely-wrapped concealing petals. And having uncovered the mystery of his hybrid treasure, he was respectful, even reverential. He had responded to her with whispered expressions of elation as if, like her, he also had never mastered the art of being casual.

Then there was Tyler. His approach had little to do with discovery, but almost everything to do with claim-staking; placing his territorial stamp on what he craved. His view was generalized, not specific. He appeared to have a talent for cloaking his true feelings by using a lifetime of theatrical training and experience as a scrim. This gauzy fabric could be lowered at a moment's notice to soften the landscape of his vulnerability. His love-making had been self-directed, an activity meant to display his masterly technique and determination. It had been impressive, breath-taking and, ultimately, impersonal. Tyler had taken her over; Henry had encouraged her to be aware. The two men had talked on the telephone and Tyler had revealed more of the state of his emotions to Henry than he had to her during the hours they spent naked together. Why was it men could find some fashion in which to communicate to each other, but not to women? Or was it she who had the reservations, the difficulties, the lack of trust?

She continued to drift, thoughts and images floating into range, then away, for what felt like hours. She remembered an afternoon—a Sunday, it must have been—when she and Henry had walked through a fine mist of winter rain all the way to Westminster Bridge. She'd left the camera back in the guest room because of the mist, and was feeling especially empty-handed, so she'd put her arm through Henry's. And he'd reached across to pat her reassuringly on the hand. The gesture had taken her off guard and she'd turned to look at him, but he'd been looking straight ahead. So she'd decided it had been an automatic gesture on his part, and she'd been angry with herself for being someone who constantly sought meanings where none existed.

"Is something wrong?" he'd asked her. "Are you cold?"

"No." She'd given him a bright, false smile. "I'm just fine, thank you."

His eyes had stayed on her then, and he'd said, "Someday, Jo, you'll tell the truth when someone asks you how you are. And then, to your utter astonishment, you'll find you get precisely the reaction you were seeking."

"What?"

"Nothing. Forget it. I have a splendid idea," he'd announced.

"What?"

"I think we should have tea at the Savoy."

"God, Henry! I'm not dressed for that."

"You think not?" He'd looked her over. "What's wrong with the way you're dressed?"

"The Savoy? They'll throw me out on my ear."

"Oh, on your ass, possibly. But never on your ear."

She'd laughed, and he'd reached out and pinched her cheek.

"You're such a twit, Jo. They'll just think you're another rich American tourist."

"Yeah. But I'll know I'm not."

"Well," he'd sighed. "I suppose it'll have to be a cuppa at some caff, then. Someplace where you'll fit right in."

"They'll be tickled to death to see you in your little three-piece number."

"I'm sure they will. Lend a bit of tone to the establishment. Tell you what. We'll compromise, and have tea and crustless sandwiches at the Ritz. We'll tell them you're blind. I'll whisper something to the effect that the poor girl thinks she's wearing her best Chanel. They'll go along. We British excel at closing our eyes to the indiscretions of the handicapped."

"Hell!" she'd laughed again. "If I'm going to be blind, let's go to the Savoy."

"Good girl!"

Gradually, she was aware of the train slowing to a stop. At once, she fell asleep, only to awaken a short while later when the train started up again. This continued throughout the night: she'd sleep when the train stopped, and come awake when it started up again.

She'd finally settled into sleep when the steward knocked with her tray. With an inward groan, she sat up, got the door unlocked, and said good morning to Mark as he slid the tray onto the table beneath the window. She then raised the shades partway to find it was raining, which meant she'd be unable to take any shots of the scenery. And that was just fine. She'd spend all the time she wanted drinking the fresh-squeezed orange juice and some of the coffee from the thermos flask; she'd sample the croissants and brioches and taste every one of the small jars of jam and marmalade. And she'd save the *International Herald Tribune* to read in the bar car. Her eyes felt too gritty, she was too tired altogether, to concentrate on reading just then.

Gazing out the rain-drenched window at the mountains—they were passing through Switzerland—she thought longingly of a hot bath or a shower. The two widows from New York had been quite crushed to learn there were no bathing facilities on board. Jo knew from her reading that there wouldn't be any. Nevertheless, it would have been good to immerse herself in a deep tub of water and scrub away some of the travel grime. But there was only the basin, and she badly needed to bathe. So she got out of her nightgown and, holding on to one of the mirrored doors for support, managed a sponge bath. It helped, as did having daylight enlarge the compartment. She no longer felt in need of medication; she was merely tired.

Dressed finally in black cotton slacks and a short-sleeved black shirt, carrying her purse and the camera bag, she made her way to the lavatory at the end of the carriage. It was again spotless. She was impressed.

Upon emerging, she came across Mark feeding pieces of wood into a small boiler at the end of the carriage just beyond the lavatory.

"What is it you're doing?" she asked as he laid the last of the wood on the fire before closing the paneled door.

"This heats the bathing water," he explained. "We use charcoal and wood." He opened a lower door to show her a store of bags of both.

"That's amazing! How often do you have to feed the fire?"

"Peak usage hours. Before dinner when we leave Boulogne, and again in the morning, then before lunch. We try to anticipate the need and keep the boiler stoked. The passengers," he confided, "sometimes get rather cross if there isn't enough hot water, especially first thing in the morning."

He was happy to stand there for an extra minute while she got a picture. She thanked him and went on to the bar car, which, with morning, had been transformed into a kind of salon. The gift items were back on sale, and several people were inspecting them. The waiters were serving juice and coffee; people sat reading newspapers; and the corpulent piano player was at his post, his music more appropriate in daytime than it had been the night before. There were couples and quartets here and there, either staring out the windows or talking quietly. Fresh flowers were on the bar and the piano top, and the air bore no trace of the previous night's tobacco smoke. This car changed character, depending on the time of day or night and on its occupants. But whatever its character, it was clearly the focal point of the train.

From a seat about two-thirds of the way down from the bar, she took in the details: cream-painted ceiling with dark wood strips, and two recessed areas adding height; dark paneling down the sides; the upholstery on the armed chairs and settees was predominantly taupe, with a paler shade of taupe in the scrollwork design; the carpet was in shades of muted green with hints of red in a curling leaf-and-flower design; in front of the settees were oblong coffee tables that had held drinks last night and now held cups of coffee; the curtains were a dusky pink, held at each side by tasseled cords; here and there were more of the pink-shaded lamps; brass handrails were regularly spaced the length of the car; and at the far end, to the right was the bar and to the left the grand piano.

Luke, the sweet-faced young waiter, came to ask what she would like. She ordered coffee, then set the camera and lenses in front of her on the fixed, round-edged table. It was still raining. She'd have to get shots of this scenery on the return trip when, with luck, the weather would be clear. She looked down the carriage again to see the fiftieth-anniversary couple entering. As they approached her, she said good morning.

"Oh, good morning! A pity it's raining," the woman said brightly as they settled opposite. "I expect you could get some quite wonderful photographs of all this."

"I'll be going back to London on the train," Jo told her, "so I'll have another chance."

"Ah, good, good," her husband said quietly, listening in on the conversation as he aligned his reading matter on the table.

"May I ask what it is you're doing?" the woman inquired.

"I'm writing a feature on the train for an American travel magazine. Primarily, I'm a photographer, but quite often I do cover articles, which means I do the photographic work as well as the writing. I'd rather just do the photos, but economically it's more practical to do the entire piece."

"How very interesting. Jimmy's quite keen on photography, aren't you?" She turned to her husband.

He had to shift slightly sideways because the space beneath the table wasn't sufficient to accommodate the length of his legs. "I prefer black and white, actually," he said to Jo. "I find color photographs rather distracting. When it comes to color, I'd much rather study paintings."

"Which is what he'll be doing throughout our stay in Venice," Anne added.

The waiter brought Jo's coffee, then, with a little bow, said, "Good morning, Sir James, Lady Arlington. You would wish something?"

Jo watched as Sir James asked for tea and his wife said she'd like some coffee. She felt like a child, awed at being with members of the British peerage, and for a few moments was rendered speechless.

"How rude of me," Lady Arlington said, correctly interpreting, and charmed by, the surprise widening Jo's eyes. "I am Anne, and this is Jimmy."

Jo told them her name, then admitted, "I'm really impressed. I've never met anyone with a title."

Anne laughed. "Hardly impressive," she said, thinking again how very like Lucia Jo was. "It's Jimmy's title. I merely tag along."

"Oh, but even so," Jo said. "To be Sir and Lady, it's so—storybook."

"How very dear of you," Anne said. "I'm afraid we're most ordinary, except for Jimmy's passion for the Venetian artists, and the Italian school in general. He'll most likely walk my feet off in Venice, taking me to out-of-the-way churches to show me works by Titian and Tintoretto and all the others."

"It's not your first trip to Venice, is it?" Jo asked them.

"First in fifty years," Jimmy said.

"We spent our honeymoon in Venice," Anne elaborated. "This is our second trip." She looked lovingly at her husband. "He's always been reluctant to return for fear of having his first impressions altered."

"But the paintings, the artwork, will still be the same, won't they?" Jo asked him.

"We'll know soon enough," he said with a smile.

"And how long will you be staying in Venice, Joanna?" Anne wanted to know.

"Just five days."

"One can see quite a great deal in five days," Jimmy said. "A number of must-sees, of course. Splendid works in Santa Maria del Giglio, including several Tintorettos; then there's the Gothic church of Santo Stefano; and—"

"I should write all this down." Jo grabbed her notebook.

"Most assuredly," Jimmy agreed. He repeated the names he'd already mentioned, then went on to include, "Santa Maria della Salute which, among others, has a number of Titians; then, of course, you simply must see the church of San Trovaso, and San Sebastiano; and, very important, San Nicolò dei Mendicoli; San Giacomo dell'Orio; San Simeone Grande; San Silvestro." He named half a dozen more churches, then wound down, saying, "Not to mention the Accademia, and all the galleries."

"You see what I mean!" Anne laughed. "I have my work cut out for me."

"You certainly do," Jo agreed. "How long are you planning to stay?"

"Several weeks," Jimmy said. "After fifty years, one really shouldn't rush through the city."

"I wouldn't think so." Jo gave him a smile, and he stared at her for just a moment, then returned it.

"Where will you be staying?" Anne asked her.

"At the Cipriani."

"Oh, so shall we!" she said. "You must dine with us one evening."

"I'd love to. Thank you very much."

"Actually, we were about to invite you to join us last evening, but we noticed you struck up an acquaintance with that most attractive French woman."

"Isn't she gorgeous?" Jo said. "She'll be staying at the Cipriani, too."

138

"In that case," Jimmy said, "we'll have to give both of you dinner."

"She's going to be getting married in Venice," Jo explained.

"Now, that's a pity," Jimmy said, and laughed when Anne slapped the back of his hand. "She is a rather fabulous creature."

For her part, Jo found these two rather fabulous. Sir James, Jimmy, was very tall, perhaps six foot two or three, with a full head of lustrous white hair, a broad forehead, wide-set blue eyes, a long well-modeled nose, high slanting cheekbones, and a relaxed mouth. This morning he was wearing navy trousers, a long-sleeved white shirt, a sleeveless cotton V-neck pullover in a Fair Isle pattern of misty blues and greens, and a jaunty light green bow tie. Anne had on another shirtwaist dress, this one of emerald green polished cotton that pointed up her fair skin and green eyes. She was shorter than her husband, about five six or seven, and wore her hair in a loosely waved bob that came just to below her ears. Again Jo couldn't help thinking what a striking pair they must have made fifty years ago, riding this train on their honeymoon.

"How," Jo asked them, "does the train seem to you fifty years later?"

"They've done a bang-up job!" Jimmy declared. "Have you noticed," he said, turning toward the window, "that even the smallest round-headed screw is of brass?" Turning back, he said, "Have to say I'm impressed. They haven't messed about with her, trying to add bits and pieces to placate those who come along expecting to find three-piece suites in every compartment. No. It's just as it was, but actually better. I don't recall there being a grand piano." He smiled. "But it's a jolly nice touch. Had a word with the train manager last evening about it. Wondering, you know, how they managed to get it inside. Took the legs off, you see, then brought the beast in on its side when the carriages were separated."

"I was going to ask about that," Jo told him. "I was wondering myself."

Luke came with Jimmy's tea and Anne's coffee, and in the lull Jo noticed that the interior of the car was growing lighter. She looked out to see that they were moving away from the rain, and automatically raised the camera. Chalets sat here and there at the base of the mountains; a river of impossible, Caribbean, blue appeared around the next bend; a sawmill with tidy stacks of lumber beside a brick retaining wall that backed onto the riverbank; a covered bridge; fields of flowers. Suddenly, the land dipped far below the tracks, spreading into a lush green valley surrounded by mist-enveloped mountains; on the rain-slick roads of a village, a man with an umbrella stood alone near an intersection watching the train go past; gliding through a town, past a block of low-rise apartments, and there was a man out on his balcony with a video camera set up to film the train's passage; on again into the countryside, where an elevated highway clogged with traffic sliced cleanly across the shaved sides of hills; red-roofed white-painted houses set like Lego bricks in graduated clusters climbing a hillside; a stone castle perched precariously at the edge of a mountain; tall spires of narrow churches poking above the treelines; an old steam locomotive parked in the garden beside a quaint little station hung all around with baskets of pink flowers; snow-covered peaks visible behind low-hanging clouds; dense stands of fir trees dwarfing a chalet positioned in a clearing; the elevated highway reappearing far above the train, curving off into the distance; a black-roofed white church halfway between the track and the highway; the sky thick with roiling gray and white clouds; sudden shafts of sunlight falling like spotlights to illuminate an isolated farm with fields whose shapes conformed to the strange configurations of the land; a small castle with two crenelated towers.

When she paused to reload, she noticed that Jimmy and Anne had gone and that the car had grown quite full. Diagonally opposite were a French quartet—three women and a man. The women all wore heavy gold jewelry—Cartier watches, thick link bracelets, necklaces, brooches. Farther along two young couples Jo hadn't seen before sat slouched in gloomy silence. One of the men, heavyset and in need of a shave, had on a Walkman and sat staring straight ahead, his legs sticking out into the aisle. The other man was in the midst of paying Luke for some drinks; the two women with them were whispering together, looking around from moment to moment as if fearful of being overheard.

The three French women were watching Jo load the Pentax, and she smiled at them, then returned her attention to the passing scenery. The clouds had pretty well dissolved, but the sun hadn't yet fully broken through. She looked at the rain-spattered window, then raised her eyes to the sliding glass panels above the fixed section of the window. Inspired, she stood up, pushed apart the panels, and found she was just tall enough to hold the camera steady in the open space.

For the next hour she stood by the window, periodically taking shots of some of the most spectacular scenery she'd ever seen. Luke came by now and then to offer her more coffee, and to warn her twice that they were approaching tunnels.

At last, cramped from standing for so long wedged between the table and her seat, she parked the camera and walked up the car to stand by the bar and chat with the young waiter.

"You like to take the pictures," he observed. "You make book on the train?"

"Not a book. Just a story for a magazine."

"Oh! You like the train?"

"It's wonderful. Do you like working on the train?"

"Is very good," he nodded vigorously. "Nice peoples. I like it."

"How long have you been working here?"

"Three year. You take my picture?"

"Yes, I'll take your picture."

"Good," he said. "Is good."

She went back for the camera, then waited at the bar while her model served some drinks. The barman smiled at her.

She smiled back. In spite of her lack of sleep, she felt extremely well and very happy. The trip so far had been highly pleasurable, and she still had Venice ahead of her.

"Where I stand?" Luke asked, returning.

She posed him against the bar so that the available light from the window hit him full on, then waited for his wonderfully sweet smile to take form before she made several exposures. She tipped him for his attentive service, said she'd see him later, and started back toward her compartment.

Returned to its daytime mode, the space no longer looked quite so confining. After stowing the camera bag on the luggage rack, she hefted her suitcase onto the seat to repack her clothes from the previous day. That done, she sat down to look out the window, wondering where Lucienne was. It was less than half an hour to lunch and there'd been no sign of her. She'd probably slept late. And if she had, then Jo silently congratulated her.

No point in procrastinating. It was time to do her notes. She began to jot down all the details she could remember of the night before and of this morning. She'd been at it for about fifteen minutes when suddenly a small, very round Japanese boy of about eight bounced into the doorway. Knees bent, body slightly crouched, chubby hands clutching an automatic camera held by a strap around his neck, he stood grinning so hard at her that his eyes all but disappeared into the creases of his face. He was dressed in a white short-sleeved shirt with epaulettes, black shorts, black knee socks, and black lace-up oxfords. He continued to hold his pose in the doorway, his feet firmly planted, hands on the camera, his face looking permanently creased into that rather bizarre, faintly maniacal grin.

Jo said, "Hi. What can I do for you?"

He shook his head, smiling all the while, cemented in place like a little Buddha. Then a tiny woman, obviously his mother, in a black and white polka dot silk dress came scurrying along the corridor—Jo could hear her faltering steps and exclamations of distress—appeared in the doorway, and at once began laughingly scolding the boy in Japanese. To

Jo, she said, "Sorry, so sorry," and offered a smile very like the one still plastered to her son's cheeky face.

"Oh, that's okay," Jo said, and watched the woman maneuver the boy out of the compartment and down the corridor. She could hear her high-pitched voice and tinkling laughter diminishing as they reached the end of the carriage.

Jo returned to her notes.

". . . bar car warm; people buying from boutique, having coffee. More families have arrived—trio of gorgeous small blond giggling kids; the scenery like melting pictures; 2 Amer. men playing backgammon; fluffy overweight young Texas woman talking at bar with Antoine, train manager, in loud voice, asking about 3 women last night, suggesting they're schoolteachers on vacation. Antoine concealing shock, tells her 1 is well-known author (thought I recognized her), other 2 important publisher and B'way producer. Bar car core of train nerve center, natural draw for passengers to meet and covertly study each other; many tunnels, sudden utter darkness enclosing car; people talking softly in Fr., and pianist plays on—'Blue Danube' often; 1 Fr. woman with huge solitaire surrounded by baguettes; 2 of the blond children go to sit behind pianist on ottoman, elbows on knees, listening; staff constantly offering service, assistance; lunch to be in 2nd dining car, 'Étoile du Nord.' L. right about Fr. couple from last night. Husband talking to little boy, wife livid, thin-lipped with anger. When the 3 Amer. women come through, wife gets up very pointedly and leaves carriage. The 3 women exchange looks, greet man and boy, and sit in far corner whispering, then laughing. Intrigue. Almost no sleep, hours staring in dark thinking about H. and T., with the feeling I must . . ."

Abruptly, she stopped, closed the notebook, recapped her pen, and washed her hands before setting off for the dining car.

11

GIUSEPPE ASKED HOW SHE WAS ENJOYING THE TRIP AS HE showed the way to her table. "Mademoiselle Denis will take lunch with you?" he asked.

"I thought so, but I haven't seen her this morning. Maybe I'll go ask her. Do you know which carriage she's in?"

"I will find this out," he said.

While she waited for him to come back, she took a few shots of the interior of the car: marquetry panels of urns of flowers, surrounded by dark wood trim; beveled mirrors set into the partitions; brass overhead lamps with tulip shades; deep green upholstery fabric on the chairs; a swirling floral-like design on the dark reddish-brown carpet; fresh flowers on every table and the usual array of polished crystal and silverware.

Giuseppe gave her Lucienne's carriage and compartment number. She thanked him, said, "I'll be right back," and returned through the bar car, the staff car where the employees slept for three or four hours during the trip, on through her own car and into the next. At the far end she found one of the stewards.

"I was wondering if you've seen Mademoiselle Denis this morning."

144

"She is still in her compartment, Madame. She did not wish to be disturbed earlier."

"Oh!" Jo looked along the corridor, wondering whether she should disturb Lucienne now.

"But that was much earlier," he added.

"Okay. Thank you."

With the decided feeling she was about to intrude, she went to knock at Lucienne's door. Hearing a response, but unable to decipher it, she said, "It's Jo. May I come in?"

This time the answer was clear. "Come!"

Jo opened the door. It was dim inside, the shades still drawn. In a long pink T-shirt, Lucienne lay curled up in a tight ball on her side on the bed.

"Are you all right?" Jo asked, at once concerned. Lucienne's face was waxy and white, her eyes darkly shadowed.

"Will you give me please some water?" she asked, and Jo at once opened a bottle of Evian.

Propping herself on an elbow, Lucienne accepted the glass and drank down the water. "Thank you." She put the glass back into Jo's hand before pushing herself up to a sitting position. "It is better now," she said. "Please sit."

Jo sat. "What's wrong?" she asked.

"I have this stupid thing, endometriosis. You know what this is?"

"Yes I do, actually," Jo answered. "It's very serious. Have you been to a doctor? Obviously, you have. But I mean, do you have anything to take for it?"

"I hate pills, and I hate doctors. Always, right away, they want to cut you open, take everything away. The pain is now," she said dismissingly, "because my period comes today or tomorrow. Then the pain will go away." She wound her arms around her knees and looked at Jo appraisingly.

"I was hoping you'd have lunch with me. When I didn't see you, I thought I'd come . . ." she trailed off.

"Mignon." Lucienne smiled and lightly touched two fingers to the underside of Jo's chin. *"Tu es très gentille, très attentive."*

"You really should see about it. You wouldn't necessarily

have to have surgery. There's medication—" She stopped because Lucienne was shaking her head.

"Already, I am much better. Also I am hungry. I will dress and we will eat, eh? You go, and I come in a few minutes."

"Are you sure?"

"*Absolument*, I am sure."

"If you're nervous about it, I'll be happy to go with you to a doctor when we get to Venice. It's really not good to ignore it."

"I know. You go now. Tell Giuseppe I come to join you."

"Okay." Reluctantly, Jo left her.

Back in the dining car, she looked over the menu (steamed deep sea fish and scampi with rock green beans; lamb medallions with zucchini flowers; green beans rolled in bacon; roast potatoes; white peach charlotte; Colombian coffee), then exchanged greetings across the aisle with Jimmy and Anne, with the two New York widows, and with the trio of women the frowzy babe from Texas had wanted to believe were schoolteachers on vacation.

Inside ten minutes Lucienne appeared looking so fit and elegant in aquamarine slacks and a matching silk shirt that Jo could hardly believe this was the same woman she'd found ashen and agonized less than half an hour before. With her blue eyes sparkling, her hair casually twisted into a knot on top of her head, she didn't look as if she'd ever had an unhealthy day in her life. Nestled in the neckline of the shirt was a diamond pendant; gold loops in her ears; a man's Rolex on her wrist; white leather ballet flats. She breezed in, bringing her wonderful scent and, again, the attention of everyone in the car.

"Not too long, eh?"

"Incredible," Jo replied. "I could spend three days working on it and I'd never look one-tenth as good as you do."

"Pah! You are young. You have no need for work. You look very fine as you are." She turned to order two glasses of white wine, then stopped the waiter. "This is Gian Paolo," she told Jo. "Gian Paolo is passionate about the train. He has the biggest collection anywhere of Orient-Express—memorabilia. This is the word?''

"That's right. You do?'' Jo asked him. "How come?''

Shyly, Gian Paolo said, "Because is only one, Signorina,'' then excused himself to fetch the wine.

"He adores the train, and being able to work on it. Charming eh? Giuseppe has told me every time the boutique has some new item to sell, Gian Paolo buys it for his collection.''

"That's great. I'll have to get his picture, work him into my piece. You know, I haven't encountered anyone who works on this train who isn't happy as Larry.''

"Who is Larry?''

"It's just an expression.''

"So somewhere,'' Lucienne said drolly, "is a happy man named Larry.''

"Somewhere.''

"So,'' Lucienne asked, "what have you done all morning, take pictures?''

"Uh-huh, dozens.''

"Very beautiful, the mountains. Good for the spirit to see all this.'' She looked out the window. "We come soon to Innsbruck. At the Brenner Pass we will get another engine, another engineer.''

"How many times have you done this?''

"Perhaps six or seven, maybe more. When I grow tired of Chez Lucienne, and the staff, and the patrons, the chef and the suppliers and the banker; when I grow tired of everyone, I come on the train, make a trip to Venice for three days, or five days, or so. Then, when I am no longer tired, I go back. It is a little gift I give to myself. And what is it you give to yourself, Joanna?''

"I don't know. Movies, I guess. And music. Books. I just finished reading a biography of Diane Arbus. Are you familiar with her?''

"No.'' Lucienne sipped at her wine, then lit a cigarette. "Who is this?''

"She was a famous American photographer who took strange pictures of strange people. According to the book, she was pretty strange herself. She committed suicide when she was forty-eight or -nine. Anyway, toward the end of her life she was mostly taking pictures of—freaks, I guess you could say. The thing that got me was she used to sleep with most of her subjects. I mean you'd have to see her work to appreciate just how weird the idea is of sleeping with some of those people. It made me think of those primitive people who didn't want to have their photographs taken because they believed their souls would get captured inside the camera. You know? Well, she seemed to be trying to get inside people's souls by sleeping with them and then taking their picture. It really bothered me. Not that I'm prudish, but it's so strange to think of giving a part of yourself to someone in order to take away an image. Maybe she was trying to punish herself. She came across in the book as very needy, very dependent. I don't know. I can't really figure it out. Maybe it's my viewpoint that's off kilter. All I know is that what you shoot is reflective; you make statements about how you see things, and how the things you see affect you. I've only once made love with someone I photographed, and I still don't know how I feel about it.''

"It is my experience," Lucienne said, "that very often you cannot get to the friendship with a man until you show them the sex will not be good, or important. So, you sleep with them because it is what they want and then, like children, they are satisfied and you are able to be friends.''

She spoke so matter-of-factly that Jo had to wonder why, in her own life, sexual issues loomed so largely. Obviously, this was one area of Lucienne's life about which she had absolute equanimity.

"What's your fiancé like?" Jo asked after Gian Paolo had presented them with their first courses.

"Oh, Paolo," she said. "He is *very* Italian, but also very American. He grew up in New York until the age of thirteen. Then his family brought him back to Italy. He is a child of— privilege. This is the word? A family of much money.''

"That's the word.''

"Good. So, they have much money, and now Paolo has

the money and is head of the family. The family," she elaborated, "do not care very much for this marriage. I am too old; I am not Italian; I have no line."

"You mean lineage?"

"Yes. I cannot make children to preserve the name."

"Why not? Lots of women in their forties are having babies these days. You're not so old."

"Perhaps not," Lucienne sighed. "But I have this stupid sickness. To make children, they say to take many pills for many months and after that *maybe* everything is okay. I hate pills."

"Would you like to have children?"

Lucienne looked away, considering. "Sometimes, again at night, I think it would be good. But when I think again at morning, I think this would be madness. Paolo is young, eh? And I think he would like the children." She gave one of her delicate little shrugs, and turned back to her seafood. "All things are complicated. We will see."

"How young is he?" Jo asked.

"Thirty-two." Lucienne laughed, showing her small, very white teeth. "My little boy. His mother and sisters are horrified he wishes to marry someone so *old*."

"Eight years isn't that much of a gap."

"To them, Mignon, it is the Grand Canyon!" She laughed hugely, enjoying herself. "To me, it is nothing; less than nothing. Ah! Here are your friends!"

"Don't wish to interrupt," Jimmy said. "Just wanted to invite the two of you to join us for dinner this evening."

"That's so nice!" Jo said. "You haven't met Lucienne. Sir James and Lady Arlington, Lucienne Denis."

Jimmy shook her hand, then Anne did, saying, "We've been admiring you. I do hope you'll be able to dine with us."

"I would adore it," Lucienne declared. "I am enchanted to accept."

"We'll book a table, say for eight?" Anne looked first at her husband then at the two women.

"That's fine," Jo said.

"Thank you so very much." Lucienne tilted her head in a graceful gesture of acceptance.

"We'll leave you to finish your meal," Anne said, taking her husband by the hand.

"The lamb's first-rate," he told them. "First-rate."

After they'd gone, Lucienne wanted to know, "How do you know them?"

"We just met."

"Everyone likes you, I think," Lucienne said. "I think this is so."

"Don't I wish."

"You don't think people like you?"

"Not everyone, that's for sure."

"Then they are foolish. You are very"—she searched for an appropriate word—"engaged, very interested in all things. You are one, I think, who cares."

"D'you mind if I ask you something?"

Lucienne grinned at her. "More questions, more curiosity." She shook her head indulgently. "Ask me something."

"Why did you invite me to join you last night?"

"Ah! Why? I have not ever done this before, but I look at you and think to myself, This one, she is being very brave. But the eyes are of the child in the corner, eh? I think you are very young, very fragile. I think you will be interesting, not difficult."

"I'm definitely not young."

"No, not so young as I think. But very interesting. I never have a dinner companion who makes photographs of the salad," Lucienne laughed.

Gian Paolo came then to remove the plates and Jo remembered to ask if he'd mind her taking his picture.

"I would be happy, Madame," he said proudly.

"After lunch?"

"Yes, Madame. You would, um, give to me one copy of your photograph?"

"I'll be glad to. Will you be making the trip back on Saturday?"

"Yes, Madame."

150

"Great. I'll get prints made while I'm in Venice and have them for you on Saturday."

"You see," Lucienne said, "everyone likes you. Royalty comes to invite you to dine; people wave to you from all corners."

"But that's just be—"

"It is because," Lucienne said firmly, "you have the eagerness—for all things, I think. And also because you say and do how you feel, and this makes others feel better in themselves. It is a little sad maybe you don't know this about yourself, because others can see it, eh? Giuseppe and Gian Paolo and the Royal Family and the two—*veuves*, the widows, and the three who sing, all see it. You must begin to think more of yourself, Mignon. You have a lover?"

Color surged into Jo's face, but she answered, "Yes and no. I don't know," she faltered, thinking how best to explain the tricky situation with Henry and Tyler. Luckily, the two widows stopped at the table at that moment to say hello.

"Isn't the food divine?" said the one.

"We just stuffed ourselves," said the other.

Jo introduced Lucienne and the first of the women leaned down and in a confiding tone said, "I want to tell you I said to May here last night when you came into the dining car, I said, 'May, is that the most stunning woman you've ever seen, or what?' And May here, she said you had some nerve, walking around with her body." The woman laughed heartily.

May gave Lucienne a guilty smile and said, "Don't mind Liz. She always blurts out whatever she's thinking. But I honest-to-God wouldn't mind being able to wear something like that black suit and look as good as you do in it."

Lucienne accepted the compliment, saying, "I will tell my *couturière* what you have said. She will be very happy. I might ask a question?" she inquired.

"Oh, sure," said May.

"You have been dancers, eh?"

The two women turned to look at each other, then burst out laughing.

"That's the best! You think we look like dancers? I *love* it! Liz here works for the New York City Board of Education. And I'm in business thirty-six years. Dancers! God love you, that makes my day! That's the best yet!"

"Enjoy your lunch," said May. "See you later."

"See!" Lucienne exclaimed when they'd gone. "Because I am with you everyone is friendly."

"You mean they wouldn't have spoken to you otherwise? Sure they would have. I would've been willing to bet they'd been show girls."

"No one has been so friendly when I have come on the train before," Lucienne said. "This is different because you are here. You jump up to take your pictures; you speak with everyone, ask many questions. And everyone is gratified, because you are having a happy time and you show it to all. And you are very charming, very pretty. Everyone responds to you. Most of the others, also me, we are soigné; we think perhaps it is déclassé to show we have a happy time. They should have you to ride the train all the time, then everyone would speak with everyone else and not worry about appearing naive. Ah! Here is Gian Paolo!"

Jo wolfed down the tender pieces of lamb, quickly cleaning her plate, then saw that Lucienne had eaten almost nothing.

"You should eat," Jo told her.

"I am not so hungry." She lit a cigarette, then drank some more of her wine. "I will eat later, when we dine"—she gave Jo a mischievous grin—"with your royal family."

"They're very dear people." Jo laughed, then explained. "I'd decided he was one of those characters in a Somerset Maugham story, with a tea plantation. And here he turns out to be *Sir James*. Of course, I don't actually know what he does, or did, so I could still be right. And she reminds me in a way of my mother. She's older than my mother would be now, and not really like Lily. I can't explain it. Have you any brothers or sisters, Lucienne?"

"One brother, older."

"Me, too. One brother who's younger."

"And your mother, she died?"

"Two years ago. She had stomach cancer. It took her a long time to die, a long, long time. I forget sometimes that she's not there anymore, that I can't phone her, or drive up to show her a couple of batches of slides, or the latest prints; I can't sit with her and ask her what she thinks about this or that."

"You were close with your mama?"

"I wanted to be, but we weren't ever really close. We just, eventually, got to be friends, I guess."

"My mama, she is close always with my papa, but not with Louis or with me. Me, I am close with Louis. But I don't see him so very often. It is strange with families, eh? All different, all the same. Me, I never cared to have my own family. Chez Lucienne is my family. My staff, they come to me with their troubles, their amours. My clientele, they confide to me exceptional facts of their lives. I have little time for anything else."

"Except for Paolo," Jo reminded her.

"Paolo, yes. I have in my baggage a marriage dress. I look at this dress and I think, Lucienne, you are crazy! What is it that you do with this dress? I think," she measured out her words, "maybe I do not believe in marriage. You believe in it, Mignon?"

Almost inaudibly, Jo answered, "No. I did, when I was little. I really did. All through my childhood, it was like something religious. You know? It was this miraculous reward you got for being female. Then, gradually, I stopped believing. And so did Beamer, my brother. When he was twelve years old, he told me he'd never get married. He swore it. At the age of twelve. I'll never forget that night. I kept thinking there had to be something I could say to get him to change his mind, but I couldn't come up with anything. Nothing."

"And now he is married?" Lucienne asked.

Very quietly, Jo said, "No. He's thirty-two years old. He's had more women than I could possibly count. But he's not married."

Lucienne watched as Jo turned to look out the window, and wondered at the younger woman's sudden and profound sadness.

"Why does this make you so unhappy?" Lucienne asked her. "Perhaps it is right he doesn't make a marriage."

Jo slowly turned back. "Maybe, but I'm not so sure. Even though I knew my mother was going to die, somehow I thought there'd still be a chance for us to talk. She'd tell me things, explain—" She stopped abruptly. "I'm sorry. I didn't mean to get into all that."

"But I *asked* you to get into it," Lucienne said.

"You know something? What you said before, about people not taking the time or making the effort to talk to you? Well, I think *they* all missed out, because *you're* very charming and sympathetic. And kind, too. I'm glad as hell you asked me to have dinner with you."

"Thank you. Now, finish for me what it is you wanted to say. I think it will be good for you, eh?"

"I'm not even sure I know what I was trying to say. It's just that ever since she died, I've been having this feeling, off and on, that I'm invisible."

"Invisible? You mean that no one sees you?"

"Sort of. I know it's ridiculous, but I think I was always waiting for her to tell me her side of the story. My mother was someone I knew for thirty-four years, Lucienne. And never, not once, did she ever explain a single thing she did."

"And you needed this explanation?" Lucienne was puzzled.

"I thought I did."

"But, Joanna, why does this make you invisible?"

"God! I sound like a mental case. I think," she said carefully, "it's because it was Lily who defined me, who decided one day who it was I should be. And I accepted it without question. But maybe I'm just something Lily made up, another version of her."

"Is that what you are?" Lucienne asked. "I think not," she went on. "I think you are who you have made yourself to be. But perhaps your mama she didn't say it was good;

she didn't say it makes her happy. And if she is the one who decides for you, then she should be the one also to say it is a good decision. Yes?''

"You mean approval? She should've given her approval?"

"Yes."

"God!" Jo said. "Maybe that's it. I'm going to have to think about that."

"It shouldn't matter to you what anyone says, Joanna. Only what *you* say."

"You're right. You're absolutely right. Thank you."

"For what?" Lucienne wanted to know.

Jo gave her a smile. "For letting me talk about it."

"Ah, well," Lucienne said with a sly smile. "Perhaps I will make you listen sometime to things I would wish to say."

"Fine. Happy to."

"*Alors, ça suffit.* Now we have coffee, eh?"

12

AFTER LUNCH LUCIENNE WENT BACK TO HER COMPARTMENT
to pack, promising to meet Jo later in the bar car. Jo, having
eaten both her own and Lucienne's dessert and feeling glut-
ted, watched Lucienne, who'd eaten almost nothing, go off.
The woman gave no external sign whatever that she was feeling less than perfectly well. While admiring Lucienne's style,
Jo was bothered by her refusal to seek medical help for a
very serious ailment. Her old friend Sally had had endometriosis and she, too, had encountered a doctor whose first
and only suggestion was that Sally have a hysterectomy. But
Sally had kept looking until she'd found a doctor who didn't
believe that the solution to every problem with the female
reproductive system was simply to remove the offending organs. This doctor put Sally on a course of uninterrupted oral
contraceptive pills for close to a year. The purpose of the
pill-taking was to inhibit ovulation, which would kill off the
endometrial tissue implants and relieve the pain. It worked.
Granted, Sally didn't have a period during that time, but she
said with a laugh it was no great loss, and since she very
much hoped to have a child someday soon—if she could just
find a suitable father—it had been a most reasonable and
humane treatment. "Course, he says it could start all over

again any time," Sally had said. "But it's almost three years and so far so good."

Jo's thinking was interrupted by the arrival of Gian Paolo for his photo session. She took his picture alone as well as with Giuseppe and several of the other waiters, promised prints for each of them, then left for the bar car. Maybe she'd phone Sally from Venice to get the name of the pills she'd taken. If she had the generic name, maybe Lucienne's doctor could obtain them for her. It had worked for Sally. Maybe it would work for Lucienne. The pain, Sally had told her, was unimaginable, agonizing. Jo couldn't bear the idea of anyone's suffering that way, especially after having seen her mother, near the end, bite right through her lower lip to keep from screaming.

The car was deserted, except for Anne, who was sitting alone smoking a cigarette. Jo went along to say hello.

"Do sit with me," Anne said. "Jimmy's having a lie-down. And I'm behaving like a delinquent, sneaking a cigarette. He loathes it when I smoke, so I encourage him to have regular naps." She laughed, then said, "I saw your friend pass through just a moment or two ago."

"She's going to pack."

"Oh, I see. Would you care for something to drink?"

Luke had come hurrying over and stood at attention, hoping to be of service.

"I'd love some coffee," Jo told him.

"You take more pictures?"

"Probably."

He shook his head like a grandfather pandering to the whims of a small child as he went to the bar to fetch her coffee.

"He's so cute," Jo said.

Anne took a long, obviously satisfying draw on her cigarette. "He has the face of a naughty choirboy. I recall finding the Italian men most attractive years ago. But back then I found most men attractive. It used to make Jimmy dreadfully apprehensive when I admired another man. He took it as a minor personal threat. He has, I'm happy to say, long since grown past that. But every now and then I suspect his overt fondness for good-looking women is his own little effort at retaliation. Men are so easily undermined, don't you find?''

"I guess they are," Jo agreed, watching and listening closely. Without her husband, Anne seemed quite different, more forceful but no less pleasant. It was as if being on her own, however temporarily, allowed her to be entirely herself without the need either to accede to her husband's wishes or to make any of the daily compromises—in behavior, in attitude, in opinion—that were an ongoing part of any marriage.

Jo knew she behaved differently in the company of other women than she did with men. Look at the things she'd said and done with Henry and Tyler! Granted, she'd been more herself with Henry, but that had been because Tyler seemed to have performance expectations. Nothing explicit, just hints. And, too, regardless of his claims of dislike for the theater and its practitioners, he was one of them. Even he admitted his entire life had been geared toward performance.

"Would you allow me to show you something?" Anne asked, reaching for her handbag.

"Sure I would." Jo finished removing the camera and lenses from the Lowe-pro, slipped the bag under the table, then waited, curious about what Anne wanted to show her. It turned out to be a photograph.

Anne removed it with care from a large well-worn but still handsome Cartier wallet. She held the photograph for a moment, looking first at it and then at Jo before passing it across the table.

Jo accepted it but didn't look at once. She was trying to read the expression on Anne's face, but couldn't. All she knew was that being shown this picture was highly significant. And when at last she did, she knew at once why. With an interior shiver of alarm and suspicion she had to study the shot for some time before she was convinced she wasn't looking at a snapshot of herself.

"Quite something, isn't it?" Anne said softly. "I've had the same reaction since first seeing you on board the ferry."

"Who is it?" Jo asked, pushing aside her things to make room for the coffee Luke set down in front of her.

"That was Lucia." She took another look before returning the photograph with the same exaggerated care to her wallet. "My daughter. She died two and a half years ago. She was thirty-two." She saw that her cigarette had burned itself out in the ashtray, and lit another.

"What happened?" Jo asked in hushed tones, wondering what it was about this train that inspired such intimate conversations. It had something to do with the isolation, and with the compression of time.

"Drug overdose," Anne said flatly. "She finally succeeded in doing what she'd spent more than half her life attempting to do: She found a way to escape reality altogether."

"My God! I'm so sorry. It must've been an awful shock, seeing me on the boat."

"Actually," Anne smiled, "it was rather wonderful, like seeing Lucia as Jimmy and I had always hoped one day we would. You have a remarkable resemblance to her. She was taller, and frightfully thin. But all in all, it's quite uncanny."

"Do you have other children?" Jo asked, sensing the woman's need to talk.

"Two sons, one in Singapore, the other in Vancouver. Lucia was the youngest. It simply shattered Jimmy. He was devoted to her. I'm afraid I wasn't ever quite so blind to her considerable problems, which were apparent to me from the time she was six or seven. It's impossible, of course, to say why, or what specifically her anger stemmed from. It has been suggested that the difficulty of her birth and temporary oxygen deprivation might have had something to do with her behavior. It's academic now. But by the time she was twelve, I knew we were in for a most difficult time with her." Suddenly apprehensive, she said, "You don't mind my telling you this? I do hope it's not an imposition."

"No, not at all. I'd really like to hear about it."

Again, Anne smiled. "I knew you'd have a sympathetic

nature. And I was made certain of it last evening when you accepted that lovely, lonely woman's invitation to her table.''

"Why would that make me sympathetic?" Jo asked, mulling over Anne's perception of Lucienne as lonely. Were other people aware of nuances she failed to see? The last thing she'd have thought of Lucienne was that she was lonely. "It might just make me someone who's overly curious, or unable to turn down invitations."

"Oh, I think quite a number of people would have found some pretext for refusing. In my experience, the majority of women are thoroughly intimidated by the good intentions of those we view as more attractive than ourselves. I've always thought truly beautiful women had to be the loneliest people on earth. And as for you," she smiled, "you may very well be overly curious, or unable to turn down invitations, but I sincerely doubt that's the case. I've been watching you," she admitted, "and it's been most interesting to see how people are drawn to you. That may have something to do with *their* curiosity. And mine," she added. "There's something quite seductive about a single woman—at least in this environment—constantly making notes and taking photographs. There is always the possibility you might actually be making notes about the very people who are watching you."

Jo gave a little laugh. "I swear it's this train. I can't think of another place where we'd all be spending so much time checking each other out. Or getting to know people in quite the same way." She paused, looking at Anne's hands, which were long and very well cared for, the hands of a much younger woman, markless and manicured and adorned only with a wide wedding band and an eternity ring of quite large round-cut diamonds. "I'd like to hear some more about your daughter, if you feel like talking about her."

Anne gazed at her for a moment before speaking. "I think," she said, "among the parents of those with children who abuse substances of one sort or another, ours is a fairly commonplace tale."

"I don't know much about it."

"Oh, the details differ, naturally. But the basic outlines

are alarmingly similar. In Lucia's case, when she was old enough to articulate her grievances, she informed us that our lifestyle, our manners and values and pastimes, were all worthy only of her contempt. She had no idea what she'd have preferred as an alternative; she simply knew we were decadent establishment fools with tedious friends, outdated values, and primitive notions of sexuality.'' She shook her head. ''The irony of that last bit of scathing invective wasn't lost on Jimmy or me, but we weren't about to reveal to her the intimate pieces of our history together in order to alter her opinion of us. Especially since everyone was so against our marriage in the first place.

''You see, when we met, Jimmy was married to someone else. Miserably unhappy, but determined to make a go of it. He's an honorable man, and when he gives his word, he's committed. He'd been married for six years, and what he wanted more than anything else just then—I'll tell you in a moment of his previous disappointment—was children. Bertie used all sorts of tactics to avoid the issue, and him. At that point, he was twenty-eight. I was eighteen. And positively wild.'' Again she smiled, and raised her eyes to Jo's. ''By the standards of the time, I was quite simply ungovernable. My parents were at their wits' end, and threatening to send me off to a cousin with a ranch in Australia. By today's standards, I was most innocent. But fifty years ago, my dear, I was considered a devil.'' She laughed, as if pleased by her rowdy past. And Jo smiled encouragingly. ''In any event, there I was in London, casting about for ways to escape the family yoke, counting down the days before I'd be shipped off to the outback. My parents insisted I accompany them to what I knew was going to be a tediously dull dinner, but I couldn't find any way to avoid it, so I went. And there was Jimmy. What a glorious man he was then! I fell in love with him instantly, on sight. I knew he was married—Bertie was right there, after all—but I simply did not care. It was, I might add, entirely mutual. We looked at one another across the room before dinner and there was an extraordinary recognition. Is this all terribly boring?'' she asked suddenly.

"God, no!" Jo said quickly. "Not at all."

Anne's eyes stayed on Jo while she tried to think what had prompted her to tell all this. She hadn't ever, with so little compunction, revealed quite so much to a comparative stranger. But the resemblance to Lucia was an inducement she could never have anticipated. And this young woman paid such close attention, seemed so eager to hear whatever Anne might choose to say. She'd never had an opportunity quite like this not only to express herself but to have so willing an audience who might have been Lucia herself.

Jo felt the woman's hestiation and said, "Go on, please."

"Yes. Well, as fate would have it, Bertie left early that evening with one of her famous headaches—Jimmy later told me she developed either headaches or food allergies in order to avoid people or menus she didn't care for—and the upshot of the evening was our creeping away together. I left first and waited at a designated corner, then he came along fifteen or twenty minutes later." She smiled, caught up again in the vivid details of that night. "We walked, talking, for hours. Then we ducked into dark corners, doorways, alleys, to touch one another, to kiss. We made arrangements to meet again, and he went home to Bertie, and I to Cadogan Square. It was all terribly intense, and we weren't as discreet as we could have been. Although, looking back, I can't see where discretion might have entered into it. It wasn't something I, at eighteen, had any interest in or knowledge of.

"It's odd, you know, but I couldn't possibly have put into words what it was I was after all those years ago. I didn't know until I first saw Jimmy, until we touched one another. And then I knew without question what I'd always wanted, and nothing could have prevented me having it. In a very real sense, we invented each other. He'd been married for six years, as I've said, but he knew nothing, *nothing*. Which could only be a comment on the lamentable terms of that marriage. And I'd certainly never been married, and had almost no experience whatever. But together we discovered ourselves, and nothing and no one else mattered. Reckless." She shook her head over the antics of the girl she'd been. "I found I was pregnant. Jimmy was ecstatic and at once started divorce proceedings. What a scandal, my dear! We were only slightly less of an outrage than Edward and Wallis. We were utterly determined, however, and succeeded in overcoming the many obstacles just six weeks before Terence was born. Our 'honeymoon' on the Orient-Express actually took place three months after Terry's birth.

"So," she sighed, "you can see that I wasn't without sympathy for Lucia. After all, I'd played actively at rebellion once upon a time myself and it cost the families involved very dearly. But no matter how hard I tried, I simply could not communicate with her."

"It must have been awful," Jo commiserated.

"It was about to become a great deal worse. She asked to go to boarding school, and we agreed. It was a dreadful mistake, dreadful! Somehow, it was at that school where she first began taking drugs. And once she'd started, we went with her down a long, terrifying road of threats and reprisals and pleas and promises. On and on.

"The problem, you see, was Lucia had her own money, inherited when she was eighteen. We couldn't control her assets, therefore we couldn't control her addiction or her access to drugs. It destroyed Jimmy. He gave up his career—something he hadn't wanted in the first place, but which he'd grown to tolerate—and spent most of his time trying to find someone who'd help Lucia; some program, some doctor, someone with knowledge and experience who would tell us how to proceed.

"And then she died. They found her in a London hotel room with the needle still in her arm. She'd been dead for more than thirty hours when they found her. And when they rang to tell us, it came as no surprise. We'd been expecting that telephone call for a very long time. We claimed Lucia's poor ruined body, and once the inquiry and the funeral were over, we were able to begin living our lives again. Tragic, but that's what it had come to. Jimmy returned to his interest in painting. He'd always wanted to be an artist, you see, but his parents had refused to allow him to study. He did architecture instead, and spent his professional life designing blocks of flats, offices, buildings about which he cared very little. The only design he's ever pointed to with pride is our home. All the others could've been destroyed at any time and he wouldn't have cared.

"He's quite happy now. At seventy-nine he's finally free to do what he wanted all along: to immerse himself in the works of other artists, and try his hand at his own."

"And what about you?" Jo asked.

"Me?" Anne took a moment to think about that. "I am free, I suppose, to . . ." For a few seconds she looked positively stricken, her eyes round as she surveyed the landscape for possibilities.

"To do anything you want," Jo offered, anxious to rescue her. "Absolutely anything."

With visible gratitude, Anne latched on to this. "Yes," she agreed. "Anything." For a second time, she extinguished a burnt-out cigarette. Jo thought that if they hadn't been on the train she'd have put her arms around this woman. But if they hadn't been on the train, they'd never have met. So she did the next best thing. She reached across the table and took hold of Anne's hand, and kept on holding it as they searched each other's eyes.

"My mother died two years ago," Jo told her. "I was trying to tell Lucienne a bit about it last night, and she made some very sensible comments that I've been thinking about. While you and I have been talking, I couldn't help realizing how much I miss being Lily's daughter. I miss that feeling I always had when I was with her of being somebody's little girl, no matter how frustrating it was or how old I got to be. And I miss the part where it started turning around so that sometimes I played mother to my mother." The hand she held was dry and cool, the skin silken. It had the thinned-down flesh and prominent bones of someone whose youth was long since gone. It also had the ability to communicate, through its grasp, all the emotions that had remained unstated. Jo now held that hand against her cheek and closed her eyes at the influx of those emotions. As she had in the kitchen with Henry, she simply opened and allowed herself to receive everything, feeling it swell her veins, pumping along in crowded communion with her blood. She didn't stop to consider how her gesture might be received, or if anyone else might see. She was fully aware of the honor Anne had bestowed upon her in divulging so much of the family's history, and she wanted more than anything else to prove herself worthy of the woman's trust. For one of the very few times in her life, she surrendered to her instincts, and accepted into herself another mother's caring.

For Anne, it was an epiphany. On the occasion of her fiftieth anniversary, long past the time when she'd believed any such thing could be possible, she was allowed to know what it might have been like to have a loving daughter. Yes, her sons had been good, devoted boys, and most rewarding. But she'd gone on hoping for too many years that she and Lucia would somehow one day be close. It never came to pass, so Anne could never be certain that the memories of the small girl she'd held so precious were accurate and not colored by her own longings. Now this young woman who too strongly bore a likeness to Lucia had appeared in her life to offer the empathy and understanding and even the overt affection that Lucia had withheld for a lifetime. Anne simply couldn't take her eyes off Jo, and had no wish to break the intense communion. For however long it lasted, she wanted to cherish the opportunity to feel valuable and loved as a mother.

It was overwhelming, she thought, utterly overwhelming. She could feel Jo's breath on the back of her captive hand, could feel the young woman's pulse beating in syncopation with her own. She felt as if she'd been drowning, but at the crucial moment had been towed to shore. And not only had she been saved, she was being transfused with some substance almost as vital as blood. If she never again saw this young woman, she'd remember her always because of these minutes when Jo held her hand pressed to her smooth, firm cheek.

At last Jo opened her eyes to look at her companion, their

hands still joined. She took a somewhat ragged breath, unsure of her ability to speak over the top of the clot of emotion in her throat, and said, "It wasn't your fault. I hope you know that. Nothing you ever did made things turn out the way they did."

Did things like this actually happen? Anne wondered, gauging the depths of Jo's eyes. Or was she a foolish and gullible old woman asking for and receiving something purely synthetic? But no. Those eyes couldn't lie. They were the eyes of a believer, of a seeker—like herself—of kindred warmth, of truth, of acceptance. Everyone paid in some way or another for their snippets of truth, their nuggets of unblemished affection. She had paid, and so had this dear young woman.

"One tells oneself that," Anne said. "But between the telling and the belief is a gap of unthinkable proportions. Thank you for the absolution. It isn't something one is able to give oneself with any real degree of success."

"I owe it," Jo tried to explain, the hand secure within hers growing warmer. "There are all kinds of debts. My mother wanted a conversation, but the timing was wrong. I was completely wrapped up in my work, too busy; and it wasn't until it was too late that I saw I'd never given her a chance to say what she'd wanted. The thing is, I asked her for an explanation of her life when I was six years old. I think she wanted to give me that explanation twenty-eight years later, but I was too preoccupied to recognize what she was offering. I thought there'd be more time, later on. But there was no later on. She died and took all the answers with her." The face opposite had grown very familiar and inestimably dear to her, and she wanted to tell this woman that she loved her, but couldn't think of any way to utter the words without sounding insincere. How did you tell someone you'd only known for a matter of hours that she'd become very important to you? She could feel it all right, but she couldn't say the words. So she closed her hand more firmly around Anne's and told her through the connection.

"I thought I'd show you the photograph. I didn't intend . . ."

"I know," Jo cut in. "It would sound crazy if either one of us tried to explain this to anyone else. But that doesn't matter. I'm *glad* you told me. I want you to know that. It means a great deal to me." She allowed her fingers to open, and the hand slowly slid away.

"I'd best go look in on Jimmy," Anne said. "And you will be with us this evening for dinner, won't you?"

"Nothing could keep me away."

Anne got up and stood with her hand on the back of the seat as she looked one long last time at Jo. "I am glad, too," she said softly, then moved off.

A few minutes later, Luke came to offer Jo fresh coffee. Distractedly, she thanked him and, sipping at the hot drink, turned to stare unseeing out the window. All of a sudden, she wanted badly to talk to Henry.

Jimmy was sleeping soundly. Anne withdrew, closing the door quietly, then stood outside in the corridor, trying to think where to go. Straightening her shoulders, she turned and walked back along the corridor to the lavatory. Once inside, with the door locked, she wrapped her arms around herself, sagged against the wall, and allowed herself to go to pieces.

Lucienne took three aspirin, then sat with her arms holding her knees tight to her chest, head bent, willing the pain away. It refused to go. Her body, like a cage of bone, contained the snarling, raging savage. Inside, behind the trap of her pelvic structure, it dug its long talons into the defenseless tissues of her deteriorating organs, into the helpless purse of her womanhood. Its fury was vicious and unrelenting. Sweat streamed down her sides, between her breasts, behind her ears. Her eyes screwed shut, her hands laced together, she pulled her knees closer, harder against her body and prayed for the blood to move, to flow, to carry away with it some portion of the pain. She could smell herself, the stink of perfume and sweat and deodorant, and was filled with disgust for her weakness. Come! she insisted. Move!

There was a tentative, reluctant, easing inside. Feeling it, she allowed her grip on her knees to ease fractionally, paying extreme attention. An interior expanding, as if the savage was growing wearied of the battle. More, then more. She allowed her arms to fall to her sides, her legs to extend themselves. A sudden cramping, then release. She opened her eyes, her head falling back against the seat; her limbs throbbed from the loss of tension. Wetting her lips, her hands twitching at her sides, she tracked the passage of the relief-giving blood, almost able to visualize its route through her system. She would have four or five days of freedom before the savage collected its strength and began again its assault on her body.

After a time, wearied, her hand rose to unfasten the shirt buttons, then the trousers. She felt bruised, fragile as she stood to remove the damp clothes, then bathed herself at the basin, stopping for a moment to study the blood-stained washcloth. Her blood, proof of her identity as a woman, evidence of a body still intact.

Jo returned to her compartment. Mark asked if she cared to have afternoon tea. She declined politely, then looked at the scenery, which had changed as the train moved now through Italy: terraced farms reaching upward along steep hillsides; fields of grapevines; pink stuccoed houses with terra-cotta-tiled roofs; stately rows of streets; once grand, now crumbling houses with green-painted shutters hanging askew; bits of rubble on the sides of the track.

And then the train very slowly came to a halt. Silence. The air conditioning went off. People came out into the corridors to stand by the open windows, talking quietly.

Lethargically, feeling grubby, Jo went to the door to look out. She was in time to see Mark pleading with the small Japanese woman and her round little boy, who was trying to climb up the wall, one hand fastened to the lowered window.

"Please, Madame," he was begging. "It's very dangerous. You must not allow him to do that."

"He wants picture," the mother explained, smiling precisely the way her son did, so that her eyes all but disappeared into the surrounding flesh. "You go, you take?" She pointed, indicating she wanted the steward to go outside the train to take a picture of herself and her son at the window.

He muttered under his breath, looked up and down the corridor as if for help, then said, "All right. But he must not climb up. You lift him." He mimed, and she nodded her comprehension. Then he raced to the end of the carriage with the boy's camera in his hand, opened the door, jumped to the trackbed, ran along to beneath the window, aimed the camera, took the picture, then tore back to climb inside.

"We thank, we thank," the woman said several times.

"You're welcome," he told her, and again mimed, this time to make sure she understood to keep the boy away from the open window.

"Bloody hell!" he said under his breath as he breezed past Jo.

"You should be getting danger pay," she whispered.

He laughed. "Too bloody true!"

The train continued to sit on the track. Jo moved to the window in the corridor. The sun cast a glaze over everything. There seemed to be no breeze at all.

Returning a few minutes later, Mark stopped to say, "There's some sort of electrical problem ahead. I'm afraid we'll be a while."

"Oh!" she said. "Thank you."

She decided she'd go visit with Lucienne, and made her way along the now-congested corridors.

Lucienne had changed clothes, and was sitting writing a letter. Upon seeing Jo, she broke into a welcoming smile and said, "Ah, good. I am very bored. Come sit! You are so good to visit. Hot, eh?"

"I don't mind. It's kind of a relief after the air conditioning."

"Soon you will mind. If we sit for long, it will get very hot."

"Has this happened before when you've been on the train?"

"One time." She gave one of her shrugs. "It makes no difference to me. I don't see Paolo for three days. He is away to Florence for business with the family money. And since we are to dine with your royal family and they are here also waiting, there is no reason to be bothered." She folded the letter, or whatever it was she'd been writing, and tucked it into her purse. "So! What have you done this afternoon? You have five hundred more photographs?"

"Maybe only a hundred."

"Wait until you see Venice! You won't have enough film, Mignon. Sometimes I think when I am old I will come to live in Venice."

"But I thought you were coming to live here now."

"Oh, no!" Lucienne said sharply. "Only to be married. We go back to Paris to live. This is the agreement. I have not consented to give up Chez Lucienne. I am not ready to do such a thing."

"I see." Jo thought this marriage seemed to have a lot of strikes against it before it had even begun.

"Did you notice?" Lucienne asked. "In all other countries, we go fast. Comes the officials, the engineer, the train goes fast-fast-fast. We come to Italy, everything is slow, slow. The officials, the engineers, they come with families, with pizza; they make a picnic." She laughed. "*Bienvenu à l'Italie*, Mignon."

13

SHE STAYED CHATTING WITH LUCIENNE FOR HALF AN HOUR. Then, all at once, she knew if she didn't get up and leave she was going to start to cry. She was suddenly overcome by emotion and fatigue, and needed some time alone.

"I think I'll head back to my compartment," she told Lucienne.

"You are all right, Mignon?" Lucienne asked, her brows drawing inward.

"Oh, sure. I'm just tired. I didn't get much sleep last night."

"Wait for me when we have arrived. We will travel together to the hotel, eh?"

"That'll be great."

Back in her compartment, she sat and fanned herself with the cabin-service menu. The heat was growing intense. She sat, fanning the air, and worked to bring her emotions into check as she watched the steady stream of people passing her open door: the three entertaining American women; the French family, the parents arguing in quiet but bitterly fierce tones, with the son trailing after looking disenchanted; the round little Japanese boy streaking past with amazing speed and followed, moments later, by his harried mother; the two

171

American men who'd spent most of the trip with their heads bent over their portable backgammon set; the handsome young British honeymooners.

Then, slowly, the train began to move. Relieved, Jo got up and went again into the corridor to stand by the open window, glad of the breeze.

Mark came by to return her passport. She tucked it into her pocket, her spirits steadily climbing as the track approached an open expanse of water. Buildings backed right up to it; a variety of boats were tethered at the shoreline. The sky was pale at the horizon and filled directly above with striated clouds.

In the remaining half-hour before the end of the line, she hurried to give tips to Giuseppe and to the waiters, to Luke in the bar, and, finally, as she was queueing up to leave the train, to Mark, the cabin steward.

She had no idea where the baggage claim area was or what the protocol might be, and followed along after the other passengers, arriving at the head of the platform to see the chef, Giuseppe, and two of the chief stewards standing in a row to say goodbye. She took a couple of quick shots of them and of curious onlookers who were there to see the train and its occupants.

A roped-off area to the left, outside the VS-O-E office, was filled with luggage, the bulk of which consisted of identical pieces of Louis Vuitton. Inside this area, several uniformed female VS-O-E employees were frowning as they attempted to match passengers to their luggage.

Lucienne appeared at Jo's side, saying, "I have arranged our transportation."

"Oh, that's good. I was beginning to wonder what I'd do if I didn't find you."

"You shouldn't worry," Lucienne said, and then laughed. "This is very amusing, eh? So many people all with the same baggage; they will break into fighting maybe."

Inside the roped-off area, the women were struggling with heavy bags, hefting them over to anxiously waiting passengers.

"I would've thought they'd have men to do this," Jo said, "the way they did in London."

"You would think," Lucienne agreed. "Me, I wait. At the end, it is not so difficult to find the luggage."

She was right. Ten minutes, and they had their bags and were turning them over to a porter Lucienne had summoned.

"Oh, brother!" Jo exclaimed. "Can you wait just a minute? I'm supposed to confirm with somebody here about going to the depot tomorrow to see the train being serviced."

"Go," Lucienne told her. "We wait."

Luckily, Antoine, the train manager, was in the area trying to sort out a mix-up in the bags. He heard her out, then said, "I knew of this. Please, I will have someone telephone to you at the Cipriani." Apologetically, he added, "You can see it is most difficult now. But the arrangements are in order. If there is any problem, here is my card. You can telephone to me."

She thanked him and rushed off in the direction Lucienne had gone, emerging from the station to find all kinds of boats traveling past the foot of the steps. Transported, she hurried down to the launch where Lucienne was waiting, climbed aboard, and at once the boat veered away from the station and into the center of the canal.

Jo sat with Lucienne inside the enclosed area for a minute or two, turning this way and that in an effort to see as much as possible. Finally, she said, "I just have to have a better view," and went to the rear to stand in the open air, awestruck. The evening light gave the buildings a peachy hue: domes and spires, arches and porticoes; mosaics and statuary. It was like moving at high speed past a series of paintings.

She kept turning, so immediately and totally taken by the city that she regretted her prior commitment to go to the depot in the morning. She'd have to spend several hours making notes, taking photographs, learning all there was to know about the train, instead of being free to wander through the streets with her camera.

From inside the boat, Lucienne was smiling at her. "You like it, eh?"

"God! It's fabulous!" Jo ducked down, shouting over the engine's roar. "No wonder you like to come here all the time. I have a hunch after this trip I'm going to spend the rest of my life figuring out ways to get back here."

"You are like a child," Lucienne said fondly.

How, Jo wondered, was she ever going to be able to identify all these buildings? She'd have to buy every guidebook going and make note of the places she photographed. With the air whipping her hair around, and spray coating her skin, she was made dizzy by the spectacle. Facing forward, she saw they were cutting across the canal to Giudecca, nearing the hotel. She ducked back inside and dropped down on the bench beside Lucienne. "I love it," she said breathlessly. "I just flat out love it!"

There was a hotel employee waiting on the small dock to assist the women from the motor launch. Jo reached for her purse, but Lucienne insisted on paying the fare. And then they walked along the winding front path toward the hotel entrance. Trees, beds of flowers, grassy areas; the pink-painted facade of the hotel with balconies running the length of the top floor; a terrace over there facing the open water.

Inside the foyer a crowd was waiting to check in. Jimmy and Anne were at the desk signing the register. A pair of porters then led them off. The line moved forward. More recent arrivals tried to work around the perimeter of the crowd but were efficiently ignored by the preoccupied staff. In the office behind the check-in desk, a number of people moved quickly, pulling reservations, reviewing telexes, making telephone calls.

"Very busy," Lucienne observed. "But it will not take long. Many people from the train."

"Quite a few," Jo agreed, recognizing the still-embattled French family, as well as the Texas quartet. The frowzy daughter was chattering away nonstop in her high, penetrating voice. Her parents and husband appeared to take no notice of her, as if they'd long since grown acclimated to her ceaseless monologue.

Lucienne was recognized by the staff, warmly greeted and in a matter of minutes had registered and was on her way to her room. "One-three-zero," she called to Jo. "I will meet with you before dinner."

Then it was Jo's turn. As she was about to identify herself, an angry middle-aged man smacked his hand on the countertop demanding attention.

"Pardon," the assistant manager said to Jo, and turned to the man who wanted currency changed.

"I am sorry," the assistant said, "but we are not able to do this now." With extended hands, he indicated the people waiting to check in. "In one hour, sir, please." He turned back to Jo, saying again, "I am sorry," took her name, and stepped back into the office area. A moment or two, and then he returned. "Signorina James, we are expecting you. Everything is arranged. You will be going to Scomenzera in the morning. A launch will come at ten to take you. Also our public relations director will meet with you for lunch, when you return." He asked her to register, then summoned a porter to show her to her room.

The first thing she saw upon entering were the flowers, two arrangements. One was from the hotel manager, Dr. Rusconi, "with best compliments," the other was from Henry. The card read, "Hotel Hart is exceedingly vacant. We eagerly await your return. Your hotelier in good faith, Henry." His card in hand, she looked around: twin beds side by side on a carpeted platform, with what looked like space command modules on either side; ranks of buttons, telephones, lights. In the center of the huge room was a console concealing a television set, on its top a ceramic ashtray. On the wall facing the bed, a refrigerator-bar, a desk, a settee and coffee table, a pair of armchairs, a side table, two standing lamps. Facing the door, floor-to-ceiling windows with sliding doors opening on to a terrace only a matter of feet from the pool. In an alcove to the left of the bed, an antique writing desk with folders of stationery, a room-service menu, a box of wrapped candies, chocolate, a ceramic penholder and pen, several brochures. Shades of cocoa and beige decor, thick carpet. To the right as one entered was a door that opened to reveal the toilet and bidet, an oval mirror on the wall with a marble shelf beneath. And to the left, the bathroom.

It was Wonderland, Jo decided, stepping into the marble bathroom to see the round sunken tub behind which was a window covered by a shade that could be opened should you wish the occupants of the bed-sitting room to witness your frolicking in the tub. Thick white towels on a heated rack, a separate shower enclosure, double sinks set in a marble countertop, built-in ultramodern hair dryer, a basket containing Emilio Pucci hand soaps, bath soap, shampoo. The bathroom wall also had a rank of buttons, with line drawings on each to signify the valet, the maid, the light for the shower stall.

On either side of the door to the bathroom were built-in closets, and in the main room, another closet, with a drawer unit that locked. She promptly placed her valuables and passport in the top drawer, locked it, and dropped the key into her purse. A few minutes, and her clothes were hung away, her suitcase stowed. Then the telephone rang.

It was Anne, to say, "Since we've arrived so late, we've put dinner back an hour to give everyone time to refresh themselves. I hope this won't affect your joining us."

"Oh, no," Jo assured her. "That's just fine."

"Good. I've told your friend as well. So we'll meet with you in the dining room at nine."

With an extra hour free, Jo got the hotel operator, gave her Henry's number, and sat on the side of the bed to wait for the call to go through.

When the phone rang, she jumped and snatched up the receiver.

"We are ready with your call," the operator said. "Please go ahead."

"Henry?" Jo spoke over the crackling line.

"Jo," he laughed. "I take it you've arrived safely."

"Henry, I love the flowers. Thank you."

"Think nothing of it. Just a token of my affection."

"Henry, there's something I want to ask you. Do you know Stanleigh Dunn?"

"Do I know her? Of course I do," he answered, sounding bemused. "You know we have an agency contract with Miles Dearborn. Why?"

"Did you know they live together?"

"Yes, I know that. Why . . . ? Oh!" There was a pause, then he said, "Are you suggesting the establishment of a trend, Jo?"

"I don't know if I'm suggesting anything, Henry. All I know is that I've thought about you a lot during the last thirty-odd hours. And I wanted to call you now, because I'm going to be up to my ears for the rest of the time I'm here. I—uh—God, Henry! Say something important!"

"What am I supposed to say?" he wanted to know, sounding suddenly distraught, even angry. "What about Tyler Emmons?"

"God! I don't know, Henry. What *about* him?"

"This isn't possible over the telephone," he protested. "I'm not sure what it is you want me to say, what you want to hear."

He was right. It was impossible. "Never mind," she said. "I just wanted to thank you for the flowers."

"How was your trip?" he asked.

"Wonderful," she said without inflection. "I met a lot of really terrific people. In fact, I'm about to go have dinner with some of them. Thanks again for the flowers, Henry. I'll see you in a week." She said goodbye, and hung up to find her hands were shaking. "Shit!" She threw off her clothes and went to take a shower.

Angry, she scrubbed her body, reapplied her makeup, pulled on a white linen pantsuit with a white cotton shirt, picked up her bag and key, and went in search of Lucienne's room. It turned out to be on the floor above and was starkly modern, with skylights at each end, and desk and storage units tucked under the eaves.

"Not too much time, eh?" Lucienne said, stepping into her shoes.

"How do you *do* that?" Jo was once again amazed at the transformation the woman had managed to achieve in about half an hour. She was dressed now in a perfectly tailored pale pink suit with hand-stitching around the notched collar, and white patent high heels.

"I am used to having very little time," she said nonchalantly.

"You look wonderful."

"You also look very fine. Come."

As they descended the stairs, Lucienne said, "You are sad again, as before, eh?"

"Pardon?"

"When the train is stopped and we sit together, I think you are sad then. Now, you are sad again."

"You don't miss much, do you?" Jo said as they went along the marble hallway toward the dining room.

"Not so very much. I think you listen to everyone, but you don't say so very much about yourself. I am here to listen if you have a wish to talk."

"Oh, it's nothing in particular. Back on the train, I got a little weepy. You know how that is. And I guess I was just feeling it again. It's lack of sleep."

"If you say," Lucienne said skeptically, stopping her before the entrance. "But perhaps you will change your mind, and then we will talk."

"Thank you."

Jimmy and Anne greeted them with affection, as if they hadn't seen one another in a long time. Anne embraced Jo, and held her for a moment, saying, "This is very good of you."

Jo hugged her, whispering, "No, it isn't. I think it's sheer necessity."

Lucienne kissed Anne on both cheeks and then, to Jimmy's delight, greeted him in the same fashion.

"What could be more perfect," he exclaimed once they were all seated, "than the company of three beautiful women!'' He asked the headwaiter to recommend the wine, then sat back to look at each woman in turn. "Quite a place this, isn't it!'' he said expansively. "Fifty years ago we stayed at the Hotel des Bains on the Lido.''

"That's the hotel where *Death in Venice* was set,'' Jo said. "I'm not sure if it was in the movie, but if it was it looked fabulous.''

"It was lovely,'' Anne said. "I'm familiar with Mann's book, but I'm afraid I didn't see the film.''

"So boring,'' Lucienne put in. "Very beautiful, the images of Venice, but so tiresome to sit for hours watching an old man looking at a young man.''

"What a pity,'' Anne said. "I'm fond of Mann's work, and that is one of my favorites. Some books really cannot be made into films.''

"I thought it was a metaphor,'' Jo said. "I mean, it was celebrated as a gay movie, you know. But I didn't think it was. I thought it was an old man wooing the lost youth the young boy represented. Of course,'' she wound down, "I didn't read the book.''

The wine was poured, and Lucienne lifted her glass in a toast. "To new friends,'' she said, which got Jo choked up again. The first swallow of wine washed her throat clear, and she was able to smile at everyone while mentally berating herself for being a fool on the telephone with Henry. Why the hell had she called? And why had she said all that stupid stuff? God! The man sends her flowers and she begs him to say something of monumental importance to her over the telephone. *God!*

"You like carpaccio?'' Lucienne asked her.

"I've never had it.''

"You like smoked salmon?''

"Sure.''

"This is the same, only beef. Very good. You must try this.''

"If you're going to order it,'' Jo hit quickly on a compromise solution, "why don't I have a taste of yours?''

"But of course,'' Lucienne agreed.

There were so many selections, Jo was having trouble deciding. After going back and forth over the four pages of the menu, she settled on the Insalata Shirley—a salad described as mixed sharp and bitter baby lettuce, foie gras, and truffles—and grilled scampi.

After they'd given their choices to the waiter, Lucienne turned to Jo, saying, "Your salad, you know what this is? This is created by Shirley Sherwood, wife of the man who makes the train."

"Indeed!" Jimmy said. "I'll have to try that." He stopped the waiter to change his order, then said, "If the salad's half as good as the train, I'm in for a treat."

"Jimmy likes continuity," Anne explained. "If one thing ties to something else, he wants it to succeed. So, you see, if the salad's a great success, he'll believe forever that the two things—the train and the appetizer—are inextricably related."

"Makes me sound a bit of an idiot," he complained to his wife.

"You are a bit." She gave him a sweet smile. "It's why I've always adored you."

Lucienne lit a cigarette, then tasted the wine. "This is very good. I must remember to ask the sommelier for the name."

"I understand you have a restaurant in Paris," Jimmy said.

"Yes. I will give you my card. When you come to Paris, I will give you dinner Chez Lucienne."

"And you're getting married," Anne said. "Congratulations."

"I am, yes. In five days."

"Will you be living here in Venice?" Anne asked.

"Oh, no! We go back to Paris. I love very much Venice, but I love Paris more. It is my home almost twenty years."

"Lucienne's from Canada," Jo clarified, and was rewarded with a smile from Lucienne.

The other three began to talk of Canada, and Jo sipped her wine, telling herself to go slowly with it. It was heightening both her fatigue and her irritation with herself. Why, *why* had she called Henry? Well, she'd done it, so she was wasting her energy being mad at herself.

Setting down her glass, she looked at Anne, admiring her gray silk dress, the long rope of slightly pink pearls around her neck, the hair brushed softly around her face. She was still a beautiful woman. And Jimmy could well have been a Malaysian planter, in his cream-colored suit, fresh white shirt, and another Liberty cotton floral tie.

Everything about this couple was of the best quality, from their clothing to their impeccable manners. And all who came into contact with them seemed to sense they were in the presence of special people. It wasn't just that Jimmy was titled. It had to do, so far as Jo was able to see, with the bond of caring between them.

After fifty years together, and much pain, they'd grown so secure in their knowledge of each other, so comfortable with one another's quirks and habits, that they were free in ways most people seldom, if ever, were to be open to others. And those who came near served in some way to reflect to Jimmy and Anne externalized images of their better selves. Jo wanted very much to photograph them, to capture their pain and dignity, their exceptional bearing, their regard for one another. She wanted to show the experience etched into the fine lines on their faces; she wanted to capture the look of Anne's hands and the subtle softening in Jimmy's eyes whenever they fixed on his wife.

"Where have you gone, Mignon?" Lucienne was tapping a long, polished fingernail on the back of Jo's hand. "Are you dreaming? Are you in love, *chérie*?"

"I'm sorry," Jo apologized to the table. "I didn't sleep too well on the train. I'm afraid it's starting to catch up with me."

"Nor did I," Anne said. "Jimmy slept like a baby. I've been convinced for years he could sleep absolutely anywhere."

"Me, also, I sleep very well on the train. I like so much the music of the train in the night, the turning of the wheels on the tracks."

"As do I," Jimmy agreed wholeheartedly. "Nothing quite like it. Minute I board a train, I'm ready to sleep."

Jo thought about the work she'd have to do the next morning, and tried to estimate what time she'd have to get up to be ready for the boat at ten. At some point she was also going to have to go through the hotel and take pictures. She'd have given anything not to have placed that embarrassing telephone call. Imagine asking Henry if he knew one of his own authors!

"I believe," Lucienne said, again tapping Jo on the back of the hand, "Mignon must be in love. This is what I think. You are in love, eh?"

Jo's face went hot, and she smiled sheepishly. "I'm trying to keep track of everything I've got to do. And I shouldn't even be thinking of that now. I really am sorry."

"Ah, well," Anne said, "you *are* working, after all. We must try to remember that." Beneath the table she took hold of Jo's hand and gave it a squeeze. Jo held on. She'd have liked to throw her arms around Anne at that moment, because the covert gesture was confirmation of their ongoing closeness.

The appetizers came. Anne smiled encouragingly, and gave Jo's hand a final squeeze before releasing it.

"One would think," Jimmy said, gazing at his plate, "after all we've eaten on the train, it wouldn't be possible to eat a single bite more. But there you are! I'm famished, and this looks most promising."

The Insalata Shirley was an inspired combination of tastes; the foie gras, rich and savory, was balanced nicely by the crisp, slightly bitter, subtly dressed lettuce. And the scampi, when they came, were large and succulently sweet, liberally basted with butter. Jimmy ordered more wine; everyone commented happily on the food. The headwaiter deferentially asked if he might suggest the dessert, and then served up a chocolate soufflé with bitter chocolate ice cream that had them all but moaning with pleasure. Espressos for Lucienne and Jimmy; Jo and Anne had cappuccinos. Then, with a meaningful look at her husband, Anne opened her bag for a cigarette. He rolled his eyes as if to say, See what I have to put up with! but gallantly struck a match and lit her cigarette.

Then the dinner was over and the four walked from the dining room together. Lucienne and Jo thanked the older couple for their hospitality. They all promised to meet, perhaps for drinks, the next evening.

Lucienne said, "I know you must work in the morning. But perhaps in the afternoon you will come with me to help buy shoes."

"Sure. I don't think I'll be back any later than one. I've got a lunch meeting with the hotel's PR director, and I should be free by two-thirty."

"Good." Lucienne hesitated, then said, "Mignon, I think perhaps I make you upset with my small joke of being in love."

"Oh, no," Jo quickly assured her.

"You are certain?"

"Honest to God!"

"*Bon*! I would not like to make you hurt with me." She gave Jo kisses on each cheek. "We are friends, eh?"

"Yes, we are."

"Good," Lucienne said, then went off up the stairs to her room.

Jo was too worn out to do more then get her clothes off and set her traveling clock before crawling into bed and plunging at once into a deep and dreamless sleep.

14

THE MORNING LIGHT WAS BRILLIANT, THE SKY CLOUDLESS as Jo stood looking out through the sliding doors at a gardener collecting leaves that had blown down in the night. No one else was around. It was one of those mornings when she'd awakened in much the same mood she'd had the night before. She was still bothered by having called Henry, and by an image she couldn't shake of someone with her face lying dead in a hotel room with a needle jammed into her vein. She didn't feel like working; she didn't even feel like moving. She had the arbitrary notion that if she just kept standing there, thinking hard, everything would suddenly make sense to her. Since her conversations on the train with Lucienne and Anne, she'd had the feeling that with a bit of time to concentrate, everything that had been bothering her for the past year or so would fall into a pattern she'd be able to interpret. But she simply wasn't free to take the time.

Hefting the Lowe-pro and her purse, she left the room and went along the empty hallway and through the gallery that faced onto the pool, stopping for a moment to admire the way the sun shone in on the enormous potted ficus trees placed at intervals the length of the area. The windows were a series of glassed archways with swagged draperies of rich brown. And on square columns between each arch sat terra cotta pots of healthy palms. The walls and ceilings were painted pale cocoa, with white trim.

To the right at the end of the gallery was a boutique, not yet open for the day, filled with VS-O-E gift items including packets of postcards—reproductions of six posters by Pierre Fix-Masseau in a bold Art Deco style with primary colors. Making a mental note to come back for the postcards, Jo proceeded to the terrace, where the maître d' greeted her by name and led her to a table overlooking the canal. It was sheltered by a white umbrella with brown trim, one of a number positioned to keep the sun from those tables out in the open.

She asked the waiter for coffee, then went to help herself from the buffet where croissants and brioches were being kept warm in an acrylic bin. A long table bore big round bowls of several kinds of dry cereal and fresh fruit. A cooler at the end of the table held yogurt and a large pitcher of cream. She took a croissant, a brioche, and an apple and returned to the table. While she waited for the coffee, she got out the Pentax and took half a dozen wide-angle shots of the area, noticing as she did that the needle on the built-in light meter wasn't holding steady. Odd, she thought, aiming at the sky to check the meter's reaction. Okay. But when she pointed down again, the needle didn't move. What the hell?! She gave the camera a shake, looked again, and the needle had dropped. Relieved, she put the KX aside.

As she ate, she spotted a number of people from the train, including the Texas foursome at a table to her right. The parents and husband of the frizzy-haired, overweight blonde were eating mechanically while she read aloud in a singsong voice from what was evidently a pop-psychology book. The mother looked up every so often to nod and smile, while the father and husband worked diligently at their food as if the grinding of their jaws might drown out the sound of her voice. The woman set the book face down and began to elaborate on one of the points she'd just read. "See," she said, "what y'all gotta get from this is a sense of how important it is for y'all to express what y'all *feel*. This here book's sayin' it's bad to *repress* your true feelin's, but it's good to speak out 'n' say what y'all're thinkin'. Get it?" The mother and father nodded obediently. The woman's husband looked at her, his mouth slightly open, as if on the verge of declaring his true feelings. Then, as if deciding that was a lousy idea, he blinked and went back to his food. His wife picked up the book and read on.

At a table to Jo's left a bearded, badly-dressed American of about thirty-five was talking loudly about the art in Venice and how disappointed he was after all the build-up. He had a flat New York accent and was talking at a couple who sat and stared at him as he ranted. "It's all dark and decadent!" he insisted, while the woman stared, her face revealing no reaction whatever, and the man with her gazed at the speaker with an expression of utter disbelief. He looked ready to leap to his feet and knock the younger man right out of his chair.

Meanwhile, an astonishing cross section of people made their way past the buffet. A second bearded man, this one with wild shoulder-length hair, was sitting alone across the way writing furiously in a notebook. Another writer? Jo wondered. Maybe, but definitely not a journalist.

A young English couple fed huge strawberries to their baby in a highchair, laughing softly as the child gobbled up the fruit. The French couple from the train were seated at the far end of the terrace, glaring at each other as they ate in silence. Their son looked back and forth at each of them, his expression both confused and resigned. Jo watched the boy with a sense of recognition, not of him but of what he was feeling. It brought back an evening—she couldn't have been more than eight or nine—when she'd sat with Beamer and her parents at the dining table listening to her parents' conversation but unable to follow it.

"You make pronouncements," her father had been saying. "You're like some kind of household oracle with your goddamned declarations, Lily. But in view of your critically limited exposure to the kind of reality the rest of us confront daily, I'd be fascinated to know just what it is you base this knowledge on.''

"You don't think my life is every bit as real as yours?" Lily had challenged him. "You don't think I know what the world's all about just because you commute into the city and I stay out here? Who ever told you that the inside of an *office* is reality? You live in your microcosm and I live in mine, but you'd like to believe that because your microcosm produces a regular check it's more valid than mine. Doesn't that strike you as just a little arrogant?''

"What's a microcosm?" Beamer had asked Jo in an undertone.

"I don't know. Something little, I think."

"What's a microcosm, Mom?" Beamer had asked loudly.

"What?" Her brow furrowed, Lily had directed her eyes to her son.

"Be quiet, Beam," Jo had whispered.

Looking now at his father, he'd asked, "Dad?"

"This is an adult conversation, Beamer," his father had said.

"Then why're you having it when we're here?" Beamer had displayed his ever-present logic.

"Ask your mother!"

"Oh, that's brilliant!" Lily had snapped. "Dump it all in *my* lap!"

"You're the one who had to bring it up now, so you answer the boy."

Jo had followed this, her head turning back and forth, feeling dizzy as she tried to comprehend what was being said. She couldn't. All she knew was that the two of them were mad at each other and if she and Beamer weren't careful they'd wind up being yelled at. It had happened a couple of times before, and she and Beam had been sent to bed way before bedtime. She didn't want to get sent to bed early tonight because she hadn't finished her school project, a topographical map she was making of American mountain ranges for geography class.

"That's okay" Beamer had said. "I don't need to know. Never mind."

But it was too late.

"Don't try to sidetrack me with the children!" Lily's voice had risen. "I spend every day of my life with those two. I know them better than you ever will." Suddenly, as if the truth of her words had managed to penetrate her anger, she'd turned to look first at Beamer, then at Jo. She'd looked so unhappy Jo had wanted to cry. "This is a travesty," Lily said thickly. "If you're finished, go to your rooms. Your father and I want to talk."

"I'm not finished," Beamer had protested.

"Take your plate to the kitchen," Lily told him.

"Come on, Beam." Jo picked up his plate and pushed through the door to the kitchen, then turned to watch Beamer follow a moment later.

"How old d'you have to be to be a mother?" Beamer had asked, settling in at the kitchen table.

"I don't know. Why?"

"Are you old enough to be my mother?"

Jo had laughed, tickled by the idea. "No, I'm not. I'm just a little kid, Beam. I think you have to be way older, maybe twenty-five. Why?"

"I just wondered." He'd stabbed his fork into the mashed potatoes, then poked the meat with the tip of his knife. After staring at the plate for a few more seconds, he abandoned the utensils and picked up a piece of meat with his fingers, eyeing his sister as he did.

"I don't care," she'd said. "But you better not let Mom catch you."

Later, when they'd gone upstairs and Beamer was sitting playing with a tennis ball while he watched Jo on her hands and knees on the floor carefully painting her flour-and-water mountain ranges with green poster paint, they'd heard their parents coming up the stairs. Jo had sat back on her knees, paintbrush poised, and Beamer dropped the tennis ball, his eyes on the door. The footsteps went past, down the hall, and then the bedroom door had closed.

Beamer had looked over at Jo and said, "They were naughty so they sent themselves to bed early." He'd nodded to himself with sober satisfaction. "Good!"

Jo poured more coffee into her cup, noticing an American family midway along the terrace in the throes of a quiet but intense argument. The parents were both in tennis clothes. The daughter, about sixteen, slouched in her chair looking peevish; the son, ten or eleven, was trying to interrupt the father, who was saying to the daughter, "We didn't come all the way here to spend entire days sitting at the pool. Now your mother and I have a game in fifteen minutes, and then we thought we'd go into town."

"Dad, I want to go now," the boy broke in. "I don't care about tennis or the stupid pool. This is *Venice*, for God's sake!"

"I *said* we'll have our game and then we'll—"

"*No way* I'm going!" the daughter interjected. "I'm staying here to work on my tan."

"Great!" the boy snapped. "Just great! I'm supposed to sit around here doing dick while you guys play tennis and Wonder Dummy soaks up rays! Terrific! If I'd known we were coming all the way here to sit around while you guys do the same dumb stuff you do at home, I wouldn't've come. I could've gone to Outward Bound. I could've done something that requires a little intelligence. This is a total, complete, absolute, colossal waste of my time, you guys!"

Jo thought the kid was bang-on. He was also very cute. Unfortunately, he lost the argument. At least it looked that way to her as she left to go to the landing stage to wait for the launch.

When it came, she went directly to the rear of the boat where she could stand and survey the view as they zipped along the canals. She had no idea what the buildings were, or what the names of the churches they passed might be; she just shot film, overcome by the magnificent architecture, by the beauty of the morning and the light that lay so gently over every surface, and by the warmth of the sun on the top of her head and on her bare arms.

As they neared the depot, Jo spotted a woman waiting by the water's edge, and waved. The woman waved back as Jo fumbled in her bag for some lire to tip the driver. He said, *"Grazie, grazie, Signora,"* gave her a hand out of the boat, then returned to the wheel and swung away.

"Hi, I'm Jo." She offered her hand.

"I am Giovanna." Her handshake was good and firm, her smile open. She looked to be in her early thirties, with short sun-streaked hair, a friendly face, and an easy manner. She was wearing a sleeveless turquoise jump suit with a white cotton cardigan. Slim and casual, she gave the impression of being accustomed to dealing with a wide variety of people. "We go around here," she told Jo, and they started off around the side of the depot to the entrance fronting on the tracks. "This is where we have our offices," she explained. "You would like some coffee?"

"I'd love some." Jo followed Giovanna up a flight of stairs to her second-floor office, which was large and airy and had all kinds of Italian-designed items Jo found most attractive: ultramodern telephones, shelf units with slick lines, an espresso machine, even good-looking wastebaskets.

Giovanna introduced Jo to another young woman, with long dark hair, who smiled warmly while Giovanna encouraged Jo to have a seat. "I make the coffee," she said, and busied herself with the espresso. Both women watched Jo openly, with frank curiosity. For a few moments, Jo felt like someone from outer space who was being given a friendly but bewildered reception.

"You enjoyed your journey?" Giovanna asked from across the room.

"It was fantastic. Absolutely fantastic. You've got a great train."

The two women laughed. Giovanna came to perch on the edge of the desk. "They don't say what it is you wish to see."

"Everything!"

"Okay." Giovanna smiled as she lit a cigarette. "We show you everything. You like sugar with your coffee?"

190

"Yes, please."

The second woman leaned on her elbows on her desk, asking, "You are writing for a magazine?"

"That's right."

"And you take the pictures, too, yes?"

"Right."

"You do this all the time, write for magazines and take pictures? This is your job?"

"Uh-huh."

"This bag you have is all cameras?"

"It has different lenses, this and that."

"Much equipment. You do this a long time?"

"Quite a long time, uh-huh."

The woman was about to ask another question, but the telephone rang and she turned to answer it.

Giovanna brought Jo a demitasse and sat again on the edge of the desk with her own cup. "Did you arrange to meet Renato and see the kitchen? You like the coffee?"

"It's delicious, thank you. I do want to see the kitchen, but I wasn't sure how to go about it."

"We do it for you." She spoke in Italian to the second woman, who covered the mouthpiece of the receiver as she listened, then went back to her call. "It is good if you go today or tomorrow," she told Jo. "She will speak with the kitchen, tell them you come. Okay?"

"Good. What exactly is it you do?" Jo asked, envying the woman's relaxed manner. There was nothing contrived about her, no concealing shadows thrown by the brim of a professional hat.

"I am the operations supervisor."

"God, that's terrific! You're in charge of all of it?"

"All." Giovanna seemed a bit taken aback by Jo's reaction. "This is unusual to you?"

"I guess I just assumed operations would be run by a man. I mean, there are no female employees on the train itself. But I like it that a woman's got the job. It says something good about the company."

"This is unusual?" Giovanna asked again.

191

"I think it is."

The other woman completed her second call and said, "Okay. They know you will come."

"Good, thanks a lot."

"I think," Giovanna said with a wry smile, "that the journalists, the *paparazzi* are all men, huh?"

"I know," Jo conceded. "Why is it women always assume men do everything?"

"I don't know, but this is true what we think."

Jo drank the last of her coffee, and Giovanna said, "We go now and you see everything."

Out again in the glaring sunshine, Giovanna put on a pair of mirrored sunglasses, fished a pack of cigarettes from the pocket of her cardigan, and lit one. Jo looked around at the various detached carriages here and there on the sidings. As they walked along the platform, headed for a short flight of steps leading down to the tracks, a man in an undershirt and blue overalls came riding up on a yellow bicycle, calling out, "*Ciao,* Giovanna!" Seeing Jo lift the camera, he obliged by holding still, gave her a beaming smile, then pushed the bicycle off around the side of the building.

Several tracks over, a woman in a pink smock was pulling a trolley laden with cleaning gear.

"This is one of the cleaners," Giovanna said, following Jo's eyes.

"They all wear pink smocks?"

"Yes."

"Are some of these extra carriages?" Jo asked, looking at the blue cars baking in the sun.

"Extra, yes. I think maybe you will want to see this." Giovanna pointed ahead to where a cluster of men were at work, using some sort of bright orange wheeled contraption.

"What're they doing?"

"They wash the carriages. You will see."

"Your English is very good. Where did you study?"

"You think so?" Giovanna looked pleased. "I studied

here, at school. I don't get to speak it very much, so you are good practice for me.''

"D'you do this often, take journalists around?"

"Never. You are my first."

Well, that explained their curiosity about her. "I would've thought you'd have them coming all the time."

"Not ever. Arrangements get made in London. When the journalists come to Venice, someone will meet with them, usually Laura at the Cipriani. You are the only one to come to Scomenzera. You have met with Laura?"

"Not yet. Boy, that's really odd. You'd think if people wanted to know the ins and outs of the train, this is where they'd come to find out. I mean, the first thing I asked was to come to the depot. What *is* that thing, anyway?" she asked of the orange machine. It had a platform upon which a man was standing, and fastened to its base was an immense roller brush that ran along the side of the carriage, spraying out water as it went.

"This is how they clean the outside. The carriages are uncoupled in pairs, then they are pulled over to this—tank? This is the word?"

"Tank, right."

"If you look under, you will see."

Jo bent down to see a cement pit filled with dirty, sudsy water. "What's that for?" she asked, straightening.

"The water from the washing is collected here. Then, once a week a special truck comes to vacuum up the water and carry it away for disposal. It used to go into the canal, but now because of the pollution laws it must be taken away. I don't know to where. When they have finished one side," Giovanna said, watching from a respectful distance as Jo took pictures, "they do the other. Then the carriages are moved, and two more come." When Jo had finished, she asked, "There is something special you would like to see?"

"Is the Lalique car here? I'd really love to see that."

"You can see, but it is very hot inside now, from the sun."

"That's okay. I don't mind."

"Hard work to get the pictures, huh?" Giovanna observed as they moved toward a carriage standing directly in front of the depot.

"I honestly don't even think about it, unless there's some problem with the equipment. Sometimes, like today, you crawl around where it's a hundred and ten degrees. Other times, you stand outside shivering, trying to keep snow off the lenses. I've been doing it for so long it's become second nature."

Jo stopped to take shots of details from several cars: the gold crest on the side of one; the words CARROZZA-PULLMAN NO. 4141 on another; then SCHLAFWAGEN NO. 3425 on a third. She also took a shot of two men laboring on an air-conditioning unit beneath a carriage, and a couple of Giovanna, who laughed for the camera.

"You put me into your story?"

"I might. It's a good angle, and I'd really like to show people the woman who's in charge of the train. Do the men give you a hard time?"

Giovanna paused to consider that. "A little," she said, "at the beginning, but not now."

"Do you feel you're the same person at home as you are at work?"

Giovanna's brows drew together. "I don't understand."

"When you come here in the morning," Jo rephrased the question, "do you feel you have to change yourself in any way to do the job, to deal with the men?"

"It's all the same," Giovanna answered, still somewhat mystified. "Are you different when you take the photographs?"

"Depending on the circumstances, I think I am," Jo said truthfully. "If I'm uncomfortable, if I'm dealing with people who put me on edge for one reason or another, then I fall back on being professional. It helps me deal with the situation."

"But it's still the same," Giovanna insisted. "It's you, the same."

"It's me, but different parts of me."

"This is confusing," Giovanna said. "Everyone has many different parts."

"I'm sorry. I didn't mean to confuse you."

"No, it is interesting," Giovanna persisted. "You are not happy with the parts?"

"I'm trying to get to the point where I *am* happy with the parts."

"Aaah! I see. I warn you it's very hot inside," Giovanna said, stepping from the platform into the carriage.

She wasn't exaggerating. Entering the car was like pushing one's way into warm Jell-O. Giovanna drew back the curtains to let in some light, and Jo sighed with pleasure at the sight of the lustrous mahogany paneling and Lalique glass inserts in single panels and in groupings of three. Each was of a bacchanalian nude set against a background of grape clusters and swirls, and above and below were pairs of smaller panels of grape clusters. She'd expected them to be quite large, but the panels were only eighteen or twenty inches high. To set them off there was a frosty bluish-gray upholstery on the chairs and silver-gray curtains that went well with the milky, faintly blue caste to the glass. At the far end was a bar, with a large plate glass window behind it; to the left of that was a single female Lalique nude and beyond that an oval frosted window the center of which was amber stained glass.

"It doesn't look the same as it did in the movie," Jo said.

"No. It is quite a story," Giovanna explained as Jo started setting up her equipment. "The Lalique panels were removed when the carriage was to be refurbished. They were stored in a shed, and the majority were stolen. So only a few panels were put into the carriage when it was finished, and the Lalique Glass Company made molds from one original to make new panels. If you look up close, you can see that the old panels are a little yellow in color."

"They never found the stolen ones?" Jo asked, unable to get a light reading from the camera.

"Never."

"That's rotten." Sweating, she got out her pocket meter, attached the cable release to the KX, which she'd mounted on the minitripod atop the bar, adjusted for a long exposure, and, praying to God nothing else was wrong, squeezed off the shot. She was suddenly nervous as hell.

"My camera's acting up," she told Giovanna, who, with a display of exceptional patience, stood calmly smoking a cigarette. "If this film's no good, I won't have any shots of this car."

"You have only the one camera?"

"Usually I carry a spare body, but I knew I'd be on foot while I'm here and I didn't want to have the extra weight, so I only brought this one." And why had she brought it? she wondered. She'd been influenced by some vague nostalgic idea that because she'd taken so many photographs of her family with this camera she might somehow forge connecting links by bringing it along. She'd been thinking about Lily when she'd packed the camera gear. Obviously, it had been a mistake.

"This carriage might be on when you travel Saturday," Giovanna said. "Then you would have time to take more pictures."

"That'd be a break. I know there are file photos, but I really prefer to take my own pictures. If you want to wait outside, I'll try not to be too long. It really is incredibly hot in here."

"It's okay. I like to watch."

"You're a good sport," Jo said apologetically.

"It's okay," Giovanna said again. "You never get to meet a woman who is operations supervisor. I never get to meet a woman who writes stories and makes photographs."

"It'd be a hell of a lot more interesting, and faster, if this camera was working properly. You see, I have to set everything manually because the built-in light meter's out of whack, and that takes longer."

"You can make pictures when it is so dark in here?"

"There's a fair amount of light coming through the panels, and that helps."

While she worked, removing the camera from the tripod to take hand-held shots of details of the interior, she wondered what Henry would think if he could see her on the job in conditions like this, with perspiration running down her ribs and soaking the hair at the back of her neck. He wouldn't think anything, she told herself. What's your problem? It didn't matter to Henry how she worked, or where. He liked the end product, and he understood there was a degree of physical labor involved. Of course he understood that! After all, Henry got out there in the garden every weekend on his hands and knees. He knew about putting an effort into the achievement of satisfactory results. Unlike Tyler, Henry had seen her with and without hats, not to mention with and without clothes.

It actually felt cool outside in the shade of the depot. Both women stood breathing deeply, blotting their faces.

"Could you give me a rundown on the schedule?" Jo asked, getting out her notebook. "I know there are two northbound departures weekly, Wednesday and Saturday. What happens in between?"

"Okay. Today, as you see, the carriages are cleaned. The dirty linens are taken off. While the outside gets washed, the inside also is done. But before the washing, the undercarriages are checked. Every four months a car must go off for one week of complete service. It is lifted off the ground with hydraulic jacks and everything is examined."

"Are there the same number of carriages each trip?"

"The computer in London takes the reservations. Then they are telexed to here, giving the number of passengers. When we have this number, we know how many cars. If there will be more than one hundred forty passengers, there will be three restaurant cars. If less, only two. The French Pullman that you love," she smiled, "becomes the third restaurant. But since it has no kitchen, it is placed between the other two and shares the kitchens.

"Later today, the coal and wood will be loaded, also the linen supply and the requisitions for the restaurant cars and the stewards' supplies. The train staff make requisition forms and these are filled here. Come, I show you the storerooms.''

Inside, Giovanna gave her a tour. One room contained coffee, tea, jams, cleaning products; another had linens, blankets, pillows, and silverware.

"What about the china?" Jo asked.

"At the beginning it was Limoges, but there was too much theft and breakage, too expensive. Now it is the same design but made in Portugal, not so very expensive.''

"What's the one thing people steal most often?"

Giovanna laughed, color rising in her face. "The toilet brushes," she replied.

"You're kidding! The *toilet brushes*? That is totally disgusting! Can you *imagine* hiding a toilet brush in your luggage? I mean, picture it!" Jo exclaimed, using her hands for emphasis. "You've got your handmade beaded evening dress with matching silk shoes, your outfits for the two days on board, not to mention your underwear, cosmetics, and all the rest of it. And you put a *used* toilet brush in there, too? God! I thought you'd say the silverware or something. The toilet brush? It makes me want to heave my heart out.''

Giovanna laughed harder. "I think the same," she said, mopping her eyes. "You are very funny."

"*I'm* not funny!" Jo howled. "*They're* funny, the ones stealing the toilet brushes. People are absolutely *amazing*!"

"Yes, I think so," Giovanna agreed, blotting her eyes on her cardigan sleeve.

"Toilet brushes! I can't get over it. What's next?"

"Okay, we go on. Wednesday morning, at seven, the food comes by boat from the Cipriani. At eight comes the staff to load supplies, prepare the tables, get extras if anything is needed. At nine-fifteen comes a diesel engine to take the train to Santa Lucia Station. By nine-thirty the train is in the station, and by ten-forty the passengers are boarding.''

There were more storerooms: one where spare basins were kept; another for various mechanical parts, including a large supply of heavy springs; an area with rolls of carpet to replace worn or damaged sections in any of the carriages; a room with bins of glass of various shapes and sizes, as well as mirrors. And outside, in an open-ended roofed area, great stacks of wood and sacks of charcoal.

"Everything's very well organized, amazingly clean and neat," Jo noted.

"You think so? Good. Thank you."

"Thank *you*. You've been incredibly patient, and I've taken up a lot of your time. I should start back to the hotel."

"I'll take you to where you can get a boat," Giovanna offered, lighting a fresh cigarette as they picked their way over the stony track bed.

"Have you been with the company long?"

"Since the beginning, in nineteen eighty-two."

"And you like it, right?"

"Yes. This is heavy, the bag with the camera?"

"I'm used to it."

"You like it, huh?"

"Yup." Jo looked over and they smiled at each other. "You're terrific," she told Giovanna. "I *still* can't get over the toilet brushes."

"You make me see everything as if for the first time," Giovanna said. "It's good." She stopped to talk to a group of men who were seated together at the water's edge, eating their lunch. The men exchanged looks, and one of them nodded and began folding the paper over his food before getting to his feet.

"He will take you back," Giovanna told Jo.

Jo gave her a kiss on the cheek, and said, "It's been a pleasure meeting you."

"For me, too. *Ciao*."

Jo climbed on board and went to sit at the rear of the boat, at once dragging out the KX to examine it and swearing under her breath as the light-meter needle fluctuated erratically. The only way to find out if the roll she'd shot was salvageable would be to have it processed. And she'd have to buy another body, because with a broken-down camera the assignment would be a write-off. What the hell, she asked herself, had she been thinking of when she'd packed this goddamned dud?

15

WITH ABOUT TEN MINUTES TO SPARE BEFORE HER MEETING
with the hotel's PR director, Jo rushed to her room to freshen
up. The air conditioning was a relief after the heat of the
depot, and she thought how nice it would be to sit for a while
on the sofa and cool down. But there wasn't time. And the
problems with the Pentax were nagging at her. She washed
her face and neck, brushed her hair, and flew back to pool-
side where lunch was being served.

The maître d' showed her to a table, saying, "Signora
Abruzzi asks you please to wait. She is delayed by a telephone call."

Jo thanked him and sat back, glad of a chance to collect
herself. Never before had she worked on a feature in such an
addled state. First there was the business with Tyler and
Henry; now she had a crippled camera. She felt impaired,
and jittery.

A tall, lean, smartly suited woman came toward the table,
extending her hand. "I am Laura. I am sorry to be late."
She pulled out a chair, asked, "You will have a drink?" and
turned to summon a waiter.

"Some mineral water, please."

Laura ordered white wine and Jo's water, glanced at her

wristwatch, then looked over at Jo. Almost as an after-thought, she smiled. "Everything is to your satisfaction?"

"Oh, yes. Very much so."

Laura had the air of someone permanently preoccupied with the pressures of her job. Her manner was one of extreme competence that was constantly being tested, and the slight lag—in her speech, her gestures, and her smiles—seemed a result of being forced repeatedly to decide if her time was being wasted. In her mid-to-late forties, she had short gray-ing hair brushed back from an attractive face with wide-set, somewhat slanted brown eyes. She was, Jo guessed, a woman who was overbooked and knew it, a woman who didn't suffer fools gladly. Her efficiency and busyness seemed designed to conceal a certain sadness her eyes couldn't quite hide. Jo made the decision to win her over, in the hope of getting past Laura's obvious professionalism.

"I have taken the liberty of making some arrangements for you," Laura began. "Tomorrow evening there is a meet-ing of the Venice Restoration Society, with a slide show and cocktails after. I thought this might be of interest to you. If you have made no other arrangements, I hope you will join me. Unfortunately, I have an engagement for dinner, so I will have to leave you after the cocktails. Then on Thursday there is a dinner sponsored by the Venice Tourist Board. I have your invitation here." She laid an envelope on the table between them. "The dinners are held twice weekly, always in fine palazzi, for perhaps twenty, two guests from each of ten hotels. This dinner on Thursday is to be held at the Malipiero Trevisan Palace, which I am told is very beautiful. The guests will meet at seven-thirty at the Caffè Florian for drinks, and then the group will be escorted to the palazzo. Since they are most anxious to have travel agents and jour-nalists in their groups, I took the liberty of recommending you for this evening. Also I have spoken with Renato and he will be happy if you wish to come to the kitchens tomorrow or the day after. So," she wound down with a tentative smile and wary eyes, "how was your visit to Scomenzera? You have seen all you wish to see?"

"Even some things I didn't think I'd see," Jo laughed. "It was very worthwhile, and Giovanna couldn't have been nicer. But I do have a bit of a problem and I hope you'll be able to help. My camera's broken down, and I need two things: a camera store, and a place that will process my film quickly so I'll know if I have to reshoot."

"This is serious," Laura said. "I think it best to talk with the concierge. He will know. We do this after lunch, okay? For now, we will be relaxed." Again she looked at her watch.

If this was her relaxed mode, Jo thought, her active mode had to be nothing short of dizzying. "I get the impression they keep you running here," Jo ventured. Not only could she see Laura's professional hat, she had the sense that it was slipping regularly.

Laura stared at her for a moment, then laughed quite heartily. "You get the correct impression," she said. "The summer is our most busy time, always too much to be done."

"I'm sure," Jo sympathized, wondering if the impression she gave was anything like Laura's.

After the waiter had brought their drinks, Laura asked, "You have seen the buffet? Or would you prefer something from the kitchen, some pasta perhaps? We make fresh pasta every day."

"I think I'll try the buffet. Have you worked here long?"

"A few years," Laura replied, sliding back into the public relations officer role.

"Have you always worked in hotels, doing PR?"

"No. I worked at this first when I lived for several years in America. Before, I was in management."

"But don't you think what you do now is a form of management? I mean, I've always thought it's the PR people who pretty well run the show. If they're no good at the job, they can really mess up a place. And you seem to be right on top of things."

"Why do you say this?" Her expression was guarded, as if fearful Jo might become critical.

God! Jo thought. This was tricky. "Only because," she answered, "of the trouble you've taken to arrange things for me, and to keep track of my comings and goings. Usually, I have to chase around, setting things up on my own. You're making my job a lot easier, and that's not only very nice, it's a major change. The attitude I get most of the time is: 'Oh, no! We've got another damned journalist on our hands.' You're also the second woman I've met today who has an important position and is right on top of it.''

"You are a feminist?" Laura asked her, still wary.

"I'm a person, that's all. But I do like to see women getting ahead. Why not? We're just as capable as men. Let me give you an example," Jo said, warming to the subject. "You're one of the very few PR people who's ever taken the time to sit down for lunch with me, never mind making arrangements to take me to a slide show because it might have something to do with the feature I'm working on.''

"This is true?" Her caution was clearly ebbing.

"I swear it."

"Hmmm." Laura drank some of her white wine, then set her glass on the table with care. "I have seen some of your work," she said. "We receive many travel journals, to clip pieces on the Cipriani. I liked very much the story you wrote about Jerusalem." She admitted this rather shyly, as someone who rarely offered personal opinions.

"You saw that?"

"It was very"—Laura searched for a word—"personal. I thought from what you wrote that you would be someone interesting to know. Also I liked the photographs, in particular the one on the roof over the market."

"That's one of my favorites," Jo said eagerly. "I wouldn't have known about the roofs, but there was this darling man who had a pottery shop in the Arab section of the market in the old city, and we got to talking—he'd been a teacher, and his English was perfect—and he took me outside and up some stairs to show me the view. You could see for miles from up there. You could also look down through arches and air vents into different parts of the market. The thing that struck me was all the TV antennas, hundreds of them. Anyway, it's exciting when you find a new view of something most people have already seen.''

"You liked it there?'' Laura asked, her guardedness replaced by interest.

"It was a beautiful and fascinating country, but it scared the hell out of me. I'd be walking around the city, and all of a sudden there'd be some kid of about eighteen in a uniform with a submachine gun. It was like constantly being jolted awake. You know? It seemed as if the minute you relaxed, a tank or some soldiers would go by to remind you where you were. I think the most moving thing I saw was the afternoon I went to the Wailing Wall, and there were all these notes tucked into the crevices between the stones. The whole lower portion of the wall was crowded with them. Like letters to God. It was very humbling.

"Then, you'd go out a ways into the newer areas, and there was all this ultramodern housing in a kind of golden stone. All the complexes had solar heating, and special window shades to keep out the sun but allow the breeze in. It was very energy-consciousness-raising. I mean, I live in a condominium in Connecticut, and the gas bills every winter are astronomical, and getting higher every year. We could save ourselves a fortune if we got together and installed solar heating systems. But I think we've grown lazy, and things always seem more trouble than they're worth. Oh, I'm as guilty of that as any of my neighbors, but after that trip to Israel, I couldn't help feeling our lethargy might one day bankrupt us. God, listen to me! I'm sorry. I didn't mean to give a lecture.''

"No. It is very interesting,'' Laura told her. "I was almost four years in America, and I liked it very much. But I saw this laziness also. It is here, too; it is everywhere in Europe. And you are right: It will ruin us. We have forgotten how to work hard. Please, go ahead to the buffet. I will have some pasta. I have my main meal at midday, and something small in the evening.'' She signaled again to the waiter as Jo got up to go to the buffet.

There were at least three or four different kinds of zucchini or eggplant dishes, as well as combinations of vegetables with shrimp; baby squid; mozzarella and tomatoes; rice-and-crab salad; fresh tuna; and traditional salads. She filled her plate, then returned into the sunshine.

People were sunbathing on lounge chairs by the pool; a few kids were splashing around in the water. A steady light wind lifted the scalloped edges of the umbrellas and the tablecloths. A variety of boats traveled past the hotel—motor launches, water taxis, fishing vessels, yachts. The Texas foursome were standing at the end of the path waiting for the hotel launch to take them across to the Piazza San Marco. The daughter was still going on about the theories put forth in her pop-psychology book. The other three were looking around, trying not to hear her.

Remembering the American family from the morning, Jo looked back at the pool area and spotted the teenage daughter alone at the far end. In a skimpy bikini, her skin shiny with tanning oil, she lay unmoving, her eyes shielded by a pair of plastic goggles, and a thick coating of zinc ointment covered her nose. Jo wondered where the young brother was, and if he'd finally gone off to tour the city with his parents.

Laura encouraged her to go ahead with her meal. "The pasta will take only a few minutes," she told Jo, stealing another look at her watch. "I am," she apologized, "in the habit of eating very quickly."

Again Jo wondered what the woman's haste and time awareness was hiding. She seemed able to relax only for minutes at a time before snapping back into hyperalertness. She certainly didn't misrepresent, however. Although her pasta arrived when Jo was halfway through her plate of salads, they finished together. Then Laura said, "If you come with me, I will ask the concierge if he knows of a camera store." Seeing Jo look around for the waiter, she said, "It isn't necessary. You enjoyed the food?"

"Very much. Thank you. If I may, I'll leave a tip for the waiter."

Laura nodded approvingly and waited—all but tapping her foot—while Jo opened her bag to find some lire.

In the foyer Laura explained Jo's problem to one of the concierges. He listened closely, then in English asked Jo if she would kindly wait while he made a telephone call to a store he knew.

"I will leave you now," Laura said. "If you have need of anything, please let me know. I look forward to seeing you tomorrow evening. We will meet here at five."

"That'll be fine. Thank you very much for the lunch."

"I enjoyed it." Laura gave one of her infrequent but sunny smiles. "Perhaps we will talk more tomorrow."

"I'd like that."

"Good!" Laura said, her body already turning away. "Good," she said again, and was off, back to her office.

The concierge spoke for a few minutes, then held his hand over the mouthpiece to ask Jo, "What is it that you are needing?"

"A body compatible with Pentax lenses, K-mounting."

The concierge repeated this in Italian into the telephone, then listened for another minute before again covering the mouthpiece to say, "He has this, Signorina, but it is very expensive. I try to make him give to you a discount."

"Thank you." She noticed the long-haired man from breakfast, sitting at the far end of the lobby, writing in his notebook. He couldn't be another journalist, she reasoned. Otherwise Laura would have stopped to talk to him. Was he working on a book?

The call completed, the concierge wrote out the name of the shop, pulled a small map from beneath the desk, and with a marker indicated the shop's location. "They will also do one-hour service for film," he told her. "You will go to see the camera. If it is suitable, the owner promises a discount. I hope this is what you need. If not, you come to me again; I make more telephone calls."

She thanked him, shook his hand, then went to get her camera bag before heading upstairs to Lucienne's room.

Lucienne came to the door saying, "I am on the telephone, Mignon. Sit, please. I will not be long."

Jo sat on the sofa at the bottom end of the room as Lucienne returned to the telephone on the bedside table and her conversation in both Italian and French. She sounded very angry, and Jo tried not to listen, even though she understood only the odd word here and there. A copy of the Orient-Express magazine was on the coffee table, and Jo leafed through it, looking up at the skylight as the first drops of rain began to fall. The sky had gone a dull gray, and the rain was coming down hard, making a lot of noise as it hit the glass. She swore under her breath, growing agitated as Lucienne's call went on and on, and the rain drummed down on the skylights at either end of the room. She had to get over to the camera store, no matter what. If Lucienne's call went on much longer, she'd leave her a note and go. She had a small folding umbrella and a lightweight raincoat in her room. She'd get them and head off.

Looking over, she saw Lucienne was seated now on the side of the bed, lighting a cigarette as she listened impatiently to the voice on the other end of the line. As if sensing Jo's eyes, she turned and signaled her inability to end the call, then barked into the receiver. Finally, after another seven or eight minutes, she slammed down the phone and stood up. *"Merde!"* she exclaimed, crushing out her most recently lit cigarette. "I am sorry, Joanna." She came down the length of the room, looked up at the skylight, then at Jo, and said, "We go anyway, eh?"

"I thought I'd stop on the way and get my raincoat and umbrella."

"I have nothing," Lucienne said furiously. *"Stupide!"*

"No problem. You can have the umbrella and I'll wear the raincoat."

"But you'll get very wet, Mignon."

"I'll dry out. Look, do you mind coming with me to a camera store? I have to buy another camera. Mine's had a nervous breakdown. Just what I needed."

"This is bad, eh?"

"It's death," Jo said flatly.

"I will come, maybe bargain for you."

"It's all arranged. The owner's going to give me a discount."

Even in the downpour, the Piazza San Marco was beautiful. And deserted. Jo and Lucienne ran, sloshing through puddles, to the far side of the square and along a narrow street to a small store that had a display of cameras and lenses in the window, as well as along the rear inside wall and within a small showcase that also served as a counter area. A young man was busy with a processing and printing machine that took up better than a quarter of the available space; an older man sat on a stool behind the counter.

When Jo announced herself, the old man smiled sadly and held up a hand to stop her, miming that he didn't speak English, and called to his son.

"The concierge of the Cipriani telephoned," she explained.

"Ah, yes. I have only one camera that will work with the Pentax lenses," the son said, reaching for a box in the rear display. "It is a good camera." He showed her an Exakta, a name with which she was only vaguely familiar. "You know this camera?" he asked.

"Not really. I know it's German, but that's about all."

"It is quite good," he said critically, removing it from the box to demonstrate its features. "Self-timer, built-in light meter, flash setting at 125, shutterspeed up to 2000. You have your lenses?"

"Yes, I do." She put the Lowe-pro down on the counter and pulled out the wide-angle. The lens snapped securely into place, and she removed the cap to have a look. The TTL meter was on the right-hand side, the opposite of the Pentax. That would take some getting used to. On the plus side, the body was lightweight and compact. She asked the price, then held her breath as the young man launched into a lengthy explanation of the normal price versus the one he would give her. When he at last named an amount, it sounded to Jo like a fortune, and she turned to Lucienne to enlist her help. All the while, the father looked on with interest.

"How much is that, do you know?"

"I know only in francs," Lucienne said. "But it is quite a lot, I think."

The father paused in lighting a cigarette to offer his package to Jo and Lucienne. Jo said thank you, but no. Lucienne gave the man a smile and took one of his cigarettes. He gazed at her lovingly, as if she were a minor miracle that had occurred in his small store.

"In dollars, it is this," the young man was saying, punching out a series of numbers on a pocket calculator, and holding it out to show her. Almost $250, a hell of a lot in terms of what that amount would buy in New York.

"That's very expensive," she protested.

"I am giving to you at a discount," he said sadly. "Three hundred thousand lire; I ask only two hundred forty-five thousand."

The father, who'd torn his attention from Lucienne to follow this exchange now said, *"Scusi, Signorina, scusi,"* and held a hurried discussion with his son.

Jo stepped away from the counter to confer with Lucienne. "What're they saying?"

"The father says to lower the price more. The son refuses. The father insists. I think they will make a compromise. The father seems to like you."

"The father," Jo corrected her, "seems to like *you*."

"That's okay," Lucienne said coolly.

The compromise consisted of an offer to process both her roll of print film and the roll of slides at no charge. Since this would have cost at least an additional twenty-five or thirty dollars, Jo gave in, turned over the two rolls of film and her American Express card, and, with a sigh, signed the charge slip.

"You come back in one hour, the prints will be ready. The slide film I give to a very good technician. He will make ready for tomorrow afternoon."

"Could you make double prints?" Jo asked.

The father wanted a translation. The son explained. The father smiled at both women and said, "Okay, okay."

"Great!" She turned to Lucienne. "Thank you for being beautiful. I'd like to have you around whenever I go shopping. We can go get your shoes now."

"First we have a drink. Okay?"

"Sure, fine."

"There is a place I know very near."

They stepped out into the still-heavy rain. The additional weight of the new camera body in Jo's bag bore down on her shoulder as she trailed Lucienne to an unprepossessing café that was, as promised, only yards from the camera store. Except for the staff, the place was empty.

Lucienne ordered a glass of red wine. Jo asked for water. Lighting a cigarette, Lucienne said, "Why is it you drink so much water?"

"When I was little, my grandmother told me if I drank at least six glasses a day, I'd always be healthy."

"And this works, eh? You are healthy?"

"Very. I don't know that it has a thing to do with the water, but I've been doing it for so long now, I think I'm almost superstitious about it."

Lucienne appeared to have stopped listening halfway through Jo's explanation. She smoked her cigarette, gazing down at the tabletop, tapping her long fingernails on the edge of the table.

"Is something the matter?" Jo asked, as the aproned waiter came with their drinks.

"This telephone call," Lucienne said. "It was with Paolo I was speaking. There are difficulties with arrangements for the marriage. It is very boring."

"What difficulties?"

Lucienne lifted her glass, her expression going hard. "His family wants an important ceremony. Church, and a priest, many guests. I have planned it, will be small and private, only me and Paolo, with witnesses. He wishes to satisfy the family. I say, to hell with his family. I would be a spectacle, eh? Forty years old in a bridal gown, with my little boy, in the church? It is *dismal*. I refuse. He declares I am impossible. I tell him I do not marry the family. Ridiculous! Absurd!'' She took a long swallow of the wine, then puffed away on her cigarette.

"So what'll you do?"

"You know what I hate? I hate when I say I will do this thing or that thing not to do what I have said."

"I'm the same way. D'you mind if I ask you something?"

"I don't mind. Ask me anything," Lucienne said disgustedly.

"It seems to me you don't really want to go ahead with this, with getting married, I mean. Maybe I'm reading it all wrong, but that's really how it seems. And if you don't want to do it, then don't! I'm one to talk, I know. But people are forever coming along after the fact to tell you they knew all the time you shouldn't do something. And you always wonder where the hell those people were before you went ahead with it—whatever it was. So what I'm saying is, if you've changed your mind, say no and forget it. Don't do it if it doesn't feel right to you."

Lucienne smoked her cigarette and stared through the smoke at Jo for quite some time. Jo wondered if she'd gone too far. What business did she have giving out with her opinions? Who was she to this woman, anyway?

Finally, Lucienne reached for her glass and looked at the wine that remained before drinking it down. The waiter came over the moment she set the glass back on the table to ask if she cared for more. When Lucienne shook her head, he retreated.

"I was thinking," Jo said, "if you like, I could call my friend Sally in New York and find out the name of the pills she took. You might be able to get a doctor here, or back in Paris, to prescribe them for you." God, why did I say anything? she asked herself. Lucienne looked ready to blow her stack.

"You take big chances, eh, Joanna?" Lucienne said hotly. "You say how you see things, what you think."

"If I'm out of line, I'm sorry," Jo said hastily.

"I don't *know* if you are out of line. I am thinking. Most people, they talk only because they have a wish to hear what they are thinking, not because they have any desire to hear the opinions of others. With you, I am not so sure. You are this way with everyone, saying what you are thinking?''

"Don't I wish!" Jo said with feeling. "I wish to God I had the guts to say what I think and how I feel, but I hardly ever do. I mean, I actually blew up at my agent, Henry, last week. But it's one of the few times I've done it. No. It's just that, from everything you've said about this Paolo and his family, it doesn't sound as if getting married is what you really want. And is it possible," she asked, treading in dangerous territory, "that you've been talking to hear your own thinking on the subject?"

"It is possible," Lucienne allowed with a sigh, unable to sustain her anger with this woman. It was so clear that Joanna was being brave, trying to be good. She was swayed by the fact that Joanna had given so much thought to all that had been said. "The difficulty is I have no wish to lose him."

"Oh, brother! If you say no, if you say you've changed your mind, what's the worst thing that'll happen?"

"He will finish with me. *Comme ça.*" She snapped her fingers.

"Then he's a jerk, Lucienne! If he'd break up with you because you've changed your mind, then maybe that'd be the best thing that could happen. I mean, would you rather break up now, or would you prefer to spend the next five or ten years being miserable because you went ahead and got married in spite of your reservations? I'll tell you something. I slept with two different men last week. Nothing planned. It just happened. Both of them are decent guys, but I've got reservations up to my hairline. Whatever happens—and God must know, because I sure as hell don't—I'm not about to let myself be talked into anything unless I'm one hundred percent sure. I want the satisfaction of knowing that whatever I do, even if it's not one damned thing, it was my decision."

"I decided this for myself," Lucienne took the defensive.

"Sure you did. And you can undecide too, if you want. God, Lucienne! You're not exactly a weakling who can't fend for herself. I mean, running away at sixteen to work in a bowling alley, starting your own restaurant and making a huge success of it. You're someone with accomplishments, someone who stops traffic, and charms little old men into giving your friends discounts. You're not exactly a woman with nothing to recommend her. Do you *want* to be pushed into a marriage you're not sure about just because—" She stopped. "I'm sorry. All of a sudden, I don't know if I'm talking about you or about myself."

Lucienne laughed. "I think maybe you talk about all women, Mignon. We are very clever, but also very stupid. I have been feeling afraid because I am not so sure as I was many months ago when I said, 'Yes, in July,' to Paolo. But for you, it is different, eh? Two men," she said with a sly smile. "This is *formidable*."

Jo flushed. "I can't believe I just blurted that out."

"Why not?" Lucienne said. "You listen to all I say, and tell too little of yourself. This is important information."

"More like confusing information."

Lucienne reached over the table to cover Jo's hand with her own. "We give to each other much to think about. I thank you for speaking the truth. And now," she said, pulling back her hand, "we go shopping, eh?" Taking some money from her bag she put it down on the table before looking out through the open door at the rainy street. Turning back, she asked, "You have plans for dinner?"

She *is* lonely, Jo realized. "Why don't we eat together at the hotel?"

At once Lucienne grew lively. "Perfect! Now, we spend money. It is good for the spirit, eh?"

16

SHE GOT TO THE HOTEL BOUTIQUE JUST BEFORE IT CLOSED, and bought three packages of the Fix-Masseau postcards. Then, back in her room, she sorted through her purchases—Fendi wallets for Beamer and her father, a gauzy blue and white Max Mara shirt for herself, and a pair of Italian-version white leather Topsiders to replace her old ones, which went directly into the trash. Then she hung away the dry cleaning and laundry that had been returned to the room in her absence, before closing herself into the shower stall.

A good forty minutes ahead of the appointed meeting time, Jo positioned herself at a small corner table in the bar to write up her notes and to take a look at the prints she'd collected from the camera shop before they'd returned to the hotel. She smiled at the images of Florella and Mai-Ling, and the shots of the train and the staff.

A good-looking man was playing quiet jazz on a grand piano at the far end of the bar. A few couples were having drinks. Outside, the rain pelted down on the terrace. A waiter came over, and she asked him what it was everyone in the bar seemed to be drinking.

"This is a Bellini," he told her. "Fresh peach juice with sparkling white wine."

"That sounds wonderful. I'll have one."

There were four small bowls on the table: one with pistachios, one with shelled hazelnuts, one with large green olives, and one with small ripe black olives. She took a black olive as she got out her address book and two packs of postcards. She wrote quickly, intermittently sipping at the drink, which was rich with the scent and taste of peaches and was a lovely pink color.

The cards done, she got out her notebook.

"Tuesday, clear in the A.M. and brilliant, hot, then rain in the afternoon; everyone huddled in sheltered parts of the piazza. Front of church w/scaffolding; repairs. Lunch, tables set out on patio near pool; buffet. Guests either very well dressed or very odd/unchic. At depot, pallet loaded with cases of Krug champagne; complete booze storeroom; special vegetarian food for passengers on request. Must ask for Cipriani menus; see VS-O-E kitchen Wed. or Thurs.; get photos of rooms, also exterior, din. rm., bar, etc. Laura says meals outside on terrace in good weather, only lunch served by pool, not dinner; chef decides daily on buffet selections. (Pick up slides Wed. aft. Maybe Thurs. for kitchen; three days prep for each trip, better Thurs. to see from start.) Told L. about H. & T., then felt stupid. Managed not to think of either one for most of day. I wish . . .'"

A hand lightly touched her shoulder, and Anne said, "Good evening, my dear."

Jo got up to kiss the woman's cheek, saying, "Hi. Will you sit with me? Did the rain ruin your day?"

"Oh, not at all. Jimmy's just having a chat with Dr. Rusconi. I'm not interrupting, am I? I see you're busy with your notes."

"I was finished." Jo swept up everything and dumped it in her bag. "Did you go to a lot of churches?"

"Several. Luckily, we got an early start. By the time the rain came I think Jimmy was secretly glad of it. He doesn't have the energy he used to. He was quite happy to come back and have his afternoon lie-down."

"Is the city the way you remember it?"

DREAM TRAIN

"It's far better. Certainly cleaner. And so many of the buildings have been restored. Jimmy's so keen on the restorations we're going to a slide show tomorrow evening, sponsored by the restoration society."

"I'm going, too. With Laura from the hotel."

"How splendid! Perhaps you'll come to dinner with us after."

"I would love that."

Jimmy appeared at the entrance to the bar, spotted his wife, and came over to say hello to Jo, then said to Anne, "It would seem we're to dine with Dr. Rusconi. He insists."

"That's good of him," Anne said.

"Very decent chap." He pulled out a chair and sat down. "Have you been to the depot?" he asked Jo.

"I went this morning. I'm rapidly becoming something of an expert on the train. It was just fascinating."

"Wouldn't have minded seeing that myself," he said. "You're not on your own for the evening, are you? We can't have you dining in solitary splendor. That wouldn't do at all."

Jo smiled at him. "I'm waiting for Lucienne. I came down early to write up my notes. And," she confided, lowering her voice, "to check out the guests. Did you *see* that woman in the black minidress with no back?"

"My dear!" Anne gave a little laugh. "I thought Jimmy was going to chase her down the corridor. But isn't it the most appalling garment you've ever seen? Horrid of me, but it truly is quite ugly."

"If you looked up ugly in the dictionary, you'd find a picture of that dress," Jo said.

Jimmy blinked, then burst out laughing. "That's very good!" he declared. "Oh, that *is* good! I really must remember that."

"He has a wicked sense of humor," Anne told Jo. "Perhaps we'll see you later on."

"Have a turn round the dance floor," Jimmy put in. "You do dance? I don't mean all that convulsive, contortionist nonsense, but actual dancing."

217

"I do a passable box step," Jo answered. "Enjoy your dinner," she said as they went off, then finished her Bellini and checked the time. Lucienne was late.

She was deliberating whether or not to call up to the room when Lucienne came striding into the bar, her angry energy galvanizing everyone into a sudden, brief silence. She paused for a moment, looking around, and everyone including Jo stared at her.

She was wearing a marvellous dress of white dotted Swiss cotton with a square-cut neckline, a close-fitting bodice, and a skirt that flared with yards of material. The sleeves were short and puffed exaggeratedly, and as she spotted Jo and came toward the table, Jo saw she was wearing a crinoline underneath. She grabbed a chair, sat down, crossed her legs, and thereby revealed layer upon layer of lace-trimmed netting. Her high heels were white leather, cut very low in the front.

"I am late! I am sorry!" She at once opened her bag for a cigarette. "What is that?" she asked of Jo's empty glass.

"A Bellini."

"Wonderful! We will have two," she told the waiter, who listened, gaping, then simply backed away.

"Your dress is heavenly."

"Thank you. I will commit a murder, or I will get drunk. I have not yet decided."

"What happened?"

Lucienne wrapped her hand around Jo's wrist, leaned across the table, and said "First, I drink, then I will talk with you. Okay?"

"Sure, fine."

Jo sat quietly, respectful of Lucienne's palpable anger, and watched people pass by in the corridor on their way to the dining room. The American family with the sunbathing daughter and frustrated young son straggled past, the boy saying, ". . . the whole morning. And then finally, *finally*, we're going to go, but it rains so you won't. I want my own table for dinner. I really do."

At the bar sat the woman in the backless dress. She was

extremely tall; several inches over six feet, fairly young, and not unattractive. But her body, which consisted of straight uninterrupted lines from shoulders to hips, was misplaced sadly in the dress. The man with her, however, seemed to like the garment, or rather, its absence. His hand stroked up and down her defenseless spine as he leaned with one elbow on the bar and spoke to her in low, insidious tones.

The Texas quartet went past, the daughter in a becomingly frilly dress that managed to disguise her bulk. "We just bought out the stores," she was saying. "Wasn't a soul around, and we had ourselves a spree. I'm goin' back tomorrow."

Beside Jo, Lucienne gulped down the Bellini, then asked the waiter for a double vodka, no ice. She lit a fresh cigarette, drew hard on it, and looked at this small American woman with her pretty doll's face—very large dark eyes; the skin of an infant, with a shine to it and genuine color in her cheeks; the mouth of a cupid; and thick dark hair cut in the style of a Dutch boy with a fringe across her forehead that tended to flow like heavy liquid back and forth from her face when she moved. At some moments she was very young; and then, most unexpectedly, she would grow serious and demonstrate a strong intelligence. She had an appreciation for clothes, Lucienne thought, but not for her own body. And so she wore the garments without certainty, as if unaware that she was nicely formed. Quite a diffident, complicated woman, yet Lucienne had confided more to her than she had to anyone in many years; they had formed a friendship, but it would come to an end Saturday when Joanna returned to London on the train. It didn't seem right, or fair, and she wondered if Joanna also had a sense of the unfairness of making a friendship with a limited future. Perhaps she had chosen to confide in her because of this limit. It was possible. Still, with the exchange of thoughts and confidences had come an understanding and even a caring that was rewarding. She wondered if Joanna had any sense of her own appeal. She had a lovely face, a sweet face, one that was like a book anyone could read. Lucienne could understand why men would wish to possess her. They would want to read themselves in her face; they would wish to make amusing remarks in order to hear her laughter, which was sweet like her face, and quite irresistible; they would be filled with desire for the very size of her—so small, but so very female. She was most American in her directness, yet not American in her openness and concern for others.

"Your grandmother, the one of the drinking water," Lucienne asked, "she was American?"

Jo pushed her hair back behind her ears. "No, she was Irish."

Look! Lucienne thought. The ears of a doll, too. "I knew it! And you were very close with her, yes?"

"Very. Why?"

"I am thinking of the ways you are American, but not. In the ways that are most important to me—I intend no insult, eh?—you are not American. And this must be because you have had an Irish grandmother."

"Could be," Jo allowed. "I've never given it much thought."

She looked again at Joanna, strongly taken by the notion that this woman was somehow half in shadow—not actually, but in spirit. She had not yet become entirely real to herself, and this was why she carried herself without pride; it was why she responded with such surprise to other people's displays of interest in her; it was perhaps also why she seemed so very young. But what a gentle person she was! And how good to look upon! If I were a man, she thought, it might be too simple to be deceived by the face into believing I could have this woman. And I would have her only to discover that this face misleads; it conceals much fear, and wisdom, and a capability of great passion. But a passion more of the mind than of the body, because Joanna has not found the connection between heart and mind.

This seemed so major a realization that Lucienne was tempted to comment on it, then thought better of it. For a woman still half in shadow, to make such an observation might cause her to return entirely into the dark. Joanna was in the process of finding her place in her own mind. And it was unwise to disturb anyone engaged in such a process. But how odd it was, she thought, that women came at different times to the finding of themselves. For herself, she had always known. For Joanna, it was coming now. It made Lucienne feel even more drawn to her, and also most protective of her.

"When do you come to Paris?" Lucienne wanted to know.

"It depends on the assignments. I don't get that many in France. But that doesn't matter. I was thinking I'd like to come visit anyway. I mean, I'd like us to stay in touch."

"I would like this, too, Mignon. It is the truth. I am just now thinking I wish to keep our friendship. So you will come to visit with me, eh?"

"Definitely."

"I have had a disastrous argument on the telephone with Paolo. He is returning immediately from Florence."

"Why?"

Lucienne drank some of the vodka, her eyes widening as the liquid flowed like clear fire down her throat. "I have told him I will *not* marry in the church with the priest and the bridal gown and the invited guests. I wish to keep the plans as we have made them. He says it is an offense to his family. I say to him I do not marry his family. He says I *do* marry his family. I say he is a child and ridiculous. He says I am stubborn and too accustomed to having my own way. I agree, and say this is so. He says he cannot have this discussion over the telephone when I am being selfish and stubborn, so he will drive from Florence immediately to speak with me in person and make me see he cannot distress the family by refusing to honor their wishes. I say he has no need to do that because I will not change my thinking. I also say that his mother and sisters deplore this marriage and believe he has gone mad to wish to marry me, and why doesn't he see this when it is the truth. He says I am hysterical because it is the wrong time of the month. And I go absolutely crazy and tell him he is a pretty little pig and if I am bleeding or not it has nothing to do with my brain. We scream at each other. And now he is returning to Venice. I will kill him! At this moment, I despise him. If he comes here, I will be out. I will not see him. I have tried to telephone to my friend in Portofino, thinking I will go there to visit for a few days, but my friend is not at home. So I will have to stay here to argue more with Paolo. And then I will kill him.''

''Oh, boy,'' Jo said softly.

''Yes, oh, boy,'' Lucienne muttered. ''You are quite right, Joanna, when you say what you do this afternoon. It is a mistake to marry the little boy. I was dreaming. I was not in my right head, only thinking I am tired of being alone. Imagine saying to me I must be deranged in my thinking because I have a period! Only a man would say something so stupid, so insulting! I am going to have to meet with him, and I dread it. It is unbelievable that I would dread seeing Paolo when yesterday I was going to marry him.''

''You might feel differently when you see him.''

''But of course I will. Because when I see him, I will like the look of him, and he will persuade me, and I will wish to make love with him because he is Italian, after all, and very handsome. I should have remained in Paris.''

''Maybe I shouldn't have said anything,'' Jo said guiltily.

''This is not your fault!'' Lucienne said sharply. ''You spoke the truth, but *you* don't decide for me. You help me to decide for myself. I am *grateful* for this. I don't *blame* you.''

''I still feel guilty.''

Lucienne shook her head, her eyes filling. ''No. Don't feel this way.'' She blinked away the tears, grabbed her glass and drank down the vodka in one gulp.

''Jesus!'' Jo said. ''How can you *do* that?''

''Because I am a crazy, hysterical woman who bleeds with her brain!'' she said, then laughed ''How ridiculous! How absolutely ridiculous!''

''We should go eat,'' Jo suggested, catching the waiter's eye and gesturing for the tab.

''It is *so* insulting,'' Lucienne persevered. ''It is the greatest insult, don't you think?''

''Are you kidding? I'd murder a guy who made a dumb-ass remark like that.''

"So you agree with me?" she asked in almost pleading fashion.

"Damned right, I agree with you. It takes guts to do what you did, Lucienne." The waiter brought the check and Jo signed it, adding in a tip. Lucienne was so distraught she didn't notice. "I made us a reservation," Jo told her. "And you should eat something."

"Joanna," Lucienne said quietly, her awareness returning, "I have not made a fool of myself here, have I?"

"No way! I'll tell you something my Irish grandmother used to say to me. She told me there was never any point in worrying about what other people might think of you because other people were always way too busy worrying about what *you* might think of *them*."

"I like your grandmother," Lucienne said with a watery smile.

"You'd have loved her. Let's go eat now. That's also good for the spirit."

"You were worried I would get drunk, eh, Mignon?" Lucienne said after dinner. They'd chosen to sit near the piano player, who shifted after the cocktail hour from the small bar adjoining the dining room to this larger one down the hall. "I think this makes you nervous."

"When people drink, I'm always afraid they're going to hurt themselves. Or that they're going to drink so much they change character and become someone I don't know."

"This has happened?"

"A few times. There was this once, when I was about fourteen. I came home from a date one night, and my mother was sitting in the dark in the living room with a full glass in her hand. I let myself into the house and jumped a mile at the sound of Lily's voice coming at me from out of the silence of this pitch-dark room. She told me not to turn on the lights. 'You can sit down and keep me company for a minute if you like, but I don't want you to see me,' she said. It gave me chills, but I went to sit on the edge of the sofa, listening very intently as if to compensate for being unable to see much

223

more than shadows, and hearing only the clink of ice cubes as Lily drank. We didn't talk. I just sat there, waiting. And after a while Lily started to cry. I didn't know what to do, so I sat there while the minutes ticked off on this four-hundred-day clock on the mantel, and my mother drank and wept. I felt like the guardian of Lily's secret misery, and I was determined to stay there in case she needed me. But finally, as she stumbled over to the bar to refill her glass, she spoke to me in this hoarse, totally unfamiliar voice. 'Go to bed, Joey,' she said. 'Nothing's going to happen.' And I said, 'No, that's okay. I'll just sit here.' I was convinced she'd need me. But she said, 'Go to bed, Joanna! Everyone has the right to be disgustingly self-pitying once in a while. Nothing's going to happen, so go to bed. I'll see you in the morning.' I asked her if anything had happened. 'Where's Dad?' I asked. And in this very harsh voice, she said, 'Don't be tedious! I want to indulge myself without being obliged to explain. *Please!* Go to bed!' So, feeling rebuked, I said okay and got up, and as if it was any other night, I said, 'Goodnight, Mom.' And, amazingly, sounding normal, she said, 'Goodnight, Joey. Sleep tight.' In the morning, when I came downstairs, there wasn't the slightest bit of evidence that the scene the night before had actually happened. Even bombed, Lily cleaned up after herself.''

"I am a good drinker," Lucienne said. "I don't drink too much, and I don't change. So there is no need to be worried, okay?"

"Okay."

Jimmy and Anne came in. Jimmy marched directly up to Lucienne and, with a bit of a bow, said, "A dance, Mademoiselle?"

"I would love it," Lucienne responded gaily.

Anne slipped into Lucienne's place beside Jo, and the two of them watched Jimmy and Lucienne dance.

"He's terrific," Jo said, noting the grace and control with which he directed Lucienne around the floor, her skirt lifting to reveal the lacy crinoline.

"A lovely dancer," Anne agreed. "And so is your friend.

224

When I was young, I'd have resented her," she said frankly. "Her beauty and her effortless charm would have undone me. One of the good things about age is the perspective one gains, and the tolerance we develop toward those we see as more appealing than ourselves."

"I'll bet you were every bit as beautiful as she is. And I can't honestly imagine you resenting anyone."

"Don't paint me in too saintly colors, my dear," Anne cautioned. "We're all human and plagued by small personal demons." She looked again at her husband and Lucienne, then in an undertone said, "She's not well, is she?"

"What makes you say that?"

"She carries herself with extreme care. I think I must have appeared very much as she does just before I had surgery many years ago. I went about for months with the sense that any sudden motion would create chaos inside me, everything would be jarred loose. It was," she explained, "an ectopic pregnancy. I was forty-four and had no idea I was pregnant. It simply didn't seem possible. I thought I was premenopausal, and there I was pregnant. In any case, it was most painful. I do hope she's looking after herself."

"I'm working on her, nagging a lot."

"Good for you! What a kind girl you are!"

"I don't know about that. It just doesn't make sense to ignore a physical problem."

The little American boy poked his head around the doorway, spotted the pianist, and stood listening. He looked small and lonely and bored, and Jo felt sorry for him. He was having a rotten vacation. With a glance around to see if he was being observed, he slid inside and sat down at the table nearest the door, his fingers beating out the tempo on the tabletop.

"That poor kid's having such a lousy time," Jo said, pointing him out to Anne. "Nobody in his family wants to do anything but hang around the pool or play tennis. And all he wants is to get into the city and see everything."

"Seems a terrible waste, doesn't it, to come all this way

and not see the city? Dear, cheeky little face he has, don't you think?''

"He's adorable," Jo agreed. "I feel like adopting him."

"He'd probably like to be adopted. Although more than once I've come across children who deserved far better than the families they had only to have the children defend those families quite violently."

"I know what you mean." She was about to wonder aloud where his family might be when they stepped into the doorway. The father made an angry jerking motion with his arm, and with a show of reluctance the boy got up and, after a last look at the piano player, went off with his family. Both parents could be heard berating the boy as they traveled down the corridor.

"Would you like to have children?" Anne asked.

"I've never thought so," Jo admitted, "but sometimes I see babies—at the supermarket, or being pushed around in a stroller—and I get this awful kind of aching feeling, and I want to pick them up and hold them. I probably won't have any." She smiled at Anne. "You need a man around, if only to get a baby started."

At that moment Lucienne and Jimmy returned to the table.

"Will you dance, darling?" Jimmy asked his wife.

"In a bit. Why not have your cognac now?"

"Good idea," he said and, breathing heavily, sank into his chair.

Mysteriously, Anne took hold of Jo's hand under the table and gave it a gentle squeeze.

17

HER DREAMS THAT NIGHT WERE MUDDLED AND UPSETTING, and revolved around Henry. In various scenarios that took place in his house, yet didn't look at all like it, they talked and talked without arriving at any agreement. At one point she curled up comfortably on Henry's bed, her arms wrapped around a heavy comforter, and dozed while Henry laughed and told her he'd better take her home. Her dream self managed to get her eyes open and to protest that she'd been waiting for ages and had no intention of going home now when they'd been planning this evening for weeks. He'd already canceled out several times, she reminded him, and then when they'd finally set a date, he'd kept her waiting for so long that she'd fallen asleep. He laughed again and said he was merely testing her interest. She kept her eyes closed while he talked, sensing his approach. He plucked the comforter from her arms and kissed her closed eyes before fitting his body against hers. The strength of her reservations and her awareness of underlying motives on both their parts distressed her, and she struggled lethargically under the weight of his body. Yet even while she pushed at him, he made her laugh, and she had to wonder how she could laugh when he made her uncomfortable in so many ways.

The alarm went off at six. She got up, still caught in the muddled mood of her dreams, plugged in the Melitta, and went to shower while the water dripped through the coffee in the paper cone. She hadn't thought to ask for a newspaper and didn't feel like reading either of the novels she'd brought along, so she slid open the doors and sat out on the shrub-enclosed patio to write a couple of notes—one to Laura saying she'd go see the kitchens tomorrow, and one for Lucienne telling her she'd be spending the day looking around before returning to dress for the slide show in the evening. The notes done, she sipped at the coffee and examined the differences between herself, Giovanna, and Laura. They were all on the job, yet of the three of them Laura was the one most outwardly role-playing, Giovanna the least. She herself was somewhere in the middle, tending to drift occasionally toward either pole. Did people actually see her change, she wondered, the way she'd seen Laura change? Did it matter if they did? And why was she all at once so obsessed with the issue?

All those years ago Lily had put a camera into her hands and said, "This is who you are." And because she'd wanted to please her mother, even to emulate her, she'd accepted the camera and the career that eventually went with it. Undeniably, she was someone who saw the world best and most clearly through a lens. But was that the sum total of Joanna James? Who the hell was she when she wasn't on the job? Was she really someone Henry could fall in love with? Was that what she wanted? The only answer she had was the regular little interior surge she felt now every time she thought of him. But did a small surge constitute the basis for caring in the long term? Who's Joanna anyway? she wondered. She's this woman who falls for babies in strollers; a woman who'd sleep with two men she likes and then run away from both of them; a woman who wasted four years of her life on a guy like Greg, waiting for the approval he was never going to give her, because he was too much like Lily on that score: incapable of demonstrating either love or approval in any overt way. God! Was that the truth?

She sat forward in the chair, both hands holding the coffee cup as, eyes on the patio flagstones, she closely examined this possibility. She was what Lily had told her to be, but Lily had never once come right out and said it was good or bad. And she'd played for a time at actually *being* Lily by burying herself in a hole with Greg. He'd never have married her although she'd always thought it was a possible option; he'd never have been willing to give her even that much approval. So she'd not only played at being Lily by involving herself in a hopeless affair, she'd compounded the game by selecting someone with whom to become involved who was a strong Lily type—with unfocused talent, with a deficient ego, and with a limitless well of resentment.

I'm not Lily! she told herself angrily. I tried it once and it didn't work. And since she died, I've been stumbling around, lost without my role model. Hell, I don't *want* to be Lily! I'm me. And just lately I've started getting close to knowing who I am. That's what's been happening; that's what the invisibility's been about. Well, okay! she thought, feeling strengthened. *Okay!*

By eight she was on her way to the lobby where she left the notes for Laura and Lucienne. The only other person waiting for the hotel motor launch was the young American boy, who said, "Hi. The boat ought to be here any minute. I just missed it before, so I've been hanging around waiting."

"Hi. Going over to have a look around?"

"Better believe it." He looked at the camera around her neck and the Lowe-pro over her shoulder and asked, "You gonna take pictures?"

"I sure am." She gave him a smile. "It's my first chance since I got here."

"Yeah, mine too. You professional?"

"Uh-huh."

"Going anywhere in particular?" He leaned comfortably against the wrought-iron gate, one Nike-shod foot propped on the other.

"Nope. Just where my feet take me, starting on the far side of the piazza."

"Me, too," he said, eyes scanning the water.

He was a very cute kid, she thought. Sandy blond hair, big round long-lashed brown eyes, freckle-splashed tidy nose, and a wide smile over teeth in the process of being straightened. He was wearing a short-sleeved white cotton shirt, Levi's, sweat socks, and the Nikes.

"Where are you from?" she asked him, thinking she couldn't possibly find a more perfect companion for the day. She had a need all at once to spend some time with someone whose view of the world was still forming, and whose opinions would be fresh. Since her conversation with herself on the patio, she'd been feeling lighter and younger and filled with curiosity about herself. With this boy she'd have no need of hats of any kind. She'd be able to be whoever she was and possibly get a fix on Lily's daughter now that she'd finally reconciled herself to the fact that Lily was gone for all time. Poor unhappy Lily with her needlepoint, her uncontrollable husband, and her compulsive cleaning.

"Indianapolis. Where're you from?"

"Connecticut."

"I've been there. We went with my dad for his twentieth reunion at Yale. You been to Yale?"

"I've seen it."

"It was cool. I think I'll probably go there when I graduate."

"Really? What grade are you in?"

"Going into tenth in September," he answered. "Surprised, right? Thought I was maybe in seventh or eighth. Right?"

"Right."

"Wrong. I know I look about eight, but I'm fourteen. Probably have arrested hormones or something: Pediatrician's been telling my mother forever that I'll have like this big growth spurt any time now. It worries the hell out of her that I'm a notch away from being a midget." He gave a little laugh. "Myself, I figure there are lots worse things than being short."

"Of course there are," Jo agreed. "And you're not *that* short."

"Right. But it's like this really major thing with her, you know? The way she sees it, my getting good grades and having a pretty decent bunch of friends are just kind of compensations. Like I'm an overachiever, and the guys I hang around with feel sorry for me. What crap! She likes to have something to worry about, so I let her believe all that stuff."

"Are you one of those brains who never studies and always pulls straight A's?"

"Oh, I study all right. Not like all the time or anything, but I put in the hours. How long've you been a professional?"

"I sold my first photographs when I was seventeen. In terms of a career, it's about fourteen years."

"Seventeen, huh?"

"Yup. Sold some stuff to the local newspaper. It was great."

"What kind of stuff?"

"Snow scenes. We had a big storm on the East Coast that year. I went out with my little brother and took pictures of frozen wires, abandoned cars, Beamer—that's my brother—making snow angels, all kinds of stuff. The paper used three of the shots in its front-page feature about the storm. Paid me a hundred and fifty dollars, which was a fortune back then. The only snag was I didn't know anything, and I let them buy the copyrights. Still, it was a big thrill. I used the money to buy an enlarger, so I could have my own darkroom in the basement."

"What does that mean, about the copyrights?"

"It meant the paper owned the rights, so I couldn't sell the pictures anywhere else. And the thing is, one of the shots got picked up by a wire service and went national. I figure the paper made a nice little profit on that deal, even if I did get the exposure. Since they owned the copyrights, they didn't even have to give me the credit, but they did. They were being kind, I guess, because I was just a kid."

"Must've been a good picture."

"Must've been. See, the thing is it's very hard to shoot in snow, because of the light. If you don't get the exposure just right, all you come out with is a dark blob and some glare."

"No kidding."

"Uh-huh."

"I never knew that. I always thought you just point the camera and take the picture."

"That's about what most people think. And with the automatic cameras, that's pretty well what happens. Except that even with the automatics, the built-in light meters take a reading that'll be accurate in the normal situation. But in a high-light situation, those TTL meters go crazy."

"What's TTL?"

"Through the lens. It's another way of saying built-in."

"Oh. Hey! Here comes the boat." He pushed away from the gate and looked away over the water. "It's about time," he said, turning back to her. "Fourteen years. How old're you, anyway? You look about twenty-five, maybe."

She smiled. "Thirty-six."

"No way! My mom's only five years older than you."

"Pretty old, huh?"

"You don't look that old at all. What's your name? I'm Jackie Watts, by the way." He wiped his open palm on his Levi's before offering his hand.

"Joanna James. Call me Jo."

He gave her hand a hearty shake and said, "Hi. It's really nice to meet you."

"It's really nice to meet you, too. Would you be interested in coming along with me? I mean, since neither of us has a set destination, we might as well head off together."

"Great! I can watch you take your pictures. Maybe I'll learn a few things. Blow dad's brain when I tell him how to improve his stuff. He's got one of those little Minolta jobs. It even loads the film. All he has to do is drop it into the back of the camera, and the thing starts to click and whirr. Amazing."

Once in the boat, Jo automatically moved to stand at the rear, and Jackie followed suit.

"Isn't it great!" he said over the noise of the motor. "I've never *seen* such a great place! I read all about it when Dad said we were going to come, got a zillion books from the library and read up on the floods in 'sixty-six and 'sixty-seven, and all the restoration and preservation work they've been doing since then; all about the carnival, and the algae problems in the lagoons. Did you know that Venice is probably the safest city in the whole of Italy? They've never even had one case of kidnapping. Nobody gets mugged. Hardly any crime here at all. And the real estate's worth an absolute fortune. There's also a ghetto. Did you know that?"

"No, I didn't." She turned to look at him. "We should definitely go see that."

"Definitely. Except I don't know where it is, and I forgot to bring my map."

"No problem. I've got one in my purse."

"Great! This is going to be great!" He was practically dancing with excitement.

She swung around and took a shot of him, then lowered the camera with a smile.

"Hey! You took my picture. Are you going to put me in a book or something?"

"I'm not doing a book, just a feature on the Orient-Express, and the hotel."

"They're owned by the same company, aren't they? Have you been on the train?"

"I came to Venice on it, and I'll be going back to London on the train Saturday morning."

"Is it sensational? What's it like?"

"It's fabulous. And the food is beyond belief. You'd love it."

"I *begged* my mom and dad to ride that train. But no. We're *flying* to London from here. It takes too long, my dad said. Not 'It costs too much,' because he couldn't get away with that one. I mean, figure what four first-class tickets round-trip have to cost from Indy to New York to Venice,

Venice to London, London to home. A fortune. We could've gone economy or even business class and had a ride on the train. But no, it would take too long. These people have no sense of adventure. I mean *none*. I mapped out this entire trip, right, with side trips to Florence and Rome; then a ride on the train to Paris; then a boat over to England, and a ride on an English train to London. I mean, think of all the stuff you could see. And what does he do? He says, 'That's nice, Jackie,' then gets this travel agent who books all his business trips, right? And she has no goddamned imagination. Four first-class tickets with as few stopovers as possible. Because he's this busy executive who doesn't want to waste any time. It's such bullshit. We've got an entire *month*. And one week's already shot with the two of them playing tennis and Wonder Dummy out by the pool defying the holes in the ozone layer. I mean, that girl uses *cooking oil*, for chrissake! She'll probably croak from massive skin cancers before she's twenty. Seriously! She wants to go home with this major tan to wow her girlfriends. Like a *Venetian tan*! Get it? I can't believe I was actually *born* into this family! No shit! They're time-sharing a brain, but they can never remember whose day it is."

Jo burst out laughing, then apologized. "I'm sorry. I'm sure it's sheer hell for you, but you've got a very funny way of expressing yourself."

"Oh, that's okay." He grinned at her, revealing two rows of metal braces. "I know. If you don't laugh, you could get ulcers."

He scampered off the boat and then, with a touching display of gallantry, turned and held out his hand to assist her ashore.

"Will you look at this!" he crowed. "You could break down and cry over a place that looks like this, no shit. What should we do first?"

"I think we should get some breakfast. By the time we've eaten, things should be open. You haven't eaten yet, have you?"

"Nope."

"Do you see any restaurants that look open?"

"Bound to be some on the other side of the square." He started off then turned back and said, "Listen, you want me to carry any of that stuff for you?"

Her first instinct was to say no, but he seemed so anxious to help that she swung the camera bag off her shoulder and let him take it.

"What's in here?" he asked as they crossed the square.

"Lenses, film, filters. I'll tell you what," she said, inspired. "I'll show you the different lenses and you can hand them to me when I need them. I'll teach you how to clean them, too."

"Okay, cool."

"There's a place just up here where we had drinks yesterday. Maybe it's open."

"I thought you said this was your first chance to look around."

"It is. I had to come over yesterday afternoon to buy a new camera. My other one had a nervous breakdown and died."

He chuckled and patted the side of the Lowe-pro. "Pretty funny yourself, Joey old girl."

She mussed his hair saying, "All my best friends call me Joey automatically. So I guess you're going to be one of my new best friends, Jackie old boy."

"Fine by me. What magazine's your story gonna be in?"

"A trade publication called *Travelogue*. Make sure you give me your address, and I'll have the magazine send you a copy."

"When's it coming out?"

"I'm not sure, probably February or March."

"This place isn't open yet." Jackie rattled the doorknob. "Guess we'll have to keep on looking. D'you *believe* how amazing this place is?" he asked, craning to look at the upper levels of the buildings they passed. "The trick is to follow the yellow guide signs. I read that you absolutely can't get lost if you follow the arrows. See!" He pointed out one of the signs appended to the wall of a building they were approaching. "That way to the Rialto. Wanna go that way?"

"Sure."

"Great!"

After several turnings they came to an open restaurant. They stopped to look at the menu posted outside.

"What d'you think that means?" she asked Jackie. "The exact same things on both sides of the menu, but two different prices."

"Oh, that's easy. The lower price is what you pay if you eat standing up. The higher price is if you want to sit down."

"Are you sure?"

"Positive. I'm telling you, I read *everything*. This is my first trip to Europe, you know."

"Is that so?"

"Yup. And next time I'm coming alone, without Wonder Dummy and the Two Stooges."

"You shouldn't talk about your family that way," she laughed.

"Keeps 'em humble. If you want to sit down, I don't mind. It's up to you."

"How about if we sit down, but we eat quickly? Sound fair?"

"Sure. That's fair."

They entered the restaurant and looked at the cheeses and cold cuts and breads and prepared sandwiches, trying to decide.

"I think I'm going to have one of those sandwiches," Jackie said. "And some espresso. I love those little cups."

"Makes you feel seriously mature, right?"

"Believe it. I've got this like major caffeine addiction. I *love* coffee. Especially first thing in the morning. I drink a couple of cups, then go stand outside to wait for the schoolbus, and I'm like *vibrating*. No kidding. All the guys I know are drinking Cokes, right, and I'm having coffee. They think I'm mondo weird, right, but I don't care. It gets me really revved, and I like it. These are the same guys, you know, who think it's major cool to drink their parents' booze and smoke J's. Then they spend the next three hours doing the old technicolor yawn. Dorks. Me, I have a couple of coffees and I'm set. Can't stand smoking; dope makes me heave. I don't mind a beer. Beer's okay, if it's good stuff and not the shit you buy at the supermarket. I mean, *imported* stuff like Tuborg, or Kronenbourg. Course I have to yack it up with old Dad and pretend we're into all this manly macho crap so he'll break into his supply and let me have one of his beers.

"Lemme ask you something. How come people grow up and turn so goddamned stupid? I mean, okay, not everybody comes out brain-damaged. You're not; you're really all right. But you should check out my family. My dad was Phi Beta Kappa at Yale. Meet him and you wouldn't buy that on a dare; you sure as hell wouldn't buy shoelaces from him. This is the same guy who, as a teenager, invested in Xerox in 1964. Feature it, *Xerox*. He totally cleaned up. Can you imagine that? This is the same guy who has conversations with my mom or with Wonder Dummy you wouldn't credit. I mean, he sounds like Eddie Murphy doing Mr. Rogers. I want to hire people to come check up on me in twenty years, and if I'm all vegged out and worrying about shit like snow-blowers and Toro lawn mowers, they've got to bounce my head off a wall a couple or three times to get me straight. You know?"

"I know."

The aproned man behind the counter went to make Jackie's espresso and Jo's cappuccino while a waitress brought over their sandwiches and two thin paper napkins. She smiled, as if in recognition, and Jo understood that the woman thought Jackie was her son. Jo liked it; it occurred to her that she wouldn't mind being mother to a boy like this. He was bright and funny and terrifically alive.

"I'll bet your folks are crazy about you."

"Why d'you say that?" he asked, looking suspiciously at his sandwich before picking up half.

"Because if I was your mother, I would be."

"Oh, yeah, but that's because you don't have to live with me. If you lived with me, you probably wouldn't see me or hear me, just the way she doesn't. I mean, they're not bad people or anything," he qualified. "I don't want to give the wrong impression. It's just that the stuff that's really important to them is totally inconsequential." He took a tentative bite of the sandwich, chewed, swallowed, said, "This is good," and proceeded to wolf down the rest while Jo watched. "I'm gonna get another one," he announced, then got up and walked with a springy step over to the counter where, with a big smile, he asked politely for another of the same. "I'm usually very fussy about what I eat," he told her, returning to the table. "When we all go to like Mc-Donald's or Burger King, I eat the salads. I wouldn't touch a Big Mac or a Whopper if you paid me. I'll bet you the next report from the surgeon general's gonna tell us junk food causes cancer."

"Everything does, from the sound of it."

"Right. So I'm very careful about my food. Which is probably why I'm not six two like my Dad. He grew up on Wonder Bread and Twinkies. Stuff's probably loaded with steroids. I mean, feature it." He started to laugh. "He didn't eat all that processed crap when he was growing up, he'd probably be a dwarf like me. Hey! Great title, right? *Dwarf Like Me*—the chilling sequel to *Short Like Me.*"

"You're not a dwarf, for God's sake."

"Okay, short."

"Maybe a little. D'you hate it?" she asked him.

"Not hate. I'm just tired of hearing about it, so you get into the joke routines, you know."

The waitress returned to the table with the coffees, and Jo indicated which went where.

Jackie said, *"Grazie, Signora,"* and the waitress pinched his cheek and said something endearing in Italian. Jackie blushed and pinched the waitress's cheek. The woman laughed loudly and went off behind the counter, telling the counterman in Italian about what had happened.

"Great people!" Jackie said, starting on the second sandwich. "I'm having the best goddamned time. Aren't you going to eat that?"

"Yes, I am." Jo picked up her sandwich, which was a rich white cheese on bread with green and black olives baked into it.

"What is that?" Jackie asked, looking suspicious again.

"I think it's fontina cheese. And the bread is heaven, with olives baked in. Want to taste?"

"No, thanks. Too much salt in olives. It's bad for you, causes hardening of the arteries and makes you retain water."

"I'll take my chances."

"Well, maybe just a little taste."

"Go ahead." She pushed the plate with the second half of the sandwich across the table.

"It *is* good," he said, returning the plate. "But it's still not good for you."

"If you worry so much about things when you're only fourteen, maybe you'll be so worried by the time you're thirty you won't be able to have any fun anymore."

He paused in his chewing to stare at her. "Jesus! You think so?"

"It's a possibility."

"Boy, that's scary! I'd hate that."

"Kids're supposed to eat junk and drink their parents' booze and then throw up. They're supposed to sneak cigarettes and then cough their hearts out. I did all that stuff and it didn't wreck me."

"Yeah?"

"Sure. You know how tiny babies can survive diseases and illnesses that would kill adults? It's because they have special built-in genetic protection. And I think it's the same for teenagers. I used to smoke with my girlfriends, but I never got into the habit. And I definitely used to raid the booze supply when my folks were out. But I didn't turn out to be an alcoholic. I don't know about the Big Macs and Twinkies, but that's only because when I was little my granny always told me never to eat hamburgers in restaurants. She implied it was seriously dangerous, and I believed her. So the only burgers I ever ate were ones my father barbecued, or that I made myself when I was a student. Now, I hardly ever eat red meat. The thing is, it's experimentation, Jackie, that's all.''

''You're pretty sharp,'' he said. ''I kind of thought so yesterday when you were taking pictures of everybody at breakfast. I made up this whole story about how you were like from the *National Enquirer*, getting the scoop on the guests.''

''The *Enquirer*? God! Do you *read* that?''

''Are you kidding? Every time I go to the supermarket with my mom, while she's in the check-out line, I head right for the rag racks they have by the cash registers and check out the Werewolf Family, and the movie-star anorexic who stabbed her manager in the hand with a pair of scissors, and the latest on Joan Collins, and all those rubes who've gone for rides in UFOs. It's the best, the absolutely best in comedy. They should have like special awards for the year's weirdest as-told-to stories, not to mention all those features about miracle diets where some totally obese guy lost four hundred pounds. Now he's down to only eight hundred and twenty.'' He started to laugh, his face twisting. ''Boy!'' he chortled, slapping his hand on the tabletop. ''I *love* that stuff, love it!''

''You're terrific,'' she told him. ''We're going to have ourselves a truly great day.''

''Count on it! Are you going to eat the other half of that?''

In answer she pushed the plate back across the table to him. She'd been right, she congratulated herself as she watched him eat. She'd picked someone to spend the day with who was exactly the companion she needed. She felt real and visible and happy, and closer to an insight into her own identity than she'd ever been.

''I wish I'd known you when I was fourteen, Jackie.''

''Oh, yeah?''

''Honestly. We'd have had a lot of fun.''

''Yeah,'' he agreed. ''Except that girls who look like you all hang out with jocks, not with the twerp brigade.''

''Not all of us.''

"Hey!" he exclaimed. "Keep that up and next thing you know you'll be giving me like serious hope for the future."

"Well, you should have. You're a seriously terrific guy."

"Maybe I'll get into a thing for older women." He did a Groucho bit with his eyebrows, one finger laid across his upper lip. "Say the magic word, sister, and the duck'll lay a hundred on you."

She laughed and went back to her half sandwich.

18

THE TRAFFIC THROUGH THE DOGE'S PALACE WAS STRICTLY one-way, with rope barriers and arrows to point out the route. This early in the day there weren't many people, so Jo was able to stop at the top of the stairs to shoot the gilt latticework above and the stonework and painted panels of the ceiling over the stairwell. Marble columns and lintels supporting statuary; ceilings thickly crusted with gilded stucco work in elaborate classical designs surrounding painted panels of religious significance; vast windows opening onto courtyards and affording unimpaired views of the canal and of the piazza; the great echoey cavern of the Sala del Maggior Consiglio with Tintoretto's *Il Paradiso* occupying an entire wall at the far end.

"It's the largest oil painting in the world," Jackie told her. "Cool, huh?"

When the guards weren't looking, Jo leaned far out one of the windows to take a picture of the Bridge of Sighs connecting the palace to the dungeons. Then they continued on through the unfurnished rooms, down stone steps into the dungeons.

"This is creepy," Jackie said quietly, with his hand to his head, measuring the low height of the heavy cell doors.

"Short people. You could like *never* break out of this place."
Tentatively, he touched the iron grillwork over the cell windows, then peered in to study the writing on the walls.

It was a relief to emerge into the sunlight of the courtyard, where he watched as she took close-ups of the stonework and the clockface, then they both stood looking up, turning slowly to take it all in: domes, more statuary perched improbably upon pointed spires; arches and decorative stonework at the roof, rainspouts; and boarded-off areas where restoration work was underway.

Back in the piazza people were milling about, snapping each other's pictures in the center, posing for one of the street photographers, or buying Venezia T-shirts and tacky souvenirs from the vendors.

"It's the most beautiful city I've ever seen," Jo said in reverent tones.

"We can get a vaporetto that'll take us to the ghetto. Then we could walk back from there. I'm not sure of the number of the boat, but there's a ticket place where we could ask."

Jo agreed, and they walked back to the canal. Again, very politely, Jackie asked his questions, bought their tickets, then told her, "He says to wait right here. Are you having a great time? I am. This is *so* cool. My folks never do anything spontaneous."

"I am having a fine time," she assured him, turning to take a shot of one of the exquisite lamp standards with its four lilac-tinted glass globes. Removing the telephoto, she handed it to him. Treating it respectfully, he replaced the lens cap, stowed it in the bag, and gave her the 50-mm.

"You learn fast," she complimented him.

"Easy as pie." He gave the side of the bag a pat. "Makes me feel kind of—official."

"Well, you are. You're my official lens handler."

"All right!" he laughed.

Once on board the vaporetto, she remained standing in order to get shots of the boats on the canal and the buildings lining either side. Efficiently, Jackie dealt with the lenses, cleaning them before replacing the caps, watching her all the while, intrigued.

"Boy," he said as they left the boat, "you see everything. I mean everything. All the other people, they're walking along looking left and right, but you, you're looking up, down, sideways, and close up. Oh, boy! Here it is."

An oblong yellow sign in Hebrew and Italian was fixed to the wall over a low square stone archway. Another sign beside it read HOSPEDALE PEDIATRICO.

"Well, that's good," Jackie said. "If I get sick, you can just drop me at the children's hospital on the way."

They went through the dark tunnel and along a walkway, emerging into a small square. To the left was a very tall building with few areas of plaster remaining on its facade; the red brick beneath was exposed, and the shutters stood open on most of the windows. Two of the second-floor windows had boxes filled with healthy red geraniums. A lone blue shirt hung on a clothesline. It was a sad-looking building, and Jo backed away to take a wide-angle shot that included the capped wellhead in the center of the square.

Following the arrows, they passed more neglected buildings that nevertheless had a certain grim beauty.

"It's one of the poorest areas of Venice," Jackie informed her, looking around. "Only about eight hundred Jewish people still live here. According to the stuff I read, the word 'ghetto' comes from the Italian *getto* which means to cast metals. See, there was a foundry here where they made cannons, right. Then, I think it was like the fourteenth century, they gave the Jews permission to live here, and they called it the 'ghetto.' It was the very first ghetto in the entire world. Did you know that?"

"No," she said, impressed by the amount of reading and research he'd done, "I didn't know any of that."

"Yeah, well, this is it." Eyes narrowed, he said, "Pretty depressing place. They had gates over those archways there, so people couldn't leave. And there's a wall around here somewhere with inscriptions. Supposedly, it's just outside, so I guess if we keep going that way"—he pointed across the square they'd just entered—"it'll be over there."

As they came out on the far side, Jackie said, "Here it is! I told you!" and ran over to the wall.

Jo followed, and looked first at the seven bronze bas-relief panels on the exposed-brick wall, and then at the two panels of writing on the same wall just beyond a wood and ornamental iron gateway. The larger of the two panels was in French, Italian, and English and read:

MEN, WOMEN, CHILDREN, MASSES FOR THE GAS CHAMBERS ADVANCING TOWARD HORROR BENEATH THE WHIP OF THE EXECUTIONER. YOUR SAD HOLOCAUST IS ENGRAVED IN HISTORY AND NOTHING SHALL PURGE YOUR DEATHS FROM OUR MEMORIES. FOR OUR MEMORIES ARE YOUR ONLY GRAVE.

The smaller plaque, also in three languages, read:

THE CITY OF VENICE REMEMBERS THE VENETIAN JEWS WHO WERE DEPORTED TO THE NAZI CONCENTRATION CAMPS ON DECEMBER 5TH, 1943, AND AUGUST 17TH, 1944.

The pictorial plaques were impressionistic depictions of massed bodies; a sole naked figure standing before an overcoated firing squad; crucified figures.

Backing away, she lifted the camera only to find herself unable to see. Tears ran from her eyes, warping the view.

"You okay?" Jackie put his hand on her arm.

She nodded, reaching into her purse for a tissue.

"Pretty goddamned terrible, huh?" he said, his hand still on her arm, his eyes on the wall.

Her voice thick, she said, "It makes me so furious when I think there are morons who go public saying none of it ever happened, that it's all propaganda."

"You kidding?"

"I'm *not* kidding," she said hotly. "Assholes who say

nobody ever got gassed in a shower, or cremated, or thrown into a mass grave. God, but it makes me mad!'' She raised the camera again and took shots of the whole wall, then close-ups. Then, shaking her head, she said, ''I've had enough. What about you?''

''Yeah, me too.''

As they were strolling along in the hot sun, she said, ''I'm sorry about that.''

''Oh, that's okay. It got to me, too. I felt like crying myself.''

She put her arm around his shoulders and hugged him against her side.

''You're one swell kid.''

''So're you.'' He put his arm around her waist and gave her a squeeze, which made her laugh. ''I'll bet you go home and you never have even one picture that has you in it. Right?''

''Right.''

''Why don't you show me what to do, and I'll take your photograph?''

''God, I look terrible in pictures.''

''Be real!'' he argued. ''Come on. Stand right here and let me do it.''

''Okay,'' she gave in. ''I'll set everything so all you have to do is turn the focusing ring here until what you're seeing is clear. Have a look.'' She gave him the camera. ''Focus on that guy sitting outside that shop there.''

He did as she said, then exclaimed, ''This is really cool! Okay. Stand where you are and give me a big veggie-burger.''

She smiled. He made the exposure, then returned the camera. ''I could really get into this,'' he said, jamming his hands into his back pockets. ''Maybe I'll sign up for the camera club this year, buy myself a camera and start snapping away. It's even worth extra credit if you take it as an option course. I could cash in a couple of my bonds, get set up. I might just do that.''

''You have bonds?''

"Oh, sure. So does Wonder Dummy. We got them for being born. I come from a family that believes heavily in liquidity, kiddo. You're nothing if you don't have tangible assets. Wonder Dummy's already used up most of her money on clothes but I've still got almost all of mine."

They went on, following the yellow signs, occasionally ducking down laneways that dead-ended at canals, then doubling back to continue on while she photographed a pair of doorbells that had been built into the mouths of two tiny brass lion's heads; gracious balconied dwellings with boats moored outside; a picture of the Virgin in a flower-decked niche behind an ornamental grille; an ornate antique watering trough that was still functioning; a bricked-in doorway at the end of an extremely narrow passage; dozens of noble stone heads positioned at the apex of archways or the undersides of windows; squares with newspaper kiosks, and squares with displays of fresh flowers in buckets, and squares with outdoor cafés; a pair of exquisite gondolas with armchairs and pillows, the pair tethered to the underside of a bridge; a restaurant situated on a bridge over a secondary canal, with yellow and white striped umbrellas protecting the diners from the midday sun; lines of washing suspended between buildings; a pair of straw-hatted gondoliers leaning against the railing on a bridge, halting their conversation to offer their services; sheets and towels draped over a balcony railing to air out in the sun; an elegant old building that turned out to be a bank, with burnt-umber walls and marble supporting corner columns; restored palazzi next to ancient churches in disrepair; thoughtful statues in the center of squares with tourists sitting on the steps at their bases feeding crumbs to the pigeons; a small-scale yacht docked between two huge houses; a row of new windows all standing open in a building whose exterior was crumbling; pointed arches over tunnels leading from a landing stage to an adjoining street; variations of the classic lamp standard with one, two, three, or four lilac globes; more gondolas, these with carvings and carpets and highly-polished bits of brass trim.

"Are you hungry?" Jackie asked her after a time. "I'm starving. I could probably eat a small whale."

"Then we'd better eat."

They sat at an aluminum table out of doors and ate thick slabs of cheese and salami on crusty bread, and drank Cokes.

"Better not breathe on anyone for several days," Jo warned him with a laugh.

"Nobody gets close enough anyway. Normally, you know, I wouldn't drink one of these if I were dying of thirst. But I'm too hot to rev up on a cup of the old caffeine right now. Maybe for dessert."

"Personally, I love Coca-Cola. It's the one American thing you can buy anywhere in the world. I wouldn't admit this to just anyone, but seeing as how you're my official lens handler and all, I'm confiding in you."

"You're putting me on."

"Yeah, I am."

"That's what I thought." He wiped crumbs from his face with the back of his hand. "It's okay being American, for the most part. But some of our foreign policy really sucks. And most of those guys in Washington make me like *very* nervous."

"You know who makes *me* really nervous?"

"Who, aside from the guys who say the Holocaust never happened?"

"All those people who take so-called moral stances on things, the ones who have whole organizations that're supposed to be religious but who're lobbying politically. They scare the hell out of me. Any group that says it's right, regardless of the issue, and thinks because it's right it can blow places up, kill people, picket and harass anybody who doesn't agree with them."

"Okay," he said, thinking. "But that's one of the good things about our country: that you're free to think what you want."

"Oh, I want people to be free, Jackie. I just don't want them trying to force *me* to believe what *they* believe. That isn't freedom; it's coercion; it's simply another, subtler, form of terrorism.''

"I never thought of it that way, but I guess you're right."

"God!" she said. "I'm getting heavy, and this isn't the time for it."

"Why not?" he wanted to know. "I hardly ever get a chance to talk about this stuff. It's one of the major disadvantages of looking ten years old. People never get serious with you, as if your brain's the size of a peanut because you're a kid and you're short. It really pisses me off. The only time my dad ever has any kind of serious conversation is with like my uncles, or with business types. Or if I give him some kind of abstracted topic, like for an essay. Usually, he brushes me off. You know: 'I'm busy'; 'I'm tired'; 'I just got home from a rough day at the office and I'm not in the mood for this'; 'I don't have time.' Being a kid's a major pain in the ass a lot of the time, no shit.''

"I know," she agreed. "Have to get all your important information from the *Enquirer*."

He smiled. "I'm really into the news, you know. I mean, Wonder Dummy'll sit there and watch reruns of 'The Partridge Family' or 'The Brady Bunch' and she thinks it's great stuff. Me, I go for CNN. I can do a couple of hours of that, then tune into Brokaw for the network poop. You've gotta know what's going on," he said earnestly. "You can't like wait until you're out of college before you start finding out what the rest of the world's doing. How come you don't like having your picture taken?"

"I'm not photogenic."

"I'll bet you are. You're really pretty." He flushed but didn't look away.

"I'm not, but thank you."

"How can you *say* that?" he asked, amazed. "You're a great-looking wench. I bet guys are all over you like a cheap suit.''

She laughed. "Not quite."

"Then they're idiots! I was older, I'd be all over you.

Boy,'' he scratched his head, confused, "I thought women all think they're great.''

"God, no! There probably aren't more than two women in the entire world who think they're great. Truly. We all have something about ourselves we hate.''

"Like what? What d'you hate about yourself?''

"I don't know. My nose. It's kind of lumpy.''

"You're nuts! Your nose is perfect. What else?''

"I need to lose at least five pounds.''

"You're *insane*! You'd be a total skeleton, you lost five pounds. What else?''

"Those are my two major bugs. D'you like everything about yourself?'' she challenged.

"Well, I'm not like in love with me or anything. But I think I'm okay. I'm short, but I'm still growing. And even if I don't grow much more, that's cool. At least my head's on right, and I'm using it. Which is more than I can say for a whole lot of people. I can't *believe* you'd say stuff like that about yourself. Your nose is great. And you're definitely not fat. If anything you're on the too-skinny side. I mean, look at your teensy little wrists.'' He took hold of her arm between his thumb and forefinger, and lifted it. "Look at that! *Little kids* have bigger wrists than that. This is too weird!'' He let go of her arm, rolling his eyes. "Wise up, Joey old girl! You're top quality. Somebody tell you one time you had a lumpy nose?''

"No. That's just how it looks to me.''

"You're a banana. It's a seriously aristocratic honker,'' he said, then laughed and waved to the waitress to ask for an espresso.

"I'll bet the girls are crazy about you.''

"Sure. They're lining up to go out with like the second shortest guy in tenth grade.''

"You don't have a girlfriend?''

"There's this girl I like, but she lives in California. We met last winter when Dad took us to Eleuthera.''

"D'you stay in touch?''

"Yeah. We write, and we talk on the phone every couple

of weeks. But it's losing steam, you know. It's hardly likely I'm gonna be going out to San Francisco anytime soon. And the world's not making a big rush on Indianapolis. Armpit of the goddamned universe. I definitely plan to go to Yale, get the hell out of Indy. Wonder Dummy'll probably get married before she graduates, so Dad'll save a fortune on her tuition. I just have to keep my grade-point average up, then look out! I'm gone. Off to old Eli Yale. Four years of English major and I'll go work in New York, or maybe Boston. Somewhere cool.''

"Doing what?"

"I don't know. Maybe I'll work for the *Enquirer*," he chuckled. "Fix up their semiliterate prose. Or maybe I'll be Jackie Watts, ace reporter, pulling the scoop on Wall Street scams, or getting guys to give me their secret papers." He shrugged as the waitress brought his espresso. "I definitely don't want to go my Dad's route into that whole corporate thing. It's so goddamned boring, rots your brain out. He never has any good stories to tell, never meets any interesting people. I'm not putting him down or anything, but I want more than the nine rooms in the suburbs with the three-and-a-half bathrooms, the Seville, and the country club. Not to mention the wife and two kids. I mean, they've been married *forever*. They've been married so long they don't even talk to each other in full sentences. They just kind of grunt. And I'm pretty well positive they don't make it anymore. If you want to know the truth, I think Dad screws around. And I'll tell you something else: I think my Mom doesn't even care. As long as she doesn't have to know about it, as long as she's got the Buick and the club and the credit cards, that's cool.''

As he spoke, she felt a chill, remembering Beamer's vow as a twelve-year-old never to marry—and for almost these exact same reasons. It was like déjà vu, but she had the power perhaps to change it this time.

"It doesn't mean they don't care about each other, Jackie."

"No," he conceded. "I guess not. The thing is, I don't

get the point. I mean, if you're gonna be married, then be married. If you're gonna screw around, why be married?''

"I'd like to tell you a little story," she said so quietly that she had his immediate and complete attention. "Years ago I was in the city, in Manhattan, one afternoon. It was just before graduation, and I was going around with my portfolio, showing editors my work, trying to get assignments. Anyway, I finished my last appointment and I was heading back across town, walking to Grand Central. I'd just missed a train, so I had plenty of time before the next one. It was in the spring, May, I guess, and the weather was perfect. For a couple of weeks every year, I just love the city. Things look cleaner, fresher than at any other time, except when there's a big snowfall. It's the best time for New York, really.''

Jackie nodded, listening closely.

"So anyway, there I was walking along, just coming up to the St. Regis. I'm waiting at the corner for the lights to change and I see this couple coming out of the hotel. The doorman goes to signal a taxi, and this couple is standing there waiting. A cab comes along, the doorman opens the car door, and these two people turn to each other, say something, and then they kiss; they *really* kiss. Then they separate, the woman gets into the cab, and the cab goes off. The man stands there watching until the cab's out of sight, then he tips the doorman, turns, and heads off down the street.

"People are bumping into me, calling me names, and I finally realize I'm holding up traffic at the intersection. So I start moving with the crowd, but I have no idea what I'm doing or where I'm going. It was terrible.''

"It was your dad?'' Jackie guessed.

"Right.''

"Shit!''

"The thing is, I'd known for years that there was something going on in my house. You know? I never knew exactly what it was until that afternoon. I just knew there was *something*. When he was twelve years old, my brother Beamer

252

said he'd never get married. He never wanted to get locked into something as messed up and confusing as our parents' marriage. At the time I told myself he'd grow out of it. But my thinking was entirely about Beamer. I wasn't really thinking how the whole thing was affecting me, probably because Beamer was outside of me, an entirely separate other person. And I could see how it all affected him, but I couldn't see that it was affecting me, too. The *really* confusing part of it was that no matter what else went on, my mother and father were devoted to each other. When my mother died, my dad totally fell apart. For an entire year he couldn't do a thing. Half the time, if you tried to talk to him, he'd start to cry. He truly loved her.

"Their marriage drove me and Beamer crazy, Jackie. Beamer's thirty-two now and he's never even come close to getting married. And to be truthful, neither have I. But you know what?"

"What?"

"I think now it's just the way things are. It's something that happens, and in a lot of ways it hardly has anything to do with the marriage. And I also think that somehow as nice as it is to be a success and have some money in the bank and a decent car, it's just not as much fun when you're all alone. Sure, you don't have to get married to have that, but it's good to have people around to make you laugh if you're bummed out, or to help you calm down when you're pissed off about something."

"You have people like that?"

"I have friends," she answered.

"Not friends. I mean like a boyfriend."

"I think maybe I do, but I don't know yet. There's someone I like an awful lot."

"Oh yeah? What's he like?"

"He's English, and very funny, and kind of sweet in a reserved British way."

"Where does he live?"

"In London."

"Yeah? You gonna move to London?"

"God knows!" she laughed.

"D'you mind if I ask you something really personal?"

"I won't know till I hear you ask it."

"D'you, um, like do it with this guy?"

To her surprise the question didn't bother her in the least. "Uh-huh," she said, "I do."

"That's what I thought. Mind if I ask you something else?"

"Go ahead."

"Is it all heavy breathing and moaning and groaning like the movies?"

"Not quite, but it's good. The thing is, it's not everything. Let me give you one big piece of advice, Jackie. Okay?"

"Sure."

"If you're ever truly interested in a girl, make sure you get to know her. Find out who she is, how she feels about things, her opinions. Do it because you like her, not because you're trying to cultivate her interest in you. If you make the effort, then making love'll be great, because people need time. All of us do. And one other thing: Don't ever make the mistake of thinking that because you're really hot for somebody that you're in love with her. Sex is definitely not love."

"Okay. I'll remember that."

"You do, and all the things that bother you now will make sense later on, I promise. And Jackie! One other thing. It's very goddamned hard sometimes to make sense out of what our parents are doing. If you understand that it's just as hard for *them* to make sense of what they're doing, if you can be a little more tolerant, life'll be easier for all of you. Don't gauge your own future on what you see of your mom and dad's marriage, because that isn't the way it has to be for you. Don't make the same mistake Beamer and I made, and mess up years of your life because your parents' marriage wasn't like 'The Brady Bunch.' The fact is, nobody has a marriage like that. *Absolutely nobody.* Okay. That's it. Ready to go?"

When he reached into his pocket for money, she said, "Listen, kiddo. You paid for breakfast, and for the vaporetto. Lunch is on me."

"Okay. Thanks."

"You're good company, Jackie."

"You, too. These have been some of the best conversations of my life. And don't ever again let me hear you say your nose is lumpy or that you need to lose weight. You're totally perfect the way you are."

She weighted the bills with one of the cups, then took his hand, saying, "So're you. And they've been some of the best conversations *I've* had, too. Don't underestimate yourself, fellow. You've got a lot to say. Now! We have at least three hours left. What say we go see the Rialto?"

"Definitely!"

19

One moment she and Jackie were outside the hotel, laughing as they reviewed the highlights of the day; the next moment they were in the heart of pandemonium.

Jackie went ahead, holding open the door, her camera bag still over his shoulder. Jo came after and stopped dead, watching and listening in a state of low-grade horror as Jackie's father, mother, and sister turned from the heated conversation they'd been having with an assistant manager and one of the concierges. Their faces seemed to twist and swell at the sight of Jackie, and they came charging across the lobby like deranged creatures, all shouting at once. Jo instinctively hunched into herself in an automatic lifelong response to unpleasantness of any kind.

"One more hour and I was calling the police!" Mr. Watts railed, red-faced. *"Where the holy hell have you been?"*

"How could you *do* this to me?" Mrs. Watts shrilled.

"Thanks a lot for messing everything up, jerk!" the sister bleated. Mr. Watts grabbed Jackie by the arm and shook him so that the Lowe-pro slid from his shoulder to the bend of his elbow where it hung, dragging the boy's arm down.

"Hey, wait a minute!" Jackie protested, with his free hand

256

trying to get hold of the bag, which was swinging back and forth between him and his father.

"Don't you wait-a-minute me, mister!" Watts roared. *"What kind of games d'you think you're playing here, sneaking off with nobody knowing where the hell you are. D'you have anything up there besides air?"* he demanded, rapping his knuckles hard against Jackie's temple.

Watching, unmoving, Jo told herself to do something. This wasn't right. She couldn't just stand there and let this happen, especially not after having established the closeness she had today with this boy. Are you going to stand here and do nothing? she asked herself. This kid meant something to you today. Do people only mean something when it's convenient for you?

"Please don't hit him," she said, but so quietly no one heard her.

Mrs. Watts now had hold of Jackie's other arm and between her and her husband it seemed as if they might literally tear the boy in two. Stunned, Jackie simply looked at them as they yanked at his arms and shouted into his face. Again, Mr. Watts rapped his knuckles against the side of Jackie's head. And Jackie blinked, wincing.

"Stop that!" Jo said more loudly. *"Please!* There's no need for this."

The assistant manager and concierge both sighed audibly, as if in agreement with this lone voice of rationality. The members of the Watts family went silent and, as one, turned to look at her.

"Who the hell're you?" Watts wanted to know.

Shaky but determined, she said, "Jackie was with me all day. Helping," she added.

"Helping you do *what*?" Watts demanded.

"I left you a note," Jackie spoke finally.

"I know all about your goddamned note," Watts blustered, and then, as if pushed beyond his limits, smacked Jackie across the face, saying, "Shut up!"

Jo broke. Her hand shot out and closed around Mr. Watts' wrist. "Please stop hitting him!" she said, her voice gone breathless and low. "Whatever you think he's done wrong, you're humiliating him in front of all these people, and you're making a fool of yourself."

Watts stared hard at her for a moment, then slowly turned. A number of hotel guests had stopped at the far end of the lobby to watch the proceedings, as had most of the front office staff. They all looked uniformly aghast. There was an awful silence as Watts absorbed this, then looked back at his hand, which was still clamped to Jackie's arm. Reason returning, he released his son. Mrs. Watts took a step back. Jo let go of the man's arm.

"If you'd like to sit down quietly somewhere, I'll be glad to help try to sort this out," Jo said evenly, taking full control of the situation, and awed by her own words and actions. "Let's go to the sitting room over there."

After looking at each member of the family in turn, she took hold of Jackie's hand and led him to the sitting room which, luckily, was unoccupied. "Sit here with me," she instructed Jackie, directing him to the sofa, "and don't say anything unless I ask you to."

The rest of the family trailed suspiciously after, casting each other baffled glances that still contained a volatile residue of anger. Jo watched them sit in the armchairs, wondering just what they were so fired up about.

"Jackie," she asked him, "*did* you leave a note?"

"Sure I did," he answered. "I left it right where Wond— Nance would find it."

"Oh, I found it all right," the girl put in sarcastically. "The idiot—"

"I don't believe I asked you a question," Jo rounded on her. "Please be quiet until your input is asked for."

The girl's mouth closed, and her face creased petulantly.

"And did you say where you were going and when you'd be back?" Jo returned to Jackie.

"Sure I did. I said I was going into town and I'd be back later this afternoon."

"So," Jo turned now to the parents, "you knew where he was."

"We did *not*!" the mother insisted.

"Now you listen," the father said. "I don't know what this has to do with you—"

"It has to do with me," Jo said, furious, "because he was with me all day, because he hasn't done anything wrong, and because he doesn't deserve to be abused in a public place in front of strangers."

"What're you talking about, abuse?" Watts asked, a slight note of uncertainty creeping into his tone.

"What do *you* call it, Mr. Watts, when three people stand in the lobby of a hotel calling someone names and hitting him? *I* call it abuse."

"Well, we were *worried* about him," Mrs. Watts defended them.

"Oh! I see. You were worried about him. Funny, I don't recall any of you shouting anything about that. Do you, Jackie?" She turned to Jackie, who shook his head. "Your son wanted to see Venice," she said, controlling her voice, "which, apparently, you've traveled thousands of miles to do. He left you a note, and did precisely what he said he wanted to do. I realize I'm a complete outsider, but it seems to me he's behaved very responsibly."

"That's right," Watts said. "You *are* an outsider. What business is this of yours?"

"What is the *matter* with you people?" Jo asked hotly. "I mean, d'you behave this way all the time? If you do, maybe you should get family counseling or something." Her anger had taken her over, but she didn't care. "I've known Jackie for one day, but I'll tell you this: If he was a kid of mine, I'd be damned proud of him. He's bright, and funny, and smart. He sure as hell doesn't deserve to be hit and humiliated. God! I'm really tired of people like you. I really am. If you don't want him, if he's just some kind of whipping boy for the three of you, there are plenty of other people who'd be happy as Larry to have him. I would, and that's for damned sure." Retrieving her purse and camera bag, she got to her feet. "You've got a great kid here, and from the looks of it you're too stupid to realize it. He doesn't drink or smoke; he's a good student; he's terrific company; and he hasn't done *one thing wrong.* I think the three of you could use a few whacks across the head, maybe smarten you up." Her hands trembling from anger, she opened her purse and got out one of her cards. Giving it to Jackie, she said, "Here's my card. You feel like leaving home sometime because they're piling too much of this crap on you, call me!" Facing the other three again, she lowered her voice to say, "You ought to wise up, you people. You're taking your problems out on him, and not only does he *not* deserve it, you don't deserve *him.* You honest-to-God make me sick! It might be a good idea if you thought a bit about the scene you just put on in the lobby. This isn't some Holiday Inn, you know, bub!" she addressed Watts. "I'd be willing to bet the management won't be too eager to have you back here again. Except maybe for Jackie. He's got beautiful manners and he knows how to behave. You all owe him an apology. You, Mr. Watts, are supposedly a shrewd businessman, a Phi Beta Kappa from Yale. If you're so damned smart, how come you don't think about your public impression a little more? Just because you're a few thousand miles away from home doesn't mean you're invisible. It also doesn't mean that word doesn't travel. Sooner or later, someone in your company's going to hear you were beating up on your kid in the lobby of the Cipriani. And the next thing you know, your personal stock might start sliding. I'll say this one last time, and then I'm leaving you to sort this mess out: If you don't want him, there are plenty of people who do, and I'm sure as hell one of them." Turning to Jackie a final time, she extended her hand to him, saying, "Thank you for today. I loved being with you." Then she marched out to the foyer.

While the concierge was getting her key and handing over a message, Jackie came hurrying up. He stopped and leaned on the counter beside her for a moment, framing his words. "That was great, what you did, Joey," he said quietly. "They've been pulling that shit on me for years, and they're probably not going to stop now, but I can handle it. I'm used to it. But you're the first person who's ever stood up for me, shut them up and put them in their place." He gave a slow shake of his head. "It was great. Did you mean it?" he asked, looking at her card. "Could I call you sometime?"

"You'd better," she said with a smile. "I can't believe I just did that, but I had to. Today was wonderful, really wonderful." She glanced defiantly toward the sitting room. "And if you want to go out again with me before I leave on Saturday, I'd be delighted."

In response he gave her a hug, then stepped back, red-faced, saying, "I'd better get back. I'll see you later, okay?"

"Okay."

He ran off to the sitting room, and Jo stood for a few moments waiting for the sound of raised voices, but it didn't come. Clutching her key and message, she took the long route—avoiding the sitting room—to her room. She had about forty-five minutes before she was to meet Laura. She could have used a few hours. She felt exhausted, and sank down on the sofa, hearing herself say, "Just because you're a few thousand miles away from home doesn't mean you're invisible," and realized, with a jolt, that people had been saying the same thing to her for ages. Well, she'd certainly just proved to everyone she was anything but invisible. And not only had she proved it unequivocally, she'd also, for the second time in a week, said exactly what she thought. It hadn't seemed as if she had any choice. So she'd taken a stance; she'd defended somebody else; she'd assumed control. And she didn't regret any of it. Sure, she was still shaky, but she'd done something she was proud of. A week ago she'd have slipped away from that scene and come back to her room to brood over her failure to do what she knew to be right. A week ago she'd stood in the doorway of Henry's living room, waiting for Tyler and Henry to notice her. What the hell had she been doing all these years? she wondered. Hiding out, keeping her thoughts to herself, never taking a position, never involved or committed. She could look back to last week and view herself with a definite objectivity, as if remembering some girl from high school she'd once known, a girl who'd made her a little sad and impatient.

She became aware she was still clutching the envelope the concierge had given her, and tore it open.

> JOANNA JAMES CIPRIANI VENICE. UPON CONSIDERA-
> TION IMPORTANT STATEMENT IS AS FOLLOWS. YOU ARE
> OF IMPORTANCE TO THE WRITER. EXTENT OF WHICH
> PRESENTLY UNCERTAIN BUT HAS GROWTH POTENTIAL.
> WRITER CONSENTS TO PORTRAIT IN GARDEN AT PHO-
> TOGRAPHER'S CONVENIENCE. LOVE HENRY.

She read it twice, then held the telex to her breast, her eyes filling. "Oh, Henry," she whispered, "you're so godamned sweet." She read it again, then went to shower.

"I do hope you won't mind if we dine at the hotel," Anne said. She looked over to where Jimmy was standing talking to Laura. "Jimmy's not feeling entirely well," she added in an undertone.

"If you'd rather," Jo said, "we can put it off to another night."

"Oh, no, dear." Anne took hold of Jo's hand. "We wouldn't dream of that. We've both been looking forward to this evening with you."

Jo's immediate reaction was to wonder why. Then, deciding this reaction was only worthy of last week's Joanna James, she discarded it and said, "So have I," and watched Anne slowly nod, her eyes still on her husband. Jo remained silent for a time, sensing something. It was a piece of knowledge lodged irritatingly in the corner of her mind—like a popcorn husk wedged between two teeth—but it wouldn't come forward. All she knew was that this was another of the moments in her life when joining hands with someone else was of great significance. And it was the second time with this woman. She thought of other times—her mother's hand hard in its grip on hers near the end; Beamer's hand linked with hers throughout the funeral services; the first time Tom Harper, her first real boyfriend, had held her hand. Now she was standing, hand in hand, with Anne, both with their eyes on Jimmy, and Jo simply couldn't make the meaning of the moment come clear. Her consciousness had no words, yet it felt bulky with information.

"Come sit with me," Anne said, at last looking away from her husband. "Obviously, he's discussing something of interest with Laura."

They sat, and Anne folded her hands on top of the handbag in her lap. Jo couldn't help being aware of Anne's every move and gesture and wished she could get a clearer fix on the situation. Caught up in her speculations as well as in the thoughtful mood of her companion, she said, "I spent the day with that boy we saw in the bar last night. He's so darling, such a dear, funny boy. I loved being with him. Several times we encountered people who assumed he was my son, and neither one of us told them otherwise. It was like a little game the two of us played. And he had as much fun as I did. Then, we got back to the hotel, and his family made the most dreadful scene, shouting and hitting him. It was a nightmare."

"So I heard," Anne interjected.

"You did?"

"A noteworthy event. One of the waiters confided the details to us. Quite a little scandal. Although I'm given to understand you were the heroine of the piece. Your stock's rising hourly among the hotel staff. Our waiter described you as a cross between a Valkyrie and Saint Joan."

"My God! I had no idea . . . They were being so horrible to him, Anne. I just couldn't stand it. Something's happening to me," she admitted. "All my life I've been—a witness, sort of. I mean, I'm there, watching things happen, but I never get involved, never put my two cents' worth in. If I don't like what's going on, I quietly disappear, go away and never come back. I've always made my 'statements' by not making them. You know? Now, all of a sudden, I've not only stopped disappearing, I've also started telling people exactly what I think. It's different and kind of scary, but it's also exciting, like I'm crashing out."

"Don't be afraid, dear," Anne said. "Speaking one's mind, provided one's mind is decently functional, is one of the great joys of life. Personally, I take a very definite delight in being regarded in some circles as opinionated and cantankerous simply because I no longer care whether or not I'm universally liked. It's a definite advantage of old age, although there are times when I simply cannot believe I'm almost seventy. My mind is sixteen and reels at the sight of this face in the mirror."

"I feel the same way," Jo said.

Anne laughed disbelievingly. "How can you possibly? You're still very young. And the face looking back at you from the mirror hasn't a line in it. Your flesh still has a close fondness for your bones." She laid her hand against Jo's cheek. "You're *very* young, Joanna. And it would appear you live a frightfully lonely life, traveling about alone from one place to the next, rarely having the time or opportunity to get to know people." She returned her hand to her lap, her eyes remaining on Jo's. "Perhaps this journey is affording you a chance to break the habits of a lifetime. And if you're not unhappy to have those habits broken, it can only be viewed as a good thing. Don't you think?"

"It does feel that way, but I can't be sure."

"Why do you doubt?" Anne asked her. "There's not a thing wrong with your powers of reasoning, or your sense of right and wrong. What you did for that boy was admirable, honorable. You know what the truth is."

"I do, but it's hard to go along with what you think is right sometimes. You get to thinking maybe your perspective is exaggerated, distorted. Something happens and you don't know what's true and what you just *want* to be true."

"Oh, you know well enough. Why do you doubt yourself?" she asked, as if the idea of this grieved her. "Don't do that, my dear. Don't." Again she grasped Jo's hand, as her eyes sought out her husband seated across the way, still in conversation with Laura, who seemed to be enjoying his company.

Jo wanted to prolong the dialogue, to move it toward a

point where she'd gain conscious understanding of that stubborn bit of knowledge still cloistered in the recesses of her mind. But the members of the panel took their seats at the front of the room just then, and the meeting began. Anne's hand slipped out of hers.

Like a small chime struck lightly and repeatedly, Jo's sense of something amiss grew during the boat ride back to the hotel. Anne seemed to be guarding her husband, not physically, but with her awareness. She kept a close watch on him, ready at any moment with words or smiles or subtle private signals. Yet for his part, Jimmy appeared oblivious to any alteration in his wife's behavior. And Jo thought she must be misreading what she was seeing. These people had grown very familiar to her—their facial expressions, their gestures and deferential displays to one another, their style of dress and manner of speaking were not only recognizable to her but somehow just as they should have been. Whether or not she wanted it, she'd very quickly become very attached to them. And so the slightest variation, every nuance, registered on her. And something was going on. It showed in the tilt of Anne's head as she listened, during the drinks before dinner, to her husband speak of the slides they'd seen of several landmark buildings in the city, before and after restoration; it showed, too, in Anne's sudden breath-held stillness when Jimmy set down his knife and fork midway through his first course and began to cough. He held a handkerchief to his mouth until the brief spasm passed, then blotted his eyes and smiled first at his wife and then at Jo, saying, "You'd think I'd have learned to swallow properly by now." Then he retrieved his utensils and went on eating.

With an impish smile, Anne said, "You've always gobbled your food. It's as if," she addressed Jo, "there's a set time allowed for each course. And if he fails to finish within that set time, a great hairy pair of arms is going to snatch away his plate."

Jimmy snorted with laughter.

Jo smiled at them both, wondering if those were really signs of strain in the lines around Anne's eyes and mouth.

"It will take decades," Jimmy was saying, "before they're able to get past all the bureaucratic rubbish and see to the work that needs doing. Their so-called Special Law from 'seventy-three has probably done more harm than good."

"Why is that?" Jo asked him.

"Ah, well. With the best intentions, of course, they set about to create a law that would guarantee protection of various and sundry buildings and so forth from pollution, floods, et cetera, in order to ensure that Venice and her environs would stay alive socially and economically. The fatal flaw in their good intentions was to involve not only city and regional delegates in this decision, but to set it down as part of the law itself that the government of Italy would have representatives in the group overseeing everything from the regulation of water levels in the canals to the restoration of buildings belonging to the state as well as to individuals. And when you have any group attempting to make decisions with wide-reaching effects, you're bound to have endless red tape to boot. From what I'm given to understand, it can take years on end simply to get permission to begin a restoration. And when one understands that the restoration itself can also take years, one is looking at vast amounts of time being wasted on bureaucratic wrangling. As I say, they meant well, but what's evolved is not ideal. Too many cooks, as it were, making a right muck-up of the broth.

"Still," he went on, "I wouldn't have minded having a hand in some of the restoration. At least I would've had the satisfaction of seeing something magnificent returned to life. Superb job they did on that spiral staircase of the Palazzo Contarini del Bovolo. One could be proud of work like that."

"There's a great deal you can be proud of," Anne reminded him. "A great deal."

He scoffed at this. "Purely functional buildings without soul."

"At least none of them has fallen down."

He gazed at Anne for a second or two, then laughed. "You

266

should have seen this woman at eighteen," he told Jo. "The most exquisite creature I'd ever seen. Masses of jet black hair and brilliant cat's eyes that, I swear, glowed in the dark. Outrageous and willful and altogether remarkable."

"The first words he ever spoke to me," Anne confided to Jo, "were to ask if I would pose nude for him. I said I'd be delighted, and he choked on his Yorkshire pudding." She laughed.

"Not quite the *first* words," he argued.

"Indeed they were! I'm not likely to forget, ever."

"Did you do it?" Jo asked, entering into their playful mood.

"Of course I did." Anne's laughter gained in intensity.

"And there I was," Jimmy guffawed, "with no bloody paper, and not a pencil to be found anywhere."

"He didn't believe for a moment I'd actually consent," Anne put in. "Of course, I had ulterior motives."

"Immediate ones, too." Jimmy was blotting his eyes with his handkerchief.

She had to be wrong, Jo told herself. She'd been reading too much into things. These two were keenly attuned to one another, and fifty years later still found each other attractive. What did it take, she wondered, to make an affair of the heart last for fifty years? She tried to picture herself fifty years down the road with Tyler, and couldn't see it. Replacing Tyler with Henry, she was surprised to be able to see possibilities. "YOU ARE OF IMPORTANCE TO THE WRITER, . . . GROWTH POTENTIAL." In thirty-six years she'd made only one real attempt to share herself with a man, and it had been a disaster. After it was over, she'd sealed herself away. She'd crept out every so often for a kind of hit-or-miss encounter but before it had any chance to prove itself good, bad, or indifferent, she'd be off and running home, or on assignment, anywhere just so long as she didn't have to deal with the implications of involvement.

"This is too terrible of me," Lucienne said, arriving at the table. "I may please sit with you to drink a glass of wine?"

"Oh, do join us!" Jimmy got quickly to his feet, breaking into a smile at the sight of her.

"Please do," Anne said graciously. "Have you had dinner? Perhaps you'd care to have something."

"You are so very kind," Lucienne said, taking the seat beside Jo. "I thought I would take dinner in my room, but I am too *agitée*."

She was very visibly agitated. Her hands were shaking so badly that Jimmy took the lighter and lit her cigarette for her.

"What happened?" Jo asked her.

"Is something wrong?" Jimmy asked at the same moment. "I think you need something stronger than wine. A brandy, perhaps?" His upheld hand kept the waiter at attention.

"Please. I am so sorry to do this," she apologized, waving away the smoke from her cigarette before stubbing it out. "Never do I do this. But I could not stay alone in my room."

"What happened?" Jo asked again.

"Ah!" Lucienne laughed ruefully. "It does not make for dinner conversation. You forgive me?"

"There is no need to apologize," Anne said. "And if you'd care to talk about it, I know we'd all like to listen."

"It is ridiculous! When I am past the unpleasantness, I think I will be very much relieved. I am no longer to be married," she said with one of her little shrugs. The waiter went off and returned with a snifter of brandy and a menu. Without consulting the menu, she said, "I will have the tournedos, rare, please," returned the menu to the waiter, took a swallow of the brandy, then said, "We will celebrate my unattachment, eh?"

"I am sorry," Anne said.

"No! It is not to be sorry. I am saved from a big mistake." She tried for a smile that didn't quite come off, and shrugged again instead.

"I'm sure it was a most difficult decision to make," Anne said gently.

"Paolo made it quite simple. He was ugly. We spent many hours arguing. He has only now gone. And my room is very noisy still from all the shouting.'' She laughed suddenly, quite gleefully. ''I think we make a great entertainment for the chambermaids.'' Her laughter escalated until the others joined in. ''Absurd!'' she declared. ''*Ciao*, Paolo!'' She raised her snifter in the direction of the door, then drank down the remainder of the brandy in one gulp.

20

LUCIENNE INSISTED ON SIGNING FOR THE DINNER DESPITE Jimmy's protests. "Please, I will do this. I come uninvited and disarrange your evening. I will feel very much better if you will permit me to give you dinner."

Jimmy would have gone on arguing, but Anne's hand on his arm stopped him. A slight shake of her head put an end to all discussion.

"Thank you very much," Anne said simply.

"You will come for a drink in the bar?" Lucienne asked.

"I think not. It's been rather a long day, and I'm afraid we're both ready for bed. Jimmy's arranged a very full schedule for tomorrow, including lunch at the Hotel des Bains, for old time's sake."

They stood to leave, and Jo got up to embrace the older woman. Anne held her close, then released her saying, "I expect we'll see you at some point tomorrow."

"I'm sure we'll run into each other."

"Perhaps you'd ring me," Anne said in an undertone. "Possibly before you set off for the day."

"Sure. I'll call you after breakfast."

The four of them left the dining room together, parting at the entrance to the bar.

Jimmy went off, cautioning them to "watch out for any stray Italian Lotharios! Don't let yourself be plied with bon-bons and amaretto!"

Lucienne and Jo waited in the corridor until the older pair were out of sight, then Lucienne said, "You will have a drink with me, Mignon?"

Jo turned to look at her. Lucienne was wearing a simple navy cotton suit, with a slim skirt and severely cut collarless jacket. The severity of the cut was redeemed by the V neck-line which revealed a respectable amount of cleavage and a strand of lustrous pearls. "Are you sure you're all right?" she asked Lucienne.

"I feel stupid," Lucienne admitted. "I am furious. I have wasted time and money and my affections. But, yes, I am all right. You have influenced me, Joanna. You know this? It is true. I have been too busy for a very long time for friends, for serious conversations. I listen to what you say, and I know you are right, eh? I think if I do not meet you, I go ahead and marry Paolo." She made a face. "This would have been tragic. So I thank you because you save me from this tragedy. And now we have champagne, to celebrate. Yes?"

"Okay, yes."

Lucienne linked her arm through Jo's and they walked into the bar, heading for a table near the piano player. Jo was aware peripherally of someone rising abruptly on the opposite side of the room but paid no attention.

"I hope you're going to invite me to join you," said a familiar voice, and Jo turned to see Tyler grinning at her.

"My God!" she exclaimed as he drew her into an embrace, then kissed her on both cheeks. As always, she was starting to pull away when he moved in with the second kiss, and she felt graceless.

"I thought I'd surprise you," he said, still grinning, "and ride back to London with you. May I join you?" he asked, looking now at Lucienne.

"Well, sure," Jo said, flustered. "This is Lucienne Denis. Tyler Emmons."

His eyes alight with appreciation, he accepted the hand

271

Lucienne offered and, to Jo's mild dismay, kissed it. *"Enchanté,"* he said, then folded himself into one of the chairs as Jo and Lucienne took seats on the opposite side of the table. "I take it," he said, "I have indeed succeeded in surprising you?"

"More like flabbergasted," Jo said. At first sight of him everything inside of her had given a startled leap, and was just beginning to subside. Here was Tyler, in a suit, no less; a very smart one of gray summer-weight wool, with an open-necked pale blue shirt, and black Gucci loafers. He did look good.

"We will have champagne," Lucienne told the waiter. "Moët et Chandon."

"Lovely!" Tyler said. "Are we celebrating something?" He looked from one woman to the other.

"We celebrate my unattachment," Lucienne said airily, trying to interpret the looks passing between this man and Joanna. "You will celebrate with us, eh?"

"Delighted."

Lucienne lit a cigarette while Jo asked Tyler, "When did you arrive?"

"Oh, an hour or so ago. Flew down, then traveled by land and sea. How has it been? Are you having a super time? You look very well indeed."

"It's been great. Busy, you know. I've still got all kinds of work to do."

"Well, I'll do my best not to get in your way. I decided on the spur of the moment. I knew you'd be busy, but I thought I'd keep you company on the train going back. I've been wanting to ride it for ages, and this seemed as opportune a time as any." As he spoke, his eyes slid away from her to Lucienne.

God! Jo thought. Things were getting unbelievably complicated. The last thing in the world she'd imagine could ever happen, but here was Tyler. It was almost too much to absorb, particularly on top of the long list of things she had left to do. And from the way he was staring at Lucienne, he might have been struck by lightning.

"Have you two just met?" he was asking Lucienne.

"We are very old friends," Lucienne lied smoothly, giving Jo's knee a squeeze beneath the table.

"We met ages ago," Jo put in gratefully. She had no idea why, but Lucienne's decision to make their friendship longstanding was exactly what Jo needed. "When I got the assignment, we decided to take the train together."

"Funny, you never mentioned that. You live in America, do you?" he asked Lucienne.

"No. I am born in Canada. I live in Paris."

"I did a piece on Lucienne's restaurant a while back," Jo compounded the lie. "She's got a marvelous place, Chez Lucienne."

"Indeed? I'll have to look it up when I'm next in Paris. So tell me, Joanna. How was the train?"

"Great," she answered, all at once filled with dread at the prospect of his expecting to sleep with her. She didn't know what she'd do if he wanted to come to her room. She had a job to do here and she hoped he really did understand that, because not only could she not spare the time to be with him, she didn't want to take the time away from Anne and Lucienne and Jackie. And just as her thoughts turned to Jackie, he came bouncing into the bar, caught sight of her, and moved right in, saying, "Hi! Can I come sit with you for a sec?"

"Sure," she said with an effortless smile. "Come meet everyone. This is Jackie. Lucienne and Tyler."

Jackie said, "Hi," and shook hands, then exclaimed, "Wow! Champagne! Can I have a taste?"

"But of course," Lucienne said, and gave him her glass. In return Jackie gave her an admiring smile of epic proportions.

"Jackie and I spent the day together today," Jo explained as he took a sip of the wine, then returned the glass to Lucienne.

"Thank you very much," he said to Lucienne, leaning for a moment with his elbow on the table, chin in his cupped hand, gazing adoringly at her so that she simply had to smile and pinch his cheek.

"I was her official lens handler," Jackie told them, coming out of his short-lived trance. "So guess what?" he said to Jo.

"What?"

"You missed the best part. Wonder Dummy and the Two Stooges were like totally chilled out by what you said. Right? I mean, I thought my dad was going to have like cardiac arrest over that bit about word getting back to his company. I bet nobody's *ever* talked that way to old John. Anyway the deal is, I can be lens handler again tomorrow, if you want."

Jo glanced guiltily at Tyler, decided he didn't dare question her actions, and told Jackie, "Perfect. I'm doing the kitchen. It's at the near end of the gallery. Meet me there at ten. Okay?"

"Okay, great! You know what my mom said, Joey?"

"What?"

"Get this! It's too amazing. She subscribes to like about a hundred magazines, right? So when I showed her your card, she had a spaz attack and got like all nervous because she recognized your name. Then she did this major number on my dad, and she actually took my part. Can you believe it? I mean, there she was, going, 'Jackie was *helping* this woman, John.' John's what she calls my dad when it's like serious, right? 'She happens to be a well-known journalist, *John*. And you *would* go and make a *scene*! I've never *been* so embarrassed!' Then the two of them got into this major don't-you-dare-raise-your-voice-to-me type number. And Wonder Dummy wants to get into the action, but the two of them turn and they both tell her to shut up. Beautiful! Anyway, they've got this important tennis date in the morning, you know. And old Nance has to get out there to soak up more rays by the pool. So I can help you out again. Great, huh?"

"Yup." Jo smiled at him.

"My mom's impressionable," he elaborated for the benefit of the other two. "She's knocked out by celebrities. Say," he said, staring at Tyler. "Aren't you the actor? You're the guy from *Lion's Gate*, right?"

"That's right," Tyler said, amused.

"I saw the whole nine episodes on PBS. It was great! *You* were great! Say, could I have an autograph? Would that be okay?"

"I'd be delighted," Tyler said.

"I'll get some paper, okay, and be right back." Jackie pushed out of his chair and went running off, sneakers squeaking on the marble floor.

"Another old friend of yours?" Tyler asked Jo.

"New friend," she corrected him, bothered a bit by what sounded like a crack. "He's a wonderful kid. I wish he was mine, if you want to know the truth."

"I like him," Lucienne said. "A pity he is so young, eh?" She looked at Jo meaningfully, and they both laughed.

Tyler followed this exchange with the sense that the two women had tacitly agreed to join forces against him for some unknown reason. It made him feel slightly foolish, somewhat defenseless, and unreasonably, albeit mildly, angry. Their complicity created an energy that was fairly commanding. He had to wonder if coming here unannounced might not have been a tactical error. Certainly, Joanna hadn't given him quite the welcome he'd anticipated.

Jackie came skidding back to the table with a piece of hotel stationery and a pen, which he put down in front of Tyler.

"Jackie, is it?" Tyler asked, at once feeling a little guilty for being condescending to this boy, taking out his anger on a kid. He tried to compensate for it by personalizing the autograph and giving the boy a genuine smile as he handed back the paper. "There you go."

"Boy, this is great! Wonder Dummy'll have a shit fit when she sees it!" He folded the paper carefully and tucked it into his pocket. "I better be going," he said. "See you tomorrow, Joey. Nice to meet you both." Again, he shook hands all around, then took off.

Lucienne was laughing. "I like him very, very much,"

she told Jo. "I like also 'shit fit.' I think this is what I have before, eh?"

"Could be," Jo laughed with her.

"It is *very* good, 'shit fit.' So, you are a famous actor?"

"I wouldn't go quite that far," Tyler said, shifting sideways in his chair to recross his long legs. "I do a fair bit of work."

"Tyler acts and directs," Jo told her. "And he works *all* the time. He's been in the theater his whole life."

"Very interesting," Lucienne said. "I see very few films except late at night on the *télé*, when I am home after Chez Lucienne is closed. I am sorry I have not seen you."

"We can always remedy that," he said, then reconsidered and added, "I mean, I'll be glad to let you know when I've got something on in Paris."

Jo was intrigued to see how attracted to Lucienne Tyler was, and even more intrigued to realize she didn't mind in the least. For her part, Lucienne handled his interest with ease, but looked questioningly every few moments at Jo, as if for permission.

"I have to go to the john," Jo announced.

"Me, also. I will come with you," Lucienne said at once.

"We'll be right back, Tyler," Jo told him, feeling like an adolescent as she and Lucienne went arm in arm down the corridor, stifling giggles.

Once inside the ladies' room, Lucienne asked, "He is one of your two men?"

"God, yes! I can't believe this!" Jo held her hands to her flushed cheeks. "He can't take his eyes off you. If he had a spoon, he'd eat you up." She laughed, then clapped her hand over her mouth. Two glasses of wine with dinner and a hastily downed glass of champagne had taken their toll.

"This bothers you?"

"Not one bit. Last week it might have. But tonight it's just funny. You want him?" she asked boldly.

"He is interesting," Lucienne conceded. "Not unattractive. But he has come to see *you*, Mignon."

"He came to see my body, not me." She laughed again, and again covered her mouth. "I think I'm a bit drunk."

"I think you are a lot drunk. What will you do?"

"God! I don't know. I really do have to work; I'm completely booked up tomorrow. Friday's pretty clear. He's planning to come back on the train with me. I just don't *believe* any of this."

"I will also come back on the train Saturday," Lucienne informed her. "I have made the arrangements today."

"Before or after the fight?"

"Before."

"Well, good for you. So, we'll all go on Saturday. That was great before, the way you said we were old friends."

"If you could see your face, you would know it is not so great. I think to myself when he comes you have gone into shock."

"That's a serious understatement."

Lucienne finished lighting a cigarette and folded her arms under her breasts. "It is the other one, eh?"

"The other one what?"

"The other one you love?"

"I don't know about that, Lucienne." Jo leaned against the wall and tried to think. The alcohol had made her brain feel huge and aerated, like Swiss cheese. "I *know* Henry. I mean, we've known each other for ten years. I know he spends a lot of evenings sitting alone in his living room with a bottle of wine and the TV set for company. I know he's dedicated to his garden. You should see him! He was out there for six solid hours last Saturday, patiently pulling weeds and pruning his plants. He never says or does the things I expect him to. But he *tries*, you know? I mean, Tyler shows up, and all I could think while the waiter was pouring the champagne was I hope to God he doesn't expect to sleep with me tonight. I'm so tired of that kind of thing. You know? Men showing up, expecting things, without bothering to think about what you might expect."

"I know." Lucienne took a puff on the cigarette, keeping her arms around herself. "I know this very well."

"What's wrong?"

Lucienne didn't answer, but continued to stand with her arms wound around herself. Then, looking fearful, she dropped the cigarette, turned, bent over the basin, and threw up. Still bent forward, she reached to turn on the faucets, while her body commenced a series of painful heaves. Jo picked up the cigarette, put it in one of the ashtrays, then went to stand by Lucienne, stroking her spine as the retching went on and on. There was a lull, during which Lucienne splashed water on her face, then turned her head sideways to say, "I am so very sorry."

"Don't be silly," Jo said, wetting a towel in cold water and placing it on the nape of Lucienne's neck before continuing to stroke her back.

Lucienne started to say something, but was overtaken by another spasm. When it ended, she drank some cold water from her cupped hand. Still hanging over the basin, she said, "I think it is finished. *Merde!* This is a disgrace." She splashed more water on her face, then straightened, removing the wet towel and setting it aside as she rinsed the basin.

Jo smoothed the hair from Lucienne's face, then held the back of her hand against Lucienne's forehead. "You're hot," she said. "You should probably go to bed."

"I think you are right."

"I'll come up with you."

"But your friend . . ."

"I'll go tell him, then come back. Don't you move! Okay? I'll be two minutes."

Lucienne had turned and was staring at her reflection in the mirror with an expression of complete disgust. "Go," she said. "I'll wait."

"Tyler," Jo said, back in the bar. "Lucienne's not feeling at all well. I'm going to take her to her room, see her into bed, then I'll be back."

He simply didn't believe her. After all, he'd heard the two of them go off laughing down the corridor. Now, a matter of minutes later, she was back with this flimsy fabrication. If she wanted to be rid of him, why didn't she come right out and say so? "If you'd rather," he said, "we can call it a night. I could meet you for breakfast."

"Would you mind terribly?" she asked anxiously. "She hasn't been well since she left Paris, and I'm really pretty worried about her."

"Go ahead. I'll finish my drink and take myself off to bed."

"Oh, God!" she said, remembering. "I'd better sign for the champagne."

"Not to worry, Joanna," he said tiredly. "My treat. Tell your friend I hope she's feeling better soon."

He didn't believe her, she thought as she hurried back to the ladies' room. Did he think she and Lucienne had nothing better to do than make up stories in order to avoid him? No, wait a minute! Would she have believed it if she were in his place? She'd apologize to him in the morning. Well, maybe not apologize, but explain. Something.

Lucienne was sitting on the floor with her head down on her drawn-up knees.

"Come on," Jo said. "We'll get you to bed."

"Not for a moment, eh?" Lucienne said weakly. "I will faint if I move now."

"Shit!" Jo knelt on the floor beside her. "You have got to see a doctor. No kidding!"

"I will be all right," Lucienne murmured.

Jo got the towel, soaked it again in cold water, then placed it once more over the back of Lucienne's neck. She shivered, her head remaining on her knees. Jo sat on the floor beside her, feeling faintly queasy herself. If she hadn't performed these same actions so many times in the early stages of her mother's cancer, she'd undoubtedly have thrown up herself in sympathetic response. She held the cold towel secure with one hand and with the other smoothed her friend's hair, marveling over how they'd gone from drunken hilarity to sober seriousness in a matter of minutes. Of course Tyler hadn't believed her when she'd gone running back to say Lucienne was ill. Well, she'd clarify matters in the morning.

"I think it was a mistake to eat," Lucienne said, her voice muffled.

"I think your big mistake is *not* eating. At least, not stuff that's good for you."

"It's like the cigarettes." Lucienne experimentally lifted her head. Her face was dreadfully pale. "You say to yourself you know they will make you die, but then something happens which is bad, eh, and you think, pah, so I will die. It is of no consequence. And it is too much difficulty to change, to give up the pleasures."

"That's crazy," Jo said softly. "You don't want to die."

"Sometimes, yes."

"But you *can't*!" Jo protested. "You've got everything going for you."

"I say this also. But just in case, eh? Things are bad, or not how you wish, so you have a cigarette and you say, Okay, I have no wish to live forever."

"God! That's terrible!" Jo said, and started to cry.

Her head propped on her hand, Lucienne looked at Jo's tear-washed face, bemused, and asked, "Why do you cry, Mignon?"

"I don't know," Jo wailed. "Everything's just so ridiculous. I mean, look at the two of us! God!"

"You care too much," Lucienne said.

"No, I don't. Most of the time, I hardly care enough. I really don't. And you make me so mad. I swear, if you don't see a doctor, I'll take you to one myself. Okay, so you're afraid. Everybody's afraid, goddamnit! But being afraid beats hell out of being dead. And I don't want you dead."

Lucienne smiled. "You have passion, Mignon," she said admiringly.

"I don't know about that. D'you think you can get up now?"

"I think so."

Jo helped her up, then dusted off her skirt.

"I am able to walk," Lucienne told her, and held herself very erect as they went through the lobby, up the stairs, and along the hallway to her room. Once inside, though, she had to sit on the edge of the bed, her arms again winding around her midriff. She swore furiously and rocked back and forth for several minutes while Jo tried to think what to do. "It would not be so bad," Lucienne said at last, "but when he was leaving, Paolo he pushed the door at me, eh? It hits me right here." She pointed to her abdomen. "*Cochon!* It hits me very hard, so I have no air."

"Come on," Jo said. "Let me help you." Getting no protest from Lucienne, she removed the suit jacket, then assisted her out of the skirt, stopping to stare at the large livid area just above her navel. "Jesus!" she whispered. "Do you know you're black and blue?"

Lucienne looked down at herself, then at Jo.

"He did *that* with the *door*? What a bastard!" Jo swore.

Lucienne stood in her filmy black brassiere and patterned panty hose, looking at herself while Jo reached for the yellow oversized T-shirt the chambermaid had arranged artfully on the bed. "Can you manage, or do you need help all the way?"

"I manage."

"I've got some Valium," Jo said, going to the coffee table for her purse. "I hate giving people stuff that was prescribed for me, but I really think you need it." She went to the bathroom for some water, then came back to the side of the bed where Lucienne was now sitting in the T-shirt. "Take this!" she ordered. Without argument, Lucienne took the tablet, then gingerly lay down. "Tomorrow, you'll go see a doctor. Please?"

"I will telephone to my doctor in Paris, make arrangements to see him when I return."

"You promise?"

"You treat me like a child," Lucienne smiled at her.

"You need it. I don't understand why you refuse to look after yourself."

"You will see: In the morning, I am fine."

Jo dropped down so they were at eye level. "Will you be able to sleep?"

"I am sure. Thank you, Mignon. I am sorry to make such a disaster of your evening."

"I don't care about the evening. I care about you. Please look after yourself." She kissed Lucienne's forehead, turned off the lamp, collected her purse from the coffee table, switched on the DO NOT DISTURB light, and opened the door. "If you need anything, call me. I'll come right away. Okay?"

"Okay."

Back in her room she sat for a time on the sofa with her feet propped on the coffee table, Henry's telex in her hand. She read it over and over until it ceased to make any sense.

It seemed as if she'd managed to get through her entire life so far without investing emotionally in anyone. Now, suddenly, like someone who'd come into an immense inheritance, she was expending her emotions on all who came near. Unaccustomed as she was to the activity, it made her nervous, and rendered her vulnerable, but she not only didn't mind, she had no desire to put an end to the spree. If anything, she wanted to perpetuate it, keep it going until she ran dry, until she'd used up every last bit of her emotional currency.

Just remember it's nighttime, she reminded herself, looking around the luxurious room. You might not feel this way come morning.

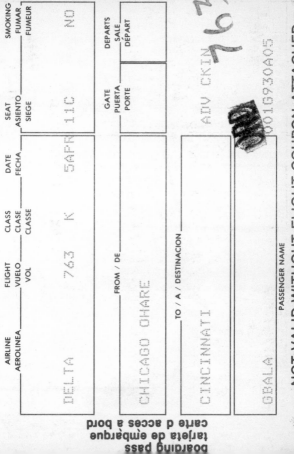

21

". . . INSIDE PALACE, HUGE EXPANSE OF ROOM WITH TIN-
toretto; J. telling about painting while parents allowing children to tear around, shrill cries echoing in vast chamber;
creepy going through dungeons; names, dates written on
dungeon walls; all roped off. City is like exotic and wonderful board game—you go forward, then double back at dead
ends; mazelike; fun finding ongoing route; so much to see,
J. terrific tour guide. Dinner last eve. at table at edge of
terrace overlooking water with splendid bldgs. in distance;
chatter from bar area adjacent; 60ish man alone 2 tables
along; all manner of boats going by, endless silent traffic;
pianist played theme from *Borsalino*, brought back memories so long ago when Lily had the sound-track album one
year and played it nonstop; after she died, I played it all the
time. Atmosphere here reminiscent of West Indies, primarily
the lushness, plantings, flowers, sandy color of hotel, flagstones, pines in planters, white tables, chairs; red and pink
geraniums in pots hanging from wall above terrace; French
windows with wooden shutters in older part of hotel; at
breakfast sm. birds come to eat off tables and flagstones, just
like Indies. Venetians v. pleasant & accommodating. L. upset, came to table; she dumped the fiancé, guy sounded like

real creep; T. showed up out of blue. Almost too much going on; every day more intense, more complicated. I feel as if I started out as one person who agreed to do a job, now daily evolving into a sort of distilled version of that same person; not sure anymore what Joanna James will say or do; can't count on her to be predictable; all the old rules gone. V. confusing.''

She closed the notebook, finished her coffee, and checked the time. Almost seven-thirty. She'd been up since six, making notes and checking the slides she'd collected the previous afternoon. They were all properly exposed. That meant she wouldn't have to reshoot anything, which was a tremendous relief. She couldn't remember when she'd been quite so tired. Just thinking of all she had to do today made her even more tired. But she had to admit she hadn't ever felt quite so fully alive.

Then there was the matter of Tyler. Without question, it was quite a gesture for him to show up the way he had. But it was an impulsive move he'd made, she was sure, without giving serious consideration to the fact that she had a job to do. Henry would never in a million years have gone charging ahead without first making sure both of his welcome and of the advisability of such a visit. Henry would be very careful about any move that might be subject to the slightest misinterpretation. He was, she thought, a lot like her in that respect. Neither of them would rush into a situation without first checking the pros and cons. And that was why he'd been unable to blurt out something "important" over the telephone when she'd asked him. She suspected Tyler would have said what he thought she wanted to hear. Not from dishonesty, but simply to please her. That was because Tyler didn't think beyond the immediate present—at least not where she was concerned. But Henry always did. Amazing, she thought, how clear things suddenly seemed to be.

Seven-forty. She returned the slides to their plastic container; notebook and pen went into her bag. Several fresh rolls of film from the minirefrigerator went into the Lowepro, and she was set to go.

As she passed through the gallery, she thought again of how she and Lucienne had sat on the floor in the ladies' room, and of how she'd started crying. All those months when she'd spent hour upon hour with her mother—before and after her several hospital stays—she'd never allowed herself to break down because she hadn't wanted Lily to see her go out of control. She'd had the idea that her breaking down would only make things more difficult for her mother. So she'd wept after the visits, but never during. Now she couldn't help thinking she shouldn't have worried so much about showing Lily a strong, cheerful face. Maybe she'd done them both a disservice in failing to allow either of them an opportunity to cry together over all they both were losing. It hadn't felt wrong or embarrassing to sit there and cry in front of Lucienne. It had been the most spontaneous demonstration of caring she'd ever made. Yes, she had friends at home. But since her move to Connecticut she no longer saw them as often as when she'd lived in the city. She was actually closer now to Anne and Jimmy, to Lucienne and Jackie, to Henry and even Tyler, than she was to most of her friends at home. She could live anywhere and it wouldn't affect the friendships that were already firmly established. If she lived, say, in London, she'd be able to perpetuate the new ones. She could even, possibly, stay in the house with Henry.

You're rushing ahead, she cautioned herself. You're building imaginary homes that can be knocked down by a telephone conversation or a negative reaction to something that might be said. Everything she was experiencing now was taking place in a kind of fantasy land. No one could live this way full-time. She'd leave on Saturday, arrive back in London Sunday evening, and all this would be over. It was temporary, time out of time; it didn't really count. Or did it? At the end, was she going to go back to being the Joanna James who hung back, waiting for other people to notice her? Was she going to return to being the silent witness who felt invisible most of the time? God! It was the last thing she wanted. But she wasn't sure what was needed to keep going forward as the new Jo. All she knew was that it had to do with people she'd come to know very well, very quickly; people she wanted to keep inside her life.

While she was waiting for the maître d' to return from the end of the terrace to seat her, Jackie's mother came along the corridor. In her tennis whites, ready for another few hours at the court, she smiled and came over to say, "I'm so glad to run into you. I wanted to say how sorry we are about that business yesterday. John tends to cover up with anger when he gets worried, and he also tends to get a little physical. But he'd never hurt Jackie. You know how men are," she smiled. "They're so bad with emotions. Jackie is John's hope for the future. He really is. It's just that he has a lot of trouble showing his feelings. And I guess, after all these years, some of it's rubbed off on me, too. Live with someone long enough and you start to become like one another. I just want you to know we appreciate your looking after Jackie. And if he gets to be a nuisance, you let us know."

She was a pretty woman, with a lot of frown lines baked into her skin from so much time spent on tennis courts, and a tendency to widen her eyes for effect, or emphasis. Jackie had her mouth, and the same shape of eyes. Jo could see him in his mother's face. It felt strange to be standing there, looking at her, watching the way her lips formed words and her eyes added the italics. She felt old enough to be this somewhat superficial woman's mother.

"Listen, Mrs. Watts," Jo said. "I meant everything I said yesterday. I think Jackie's a sensational kid. And if you want to know the truth, he looked out for me, and not the other way around. He's definitely not a nuisance, so don't worry about it. Okay?"

Mrs. Watts blinked and then, as if deciding she'd been indirectly complimented, said with pride, "He's got more energy than any ten boys."

"He's also," Jo said, "got beautiful manners and a very nice way with people. You've done a good job with him."

"Well, that's so nice of you to say." Mrs. Watts beamed. "By the way, I've read several of your pieces and they're awfully good. And your photographs are always lovely."

"Thank you. Excuse me." Jo turned to the maître d' and said, "There'll be two of us this morning."

"Very good, Signorina."

"Good talking with you," Jo said to Mrs. Watts.

"Right you are!" said the woman cheerily, and headed across the terrace to a table at the far end where the rest of the Watts family was well into their breakfast.

As Jo sat down, they all turned to smile and wave. Jo waved back, then grabbed the menu. She stared blankly for a moment at the left-hand side, which was in Italian, then shifted over and with relief read the English on the right.

THE CIPRIANI BREAKFAST. The Breakfast is served from 7 A.M. to 10:30 A.M. It is included in the room rate and offers: Coffee, Indian or China Tea, Hot Chocolate, Herbal Teas, Milk, Cream, Fruit Juice. Selections of Cereals with Milk, Fresh Bread, Homemade Plumcake and Croissants, Honey, Marmalade, Jams, fresh country Butter, 2 Eggs of the day (either Boiled, Scrambled, or Fried). THE BUFFET is served only in the Restaurant from 7 A.M. to 10 A.M. and offers a wider selection of assorted specialties (cheese, yogurts, Parma Ham, fresh fruit, etc.) in addition to the breakfast. Further requests will be charged a la Carter [sic]. . . .

She'd just started reading about those selections when Tyler arrived.

"Ah, Joanna, good morning." He sat down, bringing with him the powerful citrus scent of his after-shave.

"Good morning," she replied, taking him in.

Today he was dressed more like himself, in a pair of faded jeans and an open-necked short-sleeved Madras cotton shirt. Freshly shaved, his hair still damp, he looked loose-limbed and relaxed. His hands, she saw, were extremely large. Why hadn't she noticed before how large his hands were? Or how clean, yet neglected? It looked as if he'd taken one of those horrible nail clippers to his fingers, leaving the nails cut straight across and close to the quick, with sharp-pointed edges. As she studied his hands, she could almost hear the dreadful *cuh-lick* of the clippers. Greg had used them, whenever the notion had occurred to him, leaving his nail cuttings on the carpet or the bathroom floor for her to find. It was a habit that had repelled her, yet she'd never said a word about it. Just recalling it revived her anger.

"How's your friend?" Tyler asked, reaching for the menu.

"I haven't spoken to her yet this morning. I'm hoping she's better." That bruise had been awful, a desecration on that pure white delicately blue-veined skin. How could a door have done that? Jo wondered, trying to picture it. It hadn't been any goddamned door! she thought, appalled. That bastard had punched Lucienne! He'd taken his fists to her.

"Something wrong?" Tyler held aside his menu.

"What? No. Sorry. I was just thinking about something."

"Something nasty, from the look on your face."

"Sorry," she said again. "Forget it. It's nothing. Well, isn't this amazing! Here you are in Venice."

"Here I am!" he echoed. "Surprised?"

"Astonished."

"Good. What, by the way, seems to be wrong with your friend? She looked perfectly all right when the two of you went off to the loo."

She thought of how she'd planned to explain to him this morning, and she'd been intending to do that. But his manner and the way he asked put her off. She tried to think of some reply, couldn't, and just shrugged. "She wasn't feeling well. I think I'll go up to the buffet. I'm starving."

"Good idea. I'll come, too."

She took a croissant and some cheese, and returned to the table while Tyler loaded up with fruit and cereal, then asked for bacon and eggs. As she tore pieces from the croissant and ate it with bites of cheese between sips of coffee, she watched him consume an enormous amount of food. He did it neatly; no crumbs adhered to his mouth or chin, but there was something about the amount of food and the concentrated fashion in which he ate it that bothered her. She knew she was really bothered because of his negative reference to Lucienne, but it didn't reduce her annoyance. Since he didn't talk while he ate, she had the choice either of continuing to watch him or of looking around at the other guests. She chose to look at the other guests, noting that the Texas family had arrived and was sitting in gloomy silence as their waiter poured coffee. Where was the pop-psych self-help book? How come no reading aloud? Something going on there for sure. The son-in-law looked miserably uncomfortable, as if he'd sat in something wet and didn't have the heart or the courage to speak up. The frowzy daughter looked peevish and stared purposefully at her husband, as if she knew he'd sat in something wet and was daring him to say so. The mother and father glanced every so often at each other. When the waiter came for their order, the mother smiled, and Jo thought again what a fine-looking woman she was. Her smile was lovely and open, illuminating her face. And her husband seemed to think so, too, because he smiled as well, as if in response to the undiluted pleasure the sight of his wife gave him. Here were two handsome, worldly people who cared about each other and made an effort to present their best faces to the world. It must have been hell, Jo thought, having a daughter like that.

"I take it," Tyler said, interrupting her thoughts, "I'm being left to my own devices today."

"Afraid so. And this evening, too. I've got to go to a dinner sponsored by the Italian Tourist Board."

"Hmmmm." He sat away from the table, turning sideways to cross his legs. "Shame," he said. "Still, I expect I'll find something to do."

What did he want, pity? He couldn't show up out of the blue and expect to be entertained. "I'm sure you will," she said nicely.

"I was hoping to be able to spend some time with you," he said, briefly inspecting his critically clipped fingernails.

The waiter arrived with Tyler's bacon and eggs, and Tyler shifted back in to the table, eyeing the plate with satisfaction. He picked up his knife and fork, then looked over at her. "I think," he said slowly, his voice deeply musical, "you're a little pissed off at me, Joanna."

"Of course I'm not," she lied. "It's just that I *am* working, Tyler, and it seems as if you're trying to make me feel guilty because you've gone to all the trouble to come here and I can't spend very much time with you."

"Oh, dear," he said, frowning and smiling simultaneously. "I have no intention of trying to make you feel guilty," he lied. "And if that's the impression I've given, I'm sorry. Naturally, I'm disappointed. Winging my way here, I painted rather elaborate pictures of the sort of things the two of us might get up to. Forgetting completely, I admit, your obligations." He paused and looked at her, waiting to hear what she'd say. He did want her to feel guilty. After all, he *had* gone to a lot of trouble to make what he'd thought would be quite an impressive gesture. And while she'd been polite enough, and surprised, she was decidedly unimpressed. Which forced him to review his own actions, and to concede that as attracted as he was to her, he scarcely knew her. He, therefore, hadn't any right to expect her to perform flips for him. But knowing that didn't relieve him of his disappointment or of his mounting confusion. In the bright light of morning, from moment to moment, she seemed quite unrecognizable to him. So he had to wonder if he appeared equally unrecognizable to her. And if so, what on God's green earth had he been thinking of, coming here to take by surprise a woman whose body was more familiar to him than her face?

Was he playing out some role? she wondered. Did he have a script hidden away somewhere? And if he'd preassigned all the characters, what were her lines supposed to be? God! She didn't know a thing about this man, except that he was attractive and he made love with energy and panache. She'd gone along in conditioned blindness because he'd wanted her, and being wanted was a form of success, of acceptance. She hadn't exercised any discretion, or judgment, or selectivity; she hadn't even decided whether or not she wanted him.

"For God's sake, Tyler," she said angrily. "I'm thirty-six

years old. Of course I've got obligations. All kinds of them. Yes, I appreciate your coming here. I *am* sorry I haven't got any free time today. And you *are* trying to make me feel guilty, but I don't, and I won't. Feel guilty, I mean. I'm free tomorrow evening, and if you'd like to have dinner with me then, that'd be great. Otherwise, I'm afraid you're going to have to amuse yourself. Okay?''

He rocked back in his chair, his eyebrows lifted. "This is an entirely new view of you, Joanna. A little out of character, perhaps.''

"You don't know me, Tyler. And I don't know you.'' They were going to get into an argument, and she was dreading it. She loathed scenes and suddenly she was finding herself in the heart of them with alarming regularity.

"Ah, here you are, Mignon! And Monsieur Emmons!'' Lucienne came drifting toward the table, having undergone another of her extraordinary recoveries. She looked healthy and chic in an ankle-length gauzy white skirt and a cherry-red overblouse with very full sleeves, belted at her slim waist by a broad woven fabric belt in red and white, with white espadrilles that had satin ribbons wound over her ankles and tied in bows at the sides. Her hair was swept back from her face and caught in a loose braid at the back of her neck. "I had hoped you would still be here. I may join you?''

"Of course,'' Jo said quickly. "You look sensational. One of these days you'll have to tell me how you do it.''

"Pah!'' Lucienne passed off the compliment. "It's nothing. You are well, *chérie*? You have a good night?'' she asked Tyler.

Tyler nodded, convinced now that the two women had cooked up that story the night before. This woman looked as if she'd never had a sick day in her life.

"How are you?'' Jo asked her. "Are you all right?''

"Fine, fine. Very hungry. Now you are to tell me what healthy food I must eat.''

"Sure. You want me to come with you to the buffet?''

"But you must. Otherwise I will have coffee and a brioche, and this will not please my new doctor.''

Charlotte Vale Allen

As they approached the buffet, Lucienne took a small package from the pocket of her voluminous skirt and slipped it to Jo, saying, "This is for you, Mignon. You will open it later, eh? From me, to say thank you. What is this you give to me, yogurt? I detest it."

"It's good for you. Thank you, but you don't have to give me anything."

"I know this. I only give what I am not expected to give. Fruit also?" She made a face. "I will grow fat."

"Not on fruit and yogurt. Don't be silly!"

"Listen, Mignon. You want me to take care of that one? I keep him occupied, out of your hair for the day?"

"He can look after himself."

"I don't mind, eh? I am going to look in shops, perhaps to have a glass of wine. I take him with me, if you have no feelings about this."

"All I have is gratitude, if you're sure you don't mind."

"He is not so bad." Lucienne looked covertly over at Tyler. "Now that I am finished with Paolo, it would be amusing."

"Be my guest. He's a nice man, but he's trying to give me the gears, laying a guilt trip on me because I have no time for him today. We don't know each other, Lucienne. It's very awkward. I told him we'd have dinner tomorrow."

"Okay," Lucienne said decisively. "Leave this to me."

Upon returning to the table, Lucienne leaned over to place her hand on Tyler's arm, saying, "Our friend is too busy today for us. You would like to come with me? I take you shopping. You will hate it."

Tyler looked first at her hand on his arm, then at her cleavage, and finally at her smiling face, and said, "Have you been assigned to distract me?" then felt like a complete shit for being so ill mannered.

"Pardon?" She withdrew her hand. "What is this?" she asked Jo.

"He wants to know if he's being set up," Jo answered her. To Tyler she said, "Lucienne's inviting you to spend the day with her. If you want to, say yes. If you don't want to, don't

292

be rude. It's very good of her to offer. Don't behave like a jerk just because things aren't working out the way you hoped they would. Go on, Tyler.'' She smiled at him, suddenly understanding that he was hurt and somewhat embarrassed. "It's not every day a gorgeous woman wants to show you around Venice.''

"Too bloody true,'' he agreed with a laugh, losing his stiffness. "I apologize to both of you for my suspicious nature.'' To Lucienne he said, "I'd love to hate going shopping with you.''

"Eh, bon!" Lucienne picked up her spoon only to stop and gaze balefully at the yogurt. "I must eat this?'' she asked plaintively.

"Go on,'' Jo teased. "You French eat disgusting things like snails. What's a little yogurt?''

"Snails are delicious,'' Lucienne said haughtily.

"And frog's legs, innards of all kinds, brains, for God's sake! Eat your yogurt.''

"I'm rather partial to brains myself,'' Tyler put in. "In black butter. Bliss!''

"I'll include the English on my list of people who eat uneatables,'' Jo laughed.

"This comes,'' Lucienne told Tyler, "from a woman whose country makes a national specialty out of crushed meat on a bun.'' She shook her head and dutifully ate alternating spoonfuls of fruit and yogurt.

Everything was going to be all right, Jo thought with relief, pouring herself another cup of coffee. Jackie waved from the far end of the terrace and she waved back, then checked the time. Ten past nine. She excused herself, saying, "I've got to make a phone call,'' and went to the booth in the corridor to ask the operator to put her through to Anne and Jimmy's room.

Anne answered at once, her voice sounding deep and very cultured.

"Hi, it's Jo. I hope I'm not waking you.''

"No, dear, not at all. I've been up for some time. I was

hoping you'd ring. I don't suppose you have a few free minutes?"

"When, now?"

"If it's convenient."

"Sure. Would you like me to come to you?"

"That would be good of you."

"Okay."

"Oh, one thing. I'm on the patio, dear. Would you mind very much coming round? Just beyond the pool."

"I'll be there in five minutes."

"So good of you," Anne said, and put the phone down so quietly there was no audible disconnecting sound.

"I have an errand to do," Jo told Lucienne and Tyler. "I don't know how long I'll be, so if I don't make it back by nine-thirty, the two of you go ahead, and I'll try to check in at some point later on. Okay?"

"Go on, Mignon. I will take care of your friend."

"Yes," Tyler said, looking quite content, "I'm in very good hands." He gave her a smile with no hooks or hidden barbs, and she smiled back as she picked up her purse and the camera bag before heading across the terrace.

22

ONCE PAST THE TERRACE, IT WAS VERY QUIET, THE SUN
slanting at an oblique angle through the trees. Jo walked past
the pool, glancing at the rooms and patios to her left as she
went, and almost passed Anne by. There was a space between the enclosing shrubberies, and Jo's eye was caught by
a bit of color that caused her to back up. The color was in
Anne's dress, a royal blue shirtwaist with white piping.

Stepping into the space between the bushes, Jo said,
"Good morning."

Anne looked up with a smile. "Do come sit down, dear."

Jo put her bags on the flagstones and sat. On a low table
near Anne was a tray with coffee, and an ashtray. The telephone was on the ground within arm's reach. Which was
why, Jo thought, she'd picked up so quickly.

Looking relaxed, her legs crossed and elbows resting on
the arms of the chair, Anne was smoking a cigarette. She
seemed most serene, the movement of her hand with the
cigarette calm and slow as her eyes rested on Jo for a time
before she asked, "Would you care for some coffee?"

"No, thank you. How are you? You look wonderful."

Anne's smile returned as she reached for her coffee, then
slowly faded. She sat holding the cup with both hands, the

cigarette between the fingers of her right hand. "You look so very young," she said, her voice almost dreamy. "I think I've arrived at an age where almost everyone looks quite impossibly young. It makes me rather sentimental to look at you, and to remember the soaring energy I had at your age, and the sense I had then that everything was yet to come. Do you have that sense, Joanna?"

"Sometimes. And other times, I feel the way you said you do: unable to believe I'm not still sixteen. It's all completely relative, don't you think?"

"Yes, of course. But there does come a point when one is able to look back over the many stages of one's life and see how events, circumstances, shaped one. I've never minded growing older," Anne said. "I truly haven't. Upon turning thirty, I thought, 'Now, I will have some degree of credibility.' But I had scarcely more of it than I'd had at twenty-nine. Then, at forty, I thought, '*Now* my words and opinions will carry some weight.' And there was some evidence of that. At fifty, I was no longer concerned with credibility. I was utterly preoccupied with what appeared to be an endlessly unpleasant series of surprises nature had arranged for me." She laughed quietly. "I tried assiduously not to be horrified by my personal degeneration, by the too visible alterations to a body I'd fairly much taken for granted for the first forty-odd years of my life. Quite a number of very rude surprises! Then, by sixty, I surrendered my preoccupation for a bit of private gratification at having survived both my regrettable vanity and nature's ongoing assault. Now, here I am, mere inches away from seventy, and I cannot for the life of me think why I fussed as I did over what is, after all, a perfectly natural progression. I have come, at long last, to accept the inevitability of it all." She drank some of the coffee, then returned the cup to the tray, and put out her cigarette, only to light another at once.

Jo wished she could photograph Anne in this light. Her hair was pure silver and it glistened, as did the diamond studs in her ears. She had around her neck an exquisite long gold necklace whose detailing was set in relief by the deep blue silk of the dress. This was the first time Jo was aware of Anne wearing makeup. Very little: mascara, a bit of color on her high cheekbones, and a pink-brown lipstick. With those clear, rare green eyes, she was still an arresting woman.

"I wouldn't mind being you," Jo told her, "if I ever grow up."

"Oh, my dear, I don't think I've ever really grown up. But how kind of you to be so complimentary."

"No, it's the truth," Jo said. "I've been sitting here thinking how beautiful you are. It's more than physical; it's light and bone-structure and the way I feel about you, too." As she spoke, she thought how strange it was that her hands rested comfortably in her lap; they didn't twitch with a need to pick up the camera.

"*Is* there someone you care about?" Anne asked. "I know you were rather embarrassed when Lucienne made that comment the first evening we dined together and it's intrusive of me to ask, but is there someone?"

"I don't really know. One minute I think yes. The next I'm not sure. All I do know is I seem to care more for Henry today than I thought I ever could care about anybody a week ago. I mean, there were flowers from him in my room when I arrived. And yesterday he sent a telex. I feel as if I want to see him very much. Then I tell myself not to hope for too much because I'll be disappointed. The thing is, I've always been afraid that I'd get married and be happy, then one day find out that this man I thought I knew was seeing other women, sleeping with them afternoons in hotel rooms. My father did, and I could never understand why my mother put up with it, why she didn't leave him. But she and I never talked about it. That was the conversation we were supposed to have, but it never happened. The whole time I was growing up I wanted to hear her side of it, her reasons. The part that defeated me was that they loved each other. You could *see* it. And no matter what went on, if they argued or slammed out of the house, it didn't make a difference, because the first person either of them turned to was the other. My grandmother one time got fed up with my going on and on about it, and said, 'Who ever promised you things were going to be easy? Who ever signed that in blood for you, Joanna?' God! I was so ashamed, because in a lot of ways that's exactly what it was like: as if I'd been promised all kinds of things—understanding, happiness, an easy route straight to what I wanted. And she made me see that there were things I was just too young to understand, and other things I had no right to expect. So I stopped expecting anything. And I stopped judging situations that didn't make sense to me. And I promised myself I'd have everything I ever wanted, because I'd work myself to death to get them. But nothing anybody could ever say was going to convince me to trust any man enough to want to commit myself to him. Yet, if I were going to trust anyone, it would be Henry. And I'm not even sure I could tell you why.''

"It is well worth the pain and the effort," Anne said. "Oh, there are times when one is bound to wonder at the cost, naturally. But for the most part, one returns to the initial certainty, that instinct that told you you were about to lose a piece of yourself that you could never again retrieve, and, in return, you would have the benefit of all the drama and hilarity, all the infuriation and irritation, all the warmth and closeness that comes of making the effort to share yourself and your experiences.''

"If you can say that after fifty years, it must be true."

"One would think so. Are you sure you won't have some coffee?''

"All right, I will, thank you. I'll get it." She went to pour herself a cup and to refill Anne's, then returned to her seat, aware of Anne's eyes following her. If it were anyone else, being so closely watched would have made her uncomfortable, but with Anne she felt quite at ease. There wasn't the faintest judgmental element in the woman's gaze.

"I think every marriage that's ever been has had some degree of dishonesty in it," Anne told her. "Oh, not necessarily infidelity per se, although it's far more common than perhaps you believe. But thoughts of others, the speculation of what some man might be like, or some woman. There's a benchmark, as it were. One arrives at a plateau in the marriage where one's partner is no longer so mysterious or so compelling as he was to you at the outset. You've been overexposed to one another; you know each other's habits and propensities; you know the surface of each other's bodies more intimately than any physician ever could. At this juncture you must decide if your knowledge is going to inspire either contempt or fondness. If that basic abiding attachment is there, it isn't too terribly difficult to find the fondness. And then, my dear, if one has faith, something quite extraordinary occurs: From the fondness comes a rekindling of the love. It's as if you've set a small fire that takes hold and burns far beyond its allotted time. And having come through all the tedious, tiresome times relatively intact, you're able to go forward together because what you had at the outset was of sufficient depth and strength to see you through.

"In the case of our marriage, I was the one who, as you put it, had rendezvous in hotel rooms. Ah, I've shocked you. It isn't shocking, really. I became involved with Jimmy when I was eighteen. For twenty-five years he was the sun and the moon. And then one morning I was forty-three and fearful that I'd lost whatever appeal I might once have had. It hadn't anything to do, actually, with Jimmy, but everything to do with me. And it's never ceased to intrigue me how attractive men seem to find women who are married. It wasn't at all difficult. It was not, however, particularly rewarding. Half a dozen tension-fraught illicit meetings on visits to London under the pretext of shopping, and then I'd had enough and put a stop to it.

"I'd satisfied my vanity, you see. I'd also broken vows that I'd taken most seriously twenty-five years before. But after all those years those vows scarcely seemed relevant. I'd come to believe that remaining sexually faithful to one person for the duration of one's life was not only unrealistic but impractical. If for no other reason than to confirm the strength of my feelings for my husband, what I did outside the marriage was of infinite value. It afforded me an opportunity to reevaluate my marriage, as well as my feelings for Jimmy. It also allowed me to see that no one else—should I care to go out looking—could ever touch me, in every way, as Jimmy did. And so I went home to my husband and never again had any interest in other men, or any serious doubts about our marriage. It took being unfaithful to make me appreciate how very, very much I cared for the man I'd married."

"Did he ever know about it?" Jo asked her.

"Oh, never! I wouldn't have dreamed of hurting him by revealing what I'd done. And he'd have been devastated, because Jimmy, like the majority of men, has always believed that a woman he loved wouldn't be capable of betraying him. They, of course, wouldn't consider it a betrayal if they did those same things. But wives, especially of my generation, were property, chattel. I cannot tell you how glad I am that all that has changed. I think I railed more against the notion of being another of Jimmy's 'holdings' than I would have done had he made love to a dozen other women. And heaven only knows, he had ample opportunity. But he never took advantage of those opportunities."

"How do you know that for sure?"

"Oh, I'd have known," she said with quiet confidence. "Poor darling never had any talent for indiscretion. He was always too basically honest." She looked over at the sliding doors to the suite, then back at Jo.

"You make it sound so possible," Jo said, feeling herself strongly swayed.

"It *is* possible. I have done it, after all. And if you'll forgive me for venturing to give an opinion where none's been requested, if you have a chance to share your life, Joanna, don't let it pass you by, whatever your reservations might be. I do, with all my heart, believe people are meant to be together, not alone, locked nightly into safe little cubicles. It's too, too sad to avoid an emotional life simply because of one or two bad experiences and a set of distorted childhood memories. Tell me about him," she invited. "Is he kind to you, this young man Henry? Does he concern himself with your well-being?"

"He's not overtly demonstrative, but I think he does care.

But Anne,'' she protested, ''for all I know, I'm imagining things. For all I know, he has no feelings for me—beyond the professional ones he has to have, because I'm a client of his, after all. I keep having the feeling that I'm making this whole thing up, that all my thoughts are slightly out of whack because of this trip, the train, this hotel, this city. And it's the kind of thing single women do, you know. I mean, we embroider mental images, these perfect pictures in our heads, right to the smallest detail. And then we end up not sure what's true and what we made up.''

''He's sent you flowers and a cable, and you're of the opinion you're merely wool-gathering?'' Anne's eyebrows lifted. ''Surely not. It sounds as if he's making an effort to state his case. The question is whether you're making an equal effort.''

''Are you trying to get me married off?'' Jo asked with a little laugh. ''You're sounding an awful lot like a mother.''

Anne laughed with her, saying, ''It's what I've been for the better part of my life, after all. And you do indulge me, so it seems perfectly legitimate for me to give voice to my motherly opinions.''

''You and I have the damnedest conversations.''

''We do, don't we?'' Anne concurred. ''I can't begin to tell you how much pleasure they give me. I wonder from moment to moment if, had things been different, I would have been able to talk this way with Lucia. But it wouldn't have been possible.''

''Why not?''

Anne sighed. ''For one thing, mothers and daughters seem congenitally unable to have conversations where the entire weight of their shared history doesn't come crowding in to affect the tone and the content.''

''I guess you're right. Somehow, I'm always one hundred percent truthful with you; you keep me honest because I know you're being honest with me. With Lily I was always afraid something I'd say might inadvertently upset her. She was very complicated. I can see her so clearly, but it would take me years to describe how she was. I loved her; she fascinated me, but we were never close, not the way I was with Granny Emily. It was as if Lily used up the biggest part of her emotional resources on my father, and there just wasn't enough left over for Beamer and me. She was intuitive, but vague; she was talented, but undirected; she was inquisitive, but never persistent in terms of getting an answer. She was forward in her thinking, but I never saw her body until she was dying. And it mortified her to be so weak that she needed me to help her. Yet in helping her I finally saw the body that had made me. It seemed so strange to me, growing up, that she'd cover herself if I came into her bedroom when she was dressing. I thought for the longest time there was something wrong with her that she didn't want me to see. But there wasn't. Even dying she was really very lovely. I looked at her and tried to understand why she'd hidden herself from me all of my life. So much for that. Lily took most of her secrets with her when she died, and I'll probably get to be an old, old woman before I'm able to work out who she really was.''

"We, all of us, appear differently to different people," Anne said, putting out her cigarette and lighting another at once. She drank some of the fresh coffee, then returned the cup to the tray. "I should hate to think we wouldn't have many more of these talks together."

"I'd hate it, too. I've been meaning to ask if you'd give me your address so I could come visit you both sometime."

"I have been hoping you'd ask."

"Oh, I'm so glad," Jo said, relieved. She'd been apprehensive for a moment, thinking perhaps she was trying to create a long-term friendship out of something meant to last only a short time. "I'll tell you something," she said, leaning closer to Anne. "I've learned something important this week. It may sound ridiculous, but I've discovered I'm not my mother. Just because I accepted her definition of me and have gone along with it for all these years doesn't mean I'm supposed to be a carbon copy of a woman I never really knew. I think I believed that if I were more like her she'd confide in me. But I couldn't be her, and now that I can see what it was I've been doing, I know I don't *want* to be her. And you're not your daughter, either. You're not Lucia; you're not responsible for the way she turned out.

"If we were allowed second chances, if God or whatever power there is said, 'Okay, you can have another one, pick anyone you'd like,' I'd choose you for my mother. I can't think of anyone else I could talk with the way I do with you; I can't think of anything that would feel better or more right than being able to come to see you. It feels as if it would be like coming home."

Anne's eyes filled, and Jo thought perhaps she might cry. But she held the cigarette to her mouth and drew on it, then exhaled and said in measured tones, "Only once before have I capitulated without question to my instincts, my dear. And that was when I met Jimmy. This is the second occasion. Initially, I was taken by your uncanny resemblance to Lucia. But what I've come to love in you is the great depths of your honesty. I believe you're incapable of deceit. I don't think you've ever in your life said or done anything that violated your integrity. I'm also impressed by the enormous untapped resource of your caring. It seems to me you've never allowed yourself or anyone else to benefit from your capacity for passionate attachment—except, possibly through your camera. And I've never witnessed anything quite like your interaction with that device. Is it possible you've substituted that visual aid for something more direct? Don't answer, just consider the possibility. More motherly advice," she said with a smile. "Don't be timid about your feelings for this young man, Joanna. Even if it doesn't work out as you'd wish, you'll have lost nothing. Perhaps because you didn't come to know your mother as you'd have liked, you feel you haven't come to know yourself. It sounds to me like a reasonable hypothesis. But perhaps your Lily never knew herself. Had you considered that? No matter. You have a unique ability to give of yourself even when you're not certain why you're doing it. Very few people are willing to give anything at all, but you do, wholeheartedly and with both hands open. Meeting you, knowing you, has been a positive blessing. And nothing would make me happier than to have you come to visit.'' She reached down to open the catch of her handbag, withdrew the Cartier wallet, and took out a card. "I would be so grateful if you'd ring me upon your return to London. Perhaps you might even come to see me midweek, if you're free.''

"Midweek? I don't understand. Are you leaving?''

"I expect by this afternoon we'll have gone," Anne said.

"But what about Jimmy's schedule, lunch today at the Lido . . . ?''

Her voice still soft, her tone unchanged, Anne said, "Jimmy died several hours ago, Joanna. I will be taking him back to England later today.''

Jo didn't think she could have heard correctly. Jimmy *died*? He was dead, and they'd been sitting out here, talking? She stared at Anne and suddenly things clicked into place: Anne's answering the telephone so quickly, her asking Jo to come around to the patio, her chainsmoking, the nature of the conversation itself. "Oh, God!" Jo whispered, profoundly shaken. "I don't—''

"It was not unexpected," Anne clarified. "I had thought there would be more time, but it was not unexpected.''

Jo's immediate reaction was to offer comfort. But as she began to rise from her chair, Anne quickly said, "Please, don't, Joanna. I'd like nothing more right now than to embrace you, but if I allow myself that luxury, I will come to pieces, and I cannot do that now. There's too much to be done, and I must be all of a piece to do it. I'm sorry to put it to you so baldly, but please try not to be too upset. Jimmy was close to eighty, and he's been very happy these past few years. Most importantly, he was able to come here, to Venice, and that meant the world to him. It was a long-time dream come true, and there is a very real satisfaction to knowing he spent his final days in a place he loved.'' Anne looked at her watch. "It's almost ten, dear. You have an appointment to keep, and I'm afraid I have a great deal to do.''

Jo wanted to stay and help, yet she could see she had no

choice but to go. Feeling as if she'd just sustained a blow to the stomach, she retrieved her bags, got up, then hesitated. "I don't know what to say. I liked him so much, he was so lovable. . . . Is there anything I can do for you, anything at all? Oh, damn!" She had to stop. For Anne's sake she didn't dare let herself go.

Anne held out her hand, and Jo took hold.

"You've made this so much less difficult than it might have been," she told Jo. For a moment her eyes reflected doubt, or fear. Jo could see that she was floundering, as she had during their conversation on the train.

"I love you," Jo said inadequately. "I really do."

Anne nodded, then released her, saying, "Go along now."

"Will you be all right?"

"I am very selfish, you know. Being able to look forward to your visit will see me through what's to come. Is that unforgivable?" she wondered. "Is it too much to ask?"

"It's not nearly enough," Jo answered. "I'd be willing to do much, much more. I'll be there whenever you want me. I'll go back with you today, if it would help."

"Thank you," Anne said, her voice thinning. She drew on the cigarette, then lifted her hand to signal Jo to go. "Thank you so very much," she said in a whisper, as Jo backed through the hedges, then turned and ran off.

Jackie was leaning against the wall outside the kitchen door. Upon seeing her, he pushed away from the wall and smiled. She came over and gave him an emphatic hug. He hugged her back, then said, "Hey! What's wrong? Are you okay?"

"I'll tell you later. I don't think I can talk about it now."

"You're not sick or anything, are you?" he asked.

"No, I'm not sick."

"Is it about your friends, the English people?"

"What?"

"Everybody's talking about it. You heard, right? He died this morning."

"I heard. Everybody knows?"

"I guess. It's really too bad. He was cool. We talked for

a while the other day. He was telling me about the restorations he'd seen. Anyway, they say he just went in his sleep. If it was me, that'd be the way I'd want to go.''

''Yes,'' she said dully.

''You gonna cry, Joey?''

She shook her head.

''You want me to take off? I'll understand if you do.''

''No. I'd really like your company.''

''Sure. But if you change your mind just say the word and I'm out of here.''

''I won't change my mind. We'd better get going. I hate being late.''

''I'll take the camera bag.'' He reached to remove it from her shoulder.

She watched him for a moment, then said, ''You're a sensational guy. You know that?''

''Sure,'' he grinned. ''Everybody says so.''

''And so modest,'' she added, glad of his presence.

''Yeah, that too.'' He pushed open the kitchen door. ''After you, kiddo.''

''I don't think I'm going to be very good company today,'' she warned him.

''That's cool. I understand.''

''You really do, don't you?''

''Well, sure,'' he said quietly, then exclaimed, ''Check this out! Gives a whole new meaning to 'clean.' ''

At his bidding she turned to look at the first of the two spotless adjoining kitchens. Work to do, she reminded herself. Then, with a sigh, she adjusted the camera strap around her neck and started toward the inner kitchen, where the chef was waiting.

23

". . . THREE DAYS' WORK IN KITCHEN FOR EACH DEPARTURE.
Chef, Renato Piccolotto, young, very little Eng., patient in
miming explanations. Menus decided by group—chef, stewards. Seasonal menus: spring/summer; winter/fall. All written out on white board on wall far end of kitchen. 2 columns
each side sep. by column for brunch—1 for lunch, 1 for dinner each direction (see negs). Renato works with 2 assts., all
3 in white w/tall pleated hats; R. wears white scarf knotted
around neck, mustache & beard (like Henry's). He looks
more like artist than chef. Wed.—veg. peeled & cut, ready
to cook on train. Thurs.—1st meat, then fish made ready—
all fresh, nothing frozen. Fri. A.M.—veg. blanched & packed
airtight in heavy plastic, sealed by special machine; half-
cooked, finished on train; meat & fish then pkged. airtight.
Sat. 6 A.M.—food loaded.

"After blanching, veg. & some sauces go into quick cooler
for ½ hr., then made airtight. Cool rooms to store veg., meat,
fish; food put in foil containers, plastic over top, then airtight
machine. Very impressive, very modern equipment. Also
Thurs. A.M., potatoes cooked, scooped, inside mixed w/
egg, butter, cooked ham, returned to shell & gratinated. Fil-

lets of beef; baby zucchinis sliced at top, tomato slices inserted, artwork.

"As much done in adv. as poss. Asst. slicing beef on butcher's block, trying not to smile when I take his ph., R. showing large tray of slivered carrots; very proud of his work; all 3 enjoying themselves. Whole time J. & I in kitchen, I was thinking of Anne talking, feeling I should've known, but didn't. Such a jolt, and the way she said it, so quietly. Want to call Henry . . ."

She looked up from her notes to see Jackie with her camera, carefully turning it this way and that, then holding it to his eye. He turned, aiming the camera at her, and she waited to see what he'd do. He hesitated, his finger on the shutter release, and she said, "Go ahead. You know how it works. Don't be afraid to try it."

"You sure?"

"Yup. Just check all your settings, then ease out the winder a notch and push down lightly on the shutter release. If you get a red light on the meter, go up an F-stop. If it's green, you're all right. Check your focus and shoot. Get used to handling the camera. If you buy one for yourself, experiment. Don't be afraid to make mistakes, because you can learn a hell of a lot from the shots you mess up."

"Okay." He ran through all the steps as she'd instructed, took a shot, then replaced the lens cap and set the camera on the table, asking, "Finished?"

"Yup. I am now an authority on the Orient-Express. Ask me anything!"

"Okay." He thought for a moment. "What's the name of the engineer?"

"Which one?" she countered.

"There's more than one?"

"Yup. New ones in every country."

"Okay. Wait a minute. All right. What kind of train is it? I mean, what's the power source?"

"Electricity. All European trains are electric."

"No shit! I didn't know that."

"Well, there you go." She opened her purse to put away

the notebook and pen, and saw the package Lucienne had given her that morning. "I forgot all about this."

"What is it?" he asked, leaning with both elbows on the table.

"I don't know."

"So, open it. What is it, a present? Who from, that actor?"

"I take it you don't like him."

"Do you?" he hedged.

"No, tell me, Jackie."

"I didn't *dis*like him or anything. I just didn't like the way he put me down. 'Jackie, did you say?' " he mimicked Tyler. "I hope he's not like your main squeeze or anything."

"No. He's just a friend."

"That's good, 'cause he's got the major hots for the French lady. She a friend of yours?"

"Yes."

Jackie shook his head. "That is one stupendous-looking wench! Also really cool. I mean, letting me taste her champagne."

"You liked her, huh?"

Jackie laughed. "Are you kidding? I *loved* her! I could feel myself starting to drool." He let his tongue loll out the side of his mouth while his eyes went vague.

Jo laughed. "You're a dirty little boy."

"That's cool. At least I've got good taste. So are you going to open that or what?"

"I guess I should, shouldn't I?" She undid the paper, then said, "Oh, God!"

"What?" Jackie wanted to know, craning to see. "What?"

"It's from Cartier."

"No shit! Open it!"

"I'm afraid to."

"Why?"

"Because it's too much. I can't accept something like this."

"Don't you think," he said reasonably, "you should check it out before you say you can't accept it?"

"I'm afraid to," she said again.

"Well, I'm not. You want me to open it?" When she didn't respond, he took the red box from her and opened it. "This is cool," he said, lifting out a simple gold chain bracelet. "Look!" He held it up for her, saw the tears spilling down her cheeks, and said, "You need a drink." Putting the bracelet into her hand, he went inside the café to find a waiter. Then he came hurrying back to sit close to her, pressing his handkerchief into her hand. "It's okay, Joey," he said, patting her shoulder. "It's okay."

The waiter came quickly, carrying a glass on a tray.

"Thanks a lot," Jackie said, taking the glass from him and setting it down in front of Jo. "Drink some of that," he told her.

She sniffed and wiped her face with the handkerchief. "What is it?"

"Brandy and soda. It's what my dad drinks when everything hits the fan, so I figure it must do some good."

She picked up the glass, took a swallow, then set it back on the table and ran her finger around the rim. "This has been one bitch of a day," she said, her eyes on the bracelet.

"Any good?" Jackie asked of the drink.

"I don't know. Have a taste and tell me."

He took a sip, made a face and put it down. "I'd rather have another espresso. But I think you'd better drink it."

"I'll get bombed."

"So what?"

"You're right. So what?" She took another swallow, then picked up the bracelet. "In my whole life, nobody's ever given me anything like this."

"It was me," he said wisely, "I'd be offended if you gave it back. It was me, I'd put it on right now and wear the sucker."

She looked questioningly at him, then again at the bracelet. "You're right," she decided. "You're absolutely right." She fastened it around her right wrist, then admired the way it looked. "It's beautiful, isn't it?" she said, the tears starting up again.

"Drink some more!" he advised, pushing the glass against her hand.

She wiped her eyes, then smiled at him. "One day, kiddo, you're going to make some woman very happy."

"You think so?" he asked, looking proud.

"I know it. Whatever their faults might be, your folks have raised you to be a hell of a decent guy."

"They're not so bad," he allowed, "just kind of neurotic now and then."

"The shops ought to be opening again soon. I really wanted to take a look at the masks in that shop by the Rialto. You know the place we saw yesterday?"

"Okay. Drink up and we'll go." He reached for his wallet.

"Save your money in case you see something you want to buy."

"Okay. Thanks a lot. The lunch was really good, especially the green spaghetti."

She had to laugh. "Spinach pasta. You can't go around telling people you ate green spaghetti."

"That's what it was."

"I give up." She looked at the bill, laid some notes and coins on top of it, then collected her things.

As they started off, she said, "Jackie, d'you ever get the feeling somebody else is running your show, that you're almost incidental to the things that happen?"

"All the time," he answered. "I'm a kid, don't forget. Everybody runs me. The only thing I get to do that nobody supervises is think. Oh sure, I can go out, hang out with my friends and like that, but there's a curfew, and stuff I'm supposed to do at home, all kinds of rules. Why?"

"I don't know. Here I am, thirty-six years old, and right now I feel kind of clueless. Yesterday I thought I was really getting somewhere, breaking away from years of doing dumb-ass things, behaving like a wimp. Today, I'm back to feeling like a wimp."

"You're upset, that's all."

"That's only part of it. It feels as if my whole life's been changed by this trip. I mean, I've been more in charge of

Charlotte Vale Allen

myself this week than I've ever been before. I mean, everything that's happened, from the moment I got on the train,
has been different. All the people I've met, the new friends
I've made, this city . . . I'm not sure I can explain it. Take
you, for example.'' She turned to him. ''Aside from my
brother Beamer, and my first boyfriend, Tom Harper, who
was fifteen, I've never spent any time to speak of with kids.
But the time I've spent with you has been so wonderful.''
She had to stop and clear her throat before she was able to
go on. ''I meant what I said to your parents. I think it would
be fantastic to have a kid like you. I probably never will, but
from now on I'm never again going to be irritated when I zip
down to Darien to Baskin-Robbins for some ice cream and
there are eighteen kids hanging around outside, leaning on
their bikes, blocking the entrance.''

''They do that in Connecticut, too?'' he laughed. ''I
thought it was just us.''

''Well, next time I'll pretend you're one of those kids, and
be a little nicer about it when I ask them to move. You know
what you said about people growing up and forgetting all the
things they knew as kids? That's been me. It really has. But
no more, though. I've learned a lot about myself this past
week. And I'm through with letting people say things that
offend the hell out of me and not saying anything, just sitting
there getting madder and madder instead of telling them
they're full of shit, they don't know what they're talking
about. I loved that old man, Jackie. I felt as if I'd known him
all my life. He brought out the best in me. They both did. I
thought, somehow, they were going to be in my life from
now until forever, that I'd go visit and take Jimmy books on
the Venetian artists, or blocks of watercolor paper, or some
sable brushes, or something. I was in love with the idea of
being able to be with them, because they'd made it through
fifty years of marriage and still cared for each other. Then,
this morning, Anne and I talked, and she made me see that
I'd set standards—for myself and for others—that no one
could ever live up to. She made me see I've spent a hell of a
long time being a wimp with a serious hidden agenda. And

she also made me see that if I'd only allow a bit of room for human error—mine and anyone else's—I could have a lot more of a life than I do. She sat there and told me to take chances, to have a little faith and trust; she cared enough about me to be encouraging, and *her husband had just died*. Don't you think," she asked anxiously, "if someone cares enough to tell you the truth at a time like that, you've got a moral obligation not only to listen but to try to do something about it?"

"You'd think so," he agreed.

"Right! So before I go to that dinner tonight, I'm going to try to get hold of Henry on the phone and tell him I'm willing to give it a shot."

"Who's Henry?"

"Henry," she explained, "is the guy in London; someone, I think, who loves me."

His secretary told her Henry had gone for the day. And when Jo called the house, she got his answering machine. She thought of hanging up, decided she'd have to pay for the call anyway, so she waited for the beep and said, "It's Jo. I was really hoping to talk to you. It's been a rough day. But never mind. I'll see you Sunday night when I get back."

She'd no sooner hung up than the telephone rang.

"Mignon, you are all right?" Lucienne asked. "We come back in the afternoon and we hear. It is so very sad. I like this old man very much."

"I'm all right. How about you? Has Tyler been behaving himself?"

"You mean, does he throw me down and try to make love with me in a gondola?" Lucienne laughed. "No, he is a gentleman, and he behaves very nicely. Listen, Mignon. Laura, she comes to us at the table this morning when you have left, to say the people who are to go with you tonight cannot go, eh? And so we go with you, me and Tyler. This is okay? You have objections?"

"No, none. I've been dreading going alone, spending the evening with a bunch of strangers."

"Good! So we meet with you at six-thirty, and we go together, okay?"

"Fine. Lucienne, the bracelet's beautiful. But you shouldn't have given it to me."

"Of course I should!" Lucienne disagreed. "I want you to have this. It makes me happy to give it to you."

"Well, thank you very much. I love it."

"*Et bon!* I go now for my bath. *Au 'voir, chérie.*"

"*Au 'voir*, Lucienne."

After the call she thought again about Henry, wishing he'd been home. There was so much she wanted to say to him, and she had the feeling that if she didn't get it said very soon she might change her mind and go home to Connecticut without saying anything at all.

Since leaving Anne that morning, she'd found herself operating on a new plane. Pieces of information and knowledge seemed to home in on her at random moments, making her pause while she tried to assemble the knowledge into a recognizable whole. Everything seemed to tie into something else, yet bits hung over at the edges, dangling untidily. Now, as she went through her clothes, trying to decide what to wear, she couldn't help thinking how foolish it seemed to be fretting over what might be appropriate dress for the evening. It annoyed her to have to go through the process of selecting yet another outfit for yet another evening out. It shouldn't have mattered what she wore, but it did. Because it had been brought home to her in the strongest possible way that she *was* visible, that people *did* see her, and she'd also discovered that she wanted to be seen.

All her life she'd been buying clothes, as if in defiance of her sometime sense of invisibility. She'd taken pleasure in acquiring new things to wear, yet for the most part she'd felt something of a fraud in her clothes—as if she'd borrowed without permission items belonging to someone else that didn't quite mesh with her own personality. She'd been covering her body with garments she very much liked but which she felt were misrepresentational; she could never make the connection between the woman and her clothes. She always ended up wondering why she had so little pride in herself that even her clothes felt alien. Now she understood that with a bit of self-esteem the clothes would become secondary. And she wanted to explain this new insight to Henry. She wanted to take all the chances Anne had said she should, but it wasn't easy to break habits that had become ingrained. If only he'd been home when she'd called. The timing had been right; she'd have been able to tell him how she felt. What if she got back to London only to find she'd lost her nerve? God!

Fifteen minutes spent examining the items in the closet before selecting the short white skirt and purple-blue Claude Montana top Henry had admired; white high heels and sheer white Fogal panty hose with tiny white dots. Name brands. The shoes were Joan & David; her slip was Christian Dior. Goddamned ridiculous! she thought, laying everything out on the bed before going to take her shower. She was a mobile billboard, so she might as well use the Emilio Pucci soap, she decided, grabbing it out of the basket on the bathroom counter. One of these days, she promised herself, suddenly taken by an image of herself in Henry's garden, she was going to put on a no-name T-shirt, some good old jeans, jam her feet into a pair of ten-dollar running shoes and just be whoever the hell she was. Enough of all this brand-name consumerism.

Or did the labels mean something? They were, these quality goods, the rewards she gave herself for jobs well done. And her rewards were all over the condo, even parked outside the front door. She'd been diligently shopping, making purchases most of her adult life, in an attempt to fill a gigantic hole in her life. It was why she never said no when Gracie called to say there was another assignment. Because her work *was* her life. There was no one to come home to. It was too much trouble to stock the kitchen when she was never there long enough to eat more than a few meals. And when she did cook, she invariably wound up throwing food away. So what did she do when she was home? She rented movies and stunned her senses into obedience. Or she spent hours in the darkroom poring over the slide-and-negative files. She didn't even look after the place; the cleaning lady did that. At least Henry had the garden; he worked at it, and it was beautiful. She just sat out on her deck and watched the ducks on the pond. Some life: hanging around between jobs, waiting to get old and have the whole thing over and done with.

Well, it didn't have to be that way. Anne was right. She had choices; she could do any damned thing she wanted. And just because Henry hadn't happened to be home didn't mean she couldn't save up what she wanted to say to him for a time when he was available to hear her. One slight setback and she was ready to give up. It wasn't the only opportunity she was going to have to talk with him. It was, in fact, only the first time she'd really wanted to. Someone special had died, and she'd wanted to share her feelings and thoughts about it with Henry, because she believed he'd care. He would care, too, she thought, looking at herself in the mirror. And why not? she asked her mirror image. Look at you! You are, according to the resident fourteen-year-old authority, a comely wench with an aristocratic honker.

24

As the motor launch traveled across the canal from Giudecca toward the piazza, Jo thought about the scene in the movie *Don't Look Now* when the Donald Sutherland character saw his wife and the two strange sisters, all three in black, on a vaporetto heading down the Grand Canal. He'd been seeing the future, but hadn't known it. And at the end of the movie, after he'd been killed by the dwarf in the red cape (the small creature he'd thought was a child) there was Julie Christie, who'd played his wife, and the two sisters (one of them the blind psychic who'd predicted his death) on a vaporetto going down the canal. Strange and creepy. She imagined Anne on a boat with a coffin bearing Jimmy's body to its final resting place. Except that Anne had flown back to London in the afternoon, and Jimmy would be buried in the family plot.

"You are sad, eh?" Lucienne said quietly at her side.

"I am. But most of all, I'm worn out. It feels as if I've been in a week-long marathon, running nonstop. It's so beautiful, isn't it?" She looked at the apricot glow of the fading light, the facades of the buildings going dark as the sun dropped behind them.

"Oh, yes," Lucienne agreed, "very beautiful. This is a city to make you sentimental, eh?"

"Will you still come here, now that it's all over with you and Paolo?"

"But of course!" Lucienne looked surprised. "Why wouldn't I come? This city has nothing to do with Paolo. He is only an accident, an interruption. Venice is my holiday, my pleasure, my paradise. This is where I come when I have enough of Chez Lucienne and the days that begin at six in the morning and end at midnight. I would allow *nothing* to spoil this for me."

Jo looked over at Tyler, who was talking with the Texas couple who, for a change, were without their daughter and her husband. "I want to ask you something," Jo said, satisfied their conversation couldn't be overheard by those at the far end of the cabin. "He hit you, didn't he? You didn't get that bruise from any door. It was Paolo, wasn't it?"

Lucienne's eyes shifted, and she turned, presenting Jo with her perfect profile as she stared off into space. She closed her eyes for a second or two, then opened them and turned back to Jo. "I refused him," she said, with a look that seemed to say she could scarcely believe any of it had happened. "He would have me anyway, because he wishes to show his power. I would not fight; I would show him nothing, no anger, no fear, so he cannot be satisfied, eh, because if I do not fight, if I show no upset, he cannot see that he hurts me. He makes a fool of himself, ruining my clothes, pulling at my hair. It is incredible to me to think I would marry this man when I don't know him. And he is completely crazy. He would rape me because I refuse him. But even that is no good, eh? No rape, but he tries. I do nothing, just watch him, and say to him to go because I am exhausted after so much fighting. Please go, I tell him, and get up to cover myself, thinking he is a pig to ruin my dress, my stockings. I don't care about him. I just wish for him to go away, so I don't have to see him and think to myself how stupid I am to believe I could make a marriage with such a crazy pig. Go away, I say to him. And then he hits me. He shouts and shouts, and I am on the floor thinking he has perhaps killed me because I cannot breathe. And finally, he grows tired of shouting and he goes away. *Finis*."

Jo put her arm around Lucienne's shoulder and rested her cheek against hers. "I'm so sorry," she said, holding her for a moment before sitting back, only to be startled when Lucienne grabbed her hand and said, "You save me from making a disaster, Joanna. What happened is *nothing*! I prefer to be hit once by a madman than to have to go live with him. I didn't *see*, eh? I am looking only at my little dreams, my little wishes, but not at the madman. You say to me you are sorry, as if you are the one who caused this man to be crazy."

"No. I'm sorry because what happened was rotten, and you didn't deserve to be treated that way."

"Yes?" Lucienne gazed at her, as if to verify the sincerity of her words. "Okay, good," she said, satisfied. "Just promise to me you will stop saying to everyone you are sorry, Mignon. Okay?" She put her hands on either side of Jo's face and kissed her lightly on the lips. "I love you very much. You are sister and mama and friend, eh? And if you are sister and mama and friend, then I can say to you that you are too smart to be so stupid sometimes." She sat away and smiled. "You must only be sorry when it is something wrong you have done. You must never be sorry because maybe in your head you *think* something wrong. There are many things you make better, Mignon. Not only for me, but for the Royal Family, and for the adorable American boy, and even for this frightened man who follows after you to Venice because he fears growing old all alone."

Jo looked over at Tyler who, at that moment, turned to smile at her. She smiled back, then looked again at Lucienne. "Did he tell you that?"

"Of course not," Lucienne replied. "People do not admit to such things. But it is very easy to see."

"If it's so goddamned easy, then how come I didn't see it?"

"I don't know. Maybe you didn't wish to see, eh, because you know you are not the answer to his prayer."

"God! Maybe that's true. But what about you?"

"What of me?" Lucienne wanted to know.

"Nothing," Jo said, thinking it would be unwise to attempt to do any matchmaking. She was the last person on earth qualified to try to bring people together, even if she was sitting between two who seemed to have similar needs.

"Ah!" Lucienne said, turning away. "We have arrived."

Tyler walked between them as they went from the Cipriani's dock toward the piazza, wondering what he'd witnessed might signify. He'd turned in time to see one woman kiss another woman on the mouth, and his first reaction was shock at the notion that the two were sexually involved. His second reaction was to dismiss the first, only to have it replaced by a kind of low-grade envy. He knew that what he'd seen had nothing to do with sex and everything to do with mutual understanding and caring. And he thought, not for the first time, how very lucky women were to be able to make the displays they did of affection. Two men kissing that way could only constitute a public declaration of preference. Unless the two in question happened to be father and son. And even then, the scene might be suspect. The friendship of these two women gave him a keen sense of the deficiency endemic to being male and heterosexual. He was destined to spend the balance of his life limiting his affectionate displays to women, but even that was proving no easy thing. He'd come all this way to see Joanna, with the hope of building something out of their two prior meetings. But it was all too evident there was nothing to build upon. And here he was, walking along between two lovely, fragrant women, all too aware of past attachments and future uncertainties. He also felt more than a bit guilty at having come chasing after Joanna only to feel thunderstruck by the mere sight of her friend. And feeling guilty, he couldn't act upon any of his impulses, not even the simple, friendly ones. He felt like one of those classically silly old sods who were forever chasing after nubile young creatures, without the faintest notion of how dismal and depressing a picture they made.

They went through the Piazza San Marco, past the many tables set out in the open, past the trio of musicians on a stage surrounded by wrought-iron planters filled with pots of coleus and geraniums. Ornate standing lamps, not yet lit, would provide illumination for the musicians after dark; the three men, in flowing white shirts and gray trousers, looked content with their lot as they played violin, bass, and grand piano.

"I can just see Katharine sitting at one of these tables," Jo told Tyler.

"Ah, yes, *Summertime*. My father worked on that production with David Lean."

"He did? Doing what?"

"Postproduction." He answered and didn't elaborate.

"Oh, you must look at the little girl with her dog," Lucienne said, pointing out a pretty blond child of seven or eight in an oversized white cotton sweater and baggy white trousers, straining to keep hold of a sad-looking hound of mixed blood on a chain lead. She was watching the musicians, smiling happily. "*Charmante*, eh?"

"She's sweet," Jo agreed.

"Why not let me carry that bag for you Joanna?" Tyler said. "It looks very heavy."

"Thank you, Tyler."

"It *is* heavy," he said, adjusting the strap over his shoulder. "I can't think how you carry this about for hours at a stretch."

"Part of the job. You get used to it. So tell me. What did the two of you do all day?" She looked from Tyler to Lucienne.

"It was very amusing," Lucienne said. "We walk for a time, and Tyler says, 'If we get lost, we can take a taxi . . .' Then he stops very suddenly when he realizes this is Venice and there are no taxis, no automobiles."

"Felt like a bloody fool," Tyler admitted with a self-deprecating smile.

"Oh, but he was very good," Lucienne went on. "We walk, and he doesn't complain. We go to see the basilica of

San Marco, and the church of San Zaccaria to see the Bellini at the second altar, and to San Francesco della Vigna to see the tomb of Andrea Gritti, and then to La Pietà where Vivaldi was violin master. I would go on, but our friend confesses he is tired, his feet are hurting, he is hungry, he is thirsty. So we must stop.''

.''She walked me half to death,'' he complained good-naturedly.

"In Venice, this is what you do," Lucienne said equally good-naturedly.

"But what about the shopping?"

"This we do after we stop to rest."

"This we do," Tyler laughed, "with a bloody vengeance. There were sales in all her favorite shops. And we hit every last one of them, from Valentino to some grotty little pottery place."

"You *loved* this pottery place!" Lucienne accused. "He buys many gifts in this shop."

"It was wonderfully whimsical stuff, all hand-turned. I couldn't resist."

"Yes, so! After we have finished, we go to Harry's bar to drink Bellinis and to eat. Then we return to the hotel."

"Is the city the way you thought it would be?" Jo asked him.

"It's better than that. I simply can't think why I didn't consider all the walking we'd have to do. Wore the wrong shoes, of course. Tomorrow I'll be better prepared."

"You plan to come in again?"

"Without question," Tyler assured her. "And you did say you might have some free time."

"For dinner. I don't know yet about during the day."

The Caffè Florian was old and elegant, with round marble tables and velvet-covered banquettes. They were greeted by a man and a young woman from the tourist board, who directed them to an inner room where the people from the other hotels had gathered.

"We wait for three more, and then we go to the palazzo," the young woman told them. "Please, sit and have some

322

wine.'' She showed them to an unoccupied table, her eyes lingering admiringly for a few seconds on Lucienne before she turned to go.

Her partner from the board offered sparkling white wine in champagne flutes. Jo declined. Lucienne and Tyler each took a glass. Feeling most reluctant, and wishing she could just sit and enjoy the evening, Jo got up off the end of the banquette to take a few wide-angle shots of the group and of the interior of the café. Then she took several close-ups of Lucienne and Tyler individually and, finally, together.

As usual, Lucienne was superbly turned out, this evening in a white silk suit. The jacket was belted snugly at the waist, then flared in a peplum over her hips. The skirt was knee-length, with an alluring slit at the back. Her hair was smoothed back into a complicated chignon; her makeup was pale, with a touch of color on her cheekbones, charcoal eye-shadow, and vivid red lipstick. Large gold hoop earrings, and on her left shoulder an enameled snake brooch with gold-work around the scales and small rubies for eyes, were her only jewelry. As always, she was the focus of all eyes as she sat comfortably sipping her Asti Spumante. Tyler seemed unable to stop looking at her, his eyes straying repeatedly to the flawless column of her throat. And when Lucienne reached for a cigarette, he at once picked up a box of matches from the table to light it. Lucienne's fingertips held his hand steady, her long lacquered nails just touching the back of his hand. She thanked him, exhaled twin plumes of smoke from her nostrils, then gave him a slow smile.

Jo turned her attention to the camera, noting the number of exposures left on the roll, then cleaned the lenses before returning them to the camera bag. She suppressed a sudden strong urge to tell the other two she thought it would be a damned good idea if they got together. It was one thing for Anne to offer her motherly advice, it was something else for Jo to start manipulating people.

''Have you taken a lot of pictures, Joanna?'' Tyler asked.

''Quite a lot. About eight rolls, not counting the two I had processed when I arrived. I just wish I could've done some black and white work, too, but for that I would have needed a second camera body. Bad enough the one I brought with me went on the fritz. This is a new one," she explained to him. "It's not bad, either."

"I hope, if there's a chance, you'll show me the pictures before you leave London."

"They're slides," she said. "But sure. I'll be glad to show you."

The young woman returned with the late arrivals and announced, "If you please, we will go now."

Lucienne took time to finish both her cigarette and her wine while Jo and Tyler waited. Then the three of them joined the end of the line leaving the café and heading across the square.

"We are walking?" Lucienne said with dismay. "I did not think of this." She looked doubtfully at her black patent high heels. "I hope it is not too very far."

"I'll second that," Tyler said. "I still haven't recovered from the several hundred miles we've already walked today."

"It can't be that far," Jo reasoned. "Otherwise, we'd be going by boat."

They crossed to the right of the square, proceeding along a very cramped street and over a bridge. On the other side the street widened and they followed it through to an open square. The light was even more golden now, the air pleasantly cool. There were few people about, no traffic whatever to contend with. The man from the tourist board dropped back to say good evening and to ask, "You are from where?"

"Britain, France, and America," Tyler answered.

"And you are a journalist?"

"No, Joanna is a journalist," Tyler corrected him. "A very good, very well-known one, at that."

"Ah, yes?" The man smiled ingratiatingly at Jo. "This is very good. We are most anxious to have people who will write of Venice, speak of it."

"I'll certainly do that," Jo promised, hoping not to appear rude as she looked away from him at the dwellings they were

DREAM TRAIN

passing. In this city even the most decrepit buildings had character and charm.

"You will wish to take photographs of the palazzo," the man told her, falling into step beside Tyler in order not to obstruct her view. "It has been home of the Malipiero family, a very important family with prelates, generals, and senators. Also three doges. The palazzo becomes the property of the Trevisan family through marriage. Both very important families to Venice."

"D'you have anything on paper you can give me?" Jo asked. "Any kind of background information?"

"Of course," he replied readily. "But it will have to come from our office. We will have it to the Cipriani tomorrow. This is good?"

"Fine. If I can work anything about the palace into my piece, I will."

"Thank you. You will excuse me, please. We arrive momentarily. The palazzo is just there." He pointed, then hurried off to have a quick word with his assistant before hurrying up the steps and across the bridge leading to the entrance of the still-handsome but badly aged and stained edifice.

"It would appear we're to wait," Tyler said. "Evidently, they're not quite ready for us."

"What did you talk about with that couple on the launch?" Jo asked him. "I've been dying to know who they are."

"They're lovely people," he said, "from Oklahoma. Tulsa, I think they said. He's chairman of the board of an oil company, and she's head legal counsel for the company. The daughter"—he made a face—"whom I encountered this morning, is presently unemployed. I gathered she's never actually *been* employed. And her husband is a football coach at some boys' school. The parents are terribly concerned because the daughter's on her second marriage to this same young man, and the trip was intended to work some sort of magic and smooth over all the rough patches. It isn't working. The young man's desperate to leave and go home. The daughter's burying her sorrow in compulsive shopping. And the two together are all but destroying the parents' holiday.

They were telling me that this evening is the first chance they've had to be alone together since they left home several weeks ago. The daughter insists on having them with her constantly. The whole thing's rather sad.''

"I knew it!" Jo declared. "I had almost all of it right except for where they're from—and the mother. A lawyer. I'd never have guessed she was that.''

"You might be interested to know that Mrs. Holt was quite as intrigued by you as you were by them.''

"Oh, really?''

"Yes, indeed. She was most anxious to know what you were doing.''

"What did you tell her?''

Tyler laughed wickedly. "I told her you were Mandy Rice-Davies, in your new incarnation as a journalist.''

"Are you kidding? You didn't actually *say* that?''

He kissed her on the forehead and said, "No, I didn't. I simply told her you were doing a story on the Orient-Express.''

"Why do they keep us waiting?" Lucienne wondered, moving away from the group to have a cigarette.

"They haven't finished laying the tables or some such,'' Tyler said, hurrying to light her cigarette.

Jo had lifted the camera and was slowly scanning the scene through the lens, her eyes and the camera traveling around the square, then across the fronts of the buildings. She pressed the shutter release and cried out simultaneously at the sight of smoke drifting from two pairs of French doors giving on to a minuscule second-floor balcony. "There's a fire!" she cried, pointing wildly. She looked around, but no one appeared to have heard her. Tyler and Lucienne were some eight or ten feet away, talking. The rest of the group was clustered at the foot of the steps to the palace's bridge. People drifted over the public bridge next to it to traverse the close-walled street separating the palace from the building with the smoke wafting from the second-floor doors.

"There's a fire!" Jo cried more loudly, her pointing finger beginning to tremble.

At this, quite a number of people turned to look at her, then to where she was pointing. Seeing the smoke, which was growing thicker and darker, Tyler ran across the bridge and vanished from sight.

"Someone should call the fire department!" Jo called out to no one in particular.

Lucienne came to her side and stood looking at the windows.

"Oh, God! What if someone's in there!" Jo worried aloud, her throat going dry. "God! I hope no one's in there!"

As she and Lucienne watched, the balcony doors were suddenly, loudly, slammed shut. A crowd was collecting in the square while pedestrians coming from the other direction started across the bridge, saw the crowd, then turned to gaze up at the smoke. Heads tilted back, they continued on over the bridge, stopping to join those in the square.

"It's going on too long!" Jo said. "Every minute in the life of a fire is a very long time. And someone's in there. Whoever it is just closed the windows." Lucienne had moved nearer. Jo could smell her perfume mingling with the acrid odor of the smoke that was now pushing around the edges of the balcony doors. "Where's the damned fire department? I hope somebody's called them."

Lucienne was about to put a comforting hand on Jo's arm, when Jo abruptly moved away, the camera clicking, her hands automatically changing lenses, winding the film, clicking, clicking. She seemed, Lucienne thought, completely unaware of herself. Moving forward to keep Joanna in sight, Lucienne watched as she hurried to the edge of the canal to look both ways before pointing her camera up at the building. On the balcony of the palazzo a number of people, including a chef in white, had come out to see what all the commotion was about, and were leaning forward on the balustrade, pointing and commenting.

Tyler came pushing through the crowd and arrived at Lucienne's side, asking, "Where is Joanna?"

"She is there," Lucienne told him. "Look at her! Something is very wrong with her, eh? See how she shakes! I am afraid she will fall into the canal.''

"You wait here! I'll fetch her back." He skirted the clusters of people watching the progress of the fire and went toward the railing where Jo had positioned herself. Just as he reached her, there was the sound of sirens, and a fire patrol boat came gliding along the canal, pulling to a stop directly below where Jo was standing. Half a dozen men in bright orange coats and yellow-banded black hats scrambled out of the boat carrying axes and slinging yellow oxygen tanks over their shoulders. Tyler put both hands on her shoulders and drew Jo back, out of the way of the firemen. He could feel her quaking quite violently under his hands, yet she continued to hold the camera to her eye, taking one shot after another. "Joanna," he said directly into her ear, "what are you doing?"

"There are people in there!" she wailed, her eyes never leaving the building, the camera never leaving her eyes. "They're trapped in there!"

"Joanna," he said firmly, "there is no one in there."

"But you don't know that, you can't be sure."

"I *am* sure," he told her. "I was just in there. I closed the windows, to cut off the air so it wouldn't feed the fire."

"You were in there?" At last, she lowered the camera and looked at him. She could smell the smoke in his clothes, and there were sooty smudges on his face and hands. "There's no one in there? You're absolutely positive?"

"Positive," he told her. "The fire seems to have started in a television set."

"A television set?" She turned and looked again to the second floor, where the balcony doors were now open and two of the orange-coated firemen were signaling an all clear to the men still in the boat below. "Did you check the bathroom, Tyler? Did you? There could have been someone in there. It's important to check."

"I went through every room, Joanna. *There is no one in there.*"

"They could be pounding on the walls or the floor, and if you don't hear them—"

"*Joanna!*" he said sharply, forcing her to look at him. "*The flat is empty!*" He spoke slowly and clearly, alarmed by her eyes, which were wide and unblinking. "What is the matter?" he asked her. "You're not listening to me. *Everything*," he said even more slowly and clearly, "*is all right.*"

Her eyes stayed on him, uncomprehending, and he felt himself starting to sweat. "Joanna? Do you hear me?" He held fast to her shoulders, not allowing her to turn away. And all at once understanding seemed to penetrate. Her eyes changed, focusing. She wet her lips, said, "I thought . . . ," stopped and tried to begin again. He put his arms around her, trying to calm her and stop her quite terrible trembling.

"I thought it was all over," she cried, "that I was over it. Oh, God! I'm *not* over it. Maybe you *never* get over it. I'm so *scared.*"

"None of that," he said quietly, "prevented you from taking a whole roll of film."

She stood away from him. "What?"

He took hold of her hand, uncurled her fingers to reveal the spool of exposed film she'd been clutching. She looked at the film, then at the camera. She'd shot an entire roll and even reloaded without being cognizant of her own actions. In fact, she'd watched all of it through the lens of the Exakta. More than forty exposures—the proof was in her hand, and on the camera's counter. She stared at the spool sitting on the palm of her hand, then looked up at Tyler. She was crying, he thought, like a small child, with little hiccoughing sobs, eyes and nose streaming. He brought out his handkerchief and gently blotted her cheeks, then held the handkerchief to her nose and said, "Blow." And like a child, she did, her eyes now fixed on him as if the answers to all her questions resided in him.

"Will you be all right now?" he asked her. "It looks as if they're ready for us to go inside, and we should both find somewhere to have a quick wash."

Lucienne took hold of Jo's arm saying, "I will stay with her. Go ahead, Tyler. We will come soon."

Jo was staring at the roll of film in disbelief. "How could I *do* that? I didn't even *know* I was doing it." She turned to look at the firemen removing their orange coats, loading equipment back into the boat.

"Joanna," Lucienne said, "what is the matter?"

"I was in a fire," she explained, the residual fear thudding through her arteries. "I nearly died. It was such a long time ago. I thought I was over it. I mean, most of the time I've stopped worrying, stopped thinking I smell smoke all the time. But that's not it!" Her tears started anew. "What's so goddamned scary is the way I was shooting film, as if my brain is separate from the rest of me, as if I'm some sick kind of robot."

"But this is what you do," Lucienne said sensibly. "You make photographs. I have seen this from the beginning. Why is this so terrible?"

"It's terrible because—because it's ghoulish. I mean, here I am terrified somebody might be trapped in there, but taking pictures anyway, like a visual vampire or something. God! How could I *do* that? How could I?"

"Pay attention to me!" Lucienne said sternly. "You are being hysterical, and there is no need for this. *Listen!*" She tightened her grip on Jo's arm. "I have a restaurant, eh? Six nights of every week I greet the people who come to dine in my restaurant. I smile, I talk with these people, I ask after their children, their families. Often, I will sit to have a glass of wine with clients I have had for many years. But all the while I am smiling and talking and asking about the families, I am watching the staff, and the doors to the kitchen, and I make note of how much time passes before people are presented with their food. I look to see how well or how badly the people are responding to the staff, to the food, to the *ambiance*, to everything. It is necessary; it is part of what I do, what must be done. You are a woman who makes pictures. And while you make the pictures, you smile and you talk and you observe how things are done. It is necessary; it

330

is part of what you do. Why do you talk of yourself so badly now because you see something which distresses you but which also you have a wish to photograph? It is part of what you do, eh? Me, I don't think this is so terrible. No one is the one thing or the other thing altogether. We are each many things. And this is okay, Mignon. *You* are okay. People who love you, they know this is how you are, what you do, and it is of no consequence. Now come. We will fix the face and the hair.''

Upon entering the palace, Lucienne stopped to ask the young woman from the tourist board where there was a bathroom. The young woman showed the way, Lucienne thanked her, then directed Jo along the hallway. Inside the large marbled bathroom she seated Jo on the side of the tub, then opened Jo's bag, found a hairbrush, a compact, and some tissues. As if in a trance, Jo sat, trying to apply like a poultice Lucienne's logical words and common sense to her tangled feelings.

''That fire changed everything,'' she tried to explain. ''Afterward, my whole life was different. *I* was different.''

''But you didn't die. This is all that matters. So there is no need to be afraid now. And Tyler, he was very good, eh, to go into the fire? I am very impressed how he does this. And he has much fondness for you, Mignon. *Très gentil*, the way he speaks with you, and makes you to blow your nose, *comme une enfant*. For this, I like him very, very much.''

''I'm fond of him, too,'' Jo said, feeling she could curl up in the bathtub and go to sleep. ''I'm just not in love with him.''

''We have a good time today,'' Lucienne said, powdering Jo's nose, then studying her for a moment before closing the compact. ''You don't mind this?''

''I don't say one thing and mean something else. I think the two of you are a good match, if you want to know the truth. He's always made me kind of nervous because he seems to know what he wants and he's already going after it while I'm still trying to figure out where to sit.''

Lucienne laughed and handed her the hairbrush saying,

"Fix your hair," then lit a cigarette while Jo got up from the tub and went to stand before the mirror.

"You don't need my permission, that's for damned sure," she told Lucienne's reflection. "And you have my blessing. I just made a complete asshole of myself, and the two of you are being very decent about it. More than decent. And what you said about doing things that are necessary makes a lot of sense. It really does." She turned from the mirror and leaned against the basin. "You are one very smart woman."

"Not so very smart. Otherwise I would not come so close to making a marriage with a man who argues with his fists."

"You'd never have gone through with it," Jo said. "I could tell that from the way you talked about it at dinner the first night on the train."

"Maybe so. We must join with the others now, Mignon."

"Right." Jo returned the hairbrush and compact to her bag, picked up the camera and examined it for a few seconds, then said, "Thank you for helping me make sense of all that."

"Pah!" Lucienne laughed. "It is a fair trade, eh? I give to you advice, you give to me your attractive friend. I think this is very good. I think also you need to have more sleep."

"As soon as this dinner's over, I'm going back to the hotel to collapse. Maybe I'll even sleep late for a change."

"Maybe," Lucienne suggested shrewdly, "you should telephone to the other one, make yourself happy."

"I already tried that. He wasn't home."

"Ahh," Lucienne commiserated. "Too bad. But you will try again."

"Yeah," Jo managed a smile. "I'll try again."

25

BY NINE FORTY-FIVE THEY WERE ON THEIR WAY BACK TO the Cipriani, having been presented with a five-course meal and a hefty sales pitch on the city by the man from the tourist board. Jo had been shown only three of the rooms of the palace, the young hostess explaining rather sadly that there was a family in residence and only the dining and sitting rooms had been made available to the board for the evening. "But I show to you the bedroom," she'd said, and had, while the others were moving to the sitting room for coffee, whisked Jo down the hall to show her an enormous room to which the bed was purely incidental. Silk-shaded standing lamps, worn thin but still-regal Persian carpets, clusters of original oils on the walls, armchairs, and a rococo desk. Jo took a number of shots of the room, several more of the beamed ceiling and fabulously ornate chandeliers in the hallway, and several of the sitting room with its broad expanse of highly polished planked floors, twinned groupings of settee and armchairs, and candelabrae affixed to the walls. Then, having fulfilled her professional responsibilities, Jo had sat and tried to pay attention to a California couple who exclaimed over the palace, the dinner, and the wonders of Venice. The events of the day—beginning with Anne's disclosure of Jimmy's death and culminating in the fire—had left her in a state of exhaustion from which she had repeatedly to rouse herself in order not to offend either her hosts or the other guests. When Tyler had sympathetically suggested it was perhaps time to leave, she was deeply grateful.

"It was very interesting, eh?" Lucienne was saying. "Too much food, but not so very bad."

"Three courses with bivalves," Jo said, "is more than I can handle."

"What is this, bivalves?"

"Food that comes with shells. You know: oysters, clams, mussels."

"Ah! Yes, I think this, too. I don't mind the fish as an entrée. But also pasta with mussels, no."

"I quite enjoyed it," Tyler contributed. "Of course, we British thrive on *bivalves*." He smiled over at Jo. "And other oddities of the sea—pickled eel, and so forth. We are, as my sainted grandmother used to say, an island, after all."

"When does she say this, your sainted grandmother?" Lucienne wanted to know.

"For the last five years of her life, she said it several dozen times daily. Went a bit dotty, poor Gran did. Perfectly healthy in every regard, but she took to repeating certain key expressions sometimes five or six times in the course of a single conversation. At the start we found it rather annoying. But at the last it amused the Emmons children no end. We'd manipulate conversations to get her going. Then she'd be off, and she'd take great umbrage when we'd roll about laughing."

"I think this is cruel," Lucienne said.

"Perhaps. But we were children, and children are, for the most part, oblivious to their cruelty. They are the center of their small universes and believe devoutly that only they are capable of feeling hurt. My son is a perfect example. He has little time for the things his mother or I say to him, and goes into a huff when we fail to pay him what he believes is his due portion of attention."

"And how old is your son?" she asked him.

"Twelve, nearly thirteen."

Jo walked along mechanically, tuning in and out of their conversation, listening to the sound of their footsteps on the paving stones, and smiling at passers-by who nodded and said, *"Buona sera."* They'd reached the canal, and the light shone gently through the lovely tinted-glass lamps she'd previously seen only in daylight. The air smelled of salt and the sea, with wisps of Lucienne's perfume and lemony tendrils of Tyler's after-shave. She felt as if she were sleepwalking; her ability to concentrate was down almost to zero. All she wanted was to get back to the hotel and into her bed.

"Look," Lucienne said to Tyler. "She goes in a dream."

"Joanna!" Tyler laughed. "The boat is back here."

Jo stopped, turned, and saw she'd gone some twenty yards beyond the hotel's dock. She'd probably have kept on going if they hadn't stopped her. She went back, following after them along the wooden walkway to the motor launch.

In the hotel lobby, while Jo was getting her key and several messages from the concierge, Tyler suggested going to the bar for a drink.

"I just couldn't," Jo told him. "I've got to go to bed. I'm only barely conscious."

"I go as well," Lucienne announced.

"Well," Tyler said, "I'll see you to your room, Joanna."

"Your eyes are closing, Mignon." Lucienne drew her close. "We will meet for breakfast?"

"Absolutely. Is eight-thirty too early?"

"It is perfect. Sleep well." She kissed Jo on both cheeks, released her, and then turned to say *au'voir* to Tyler.

"It was a pleasure having your company today," he said to her. "Perhaps I'll have that pleasure again tomorrow."

"Perhaps. I have made no plans. Take care of *ma petite* Joanna."

"Night, Lucienne," Jo said, then allowed Tyler to direct her to her room.

She got the door open and reached inside to turn on the lights, saying, "Come in for a minute, Tyler." Inside, she stepped out of her shoes and proceeded to the sofa, dropping the key and her messages on the coffee table.

Tyler closed the door and held out the Lowe-pro, asking, "Where do you want this?"

"Anywhere."

He put it beside the other things on the coffee table, then came around to sit with her on the sofa.

"There's something I want to say to you," she said, stifling a yawn.

"And what might that be?" he asked pleasantly.

"What I said this morning is true, Tyler. You and I hardly know each other. I do like you a lot, and your coming here was a wonderful thing to do. You were heroic this evening, running into that place the way you did."

"Oh, I don't know about that. In some circles that act might be construed as sheer lunacy."

"Well, I don't think so. And you were very nice to me while I was having what Jackie would call a spaz attack. The thing is, I want us to be friends. I really do, if that's possible. It's just that, well, you've met Henry, and I think something's happening, if you know what I mean."

"There's no need to explain, Joanna. I understand."

"You do?"

"I think so. And I can't see any reason why we can't be good friends."

"Good. I'm glad. Because you are a nice man and I like you."

"Joanna, it's time for you to go to bed, luv. Your eyes actually are closing, so I'll leave you to it and, if I may, I'll join you for breakfast in the morning."

"Okay."

He got up and walked around the coffee table, on his way to the door.

She trailed after, colliding with him when he stopped and turned.

He laughed and reached to stroke her hair. "I do think you're a dear little person. You're not still bothered about the fire, are you?"

She shook her head. "I'm okay. I'm sorry to have behaved like such a crazy person."

"Not at all. Good night, Joanna." He gave her kisses on both cheeks, then opened the door. "Sleep well," he said, and went off down the hall.

"Night," she said, and closed the door.

He stood in the lobby debating whether or not to go to the bar, decided he would, started on his way, and found himself swinging in the opposite direction, climbing the stairs to the second floor. His footsteps were inaudible as he walked along the carpeted hallway, halted, and knocked at the door. A few seconds, the door opened, and a bare arm reached out, took hold of the front of his jacket, and pulled him inside to the sound of laughter.

The only light came from the bathroom, and it took a few moments for his eyes to adjust. During those few moments Lucienne said, "I knew you would come," looped her arms around his neck, and kissed him on the mouth.

"You did, did you?"

"But of course."

Her hair was hanging free and she was wearing some kind of sleep shirt. He put his hands on her hips and she came closer.

"I thought you might change your mind and come for a drink," he said, bending to breathe in the scent of her hair, touching his lips to her temple.

"I have no wish for a drink," she said, her hips subtly shifting under his hands as she lifted her mouth again to his, biting lightly on his lower lip.

The kiss evolved as if in stages so that it seemed to last a very long time. She tasted of mint and tobacco, and her hipbones were prominent against his hands.

"I knew also you would be good to kiss," she said, unwinding her arms from his neck and placing them around his waist.

"Quite a lot you seem to know," he said, as his hands searched for the bottom of the shirt, found it, and slipped underneath. Starting at the tops of her thighs, he drew his hands upward slowly until they covered her breasts, his thumbs pressing into her nipples.

"I knew you would have very good hands," she told him. "I have watched how you use them."

"*I* knew how you'd feel," he countered, pulling the shirt off over her head and letting it drop to the floor. Her hips shifted again and she pressed into him.

"You like me, eh?" she asked, taking hold of his hands, holding first the left and then the right one to her mouth.

"I more than like you." He freed one hand and placed it against the small of her back as he lowered his head to her throat, breathing deeply of her perfume as he left a trail of kisses along her shoulder, partway down her arm, and across to her breast.

She sighed, an appreciative sound, as her hand went over the back of his head, holding him to her. "Come, take these off," she whispered. And he straightened while she busied herself with the buttons on his shirt and he struggled out of the jacket. Then she moved away, into the deeper darkness of the room, whispering, "Come here!" and laughed again. *"Vite!"*

He had a moment of complete paranoia standing there in the dark with his clothes off, wondering if the two women had cooked up some grotesque scheme to humiliate him. Then he told himself not to be such a bloody fool, and followed the sound of her voice to the bed. This simply had to happen, he thought with slight desperation. As they had discussed earlier, he truly believed only children were intentionally cruel. He lay down at her side and threaded his fingers through the silky abundance of her hair. "Am I really so predictable?" he asked her.

"Ah, no! It is only that I can see you wish to make love

with me. And so now we do. Come!'' she urged, and stretched briefly against the length of his body before rising over top of him to kiss his forehead, his nose, and then his mouth. ''It is a long time since I make love with a man who loves women. And you love women, don't you, Monsieur?''

''Oh, yes I do. Particularly exotic French women with ebony hair and fine long legs and impertinent breasts.''

''What is this 'impertinent'?''

''It means perfect and proud.''

She laughed and drew her nails lightly down the length of his inner arms, giving him goose bumps. ''I like English men with not enough flesh and big hands and very little hair at all.'' She swayed above him so that her breasts just touched against his chest, then she ducked her head and her hair tickled across his ribs, down his belly. ''You are very nice,'' she said after a moment, her hand playing over him, then she ducked her head again.

He could scarcely believe they'd moved so quickly, with no preamble, to so intense an intimacy. A minute or two, then he sat up, took hold of her, turned her and put her belly-down on the bed so that he could take his hands and mouth on a slow tour from the nape of her neck down the length of her body to her feet before turning her over in order to repeat this investigation with even more deliberation.

''I love this,'' she murmured. ''This is wonderful, wonderful.''

''Is there a need for precautions?'' he asked, his mouth against hers.

''No need.''

''Lovely.'' Wrapping her in his arms, they rolled over so that she lay above him.

She raised herself up and sat astride his hips, guiding him inside her. ''Just touch me here, *chéri*. Ah, yes.''

Her body a curved-back arc, she lifted and fell sinuously, knowingly, reading the pressure of his hands and the thrust of his body, gradually increasing the tempo until she froze, her fingers digging into his flesh as she drew at him, deep interior waves he found irresistible. And then she came toppling down on his chest to bury her face in the side of his neck, laughing softly.

"I knew you would be good," she told him with a kiss.

"You are beyond my wildest, Mademoiselle."

"Ah, yes?"

"Oh, yes, indeed."

"There is much to say for older women, eh?"

"Very definitely. You are a wonder."

"You also are a wonder," she said, and eased away from him to reach for her cigarettes, then changed her mind and settled her head on the pillow.

"You prefer the dark, do you?"

"Only sometimes."

"That's good, because I'd like to be able to see you next time."

She didn't respond, but he thought nothing of it, and folded his arms under his head, temporarily sated and very happy. He was aware of her moving beside him and assumed she was making herself comfortable. Then she groaned, and the sound was so unmistakably one of pain that the hair rose on his arms and he asked, "Are you all right, Lucienne?" When she failed to answer, he felt for the switch on the bedside lamp, found it, and turned on the light to see her wound into a knot, her forehead on her knees, her arms locked tightly around her drawn-up legs. "What is it?" he asked anxiously, watching her rock from side to side in obvious and terrible pain. "Jesus Christ! You really were ill last evening."

"You didn't believe this?" She raised her head slightly to look at him, and he was shocked by the waxy look of her skin and the beads of perspiration gathering at her hairline.

"What can I do?" he asked, on his knees beside her. "Perhaps I should fetch Joanna—"

"No!" she got out, then groaned again, shutting her eyes tightly.

"The hotel doctor, then."

"No!"

"Well, at least tell me what it is, if you know, so I can try

340

to be of some help here. I can't just sit and *watch*. Let me help."

"It is endo—in the womb," she gasped.

"Right!" he said decisively, and sprang into action. In the bathroom he turned on the cold-water faucet, snatched up one of the hand towels, then tested the water. Tepid. "Bloody hell!" He turned off the faucet and went to the small refrigerator, relieved to find two full trays of ice. He pulled one of the plastic dry cleaning bags from a hanger in the closet, then carried the plastic and the two trays of ice back to the bed. "First thing, you've got to lie back, straighten out."

"I cannot!"

"You're going to have to." Putting everything down on the floor, he sat beside her and began trying to get her to unwind her arms and legs. "You must try," he said. "I'm sure it comforts you to fold yourself into a knot, but it can only heighten the pain. Come on now." Keeping his voice low, he encouraged her to lie back. "Please trust me," he said, his eyes on the terrible bruise above her navel as he laid the plastic across her midriff, then emptied the ice from both trays on top of it. Centering the ice, he closed the sides of the plastic bag over the cubes, then held his hand flat on top of the package he'd created. "In a minute or two, you'll feel much better," he promised.

"If I do not," she said between her teeth, "I will die."

"What a thing to say!" he chided with a smile. "Try to untense your muscles," he instructed, caressing her brow with his free hand. "I know it's dreadful, but you must try. The more tense you are, trying to fight it, the more painful it's going to be."

"How do you know this?" she challenged, starting to feel the cold penetrating her abdomen.

"In my long-departed youth I put in my time with the National Service. Conscription," he explained. "I did my stint with a medical corps. Learned quite a few useful things. This is one of them. Any better?"

"A little."

"You see," he smiled again. "I'm more than just another pretty face, my lovely. How did you get that nasty bruise?"

"Some other time I will tell you."

"Fair enough. Have you seen a doctor about this problem?"

"I have."

"And nothing was prescribed?"

"I refused."

"What did you refuse?"

"Everything."

"I see. You prefer pain to some sort of remedy?"

"Please!"

"You'll forgive me, I hope, if I suggest you should see another doctor?"

"I have made an appointment. I go Monday."

"I see. And how long has this been going on?" he asked, checking to make sure the ice wasn't leaking.

"Some time."

"Some time," he repeated. "I'm beginning to acquire some skill at translating your cryptic answers. Some time undoutedly means *quite* some time."

"I detest doctors!"

"That's sensible."

"You make fun of me!" she accused.

"Only a bit. You really should have this seen to, you know."

"I am seeing to it. On Monday."

"You know what I think? I think if you're feeling reasonably well come Monday you won't bother to keep that appointment. And I suspect that if you don't keep the appointment, you're going to end up in a lot of trouble. So I think it might be a good idea if someone came along to make sure you do keep the appointment."

"What are you saying?"

"I'm saying, I'll go with you, hold your hand should it prove necessary."

"Why would you do this?"

"I suppose because I like you. Better, isn't it?"

She nodded, her features slowly relaxing, her eyelids beginning to droop.

"We'll give it a few more minutes, then tuck you up."

"I want a cigarette," she said, moving to reach for the pack on the bedside table.

"I'll get it. You stay still." He lit a cigarette, handed it to her, then placed an ashtray close by.

"You are very kind," she said. "Men are not usually good with illness."

"I wouldn't say I was good with it. It just doesn't frighten me. And I've got some interest in your well-being. I'd like to think we'd see one another again."

"You would like this, eh?" She managed a smile.

"Wouldn't you?"

"Yes, I would like this. You make good love."

"I was inspired. I think you should put that cigarette out and try to get some sleep. I'll get rid of the ice, then make sure you're settled for the night."

Returning from the bathroom, he plucked the cigarette from her fingers, surprised her by taking a puff and inhaling deeply, then put it out.

"You are going now?" she asked.

"Well, I thought . . ."

"Stay," she said, then added, "Please."

"Mademoiselle says stay, therefore I must stay." He climbed into the bed, gathered her up as if she were weightless, and cradled her in his arms like a child, his hands smoothing and stroking as he said, "Go to sleep now. I'll stay for a bit."

"A kiss?"

He kissed her softly, then eased her back against his chest. "Pain gone?"

"Tyler, I like you very much. Thank you for caring for me."

It was a matter of semantics, of course. What she meant was "Thank you for looking after me." But he much preferred her words, finding in them a somewhat ironic potential.

"Thank *you*, Mademoiselle, for a most memorable experience. It is my great pleasure and privilege to care for you."

"You are so English," she said sleepily.

"And you are so deliciously French. Sleep now."

26

JO WAS JUST ABOUT TO GO TO BREAKFAST WHEN SHE REMEM-
bered the messages she'd collected the night before. One was
from Laura, asking her to stop by her office in the morning.
Another was from Jackie, saying he'd finally managed to
convince his family to spend a few hours away from the
hotel, and he hoped maybe to see her at dinner. The third
was a telex from Henry that had obviously been sent before
she'd left her message on his machine. PLEASE RING ME AT
THE OFFICE FRIDAY. HENRY.

From the brevity and terseness it seemed likely it was
business he wanted to discuss with her. She'd call after breakfast, and no doubt he'd be every bit as brief and terse as his
telex. Talking to Henry in person was one thing; talking to
him over the telephone quite another. Over the telephone he
usually sounded somewhat irritable and even unfriendly. In
the years that she'd known him, she'd come to accept that
telephones and Henry were not compatible. Yet she'd been
hoping—foolishly, she now told herself—that this would
change because of last week's events. As she headed for the
terrace, she was gearing up for what she believed was bound
to be a not especially heartwarming telephone conversation,
and wondered, too, why, just because her feelings had un-

dergone a change, she thought that Henry's would as well. She hadn't actually declared herself to him.

Tyler was already there. She went directly to his table, saying, "Hi. You're early. I was thinking I'd have some coffee and get my notes done before you came."

"Joanna." He half stood as she pulled out a chair, then sank back into his seat. He looked frazzled, although he was freshly shaved and smelled nicely of his lemony after-shave.

The waiter came, she asked for coffee, then turned back to Tyler, who was sitting with his hands laced together on the tabletop.

"You look worn out, Tyler. Didn't you sleep well?"

"I scarcely slept at all. Look, Joanna. This is rather awkward, and I hope you won't misunderstand."

"Don't confess, okay?" she said with a smile. "Whatever you do on your own time is none of my business, and it's not up to me to judge it one way or another."

"That does make it a bit easier. You see, I didn't believe you the other evening, about Lucienne's being ill. And I apologize for that, because there's no question that she is. I spent much of the night trying to help her with the pain. Unfortunately, as you undoubtedly know already, she has a complete and, to me, bewildering aversion to the medical profession."

"I know how she is."

"Yes, well. I finally succeeded in convincing her at four this morning that she really must see someone, and soon. I rang her doctor in Paris. Luckily, he speaks quite good English. And after explaining the situation, he said he'd see her later this afternoon. So I've booked tickets on the first available flight, and I'm taking her back to Paris. All the arrangements have been made, and a water taxi's coming in half an hour."

"My God!" Jo exclaimed. "How bad is it? Where is she?"

"It's pretty bloody bad. She's just organizing the last of her bits and pieces, then she'll join us. The thing is, I felt if I didn't escort her, she simply wouldn't go."

"I think you're right about that."

He looked at his hands, and unlaced his fingers. "I didn't want you to think I was jumping from one woman to another, that sort of thing. I truly did, and do, feel something needed to be done. She's really very ill, Joanna."

"Did you think I was going to be mad, or jealous, or something?" she asked him. "And why would I be? I mean, I know she's not well. And if you've managed to talk her into seeing a doctor, then good for you. The fact that you'd take her personally is very goddamned impressive, Tyler."

"The last thing I imagined, when I set out on this trip, was that I'd be accompanying a woman I've only just met to a hospital in Paris."

"You're taking her to a *hospital*? And she agreed?"

"I omitted some of the details. I simply said her doctor would see her. I had the decided impression that if I mentioned the word 'hospital' she'd refuse in no uncertain terms. Given the struggle I had to get her permission to ring the doctor in the first place, I hardly thought it wise to say more than was needed."

"Why are you doing this, Tyler?"

"Haven't the faintest," he admitted. "It needs to be done, and there isn't anyone else. You're not available; you have commitments. Although I'm sure you'd chuck it all and go with her. But my time happens to be free at the moment, and it seems the only decent thing to do. Being truthful, I have to tell you I was frightened for her."

"She's terrified they'll insist on her having surgery of some kind, even a hysterectomy."

"From what her doctor told me, I gather she may not have a choice in the matter. She's left it a very long time. He first saw her for the problem close to three years ago. I'm ignorant on the subject, suffice it to say, but I am able to recognize great pain when I see it, and she's in absolute bloody agony. It's nothing short of amazing that she's managed to function at all in her condition, let alone turn herself out as she does to such dazzling effect.

"I know it sounds unlikely," he said, his eyes on hers, "but I've come to care rather a lot for her in a very short

Charlotte Vale Allen

period of time.'' He emitted a grim laugh. ''Last night was like being in the trenches together—a great deal compressed into a very short time. We talked for hours, or rather, I talked, trying to distract her. I admitted things out loud I've never admitted to anyone, not even to myself. Especially not to myself. It may not lead anywhere, but I feel obliged to see this through.'' He glanced away, then dropped his voice to say, ''Don't say anything to her, please. She's coming now.''

Even if he hadn't warned her, Jo would have known. Lucienne looked unwell, even with the artful application of makeup. Her eyes were sunken and there was a tightness around her mouth as she sat down and said a subdued good morning.

''Tyler says you're leaving,'' Jo said cheerily, ''the two of you running off together. Very nice.''

''Does he tell you how I have disgraced myself?'' Lucienne asked, looking at Tyler. ''Has he told you he has become my nurse?''

''No,'' Jo lied, also looking at Tyler. ''He hasn't said a thing.''

''Well, it is true. I am falling in pieces and he is very kind to stay with me.''

''Tyler's a very kind man,'' Jo said.

''Mignon, this looks bad,'' she said, taking hold of Jo's hand. ''Please don't be angry.''

''Why would I be angry?'' Jo asked with genuine candor. ''If anything, I'm glad somebody's finally looking after you, because you sure as hell aren't doing much of a job of looking after yourself. I just want the two of you to promise you'll call me and let me know how it goes.''

''Oh, of course!'' Tyler said quickly. ''I intended all along to do that.''

''Are you going to have something to eat before you go?'' Jo asked, ''Is there time?''

''I will have coffee with you,'' Lucienne said, her hand very tight around Jo's. ''And this man is complaining of hunger for hours. Eat!'' she told Tyler. ''I will not run away.''

The moment he was out of earshot at the buffet, Lucienne

348

whispered, "I thought it would be a diversion, eh? But he has been so good, and I am very afraid. You think I am bad to allow him to come with me? I am thinking only weak women, silly women, fall on men this way."

"You're not weak or silly. And maybe *he* needs to do this," Jo told her.

"I know they will cut me, Joanna; they will take everything away, and I am very much afraid."

"Tyler will stay with you. He'll make sure you're all right."

"He will stay, but he cannot make sure I am all right," she said sagely. "And he cannot take away the fear. But I am so grateful that he would do this for me. And I am sad to leave you. You will telephone to me, come to see me?"

"You know I will," Jo assured her.

"He makes me to care for him, eh? Big surprise. If it was Paolo and I was sick, he would run away. But this man, he is like my papa. He holds me like a baby, and he *sings* to me." She smiled and shook her head.

"He sang to you?"

"Unbelievable, eh? He rocks me, and he sings, and I am able to sleep."

"God, Lucienne. Maybe the two of you have found what you've both been needing."

"I do not need," Lucienne declared.

"Oh, *please*! We all need, Lucienne. Every last one of us wants to be special to somebody else. And I'll tell you one thing I know for sure: Tyler's not some half-assed jerk who's going to belt you around if you say or do something he doesn't like."

Lucienne's grip was suddenly fierce, her cheeks sucked in, her eyes clamped shut.

"God, it's really bad, isn't it?" Jo said worriedly. "Let me give you another one of my Valium. Maybe it'll help."

"Please," Lucienne whispered. "I will take anything now to help with the pain."

Jo freed her hand to open her bag. She gave Lucienne a tablet, then poured some water for her.

"How is it that you have these?" Lucienne asked after she'd swallowed the tablet.

"They're muscle relaxants, for my neck and shoulder. Listen, even if it turns out you do have to have surgery, at least you won't suffer anymore. You'll be able to enjoy your life again. And if you change your mind and decide sometime you want to have a child, there are lots of kids waiting to be adopted. Your life is important. It's important to me. I don't want to lose you."

Tyler came back to the table with a heaped plate. "I know it's obscene, but I'm ravenous."

"He eats everything they put into the room—the chocolate, and the crackers, the sweets, all," Lucienne told Jo. "When we are home, I will have to feed him."

Around a mouthful of cereal Tyler said, "She's going to give me my very own table Chez Lucienne."

"I have not said I would do this."

"You'll have to," he grinned at her. "It's my nursing fee. And cheap at half the price."

"You are not eating, Mignon?"

"I'll see you two off first. God, I'm going to miss you both. My last day in Venice, and no one to play with."

"Pah! You will go out and take hundreds of pictures. And tomorrow you will go on the train and make many new friends."

"Maybe," Jo said, doubting this. "It won't be the same without you. And I'm getting a little tired of looking at everything through the camera. I might just give myself and my eyes a break and go sightseeing empty-handed."

"Impossible," Tyler said. "Joanna without her camera is like a vase without flowers."

"What?" Jo laughed.

"It's part of you. Surely you accept that," he told her.

"I do, but that doesn't mean I can't get tired of it."

"True," he conceded. "But it's also probably your very dearest friend, and you take it with you for company and protection, even consolation."

"Very profound, Tyler."

"Profound and true. I envy you your camera and your lenses and your built-in armor. Most of us go about with no protection at all."

"It's too early in the morning for this," she said. "Give me a break and just eat."

At that moment one of the assistant managers came to the table to say, "Signor Emmons, your water taxi is come."

"Thank you. Would you tell him we'll be just a few minutes?"

"Very good."

"Bloody hell!" Tyler groused. "I haven't finished."

"Take your croissants with you," Jo said, "and eat them in the taxi."

"Brilliant. You *are* clever!" He scooped up the last of the yogurt, wiped his mouth, plonked the napkin on the table, and said to Lucienne, *"Mademoiselle, nous départons."*

Lucienne shook her head. "His French is deplorable."

Jo told the waiter she'd be returning, then walked with Tyler and Lucienne to the landing stage. At the foot of the walkway, Lucienne turned abruptly and embraced Jo, fervently whispering, "Don't forget me, Mignon."

"Never! Take care of yourself, and be well. I'll be thinking about you."

Her arms still around Jo, Lucienne leaned away to say, "Only good things have happened since I meet you, Mignon. *I* will not lose *you* now, eh? You will telephone to me, come to visit?"

"I will, I promise."

"Bon!" She kissed Jo on both cheeks, then turned and allowed the boatman to assist her into the water taxi.

"I'll ring you first chance I have," Tyler told Jo.

"Please do. I'm so worried about her."

"So am I," he confessed, then gave her a pair of kisses, and followed Lucienne into the boat.

Jo's hands went automatically to the camera. She lifted it and took a few shots of the two of them standing in the taxi, then lowered the camera and waved until they were out of

351

sight. And once they were gone, she let out her breath slowly before turning to go back to the terrace.

While she tore a croissant into small pieces, she tried to write up her notes, but couldn't begin. All she could think about was Jimmy's death and Lucienne's illness. The pleasure she'd experienced on this trip was suddenly overshadowed by sadness and by a feeling of aloneness. There was no one on the terrace she recognized, and the people she'd come to know so well since leaving London had all gone. She gave up on the notes and was tucking the book into her bag when Laura came over and stood with her hands on the back of one of the chairs. "Good morning, Joanna. How are you?"

"Oh, I'm fine. I was about to come to see you."

"Yes? Good. I am free today," she said. "I thought you might like to come with me to see some of Venice you would perhaps not have a chance to see otherwise."

"I'd love that. I've just been sitting here trying not to feel sorry for myself."

"Your friends have had bad luck," she said. "Everyone is sad about Sir James. And now Lucienne goes. Always she is so much fun."

"I take it you know her from her previous visits."

"Oh, yes," Laura said brightly. "And I have been to her restaurant in Paris. You have been?"

"Not yet, but I hope to get there soon."

"It is very special. And the food is magnificent. But the people, they come because of Lucienne. She is most charming, *molto bella*. Such clothes, uh?"

"Fabulous," Jo agreed. "I'm really going to hate to leave here, you know. Everybody's been so nice, all the Orient-Express people, and the hotel staff."

"They like you," Laura said simply. "You show you are pleased, so we all wish to please you more. Now! I have some little work to do in my office, then we go. Yes?"

"Great. By the way, do you think I could have a couple of the menus to refer to for my piece?"

"I will make a package," Laura told her, and went off.

Jo returned to her room to put in a call to Henry. As she waited for the operator to ring her back, she drummed her fingers on her thighs, hoping his call to her had been personal and not about business.

When he came on the line, he sounded very cheerful. "How are you?" he asked. "I did get your message last evening. Seems we crossed wires," he chuckled, and there was the slightest edge to the sound.

"I'm kind of blue, Henry. Tell me about you, about what you've been doing."

"Oh, the usual, you know. The garden's doing beautifully. Weather's still glorious. And have you had a smashing time?"

"Yup, smashing. Do you miss me, Henry?"

A pause. Then, "Yes, I do, actually."

"Look, I know you're at the office, and I know you hate taking personal calls at the office; furthermore, I'm beginning to realize you hate telephone calls in general. But will you, just this once, please, try to overcome your hatred and say something nice to me? I feel really shaky right now—I'll explain why when I see you. But if you'll humor me, I'll say something nice to you."

Another pause. Then: "I was thinking there's ample room below stairs for a darkroom. I went down the other evening to have a look round, and thought it would do rather nicely. There's access to running water and, all in all, it's not bad. I've never done anything about it, you see, and there's quite a lot of usable space."

"Ah," she said. "That's nice, but it's not *nice*."

"Sorry you don't think so," he said curtly. "You're quite correct in assuming this is not my favorite pastime."

"You're definitely not a star on the telephone, that's for sure."

"*One* does *one's* best," he said. "And having done it, I do believe you are now obliged to say something nice to me."

"Are you kidding?" she laughed.

"No, I am not. And I've another call waiting, so hurry it

along. I mean, really, Jo! First, it's 'important,' now it's 'nice.' What, *one* wonders, will be next?''

"I don't know. I'm not there yet."

"Come along. I did do my best, and it's now your turn."

"Okay, here goes. I want to stay," she said, then quickly added, "another week. At least. Would that be okay?"

"Not much of a star turn yourself, Jo dear. But yes, naturally, it's okay."

"Thank you."

"I am still waiting to hear your something 'nice,' " he reminded her.

"Okay. Henry?"

"Yes, Jo?"

She gulped down some air, said, "I think I love you," then slammed down the receiver and sat staring at it, her heart pounding. "Jesus H. Christ!" she said to the telephone. *"Christ!"* She sat for a few moments, then thought he might call her back, so she jumped up, snatched her things, and went to find Laura.

The sadness hit her again late that afternoon while she packed. She'd bought gifts the day before for Tyler and Lucienne, but hadn't had a chance to give them. Now they sat, wrapped and set aside, somehow reproaching her for her forgetfulness. Then she wondered about the mask she'd bought for Henry, a pale Pierrot's face with burgundy lips and eye slits decorated in such a way as to make the mask appear to be shedding tears. It was a beautiful creation, with black satin ribbons, that she'd selected because she could visualize it on Henry's living room wall. And maybe, she thought, that was presumptuous. Oh, no more presumptuous than blurting out what she had over the telephone before severing the connection in order not to have to hear his response. But she wasn't sorry she'd said it. It was how she seemed to feel, so she'd told him. It was now up to him to show her, one way or another, if it was what he'd wanted to hear.

The bulk of her packing completed, she looked at her luggage and then at the room, sadder still at the knowledge that it was over. She'd have dinner now, come back here to sleep one last time, and then, in the morning, climb on board the train. She didn't want to leave Venice. Who knew what Henry might have to say to her? There was a fair degree of uncertainty facing her, yet she had to go. All journeys had to come to an end. She'd already shot the train, so she'd be free, if she wished, to sit in her compartment and stare out the window at the scenery. If she wanted, she could go sit in the bar car and have a drink and listen to the piano music. She almost wished the Pentax had failed on the southbound trip so that she'd be forced to pay as close attention to details as she had on the way out. The need to work would again lend purpose and meaning to her presence on the train.

In the shower she told herself none of it mattered. She'd get back to London to find Gracie had lined up five more jobs, and she'd have to be in Montana a week from Wednesday, or in Auckland two weeks from tomorrow to cover some goddamned kiwi festival or something. Then she'd be bitching and groaning about that. You chose it, kiddo! You were the one who said you'd be glad to travel on assignment; you were the one who could see money, and success, and potential, in going to twenty different places in any given year. But what'll you do when you're fifty, huh? Are you still going to be hopping on planes with the camera bag, rushing to meet some magazine's deadline because you've got no personal deadline of your own? Is this what you're going to do until you're too old, or too wrecked from dragging the equipment around, to go on the road anymore? Or do you want to follow through, find out what Henry's got in mind?

I want Henry! she thought, and felt a jolt of something awfully like dread at the idea that she was putting so much store in the events of so short a period of time. But he was so goddamned sweet—the way he'd put her to bed that first night in London; the way he'd looked on his knees in the garden; the way he'd pleaded his case on the bench in the park. No. If she had a choice, and everyone insisted that she did, then she'd choose Henry, take her chances with

Henry. She'd still be hopping on planes, and dragging equipment around, but someone would be waiting for her. The only question was: Would Henry choose her? Did saying some space would make a good darkroom constitute any kind of commitment?

The maître d' gave her a table at the edge of the terrace, from which she could look out at the Canale San Giorgio and watch the water traffic. As she ate the fresh spinach pasta in a basil-and-tomato sauce, and the salad nutty with arugula, which the waiter had made for her from the cart, she watched ominous clouds gather over the city in the distance, and sizzling streaks of lightning illuminate the buildings. A rising breeze lifted the tablecloths and turned the pages of her notebook on the table. She was the only guest seated out in the open. Everyone else had been placed beneath the canopy extending from the hotel wall. She didn't mind. From this vantage point, she was able to view the tremendous storm as it slowly approached over the canal. She ate slowly, winding the pasta around her fork the way the Italians did, the way she'd seen Laura do it at lunch. A glass of crisp white wine to wash it down, then a mouthful of the best salad she'd ever had.

The boom of thunder was coming closer, the breeze increasing to a wind. She felt quite bold, out there unprotected from the elements. She was determined to stay until the storm was ready to break directly overhead, and she wouldn't move a moment sooner. She hadn't watched a storm this way since that summer years and years ago when her parents had rented a house on Fishers Island, and she and Beamer had crouched on the balcony outside her bedroom to exclaim over a ferocious storm they could see across Hay Harbor. She'd never forgotten the excitement of being secure and sheltered while the sky was split by zagging streaks of lightning and the house behind them seemed to shake with the thunder. She'd held Beamer's hand, and the two of them had laughed, pointing and shouting, "Look over there! Oh, over there! Look!" until her mother had come to stand at the door behind them saying, "Are the two of you aware that it's three in the morning, and some people are trying to sleep? Could you possibly try not to shriek?" And then she'd stood behind them to watch, so silent, so wonderfully fragrant, that it was quite some time before they realized she was no longer there. Now, she was gone forever. *Goodbye, Lily. Be happy, Mom.*

She was finishing her coffee when the storm broke overhead and one of the concierges came to the table to say, "Signorina James, a telephone call, please."

She picked up her bag, stood, and began moving toward the door just as the rain came cascading down. Perfect timing, she congratulated herself, and went to the booth in the hall.

"Joanna, it's Tyler."

"Tyler! How is everything? How is Lucienne?"

He sighed tiredly. "It's been quite a day, Joanna. As we both knew she would, she got quite hysterical when she saw I was taking her to the hospital and not to the doctor's office. The only way I could induce her to go through the front door was to promise I'd stay with her, no matter what. I have *never* seen anyone so cataleptically terrified of a *place*. But I gave her my word I would stay, and I did. I had to hold her hand through the examination, and she refused to allow me to leave for so much as a minute, so the doctor—a very decent chap, by the way, and most tolerant, under the circumstances—had to give us both the news. Which was that she was in fairly desperate condition and he wanted to perform emergency surgery, which, he said, was the only chance she was going to have, very literally, to save her life. Then, it took the two of us the better part of an hour to convince her her life was worth saving and that a short period under anesthetic wasn't the torture she somehow imagined it to be. And, of course, the only way she could be persuaded to sign the consent form was if I swore to her I would go with her right into the operating theater. You can well imagine the doctor's delight at this. But he was so concerned, and so determined, that he agreed."

"My God, Tyler! It sounds awful."

"You haven't heard the worst. We had to get a nurse to stay with her, to talk to her and hold her hand while the doctor went off to prepare for the surgery and I got rigged out in surgical gear. Anyway," he sighed again, "half an hour later there we were in the operating theater. And while they were getting everything ready, she clung to my hand and, convinced, utterly convinced, she wouldn't survive the procedure, told me why she was so afraid. It seems that her parents had, when she was nine years old, placed her in the care of a young nephew in order that she could have her tonsils removed at a Montreal hospital. The nephew was apparently perfectly charming to the parents, and acted the soul of discretion during her overnight stay at the hospital. However, upon taking her home with him where she was to recuperate for a week before a checkup with the doctor followed by her return home, the son of a bitch proceeded to rape her. And not just once, but repeatedly. Then, after threatening to find her and kill her if she told anyone, he took her home.

"Somehow, in the years after, she substituted her hospital stay for the events that came after, and associated hospitals in general with gross abuse. Hence her terror. Hence her soliciting my promise not only to remain with her but to be there when she came round from the anesthetic. I could hardly refuse," he said, his voice starting to break.

"Joanna, it was a horror show! They had to double the normal dosage of anesthetic because she struggled so hard against it that the doctor had already started the incision and she was still awake."

"Oh, my God!"

"It was dreadful, dreadful," he said, starting to weep in noisy sobs. 'I'm sorry," he apologized. "Just one moment."

She could hear him put the telephone down, then he blew his nose, coughed, and came back on the line.

"Sorry," he said again. "The doctor," he continued, "as if to prove to me how urgent the need was for the surgery, was good enough to show me, in an enamel basin, the condition of the organs he removed from her body. As if I were another doctor, or someone accustomed to the sight of such things. Christ! They were literally, and I mean literally, disintegrating. He touched an instrument to them, to illustrate, and they simply came apart. I very nearly passed out, and one of the nurses had to give me a whiff of ammonia. Anyway, after telling me she was very fortunate to have come in when she did, he sent the lot off for biopsy, sewed her back up, and said she'd be right as rain in a matter of weeks. Provided, of course, the biopsy came back negative. Which, thank God, it did."

"Poor you," Jo said. "Poor Lucienne. How is she now?"

"She's sleeping. They've shot her full of all sorts of drugs, and she's out of the recovery ward and into a regular room. I'm stopping the night with her."

"You sound so worn out. Are you all right?"

"Never mind me!" he said impatiently. "I want to fly to Canada, find the child-raping son of a bitch, and strangle him with my bare hands. I have *never* felt such helpless, overwhelming rage. I want to *do* something, but there's nothing I can do," he ranted. "I want to put my fist through a wall, kill someone. I've never *been* so angry."

"You *are* doing something," she told him. "You've done it, Tyler. There isn't anything else."

"Christ!" he cried. "While she was on that table, Joanna, I stood there and I prayed. I didn't know what I'd do if she didn't come round. I imagined her dead, and was suddenly terrified that I'd never see her laugh, or hear her voice again, have her tease me the way she does, taking the Mickey. Am I mad?" he asked. "Have I lost my senses? I'm here in a hospital in Paris with a woman I've known for what, three days, four? And if anything happens to her, I simply don't know what I'll do."

"Is there something wrong with that?" she asked him. "Do you have some objection to caring?" Listen to me! she thought. I sound like Anne. "Life's too goddamned short, Tyler. *It is too goddamned short.*"

"It is," he said, sounding less frenzied. "You're right, it

Charlotte Vale Allen

is. We've been through so much. It feels as if it's been going on for weeks, months. I've known her all my life, and I can't possibly let go now.''

''Then don't. It isn't written anywhere that you have to.''

''I must get back,'' he said suddenly, ''in case she awakens and I'm not there.''

''When she does wake up, tell her I love her. And I'll be coming to see her. Both of you, if you're still there.''

''I think I'll be here, Joanna. I think I'm going to be here for quite some time.

''That's good, Tyler. It really is. And I love you for seeing her through this.''

''Thank you for letting me rant and rave. I know it wasn't quite what any of us had in mind.''

''*Please don't thank me*, Tyler. Will you keep me posted?''

''My word on it. Good night, Jo.''

''Bye, Tyler. Don't forget to give her my love. And try to get some rest.''

The air inside the booth had grown very warm and stuffy, and it was a relief to open the door and step outside. She was far too distressed by what Tyler had told her to go back to her room for the early night's sleep she'd planned. So she went along to the bar. And on her way inside she stopped to place some lire on the piano top, and asked the pianist to play the theme from *Borsalino*.

360

27

AFTER TWO BELLINIS IN THE BAR, A STOP AT THE CON-
cierge's desk to order a water taxi to take her to the station
in the morning and to pick up the envelope left for her by the
tourist board with information on the Malipiero Trevisan Palace, she returned to her room and stood for a long time at
the patio doors watching the storm whipping the trees at the
front of the hotel. Then she went to bed and had anxiety-
ridden dreams of death and diseased organs and angry con-
frontations. She saw her dream self sitting with a bottle of
gin in the dark of Henry's living room, telling a small child,
who was also her, to go away. Lucienne stood naked in a
boat, a gaping hole beneath her ribs and her spinal column
visible. Tyler shouted down the length of an ornate and
gleaming coffin whose top sat open to reveal Anne's corpse,
while Jimmy pushed at him, asking him please to be a little
more respectful.

Twice in the night she got up to go to the bathroom, where
she drank several glasses of water, then stood holding the
glass, gazing at her fuzzy reflection while she waited for the
latest dream siege to recede.

By six she was sitting in her nightgown on the sofa with
her notebook, writing about what she'd seen on her two-hour

tour with Laura the day before. The time constraints had been considerable, since everything closed at noon, and she'd chased after Laura from one place to the next, taking pictures on the run and hoping she'd be able to find guide books that would tell her where she'd been.

Now all she could recall were random details—a miniature statue of some saint; a haunting triptych of religious significance; glass cases of hand-embroidered antique religious garments; a darkened vestry with a window in one corner through which light fell like an ax, cutting the room into two separate segments.

By seven-fifteen she was in the dining room—it had stopped raining, but the outdoor furniture was still wet—helping herself to croissants from the acrylic warming bin. There were few people about this early; the dining room was very quiet. The terrace bore a litter of stripped leaves, broken blossoms, and evaporating puddles of rain water. She ate, feeling drugged and sluggish—the cumulative effects of more than a week with little sleep making themselves felt. She checked to make sure she'd put the Dramamine pills in her purse. If she spent one more sleepless night, especially on the train, she'd collapse. And she couldn't afford the luxury of taking to her bed for a few days, not with a visit promised to Anne, and one certain trip to see Lucienne in Paris. And then, of course, there was Henry. So she'd take some Dramamine and knock herself out on the train in order to have the energy she'd need.

After breakfast she went to give the concierge his tip along with the equivalent of fifty dollars and the name of Lucienne's hospital, and received his solemn guarantee that he would make all the arrangements for flowers to be sent in her name. Then she stopped in the kitchen to shake hands with and say goodbye to Renato and his assistants.

As she double-checked the drawers and closets of her room, she wondered where Jackie was. She hoped to be able to say goodbye to him, but just in case he wasn't around, she wrote a note saying how much she'd enjoyed their time together and asking him to stay in touch.

She cleaned the portable Melitta and packed it into a corner of the Hartmann. She made sure she put the Walkman and the microspeakers into her carry-on bag. And then the concierge rang to say her water taxi had arrived. She asked for a porter to come for her luggage, laid some lire on the TV console where the maid would be sure to find it, then followed the porter to the lobby, where a small group had assembled to see her off: Laura, Jackie, the concierge who'd arranged her camera purchase, and the maître d'. The concierge and the maître d' expressed their pleasure at meeting her, then excused themselves to return to work. Jackie and Laura walked with her to the landing stage.

"Come back again very soon," Laura said, giving her a hug before presenting her with a gift-wrapped package. "Something to remember us by."

"Thank you for everything," Jo told her.

"Don't forget to send me some pictures," Jackie said, also giving her a wrapped package. "And thanks a lot for taking me around, and for showing me how to take pictures, Joey. You're really cool."

Jo hugged him and mussed his hair, saying with a smile, "You've given me hope for the future, Jackie old boy. If the other kids turn out half as terrific as you, we're looking pretty good."

"Wait till I start sending you *my* pictures," he threatened. "Maybe you'll change your mind."

"No, I won't," she told him. "I'll just write back with helpful hints. Seriously, Jackie," she said, taking his hand, "I had some of the best times of my life with you. Just eat some junk every now and then. It's good for you."

He laughed and said, "The minute you're gone, I'll order a burger and fries."

"Right!" She climbed into the boat and waved to Laura and Jackie until she could no longer see them. Then she went to the rear of the taxi for her last look at the city.

When she arrived at Santa Lucia, a stocky man wearing a CIGA Hotels badge came racing down the steps to the taxi.

"Signorina James? I am asked by the Cipriani to assist you in checking in."

"That's great," she said, glad not to have to cope alone with her bags as well as with the crush of people in the station. "Thank you." She paid the boatman, then had to rush to keep up with the CIGA representative, who'd taken the Hartmann as well as her carry-on bag and was racing back up the steps and into the station.

At the VS-O-E check-in, he left her, apologizing for his haste, and explaining, "I have other boats I must meet. *Scusi, scusi.*"

She pulled out some money to tip him, but he held up his hands, shaking his head and smiling, then tore off.

"*Ciao*, Joanna!"

Jo turned to see Giovanna and said, "Hi! How are you? It's great to see you."

"I come to see you off," she said. "Also, the Lalique carriage is on today and I thought if your pictures are not good, maybe you like to take more."

"They're okay, but I wouldn't mind taking a few more."

"Okay. We check your bag, and I take you on."

As they were walking down the platform, Giovanna said, "I have told them to put you into a different carriage, so you are not freezing this time with the air conditioning."

"Bless your heart."

"So now first we put away your bag, then we go to see the Lalique. Okay?"

"Great. This is so sweet of you."

"I wanted to see you to say goodbye. You have a good time in Venice?"

"The best. I have enough material for about five features."

"Maybe you should make a book. Here is your carriage."

Giovanna stayed until Jo had had a chance to admire the Lalique carriage in full sunlight with the curtains open and everything freshly cleaned and polished. Then she said that she had to get back to the depot, and Jo descended onto the platform with her to exchange hugs and say goodbye.

"Have a good trip, Joanna," Giovanna said. "You come back, huh?"

Jo stayed on the platform to get some shots of the arriving passengers and the stewards with their clipboards waiting to direct them to their compartments. Then she went back on board to unpack her clothes for the evening and the next day. That done, she set up the Walkman and the speakers, popped in the sound track of *Manhattan*—Gershwin music that felt most appropriate for the train—and sat down to open her gifts. Laura had given her a journal with painted scenes of Venice at the top of every page. And Jackie's gift was a pointy-headed pottery Viking, complete with spear. A note inside said, "He's also a whistle. You can blow his head, if you'll excuse the expression. Love, Jackie."

Just as the train began to move, a handsome young man knocked at her open door and introduced himself as Adrian, the chief steward. "Is there anything you need? I've been told I'm to look after you." He said it with a smile that dimpled his cheeks.

"I can't think of a thing," she smiled back at him. "But if I do, I'll let you know."

"Be sure you do," he said, and went on his way.

All the staff she met on the southbound journey greeted her effusively, and were most appreciative of the prints she'd brought for them. Luke, the waiter from the bar, beamed at her; Gian Paolo, the waiter with the memorabilia collection thanked her shyly but profusely; Giuseppi welcomed her with a deep bow. It made her feel as if she belonged to an elite minority of people privy to the innermost workings of the train. She felt proud and quite humbled at being on her second trip on this extraordinary vehicle and wished she could, as Lucienne did, ride it whenever she was in need of cosseting or diversion.

To give herself courage at dinner, because she was not only eating alone but also didn't have a camera with her, she ordered a half-bottle of St. Émilion to drink with the salad she had in lieu of St. Peter's fish steamed with carrots and zucchini, and the roast duckling breast and duck liver sautéed in muscat wine, with mange-tout peas, thin-sliced pan-fried potatoes, and the brie she selected in preference to the caramelized walnut sponge cake listed on the menu. By the time her coffee came, she was having trouble staying awake. She took two Dramamine, paid in sterling for the wine, and headed along to the bar car to see what was going on.

There were perhaps two dozen people in evening dress having aperitifs before the second dinner sitting. The atmosphere in the car was subdued, and the pianist's rendering of a Viennese waltz seemed to be making people comatose. Luke greeted her happily, asking if she was going to stay for a drink or some coffee, but she told him she was off to bed and would see him in the morning. She wasn't up to sitting alone in the bar car.

Again she had to undress in stages, noting as she did how small the compartment felt in its nighttime configuration. But at least this time she wasn't cold, and she'd sleep, thanks to the Dramamine. By the time she'd bathed at the basin and packed away the clothes she'd just removed, her mouth had gone into the familiar dry stage the pills always created before they knocked her out.

She lay down, settled the blankets around herself, closed her eyes, and at once fell asleep.

The steward's knock awakened her at eight-thirty, and she sat up to let him in, thanked him, then raised the shades to see that it was raining as they passed through the French countryside. Another half-hour and they'd be in Paris. While she ate, she toyed briefly with the idea of dressing quickly and leaving the train in Paris to go to see Lucienne. Impossible. Even as she was considering the idea, the train was speeding through the outlying areas of the city. At just before one in the afternoon they'd get to Boulogne and transfer to the Sealink. Venice was a day and a night behind her. London, and Henry, were ahead.

God! she thought, pausing with a half-dipped fragment of croissant poised over her coffee cup. What if his primary reaction to her abrupt declaration was discomfort? Oh, come *on*, Joanna! Two telexes, flowers, and the phone calls proved his interest. And Anne was right. She had to take this chance because she really didn't want to get to be a fifty-year-old photographer running around the world because there was no one to come home to. The photographer part was fine, but the rest of it wasn't.

Don't let me down, Henry! If this whole thing's only in my head, I'm going to feel like the biggest fool of all time.

There were eighty-seven passengers on this northbound journey, and better than a third of them left the train in Paris, while only twelve got on for the ride to London. Hence the bar car was very quiet. And the brunch—she simply couldn't believe how consistently hungry she was on the train—was also quiet.

She tried not to wolf down the scrambled-eggs-with-smoked-salmon appetizer, followed by broiled lobster in butter sauce accompanied by one of the baked, stuffed potatoes she'd watched Renato prepare. The caramelized apple tartlets were heavenly. She drank two cups of coffee, then tipped the dining car staff and Giuseppe before returning to her compartment to prepare for their arrival in Boulogne. The time had flown by. It seemed as if she'd only just climbed on board and already she was following the others to the ferry. And as on her previous crossing, she was lulled to sleep by the all but unnoticeable motion of the ship as it surged across the Channel.

One of the lounge staff came to tap her on the shoulder, saying, "We've arrived at Folkestone. We'll be leaving the ship momentarily."

Jo sat up, her mouth still dry from last night's Dramamine, and collected her belongings. She made a mental note to mention somewhere in her article something about arriving to ride the train in a well-rested state. It was all too easy to sleep the trip away.

The cream and brown British Pullmans were waiting. And once the passengers were settled in the coaches, the white-suited waiters at once began serving an afternoon tea of dainty finger sandwiches, scones with clotted cream and strawberry jam, chocolate shortbread, and Ceylon tea. She ate yet again, wondering what it was about train travel that provoked such enormous hunger. She could see herself dieting for the next six months as a result of this sustained gluttony. And no sooner had she finished the last of her tea than she fell asleep, only to jerk awake as the train rounded a bend in the tracks. She looked around guiltily, hoping no one had seen her asleep with her mouth hanging open. She was turning into a gorging narcoleptic, she thought, staring out the window as the train brought her closer by the minute to London.

Undoubtedly, Henry would have left dozens of Post-its appended to every available surface. Eat-me chicken, and chocolate biccies, and cream in fridge. Henry Hart, Hotelier with the three-piece suits and the Vandyke beard, who looked so dear when he slept.

They were slowing to pull into Victoria, the rails branching to reach the many platforms. An hour, perhaps, and she'd be at the house in Chelsea. She checked herself in her compact mirror, put on fresh lipstick, then got out money to tip the waiters. She was back. It was over. She took a long last look around the magnificent parlor car and prepared to leave the train.

After so many hours in motion it felt odd to walk on firm ground. She started down the long platform, bags in both hands, moving carefully until she could get used to the lack of sway. She looked up to see how much farther it was to where they were off-loading the luggage, and there was Henry, one hand raised to catch her attention. Suddenly, she was smiling so hard it made her cheeks ache, while he worked his way among the passengers and threw his arms wide as he came toward her. She put her things down on the platform and walked right into his embrace.

After a moment she said, "God, Henry! I was worried you'd think I was crazy or something."

"I am well aware that you're crazy."

"That's nice, thank you. Give me a kiss."

He held her away to have a look at her, saying, "You look well, but a bit tired."

"All I did on the way back here is sleep. Give me a kiss, Henry, or I'll stop asking."

"Don't do that," he said, and kissed her. Then he said, "An entire week you've been putting me through my paces."

"You know what I think? I think you liked it," she said, her nose touching his. "And you like me, too, don't you, Henry?"

"Of course I like you. Although I do believe you're even crazier than I thought."

"But do you really, honestly, like me?"

"Don't be a ninny, Jo. I've always liked you. In fact," he said a bit slyly, "I *think* I love you."

"Henry!" She laughed and hugged him again. His neck was smooth and soft; he smelled wonderful. "I can hardly believe it," she said. "Here you are, in one of your famous three-piece suits, Henry Hart, Hotelier."

"Hardly famous. You do realize people are bestowing slightly fatuous, rather doting smiles upon us?"

"I don't care. Do you care?"

"Not if you don't. You're getting me to do things I'd never do for another living soul."

"Such as?"

"Making me say 'nice' things, 'important' things. Do you put everyone through such rigorous testing, Jo dear?"

"Is that what you think I was doing?"

"Wasn't it?"

"No. I just wanted to know where I stood. So! What do we do now?"

"First things first. We'll collect the rest of your luggage. Then we'll go out and get a taxi."

"What if I never want to leave, Henry?" she asked, as he picked up her carry-on bag.

"Were you planning to? I mean to say, I've already been onto the chap who did the work on the house, and he's drawing up an estimate for your darkroom. I've also been making inquiries about a work permit for you."

"You're kidding!" she said as they moved several yards along the platform, then stopped. You care about me, she thought; you're concerned with my well-being.

"Of course I'm not kidding. Do you honestly think I'd joke about taking time away from the office, from my many other clients?"

"Oh, good heavens, no!" she quipped. "Seriously. Why would you do all that?"

"Well," he shot her a grin, "it isn't every day someone rings me from Venice to say she *thinks* she loves me."

"No, I suppose not."

"From Leeds perhaps, or even Manchester. But never from Venice."

She hooked her arm around his neck and kissed him once more. "You know what, Henry?"

"What, Jo?"

"I think it's taken me too damned long to figure things out."

"Ah, well. I'm noted for my patience. And better late, as they say, than never."

"There are some people I really want you to meet, Henry."

"I always enjoy meeting new people."

"You'll love them."

"I will, will I?" He ran his hand over her hair.

"You know what I mean."

"Yes, I do. Before we do anything, however, you simply must see the astonishing new improvements to the kitchen."

"Oh, yeah? Like what?"

"Super things: cushions on the countertops, scented candles, incense, that sort of thing."

She laughed loudly. "Can't wait to check it all out!"

"I'm sure you'll find everything to your satisfaction."

"I'm sure I will," she murmured into his neck.

"We should look for your bag," he said.

"It'll wait another moment. Say something significant, Henry."

"I knew it! Didn't I just know it!" He held her away again.

"Let me take you home now, Jo. I'd really hate to go to the trouble of dragging you into one of those empty carriages and risk having some waiter come upon us in the fragrant delicious."

"In the *what*?" she roared with laughter.

"You heard me."

"Yup, I did."

"You seem quite—different, somehow; changed."

"Yes, I am. Say, 'Thank you, Train.' "

"I beg your pardon?"

"Nothing." She kissed him on the tip of the nose, then turned inside the circle of his arm to point, saying, "That's my bag right over there. Let's grab it and go."

"Don't you want to hear my 'significant' something?"

"I already heard." She smiled at him. "Every single word. Now come on. Take me home, Henry."

ABOUT THE AUTHOR

CHARLOTTE VALE ALLEN is the author of several novels and of a nonfiction book, DADDY'S GIRL. She has one teenage daughter. Charlotte Vale Allen was born in Canada and makes her home in Norwalk, Connecticut.